Many a Voyage

Other books by Loula Grace Erdman

THE YEARS OF THE LOCUST

LONELY PASSAGE

THE EDGE OF TIME

THREE AT THE WEDDING

THE FAR JOURNEY

THE SHORT SUMMER

THE WIND BLOWS FREE

THE WIDE HORIZON

THE GOOD LAND

LOULA GRACE ERDMAN

Many a Voyage

DODD, MEAD & COMPANY
New York

Library of Congress Catalog Card Number: 60-8440
Printed in the United States of America

For Raymond T. Bond, who knew I would do this book because he thought I could; and for Barbara Kamb, who gave me help above and beyond the call of duty

Contents

She knew she was dying, although they were all busy trying to pretend it was not so. A pleasant fiction which made things easier for everyone, especially for her because it relieved her from the necessity of trying to comfort them. But why else had all the children gathered here? Her children, grown now, with children of their own. Such a lot of people, and yet she felt a lack. She had borne seven children. Flint—no, of course, Flint was not here.

The grandchildren tiptoed about, their very quietness a betrayal. Perhaps it was to offset this unnatural restraint that Edmund suggested they, young and old alike, gather around the piano evenings and sing, with Lillie to accompany them.

No matter how many people might be around, Edmund still dominated any group of which he was a part. He moved among them, erect, dignified, frock-coated, his hair white now but as abundant and carefully groomed as it had been in young manhood. When he spoke his voice was deep and rich as ever, and when he joined in the singing, his voice sounded clearest and best of all. An unusual thing for a man past seventy. But then, Edmund was an unusual man. For instance, it was clever of him to manage the singing in such a way that, although the piano was in the living room just off her bedroom, the group congregated close to her door with Edmund himself standing near her bed so that she did not feel apart from the children nor they from her.

"Try 'Come Where My Love Lies Dreaming,'" he suggested.

Before long, even the grandchildren had joined in. Fannie herself lay listening. Singing was rather more effort than she wanted to expend at the moment. Then Lillie, perhaps not realizing the import of it, slipped into "God Be With You 'Til We Meet Again," which was a mistake, for midway Eddie broke down and fled the room (Eddie was always the tenderhearted one). Fannie threw herself into the awkwardness of the moment and joined in the singing, surprised to find her voice still clear, and strong enough, too, after all these years and her illness. She and Edmund carried the song through without faltering, straight to the end. It was a great satisfaction to see that once more they could rally the children back to poise and self-control.

At the end, however, she found the experience had tired her more than she had realized. In fact, she felt a little lightheaded, a sense of being unrelated to time or place. She turned her head to look out the window where she could see the high peaks of the Sandia Mountains and, above and beyond them, the pale green and purple and rose sunset splashed across the sky and, in the middle distance, the river. Strange that most of her life had been lived within the sight of water. Put-in Bay, gently blue against the horizon back in Sandusky; Lake Michigan, sweeping almost up to her door in Milwaukee; the winding blue thread of the Kaw with its girdle of green trees in Topeka and Lawrence. Even when she visited Edmund in Washington, she could see the Potomac from the window of his room. And when they went to live at the Old Palace in Santa Fe, she had been delighted with the turbulent little stream they called a river, tumbling past the Cathedral. She was glad the pattern held in Albuquerque. She would have felt lonely away from the sight of water. In some ways it was like her life—changing, fluid, always moving, pushed about by winds and tides of circumstance.

For more than fifty years she had been Edmund's wife. Such a long time together; so many things shared. It seemed strange to think that, in only a few weeks, a new century would be coming in. But she would not see it.

The feeling of unreality, of disassociation, still possessed her. She moved restlessly and Pitt, who had been standing at his father's side, turned to ask, "Are you comfortable, Mother?"

At his words, Edmund came rapidly to her side. He took her hand, holding it in a warm strong clasp. She gave his hand a slight pressure and the children, who had stopped singing and stood clustered helplessly about the door, watched, apparently reassured by the sight of their parents, two old people, holding hands from force of habit.

"Yes," she said. She hesitated, not from reluctance to make the request, but because she must think first so she could tell them where to look. She knew now. The trunk in the attic, under the baby bonnets and the scuffed little shoes and Flint's blouse.

"What do you want, Mother?" Pitt asked.

"The quilt," she said, speaking distinctly. They must not think her an old woman, wandering in her mind. She was very much aware of everything. She had been sick a long time; she could see what a small mound she made under the bedclothes. She could see her hair, braided into two pigtails, still brown with only a little gray in it. (How proud Edmund had always been of her hair.) She knew all of them, there in the room; she could almost read their thoughts. She was not going to allow them to think she was not clear in her mind. "The quilt," she repeated firmly. "The one I pieced—"

"But Mother—" Pitt's wife protested. "It hasn't been aired for years! If you are cold, I'll get a clean one."

Clemmie had not asked, "What quilt?" None of them did. They knew quite well what she meant.

"Bring her the quilt, Clemmie," Edmund said quietly.

At his words, she rose and left the room. In only a little while the quilt was there and Edmund himself was spreading it over her.

Sure enough, it did smell a little musty, but not unpleasantly so. She traced a piece with her finger. It was faded almost white now, but she could remember when it had been very new and bright.

"I wore that dress in Sandusky," she said.

"I remember it," Edmund told her.

"I remember so much," she went on, touching another piece.

The children were silent. Why should they speak? The memories went back and beyond them. But not beyond Edmund. Always he had been a part of her life. And there was, as she had said, a great deal to remember.

PART ONE

THE EARLY YEARS

I

Sandusky

1848–1851

SHE HAD TAKEN her place on the front porch, a bit of needlework in her hands, sitting so that she had only to raise her eyes to see the sweep of the turnpike westward, the direction from which the stage coach would come. Her dark brown hair, soft and abundant, was drawn upward from her face and looped with a ribbon. The high cheekbones and her eyes, very dark under strongly marked brows, gave her face a look of strength and determination, an effect somewhat minimized by the nose, broad at the base but still a little on the perky side. Now and then she made a few quick stitches, her delicate hands both deft and graceful. Occasionally her mouth, full and generous in her small face, curved into a secret, happy smile.

Even before it swept into sight, she heard the clatter of the stagecoach, the six horses at a smart lope, the driver jaunty and important in his seat with some privileged passenger beside him. The less fortunate ones rode inside with the panels opened because of the midsummer heat. Her eyes flicked quickly past the baggage riding on top to the back platform where the mail, covered with its leather apron, would ride. Sure enough, the pouches were there. She stood up quickly. Folding her work into a neat little bundle, she walked into the house.

"Are you finished, Fannie?" her mother asked.

"For a while, yes. I'm going downtown, Ma. Do you want anything?"

"Uhmn-mm—" her mother said, smiling knowingly, "so there *was* mail on that coach."

The girl smiled back, her face gay and her eyes twinkling. She turned to survey herself carefully in the little mirror hanging over the washstand.

"You're a pretty girl, Fannie," her mother told her.

"Everyone says I look like you, Ma," she said. And then, "I'll be back after a while."

"No hurry," her mother assured her.

The girl walked down the path, past where her small sisters were playing, out to the board sidewalk which led to town. She went with purpose but no particular haste, showing no impatience when she had to wait for a dozen wagons to pass before she could cross the street. The oxen strained with the weight of the grain piled into the wagons and the drivers plodded along beside them, their own faces filled with wonder at the richness of the cargoes they guided, wheat to be shipped from Sandusky all over the world. *The Mirror* printed statistics—two million bushels of wheat and a quarter as much corn had been sent from this port last year.

She smiled, thinking of *The Mirror*.

Beyond her the lake glittered, blue and shining in the sun, with trees growing down to the very edge of the harbor. In almost every yard vineyards and gardens flourished. She was sure Sandusky was the prettiest town in the country. Of course, Mr. Charles Dickens hadn't liked it when he came to lecture six years ago. He went away to write hard things about the town. But nobody minded what Mr. Dickens said. Plenty of people liked the town. Mr. Sylvester Ross, editor of *The Mirror* (and again she smiled), said there was a population of at least five thousand here. He was always pointing out the good things about the town—boats docking regularly and stagecoach service. A high school and churches and literary societies.

"Good morning, Miss Fannie."

Mr. Basil Courtney stood in front of her, his hat in his hand.

"Good morning, Mr. Courtney."

"I have just received a shipment of new calicoes. You must come in and look at them."

"Thank you, I will," she said, as he walked on.

What a nice man Mr. Courtney was. He always acted as if you were doing him a real favor just by walking into his store and looking around. Uncle Elial said he was a true gentleman, even if he did keep pretty much to himself. Uncle Elial was never one to do that; he was always joking and teasing. He pretended to be worried about Fannie.

"Twenty years old and not married yet," he had said the last time he came. "I hope we aren't going to have an old maid on our hands."

She came to the post office now, stopped in front of it.

She tried to tell herself that perhaps the letter hadn't come; that even if it had, its contents might not be at all to her liking. She felt herself flushing. A girl couldn't lay down conditions to a man who hadn't even asked for her hand—yet. Her letter had been a very difficult one for her to write. But she had to say something. His letters had been gaining in warmth all spring. She had to make him understand how she felt. Why shouldn't he know how she felt about him? It was a fact assumed by both of them down the years, and by their families and friends as well. Everyone said "Fannie and Edmund" together, as if there was no way of thinking of the two of them separately.

She walked inside the post office.

"Oh, good morning, Miss Fannie," Mr. Evans said. He was sorting out the mail, peering through his steel-rimmed glasses which were almost lost in the soft roundness of his face, but he looked up now to smile at her archly, "I don't suppose by any chance you were expecting anything?"

She smiled confidently, reaching for the letter he extended toward her. The writing on the envelope—small, clear, almost of steel-engraving precision—seemed to leap out at her.

Miss Fannie Lathrop
c/o Rodney Lathrop
Sandusky, Ohio

"Thank you," she remembered to say before she went out into the hot brightness of the street. She turned in the direction of home, then suddenly changing her mind, walked down the street which led to the bay. She wanted to be alone when she read this letter. It would be different from the others. She found a quiet place close to the water, sat down, and opened the letter.

"My dear Fannie—" Her eyes slipped along the pages, following the closely written words. His letters were the ties which had held them together during this year he had been gone. All across the wild country he had written to her. From Indiana, and Illinois, and Ohio. Towns whose names she had never heard before but, because he had been there, became real. This one came from Janesville, Wisconsin, where his parents had taken up a homestead. Those Rosses—always on the move.

"I had your letter," she read. "I think it says what I want to hear. I'm coming to see for myself—by stagecoach, the fastest way there is. Even that will be too slow, knowing you are there waiting for me. Your letter does say that, doesn't it?"

And when she came to the end and read the signature, her face grew hot with blushes. He had signed it, "Your betrothed, Edmund."

"Oh my goodness," she whispered and laughed softly to herself.

After reading the letter again, she folded it and put it back into the envelope, which she slipped down inside the front of her dress, where it rested, smooth and crisp against her skin.

Well, she had evidently made herself clear enough in her letter. If he wanted to come home and ask for her hand, she'd listen to him. She wondered if she had made the rest of her letter equally as clear. She was willing to marry him, all right—she was immodestly, unmaidenly willing. But she didn't have any intentions of following him all around the country while he worked on little county newspapers. Sandusky was a good town. His brother Sylvester owned the paper here and would give Edmund a job. All the time Edmund was in high school he had worked for Sylvester on *The Mirror*. If newspaper work was what Edmund wanted, he had it waiting for him right here in Sandusky.

One of the first memories Fannie had of Sandusky, after the Lathrop family came here from New York, was of Edmund Ross, working on his brother's newspaper, *The Mirror*. Unless you knew him better, you would have thought him a frail lad. He had been a delicate baby, his mother said. Perhaps that was why he never grew to be a big man, although, some way, he gave the impression of height, an effect which came, perhaps, because he carried himself proudly. She was glad he was neither tall nor massive—beside such a man she would have felt dwarfed entirely, since she herself was only a few inches over five feet. His features were regular, with a fine drawn precision to them. A very good looking young man, Edmund Gibson Ross.

She remembered so well the first time she was really conscious of this fact. She went with Ma and Pa to a program at the high school where Edmund read a paper. She didn't in the least remember what it was about; she did remember, however, that he got a great deal of applause.

The next time she saw Edmund Ross, she stopped to talk. "Your paper was the best of all at the program," she told him, smiling directly at him. "Ever so many people have said so."

He smiled back at her, seeming both pleased and proud.

"Thank you," he said. He looked at her more closely. "You sing, don't you? I've heard you at church. My brother and I are looking for a fourth to a quartet. He and his girl and I. Want to join us?"

"Oh, yes—" she told him shyly.

After that they sang together on all sorts of occasions. You'd think Edmund had enough to do, working in the office of his brother's newspaper and going to high school. But no, he had time to go with the quartet whenever they were called to perform.

There was always that strain of restlessness in his blood. Pa said he got that from the Rosses.

After Edmund finished high school, he announced that he was going traveling about the country for a year, earning his way by working as a printer.

"I'll be coming back. Don't forget that," he said when he came to bid Fannie farewell.

"Oh, I won't," she assured him, working to keep her voice light.

"I'll expect to find you waiting here for me," he went on with what she thought was impudent assurance.

"I'll be waiting at the gate," she said, very proud that she managed to say this with a mock levity which gave the lie to her promise. Indeed, she did not intend to let him know what he seemed to take for granted—that when he was gone, however teeming the town might be with eligible young men, for her it was empty.

"I'll depend on that," he said, looking at her searchingly. He made a slight motion in her direction and for one frightened, delightful moment she thought he meant to put his arms around her. Instead, he took both her hands between his, gave them a strong warm pressure and said, "Good-by, I'll write you often."

Then he was gone, leaving her with a sense of annoyance and disappointment. Of course, she wouldn't have *let* him kiss her good-by, with no promise between them, but at least, he might have *tried*. It didn't help any to know that he probably suspected how she felt.

Well, he had now had his year of wandering, and had probably seen for himself there was nothing to this roaming.

She rose and walked home, thinking deeply. She had scarcely opened the front door when she said to her mother, still working in the kitchen, "Ma, I want a new dress. Mr. Courtney said he had some new patterns in."

"So he's coming back," her mother said softly. "When?"

"I don't know exactly. Soon. But we'll have time to make the dress."

"Of course, dear. We'll go down and select the material this very day."

2

She sat in the parlor, her ankles crossed, her hair neatly combed, proper and demure as a young lady should be on such an occasion. She wore the new dress, calico sprigged with small green flowers and delicate black leaves. The pointed bodice was long and tightly fitted. There was a small lace collar and lace at the sleeves.

"Do you want to meet him at the door, or shall I?" her mother asked.

"I think you'd better," she said, struck with sudden shyness. When she received Edmund's note this morning, delivered by a small boy who also worked on the paper, saying that he wanted to "do himself the honor of calling this afternoon," she had been so excited she thought she could not wait the two hours which must pass before he would arrive. And now that the time had come, she felt a wish to run off and leave her mother to cope with the situation.

At that moment they heard his knock, quick, determined, businesslike. Mrs. Lathrop looked at her daughter, who nodded, and the older woman made her way to the door. She opened it, and Fannie could see Edmund standing there on the threshold.

"Oh, Edmund, do come in," Mrs. Lathrop said. "How are you?"

"I'm fine, Mrs. Lathrop. Just fine. And you?"

There was a real warmth and cordiality in their greeting. Somewhere Fannie had read that it was a good sign for a mother and a young man caller to get along well. When Ma said, "It is good to have you back with us," it was as if she meant it; and when Edmund told her, "It's good to be back," he sounded as if she was one of the things which made homecoming pleasant.

But for all his liking for Ma, he looked around her now, his eyes eager and searching. "Is Fannie here?" he asked.

"Yes—she's in the parlor. Go right in—"

Ma slipped away and Edmund came into the room.

"Fannie—" he said, moving quickly across the distance which separated them.

"Edmund," she said, putting out her hands. He took them in a quick, decisive gesture.

"You weren't at the gate," he said accusingly.

She looked at him quickly. Surely he didn't think she had *meant* those words, spoken with lightness in order to cover up her real concern at his leaving. And yet, he wasn't smiling. Perhaps he suspected the truth—that, had she followed her own wishes she would have been at the gate or perhaps halfway down the street, running to meet him.

"I had forgotten," she said. She spoke too fast and he probably knew the reason for it. "That was a long time ago."

"Then it seemed long to you, too?"

There was no way of pretending around him. She might as well be forthright and honest; especially, since that was what she wanted to do.

"Very long," she said simply. "Now, sit down and tell me all about it."

He seated himself, his motion effortless and controlled. Now that she thought about it, she didn't remember ever seeing him go through what was called in other boys "the awkward age." She looked at him closely. At first she thought he had not changed at all, but now she could see he had. He looked different—older, perhaps, and certainly more mature. She recalled the oft-repeated story of his mother that, as a baby, he had been so small one of her blue teacups would have fitted over his small face. He certainly looked healthy enough now.

"You look well," she told him, filling in conversation.

"I'm as strong as an ox," he said. "I've done a lot of walking between towns these past months, and plenty of times I slept out under the stars."

"You certainly were moving," she agreed, smiling at him. "Your letters were always coming from some new town."

"I stayed in a place just long enough to make money to live on.

It was an exciting experience. I got to know the people, and what they were thinking. They *are* thinking, Fannie. They are restless and changing, getting rid of a lot of old notions. The newspapers help them in this, by passing on new ideas."

"Maybe you're just seeing yourself in others," she suggested, playfully.

"Now, Fannie," he protested. Always there was this literal streak in him which could not take teasing well; especially was it evident when he knew her remarks were grounded in deep seriousness, as, indeed, they were now. "I know you think I'm just a tramp printer, wandering for the sake of being on the move. That's not it. I'm not a tramp. I stayed at the Tremont Hotel while I was in Chicago. By the way, Chicago is getting to be quite a town."

"Sandusky is a good town, too," she told him quickly. "People keep pouring in here—"

"Oh, yes—of course," he agreed absently.

"And there's a newspaper *here*," she said. "Your brother has made a good thing out of *The Mirror*. Every one is talking about it."

"That's just the point," Edmund said. "Sandusky *has* a paper. But we've got to have them everywhere. The way people are moving around these days—hardly get settled before they decide to move on somewhere else—there has to be some sort of a cement to hold them together, and to the nation."

No matter how substantial Fannie's arguments might have been when she lined them up in her own mind, once he began talking he made them seem inconsequential. Her father said that rarely could a man both speak and write well, but Edmund used tongue and pen with equal skill.

"It's as if—" he hesitated a moment then went on, "—as if in helping people to have their newspapers I am preserving the bright shape of freedom, both for them and for myself. You'd understand, if you went with me on one of these trips."

"Perhaps," she agreed, not dropping her eyes.

"You don't realize, Fannie, that newspapers mean everything

to a region. In the Middle West, for the most part there are only weeklies. For the men who edit them, the job is a sort of crusade. Sometimes they bring their presses part of the way in river boats and then finish up hauling them by ox cart overland. Always, someway, they get them to the town and set them up somewhere. A few months ago I helped some settlers bring a hand press up the river on a homemade raft. Once we go it there, we set it up in a cow shed."

"And then you had to stay and set the type," she said, faint irony in her voice.

"Of course," he told her simply. "There was no one else who knew how. I stayed long enough to teach a boy to do it, and then I went on."

He had been gone almost a year and all he could talk about was newspapers.

"We have a newspaper here in Sandusky," she repeated softly. "Someone has to work on it, too."

He looked at her keenly. "I read between the lines in your letter," he told her. "You made me see your position without putting it into words. Why else do you think I came back as quickly as I did?"

She felt the blood rush to her face. Without actually putting anything into words, she had set down the conditions under which she would accept him. He was too clever not to sense this.

"Fannie," he said, his voice rough with tenderness, "I made it clear in my letters how I feel about you. But even when we were in school together, when we sang together, I never hid what was in my heart."

He moved closer toward her, and instinctively, she drew away. "I have come back," he said. "I am going to work for Sylvester on *The Mirror*. Fannie, will you marry me?"

Edmund was going to stay here in Sandusky. Together they would live in this lovely town, with her family and friends nearby, with the flowers and trees and lake and sky around them. Secure and content. A house set back in a neat yard; church and school at hand. Dear, familiar things—all the ingredients for a good life.

Here was Fannie's freedom; it was not a nebulous thing, beyond the horizon of home and family.

"Will you?" he repeated.

How well she should know her answer. Across the width of half a dozen states her heart had followed him these past months. Yet she hesitated now when the thing she wanted most was being offered her.

"You don't believe I'll stay here, do you?" he asked her gently. It did not occur to him to say, "You don't love me." He knew better than that. "You think—after a while—I'll want to roam."

"Yes," she told him. "That's it."

He hesitated. Perhaps, she thought wildly, he's getting ready to promise me he'll never leave here. And suddenly she knew she could not ask that of him. She loved Sandusky, but she loved Edmund more. She loved him enough to take him just the way he was without binding him to any promise. "The bright shape of freedom," he had said, was the thing which newspapers meant to him. Freedom must be his. Now, and always.

"Yes," she broke in with what probably sounded like unmaidenly haste, but she didn't give that a worry. She had to forestall any promise he might make and later regret. "Yes, I'll marry you, Edmund."

He took her in his arms, and kissed her. And she thought, this is better than letters. Oh, much—much better—

3

Fannie Maria Lathrop and Edmund Gibson Ross were married on October 15, 1848. The journey from Janesville was rather a long one for Edmund's parents and younger sisters and brothers to make, so they did not come. But Sylvester was there to represent the family.

Uncle Elial Rice came over from Sullivan. "Prettiest bride I ever saw," he told Fannie, his face alight with love and good humor. "Bet you made that dress yourself. Does Edmund know how lucky he is, getting a girl who can sew and cook and keep house and look as pretty as a picture?"

"Maybe you should remind him," Fannie laughed.

She had helped her mother make the dress and she knew it was pretty. A green silk, richly braided, it had white undersleeves and a lace collar. The material had come from Mr. Courtney's store, and he had been as pleased as Fannie herself that it turned out so well.

The petticoat, of finest muslin, fell over crinoline, so that the skirt of the dress stood out from Fannie's small figure, almost as if it had a will of its own. The bodice, slightly pointed, showed her small waist to advantage. She looped her hair up carefully, disciplining the curls, and when she saw herself in the mirror, she was content. Edmund was going to think she looked pretty.

When the time for the ceremony came, she had no such vain thoughts, however. She was conscious of her parents—her mother cheerful and matter-of-fact and her father close to tears, restrained only by the fact that men did not cry. Dear, dear Pa—for a moment she wanted to comfort him, telling him he must not feel bad. Edmund was so good, and she was so happy. And then the words of the service started and she was listening, so she would not miss any, and would answer at the right time.

"I, Fannie, take thee, Edmund—"

A few phrases, a few minutes, a few promises—and she was no longer Fannie Lathrop, but Mrs. Edmund Gibson Ross ". . . as long as you both shall live."

And that is all too short a time, she thought, as Edmund kissed her. She touched his ring on her finger. *Too short a time—*

They settled down comfortably in a little house not too far from Fannie's parents. Edmund went daily to *The Mirror* and seemed content enough, although there were times when Fannie thought she detected a hint of the old restlessness.

No matter how late he came home, he usually brought a book with him or some newspapers from other towns. He would pore over them while the candle sputtered and flamed and shadows danced on the walls. She schooled herself to sit quietly, her sewing in her hands, until he wanted to talk.

One evening he looked up from a copy of the New York *Tribune*.

"The editor, Horace Greeley," Edmund said thoughtfully, "has some good sense in what he says. He thinks there's no end to the possibilities of the West."

She didn't answer that.

"The thing we have to watch," he continued thoughtfully, "is this business of slavery. Every new region that opens up must take a firm stand in the matter."

"Slavery?" Fannie looked up from her mending. "I thought the people who went West were not slave owners."

"That's not the point," he told her. "With all the people pushing West, we'll have new states asking for admission. Already the trouble has started—the politicians from both North and South, squaring off, fighting to bring in the new states—even the territories—on their side."

"You've chosen your side, I take it."

"I'm on the side of right, Fannie. When an issue is as clear cut as this one, there's no difficulty in making a decision. Slavery is wrong and I am against it."

It was a position which Edmund made clear in his editorials for *The Mirror*. These, he not only wrote, but also set in type. Because of his pronouncements Fannie herself became more fully aware of the situation. There were times when it seemed to her that the whole country was in a giant tug-of-war, each section pulling against the other, each declaring its own stand the right one. Minnesota was established as a territory where slavery was to be forever prohibited. Edmund counted that as a great gain, setting the type which so proclaimed it. But the Missouri legislators had taken the position that the right to prohibit slavery in any territory belonged exclusively to the people thereof. Edmund proclaimed this compromise, if not actual loss.

He had been a Democrat, but now he found much to criticize in the party's leniency toward slavery.

"I think I'll shift to the Free Soil bunch," he said. "They want the spread of slavery stopped, and they want railroads. If we can build railroads from ocean to ocean, the country will grow. As you said, people traveling west won't want slaves. Railroads are the answer."

He talked about this to anyone who would listen.

But there were other things going on in Sandusky which people discussed little, and then in guarded tones and only to the right people.

In the dead of night knocks were heard on doors which opened stealthily, showing no band of light. People were drawn inside, people as dark as the night through which they fled. And although no word was said, one still knew what went on within those houses. Food was brought and set before weary travelers; hushed voices gave plans; and then the dusky visitors were put to bed in attic or basement or barn loft. By morning the house looked just as it did any other day. Then, again with the coming of night, there was more hushed activity. A man came with a closed carriage, or a wagon which would look no different from any of those others carrying produce to town. But those who knew could have told of travelers hidden beneath empty grain sacks. Under the shadow of night these carriages and wagons were driven away by strong, silent, trustworthy men. They drove swiftly until they came to some prearranged place where the passengers were turned over to others who knew what they received. Thus the human cargo was passed on, like a sacred trust, taking those dark travelers each day closer to Canada and freedom.

Sandusky was an important station in the "Underground Railway," the system which helped escaped slaves to get to Canada. When Fannie went to Mr. Courtney's store some mornings and found him red-eyed from lack of sleep, she knew the reason why. He himself had driven all night long, pushing his team and carriage as fast as was possible, and then had driven back in time to open the store. But she said nothing except, "Good morning, Mr. Courtney. I think I'll have some sugar and molasses today." And he would fill her order, courteous and thoughtful as always.

4

But suddenly, all talk of politics and slavery ceased.

Cholera struck Sandusky.

It had started half a world away, in India, and had spread westward to Persia and to Russia. At first, people here had mentioned it briefly—a distant, terrible thing which happened to other people who had no notions of sanitation or health. Then it was no longer far-off; it had come to the eastern shores of the United States. It moved closer still, having made itself an unwelcome passenger on the ships sailing the Great Lakes. It came to Sandusky in June 1849.

So suddenly it came, no one was prepared. But none could mistake the nature of the seizure; the agonizing cramps; the dry and wrinkled skin; the eyes deeply sunken; the pulse so weak as to be almost imperceptible; the voice lowered to a hoarse whisper. Those in each family who had not yet succumbed treated the sick, giving them ice water to drink, putting mustard and turpentine plasters on the abdomen, and rubbing the flesh already turned cold and blue. Most of the time these ministrations were in vain: the patient died. Frequently the very ones who had nursed their sick would themselves fall ill; and perhaps there would be a double funeral, so quickly did death come.

Every day there was an account of deaths of friends. Fannie's mother would come briefly to tell her of those who had gone. She kept her two younger children at home, as every mother did. Yet nothing seemed to help. The plague spread—and with it, panic. Each evening when Edmund returned from the newspaper, he too brought news of more seizures. As Fannie listened to them, a knowledge was coming to her that made the news seem even more horrible, the epidemic a thing to be more greatly feared.

When Edmund came home one night, his face looked tired and white with despair.

"What's wrong?" she asked, thinking one of the family—his or hers—had been stricken.

"Mr. Courtney—" he said.

"Oh, no—" she cried. "Not Mr. Courtney!" Not the good, kind storekeeper who made everyone's welfare his own. Men like him could not be spared. Surely death would realize this and pass him by.

"He was at the store," Edmund went on dully, "and became ill. He knew what it was—"

Well he might; there could be no doubt when the symptoms, now so familiar, came.

"So he walked out of the store to the cabinet warehouse where he chose his coffin. Then he went home and lay down. By the time the coffin was delivered, he was dead."

Poor, poor Mr. Courtney, she thought. And poor Edmund. I have to tell him now. It was going to be such a happy thing to tell— She began to shiver a little, although the July day was warm.

He put his arms around her, his face white. "What's wrong, Fannie?" he asked, terror in his voice, such terror as everyone in Sandusky felt now when a loved one acted less than his usual self.

"I'm going to have a baby," she whispered. "What if—"

"Hush," he said. "Don't talk like that." He held her close as if he, by his own might, would keep away the danger and her fear.

The scourge struck home in August. Sylvester Ross caught it and died in the quick agony all victims experienced. Fannie felt his death deeply. He had been friend and benefactor as well as brother. First he had taught Edmund the printing trade, back in Huron and then, when he came to Sandusky and bought *The Mirror* he gave the younger brother the job which enabled him to go to high school. Without Sylvester, Fannie and Edmund might never have met.

The horror mounted. Victims died and lay where they fell because the members of their families were too ill to bury them properly. In such cases, anyone well and brave enough to do so wrapped the body in a sheet and bore it to a common grave at the foot of Harrison Street. There were no prayers or service, unless the bearer said one for himself. And then, in gray sorrow, he walked back home and once there, like as not, found another friend or loved one had died in his absence.

Fannie wished to be away from this spot on which the curse of death had fallen. She could scarcely bring herself to look at the lake or Put-in Bay, once spots greatly loved, because it seemed almost as if the plague hovered over the water, waiting to strike again.

Even as she wondered how to tell Edmund her fears, grown almost too great now for concealing, Uncle Elial Rice came over from Sullivan.

"I couldn't get a word out of the town," he said, "so I came to see for myself."

They told him of all the deaths. Of course, they told him about Sylvester. He looked at Fannie shrewdly.

"You've no business to be here, child, in your condition. I'm going to take you back with me."

Fannie looked swiftly at Edmund. Frightened she was, but she would not leave this doomed town unless he went with her.

"Edmund will come, too. Won't you, Ed?"

Edmund did not hesitate. "Yes, we'll go," he said.

5

It was fall before they came back, to enter a city of the dead. Four hundred townspeople had died, including Fannie's father and the two younger sisters. She went to her mother swiftly and for a long time they stood, not speaking, their arms around each other. There were no words to use at times like this.

Once more they settled into the routine of the town's life, trying to take up where they had left off. It was a thing difficult to accomplish. So many good friends had died. Many, having been spared, wanted no part of the town and had moved away. Sandusky had become a ghost town.

The baby, a girl, was born in December. They named her Lillie. Such a good baby, little Lillie Ross. Bright and sweet and pretty. She should have filled her parents' hearts with pure delight, had not delight been a thing now foreign to this town. When Fannie walked to her mother's house, carrying baby Lillie with her, she averted her eyes, trying not to see the mass burial ground and the empty houses where once good friends had lived. There was, however, no escaping the sight of the water lapping at the streets of the town, the water which was suspected of carrying the plague. If it had come once, what was there to prevent it from coming again? She shivered a little, thinking of this. She was not strong like Ma; she could not live on if Lillie or Edmund were taken from her.

Edmund, too, showed signs of restlessness, and no wonder. Every day he set type for the stories which bore out the things he had told Fannie before their marriage. Going West was a fever in men's blood. Every issue of Mr. Greeley's paper advised young men to "Go West and grow up with the country." Mr. Thoreau and Mr. Longfellow and Mr. Whitman wrote about the region. Congress talked endlessly about it. Everyone, however, agreed that John Frémont was the one who knew it best, and why shouldn't he, always off exploring it, gone months at a time and nearly losing his life in storms and blizzards. How did his wife, Jessie Benton Frémont, stand to have him gone so much?

Now, when gold was discovered in California, Frémont had gone there, too, taking Jessie with him. Edmund said he could do a great deal to influence the territory to come into the Union as a free state. He took this matter of the extension of slavery so seriously; as if, perhaps, he felt that he himself should do something to curb it.

Strange, wasn't it, that when they did leave Sandusky, the decision was hers, not Edmund's?

It came about because one day Lillie ran a slight temperature. Nothing alarming—her mother assured Fannie that all babies did this occasionally. But it could have been—oh, it could have been! When Edmund came home for dinner, the stove was cold and there was nothing on the table at all. Fannie sat in a small rocking chair, holding Lillie, sleeping now, in her arms. Tears were streaming down her face.

"Let's get away from here," she burst out.

Edmund looked at her sharply, interest and hope in his eyes. It was as if he wanted her to remember, afterward, that he had not broken his promise; he had not suggested their leaving Sandusky. Even so, his face could not hide how great his wish had been.

"We could go to Janesville, where Ma and Pa are," he said. He spoke so quickly, she could tell easily enough that the plan had been in his own mind for a long time.

"What could you do there?" she asked. His parents were living on a farm. Edmund was no farmer.

"Oh, we'd stay there only long enough to get our bearings. I can find a job. Maybe in Chicago. I liked that town. Don't worry, ever, about my getting work. Any man with a shirttail full of type can get a job on a newspaper anywhere he goes."

The old way of life. The one she hadn't liked. And now, she had pushed him back into it.

"How would we go?" she asked.

"By boat, of course."

She had wanted to leave because she was afraid of what the water might bring to them! Still, there was no turning back and she knew it. She looked at Lillie asleep in her arms. Such a little girl to start moving. But then, smaller ones were going away every day with their parents. Babies were born along the trail to the West. The westward movement was too big to be stopped by a frail thing like a baby.

"I'll tell you what, Fannie," he said. "Why don't we ask your mother to go, too?"

Fannie was glad he had suggested it. It would be good to have Ma in a new, strange country.

"I think she'll want to go with us," Fannie said. "There's nothing to hold her here now."

Edmund helped Fannie pack. He was brisk and excited, a tremendous eagerness in everything he did. Sandusky was, for him, a book whose covers he could now close.

Finally they were ready. Friends and neighbors came down to see them off as they boarded the boat.

"Good-by—" they said. And, "Good luck."

They did not say, "Come back to us." People did not turn their faces eastward, once they had gone West.

"Good-by—" Fannie said, her mother and Edmund echoing her. They called as long as the voices carried, the sound tenuous webs binding them to the shore.

Edmund and Ma, with little Lillie, went down to the stateroom, but Fannie remained on the deck, her face still turned, like Lot's wife, back toward the town she had left.

Northward the boat went, across the long and narrow Sandusky Bay. Skirting Cedar Point, it passed Marblehead peninsula. On it slipped, leaving behind the gray shoreline of upturned rocks and masses of trees with the contrasting browns and greens; passing ship-shaped Kelleys Island, its shores rock-ribbed and bay-indented, its limestone boulders rising out of the blue water. Huge white rocks showed stark against the girdle of red cedars which bound the island. The boat moved on until, at last, it went into the open lake.

Even then Fannie stood, believing she still could glimpse the outlines of Sandusky, knowing in her heart she would never see it again.

II

Milwaukee

1851–1854

FANNIE ROSS set the table for supper, an edge of exasperation in her movements. One, two, three, four places and a highchair for little Arthur. She probably should go on and feed the children, for there was no telling when Edmund and William would come. Honestly, for weeks now she might as well have been running a hotel, with the irregular hours the two kept.

Lillie stood hopefully at the window, a small pickaninny doll clutched in her arms. Arthur, so recently started walking that the whole business had a tremendous fascination for him, was exploring the room with eager curiosity. Fannie smiled at them with absent tenderness, and looked out the window once more. She saw Lake Michigan, dull gray under a sullen March sky, and the Wisconsin River cutting through the middle of the town, but she did not see either Edmund or his brother William.

"Where are Papa and Uncle William?" Lillie asked, growing impatient in her vigil.

"They'll be here any minute now," Fannie told her. "They probably had to do some extra work on the paper."

Her reassuring words sounded good to her own ears. Here they were in Milwaukee in a snug little house, with Edmund and

William working on the *Free Democrat* (because William knew the editor and publisher, Mr. Sherman Booth). Lillie, four years old now, and baby Arthur were strong and healthy; and Ma lived close by—oh, she should be counting her blessings.

One would have to work hard to find fault with Milwaukee. There must be thirty thousand people living here, with more arriving every day. When summer and harvest time came Fannie looked out her kitchen window to see the harbor filled with wheat barges. (It was the largest wheat shipping port in the world, Edmund bragged.) Other boats, carrying people and freight, steamed in and out all the time. If you liked music, drama, or lecturers, there were societies organized for those purposes. Oh, it was foolish for her to feel uneasy. Yet she was, and with good reason.

Scarcely had they settled in the town before she learned that Milwaukee, like Sandusky, was an important station in the Underground Railway. Waukesha, twenty miles away, was the heart of the movement ("that abolition hole," the proslavery forces called the town). In Waukesha *The American Freeman* was published, stirring up its readers to such good effect that farmers and tradesmen were willing to leave farms and counters to drive all night in order to take the fugitives to the next station.

When Fannie first heard about the part Milwaukee and Waukesha played in the Underground Railway, she gave the matter little thought, taking it for granted just as she had done in Sandusky. It had no personal meaning for her; the whole question of slavery did not touch her, for all the strong convictions Edmund had in the matter. They owned no slaves, nor wanted to. But now, three years later, she could feel a shadow falling menacingly across her path.

Mr. Booth was one of the foremost men in the movement. In the pages of his paper, and in his own personal utterances, he made no effort to conceal his beliefs. Every lover of freedom and justice, he said, should aid slaves to escape their masters. For four years Mr. Booth had been thundering out against the Compromise of 1850, when the Fugitive Slave Law had included a provision which made it the duty of the Federal officers to capture and return escaped slaves to their masters; it also decreed that anyone helping a slave escape was guilty of treason.

Edmund and William, working for Mr. Booth, admired him greatly—oh, Fannie knew she was right when she feared for them.

In the past weeks, her fears had been given much to feed upon. There was an undercurrent of excitement, of preoccupation, about Edmund. He was late for meals; he often worked nights at the paper. And the editorials he wrote—my goodness, any proslave man would suspect him, even though he was innocent of anything save expressing an opinion which might be that of his employer and not his own at all.

But the opinions were his own. Edmund believed what he said. He wouldn't write a word he didn't believe with all his heart.

"There's Papa now," Lillie cried, running to the door to meet him, Arthur at her heels.

Edmund opened the door, bent to kiss the children. Over their heads his eyes met Fannie's.

"M-m-mmm—something smells good," he said.

"Potatoes and onions," she told him, knowing it was not food alone he meant, but the warm cleanliness of the kitchen, the spicy pungency of geraniums in the window. The home smell.

How well Edmund looked. Like so many young men of the day he had allowed his beard to grow after the fashion of Kossuth, the Hungarian patriot whose visit to New York had made him a hero to all freedom lovers. A beard was becoming to Edmund. It made him look more handsome and distinguished than ever. He probably knew she was thinking this as she smiled at him. He walked over to kiss her.

"Where's William?" she asked, trying not to sound concerned.

"He'll be along in a minute. He stopped by to have a word with Mary Elizabeth Berry."

"Oh, those two—" Fannie said, relief flooding her voice. "What's that you have under your arm?"

"A book—Mr. Booth sent it to you."

"That was kind of him," Fannie said. Mr. Booth was always sending her little presents, and never forgot to ask about the children when he saw her. She should be ashamed of herself for thinking he would bring any sort of trouble on Edmund.

She took the volume which he handed her, scarcely looking at it. She was more interested in him than in any book.

"It was written by a married woman with a family," he told her.

Fannie looked at the title—*Uncle Tom's Cabin*—and wondered briefly how a wife and mother could find time to write a book.

"Sit down and eat your supper before it gets cold," she said.

Edmund did as she suggested, but he had not forgotten the book. "We'll read it aloud tonight," he promised.

"Good," she said. If Edmund read aloud, that meant he'd be home. The evening promised to be a pleasant one.

After the children were in bed, Fannie and Edmund settled down in the sitting room. The candlelight flickered, reflecting itself on the polished wood of the organ, their one luxury (and how proud Edmund was that she could play it), and on Edmund's face as he read. His voice was like music, even when he spoke. Fannie's head was bowed over a pinafore for Lillie in which she was making buttonholes.

The story was certainly not a pleasant one to hear. How vividly Mrs. Stowe told about it all—Uncle Tom, best of the lot, although he was black; Topsy, so stupid and yet so discerning; poor desperate Eliza who must escape with her child; and the terrible Simon Legree. The characters seemed very real to Fannie, almost as if she knew them.

"Poor, poor, Eliza," she said, dropping her work to wipe tears from her eyes. "I am glad it's only a story."

"It may be a story," Edmund told her, "but things like that are happening all the time to the slaves. Families separated, never to see each other again. Beatings, and worse. And always the knowledge that they are property—something to be bought and sold at will."

"But," Fannie said uncertainly, "there must be some good slaveholders. There is even one in this book."

"There is little difference, really, between being owned by a good or a bad man. In either case, a slave is not free. It's like—" he hesitated, wanting to find words to bring the situation down to Fannie's own experience—"it's like that pickaninny doll Lillie has. She loves it, and takes good care of it. But if she decides to throw it into the stove some day she can, because she owns it."

The next evening Edmund and William were very late for supper. Fannie kept things warm as best she could, trying not to be impatient, knowing something important was keeping them. A newspaperman was like a doctor, at the beck and call of the public, never able to set a definite schedule for himself. She had resigned herself to the fact that the steak was quite ruined—dry as a bone and flavorless—when Edmund came alone. He was much too concerned to notice that the food she set before him was less than perfect.

"What's wrong?" she asked anxiously.

"Remember the former slave living in Racine—Joshua Glover?"

"Of course." Mr. Booth had discussed the case of the runaway slave with William and Edmund in her presence. Several years ago Glover, fleeing from his master in Missouri, had come to Racine, not more than fifty miles from Milwaukee. Once there, his way was made easy. He found work in a sawmill and was given a small shack in which to live. Although a number of people knew about him, everyone seemed to think the secret would be kept.

"They've caught him," Edmund told her. "Someone must have tipped off Garland, the owner. Last night a United States marshal named Catton, with another man to help him, went to Glover's shack in Racine and dragged him out. They handcuffed him and are bringing him here to the jail in Milwaukee because feeling was running so high in Racine they didn't dare try to hold him there."

"What will happen now?" Fannie asked.

"He's supposed to be turned over to Garland tomorrow afternoon at two o'clock. But from the way people are talking, Catton may not find the transfer as easy as he thinks."

"But Edmund," she said, "after all, Glover is an escaped slave, and anyone who interferes now—anyone who has been helping him, as far as that goes—is breaking the Fugitive Slave Law."

Everyone knew about the penalties for helping a slave escape. Any citizen refusing to aid in capturing and returning escaped slaves was declared guilty of treason, and the laws of the land did not deal lightly with traitors.

"In this case," Edmund retorted hotly, "the law is wrong. It asks us to align ourselves with a sin against man and God."

He was growing angry. To him, freedom was a sort of religion. Once Edmund was convinced of a thing, there was no way of swaying him from the course which he believed to be the right one. She should be glad he was like this—too many men walked weakly on the other side of any issue, averting their eyes to obvious wrongs, refusing to take a stand.

"I'll go on and eat," he told her. "William may not come at all."

Edmund might as well have stayed away himself. As soon as the last bite of supper was swallowed, he got up from the table and started toward the door.

"Don't wait up for me," he told her, over his shoulder. "There's no telling when I'll be home."

He was off, his footsteps very quick and determined on the wooden sidewalk. Fannie cleared up after the meal, feeling uneasy and apprehensive. She didn't like the way things were going. Not one little bit, she didn't. Edmund was keyed up to the point where he could easily do something rash and impractical. Her mind couldn't quite name the nature of the indiscretion she feared, but her heart told her it was not only possible but imminent.

He did not come in until after midnight. She had finally taken him at his word and gone to bed, although she was still awake. By the way he slipped around the room quietly, undressing in the dark and not saying a word, she knew he didn't want to talk. Perhaps it was just as well. Disturbed as she was, anything she might say would only serve to upset him and, like as not, provoke a quarrel.

He seemed no more anxious to talk the next morning, nor was William inclined to conversation, either. The two men ate hastily, exchanging only monosyllables, and those about such matters as passing sugar and cream. Before Fannie could make up her mind how to start asking questions, they were up and away.

Edmund came home for dinner alone. At last, he not only had news but seemed willing to talk about it.

"A hundred men just rode in from Racine," he told her. "They said that when they left there, the church bells were all ringing as if for a death. The town is greatly upset by the Glover affair."

"Where are the Racine men now?" she asked, setting a cup of coffee beside him.

"In the courthouse square, milling around the jail where Glover is being held. The people of Milwaukee are joining them. Must have been several hundred people there when I left."

Glover had been brought from Racine because the feeling was so high there; it seemed to be no less so here in Milwaukee. Fannie's concern spilled over into her question. "What is going to happen?"

"I don't know exactly," Edmund told her. "But it looks to me as if the people of Milwaukee mean to join the group from Racine in seeing that Glover is not handed back to Garland."

"Edmund," she protested, "you won't get mixed up in this, will you?"

He looked at her quietly. Something about that level, intent glance frightened her more than a burst of argument might have done.

"Why not?"

"Because," she said simply, "it would be treason."

"Patrick Henry had something to say about that word 'treason,'" Edmund told her. "If he hadn't taken the stand he did, none of us might be here."

Even as he was speaking, he moved toward the door. "I must go," he said. "If I don't come home for supper, don't worry. I'll be all right."

She went to his side, put her hand on his arm. "Please, Edmund—" she begged.

He released her hand gently.

"Now Fannie," he said soothingly. It wasn't an answer at all, and yet, to her it was a very definite one. He put his arms around her and held her close and she clung to him, the very tenseness of her clasp an entreaty. He kissed her quickly. And then he took his hands and pulled her clinging arms loose—not roughly, but with decision. He kissed her again, and then he was outside the door and gone, walking very fast in the direction of the courthouse.

2

Fannie tried to go about her work, but whatever she did she found herself listening, for what she did not quite know but feared nonetheless. Lillie, sitting in her little rocking chair beside the window, was dressing and undressing the pickaninny doll with motherly tenderness and Arthur, bedded down for his nap, was protesting indignantly.

"Mama," Lillie said, "someone's coming down the street, awful fast—"

Fannie ran to the front door and jerked it open. Sure enough a man was riding as if the very fiends of hell were loose upon his trail. One glance told her it was Mr. Sherman Booth. And, as he rode he cried, "Freemen, arise. Come to the rescue! There are slave catchers in our midst. Be at the courthouse at two o'clock."

"What's he saying, Mama?" Lillie asked.

"He's—" Fannie searched for words to explain to the child, words which would have the conviction Edmund expressed and yet would not repudiate her own feelings. The situation was very clear now. Mr. Booth himself was arousing the people of Milwaukee, already in a turmoil, bringing them to a state of determination which would result in the freeing of Glover. In doing this, he would be setting himself against the laws of his country; not only that, but he would be involving his own fellow townspeople in the act. The thing she had feared had become a terrible, menacing reality. Two o'clock. That was the hour set for the release of the slave to his master. Mr. Booth, apparently, had other ideas.

They went back inside the house, but Fannie could not longer control her restlessness. As the hands of the clock drew nearer the fateful hour, she knew she could not remain away from the courthouse. Some inner urge, deeper than thought or reason, pushed her on. Picking up little Arthur, she bundled him in a blanket and found Lillie's mittens and cap and coat. She wrapped herself warmly against the chill March air.

"Are we going to Mr. Booth's meeting, Mama?" Lillie asked.

"No," Fannie said, "you're going to Grandma's. That will be ever so much nicer."

She was quite sure the courthouse square would be no place for children the rest of the afternoon.

Edmund had been right. A huge crowd—by this time there must be several thousands—had congregated in the courthouse yard and the square around it, presenting itself as a common unit of protest. Fannie decided that the American House, with its three stories rising proudly against the sky, would be a good vantage point. Here she would be a little removed from the crush, yet just across the street from the courthouse yard. She took her place on the portico. From where she stood she could see the jail—two small wooden cabins, surrounded by a rickety picket fence. Glover was inside one of them.

"Has anything happened?" she asked a man standing next to her.

"No," he said, not taking his eyes off the jail. "Garland was supposed to be here for Glover at two, but he hasn't shown up yet."

"Do they—" she was not quite sure who she meant by "they," but she went on, "—do *they* mean to let him go?"

The man looked at her curiously as if he wanted to ask where she had been these past hours if she could ask such a question.

"The sheriff from Racine just rode in," the man told her. "He has a warrant for the arrest of Catton and Garland, Glover's owner, for assault and battery. You should have seen Glover when he got here—his face streaming with blood and his hair matted with it."

Seeking Edmund and William, Fannie stood on tiptoe, trying to see over the heads of the crowd. Oh, it was a great nuisance, being so short.

"Do you know where Mr. Booth is?" Fannie asked the man still standing beside her.

"He's inside—" Her companion indicated the American House by a jerk of his thumb. "He's got a bunch of men with him. They must be planning something."

A bunch of men with him! No wonder she did not see either Edmund or William in the crowd. Good and well she knew they were with Mr. Booth, working on whatever plan was to be carried out.

People continued to converge on the courthouse, some joining her on the portico of the American House. One did not need a second look at their angry faces to know in which direction their sympathies lay. The steps of St. James Cathedral, so recently completed that piles of lumber were still scattered around, were thick with people.

Time dragged on; it was well past the hour when Glover was supposed to have been turned over to his owner, and yet nothing had happened. Already the light of the short March day was beginning to dim. Fannie shivered, but not from cold, although there was a rawness in the air.

Then suddenly the doors in the American House opened and Sherman Booth strode out, a dozen or so men following him. Fannie caught her breath quickly. Yes, Edmund and William were in the group. They passed so close to her she could have reached out and touched Edmund; she half-extended her hand, and then let it fall at her side.

The crowd, until now restless and noisy, grew quiet, sensing that something tremendous was about to happen. Mr. Booth and his group moved across the street to the Cathedral. Together, as if by prearranged signal, they bent to pick up a long piece of timber and then, with it on their shoulders, they started toward the jail.

"They're rushing the jail—"

People caught up the words, tossed them back over their shoulders, to have them repeated by other waves of people. All eyes were on those men with the huge piece of timber on their shoulders, making their way toward the cabin which held Glover. Once there, they swung their weapon back and forth, like a battering ram.

There was a sound of wood on wood—that would be the door crashing. And then, so quickly it did not seem possible for anything to have happened, the rescuers were coming back from the jail. Booth was in the lead, with Edmund and William immediately behind him. Following them was the slave, Joshua Glover, his hands manacled, tears streaming down his face. Swiftly the men ran, and Fannie, on her tiptoes, watched their flight. A small light wagon had appeared as if by magic in the street, and into this Glover was hoisted. He stood upright, lifting his manacled hands above his head. "Glory, glory hallelujah," he shouted.

As the wagon dashed off, people made way for it. Once it passed they fell in line behind it, and as they followed they took up the cry of the slave. Fannie could hear them, even after the wagon was out of sight. "Hallelujah," the words came back faintly. "Glory, glory hallelujah."

"They'll make it to Canada safe enough," the man next to her said. "It all worked out slick as a whistle."

A great relief came to Fannie, but not because of the assurance of the slave's safety. Edmund and William had not been on the wagon; they would be home this evening. She turned and started off toward Ma's to pick up the children. She must have something good for supper, a hot and nourishing meal. Edmund and William had eaten little in the past two days.

It was not until she was back home, with preparations well under way for the meal, that her relief was canceled out. Edmund might not have been on that wagon which bore Joshua Glover away, but he had taken part in the rescue. He and William. With her own eyes she had seen them. If Glover's owner wanted to prefer charges against the Ross brothers, he had a clear case.

3

Garland did prefer charges against Booth, omitting, however, to name anyone else even though there were some—the Ross brothers, for instance—whose guilt was equally clear. Booth was arrested and a legal battle followed, one which was fought through state and federal courts. The case aroused the nation. The Wisconsin legislature defiantly denounced the United States Supreme Court for its decision, which was against Booth, and openly urged resistance to the mandate. Garland sued Booth for two hundred dollars, the value of the slave. These and other court costs mounted up until the *Free Democrat* had to be sold to satisfy judgment and pay costs.

And there were Edmund and William without work.

"What are we going to do now?" Fannie asked, a note of desperation in her voice. It was all right to take a stand for conscience's sake, but that did not buy food and shelter for a family.

"We'll find something," Edmund assured her.

She wanted to tell him that he had gone too far for the sake of a Negro who, until the day of the rescue, was scarcely more than a name to him. But she refrained.

"No one suffers permanently for standing up for what he believes to be right," he told her, evidently sensing her rebellious thoughts.

"I can't see what poor Mr. Booth gained," Fannie couldn't help pointing out.

"The end of the story hasn't been written yet," Edmund said. "And anyway, he is rewarded by his own conscience, as I have been."

She started to retort that such reward did not fill a rapidly emptying flour barrel, but was held back by the knowledge that Edmund knew this as well as she did. He was no wide-eyed dreamer who thought that, once he had done his duty, manna would fall from Heaven to meet the needs of wife and children. He wanted another job and she should be thinking of ways to keep his hopes high instead of reproaching him. Besides, since Mr. Booth engineered the rescue, the *Free Democrat* would have folded even if Edmund had remained home drinking coffee the day Glover was freed.

For a man without work, Edmund seemed to be extremely busy. Once when he failed to come home with William for supper, Fannie asked her brother-in-law point-blank what her husband was doing. William hesitated and shifted in his chair before he finally answered, "I left him with Mr. Holton."

"Mr. Edward Holton?"

"Yes—" William slanted his eyes away from her, but she knew a great deal just by hearing the name. Edward Holton—banker, promoter, abolitionist. And an active figure in the Underground movement.

"Now don't you worry, Fannie," William advised her kindly. "Edmund is all right."

She made no answer. It would take more than William's assurances to allay her fears in the matter. When Edmund came, much later, Fannie put the remains of the warmed-over meal before him and said, "All right—I know. But you might have told me yourself."

"I meant to," he said, laying down his fork and looking straight at her. "I was going to tell you tonight. Until this evening, there was really nothing definite."

"You are going to help—to help—"

In your own home, in the bosom of your family, you hesitated about coming out and saying the words. Even in a town where you knew almost everyone was sympathetic to the movement. That sympathy had done nothing to save poor Mr. Booth.

"Yes, I've agreed to help Mr. Holton. If I had not, Fannie, I could never have faced myself again." He reached out to put his hand over her wrist, holding it fast. "You understand, don't you?"

"Oh, I suppose I do," she said. She wanted to jerk free of him and cry out, *But, oh, the risk, Edmund. You have a wife and two small children. Think what it would mean to them if you were caught*. One look at his face—earnest, sober, quietly confident—prevented her from doing either. Edmund had acted as he felt he must and there was nothing for her to do but accept things as they were.

"Yes," she said softly, "I think I understand. Now eat your supper and tell me what your job will be."

Edmund released her wrist and began to eat.

"I don't know exactly, as yet," he said truthfully. "It may be much, it may be little. It could be nothing. But when the time comes, if it does, I'll have to do—well, whatever there is to do."

If his purpose had been to relieve her concern, he had certainly failed. Better, she thought, a definite responsibility than a nebulous uncertainty.

Edmund got up from the table. "Fannie," he said, "I want you to find me some old bedding. Something warm, but not fancy. And you might collect some old clothes, as well."

"What for?" she asked fearfully.

"I am going to prepare a shelter in the barn loft. It may never be needed, but in case it is, I must have it ready."

"You mean—" She could not bring herself to finish the sentence whose import was so great.

"Yes," he said. "I know. I thought it all through before I decided to help Mr. Booth. I have from the first not doubted the cost or risk in aiding the oppressed. I know I must help Mr. Holton, just as I helped Mr. Booth."

When he talked like that, there was no way of answering him.

4

Fannie watched the summer days melt away, dreading what the coming of winter could mean to a family whose breadwinner had no work. To occupy her mind, as well as to build up some bulwark against the possibilities, she began to sort through the family wardrobe. Thank goodness she was clever with the needle. She could repair, refurbish and make do with what they had. The children were growing so fast—for them she would have to manage new clothes by cutting down articles from Edmund's and her own wardrobe. This shirt, for instance, worn only at the collar and cuffs, would make a good dress for Arthur. There was a big bundle of scraps packed in a trunk which had not been opened since they moved from Sandusky. More than likely she could find many useful remnants there.

She was sitting down on the floor, surrounded by the contents of the trunk, when her mother came in.

"What are you doing?" she asked. "Fixing to piece a quilt?"

"I'm looking for materials to sew into clothes for the children. Look, Ma—here's a length of that green flowered dress I wore when Edmund came home. Remember—we were so afraid we wouldn't have enough to make it right and bought too much!"

"You're such a little thing," her mother said fondly, "it just naturally didn't take as much material for you as it did for most girls."

"And those yards of white stuff left over from my wedding petticoat—" She fingered the material gently, her mind and heart not here in Milwaukee at all, but back in Sandusky once more with the girl who had been Fannie Lathrop.

"You know, Ma," she said, "I think I *will* piece a quilt."

"Use only good, strong material," her mother advised. "A quilt is no better than its weakest block."

"I will," Fannie promised.

And so she would, but not quite in the way her mother meant. She would use only scraps from such garments as had meaning in their lives. Of course, the dress she had worn when Edmund came home from his wanderings to ask her to marry him. A bit of the pinafore in which Lillie had taken her first staggering steps; another from Arthur's little dress, the one Edmund had insisted must be a boy's outfit without lace or frills. She would set the blocks together with material from her wedding petticoat, which was white and strong and ideal for the purpose, besides having a pretty symbolism.

"It's good for you to keep busy," Ma said. She did not add what was most certainly in her mind—that work kept one from worrying—an omission for which Fannie was grateful. Even to

Ma, dear as she was, Fannie did not want to speak overmuch of their present situation lest her words imply a criticism of Edmund.

Fannie kept busy enough. But every time she went to the barn —to gather eggs or bring in wood for the stove or feed the chickens—she remembered the loft and the secret preparations Edmund had made for the comfort of guests who had not yet arrived (and in her heart she prayed they would never come). At such times, she hastened away from the barn.

Then gradually the keenest edge of her unquiet began to wear off and she almost—but not quite—forgot about the loft.

Fall settled over Milwaukee. The scarlet of the maples and the brown of the oaks drifted down to mingle with the dun grass. The lake was brightly, intensely blue in the sunshine. Then a period of cold drizzle set in, making it hard to believe the sun had shone so recently or, indeed, that it would ever shine again.

William and Edmund went about their ways, and Fannie did not question them. She felt that William, as an unmarried man, might well be taking even greater risks than those incurred by Edmund, and she wondered fleetingly how much Mary Elizabeth knew of the situation. One bright spot in the whole business was that Edmund spent most of his evenings at home now. He often read aloud while Fannie worked on quilt pieces or, with winter coming on, busied herself sewing warm things for the children.

She had planned to work on a coat for Arthur that evening in late October, using material from one of Edmund's old ones. Supper was finished and the children in bed although, goodness knows, it had been difficult enough to get Arthur there. Lillie, more biddable, had gone with little protest although she might lie awake for ages and then finally get up to trail into the sitting room to join her parents. But, at the moment, things were quiet.

Outside a storm lashed the town. The wind swept around the corners of the house; cold sleet dashed against the windowpanes. Inside all was warm and pleasant, with a fire in the grate and candles burning, and Edmund looking over a copy of the Milwaukee *Sentinel.* She started for her sewing, when he looked up to say, "Wouldn't this be a good evening for some music?"

She put aside any thought of sewing and went to the organ.

"Try this one," Edmund suggested, humming a few bars of a song which was very popular now, one written by a young composer named Stephen Foster.

"Come where my love lies dreaming—" he sang, and she followed hesitantly, until she had the rhythm and then swung into the melody with confidence, joining in the song.

"—the happy hours away," they sang together.

What a good voice Edmund had. It helped to cover hers, weak now from lack of practice and little knowledge of the song. She felt happy and relaxed and lifted up by the music. Her mind went back to old scenes—picnics on Put-in Bay with the yellow moon high in the heavens repeating itself in the waters of the bay. Two moons for the price of one, the girl Fannie Lathrop and the boy Edmund Ross used to say as they floated along in a canoe, singing together. Now here they were, man and wife, singing in another town far removed from Sandusky, their children asleep in the next room. Life had been good to her. At the moment it didn't seem to matter that Edmund had no job save a secret, uncertain thing about which they rarely talked.

"Come where my love—"

Edmund stopped, putting his head to one side and listening intently. Fannie, her fingers suspended over the keyboard, listened too. A noise—no, not so much a noise as an awareness of something outside. Swiftly Edmund went to the candle and extinguished it. Then, so surely and unerringly that he must have rehearsed the act mentally dozens of times he went through the kitchen to the back door. Fannie followed him; by the time she reached his side his hand was on the doorknob.

"Who's there?" he asked in a hushed, guarded voice. The answer, barely audible, must have satisfied him, for he opened the door.

Out of the darkness came darkness—two shrouded forms, the blackness of their skin and clothing one with the blackness of the night. Edmund reached a hand to pull them into the room and then closed the door after them.

"Do you think you were followed?" he asked.

"No—" a man's voice answered, low and strained as if the very kitchen walls might overhear.

Fannie stood paralyzed while Edmund drew the kitchen curtains and then lighted a candle. This done, he turned to her.

"Give them food, Fannie," he said as matter-of-factly as if they were only neighbors dropping in.

She could not seem to move. Instead she gazed at the newcomers. Here were runaway slaves right in her own kitchen! The man, for all his terror, had a certain dignity about him; the woman's face had a poignant beauty. She was fumbling now with her shawl and finally uncovered a small child—a boy, whom she inspected with anxious care.

A baby, out on a night like this! Fannie's fears gave way to action.

"I'll have something right away," she said.

Hastily she assembled whatever food she could find. The woman sat holding her baby, her eyes following Fannie's movements. Edmund and the man talked softly together, evidently getting, and giving, the necessary information.

"Come eat," Fannie said.

The two visitors made their way to the table, the woman still holding the baby. When Fannie reached to take the child, instinctively the mother drew back, clutching the baby closer to her.

"I won't hurt him," Fannie told her softly. After a moment, the woman surrendered the child. He was light, almost no weight at all in Fannie's arms. The brown eyes looked enormous in his little face as he regarded her gravely.

"How old is he?" Fannie asked the age-old question of mothers.

"He's almost a year." The mother's voice was soft and liquid. And troubled. She knew the child was too small for his age and too frail. He ought to be laughing and crowing and gurgling, reaching out his arms to go back to his mother. But instead he lay still in Fannie's arms.

"I'll warm some milk for him," Fannie said, getting to her feet, holding the baby cradled on her hip as she would have done with a child of her own. She poured the warm milk into a bowl, broke bits of bread into it, and spooned bites into the child's mouth. He liked this new game, leaning forward eagerly, opening his mouth like a fledgling in a nest. The mother ceased eating to watch the wonderful thing which was happening to her child.

"He's never been strong," she said gently.

Not strong. Yet perhaps the parents had been traveling for weeks.

"That's part of why we ran away," the woman went on.

Her soft, plaintive voice continued their story. Their names were Tilda and Mart. The baby was named Barney. They lived in Kentucky and their master was going to sell them, but not to the same man. Barney was sickly and the master didn't care if he died. Tilda was more valuable without an ailing child. When he wouldn't get a doctor she and Mart decided to run off. It had been awful hard, but now that they were here—

"You know what to do?" Edmund asked.

They nodded.

"You'll stay here until tomorrow night. Then you'll move on."

"More coffee?" Fannie broke in, unwilling to face the responsibility entailed in Edmund's statement.

She refilled the cups, still holding the baby crooked in one arm. Tilda's face was warm with content. She and Mart continued eating, slowly, although they must have been very hungry. Edmund asked no more questions, either because he knew all that was necessary or wanted them to eat in peace. Little Barney dropped off to sleep, and Fannie stood up, still holding him, and started toward the couch to lay him down. The room was very still.

Then it was that the door from the bedroom opened. Everyone jumped—the visitors with their forks halfway to their mouths, Fannie on her way to the couch, Edmund in his chair. As one person, they whirled to face danger. And there stood Lillie, her hair hanging loose about her face, her long nightgown held up in one little hand.

"I woke up," she explained, "and I was lonesome." She paused, as she saw the visitors and the baby in her mother's arms. "Oh," she cried, "a little black baby! Just like my doll—"

No one spoke. Of all the threats which might have come through the door, this was the one least expected.

"What are these—these black people doing here?" she asked. "Have they come to see us?"

Edmund was first to get hold of himself. He walked over to his daughter and gathered her up in his arms. "Yes, in a way," he told her. "Now you must go back to bed. I'll sing a little song to you so you can go to sleep." He walked into the bedroom, carrying her with him. It was over so quickly, it might have been a dream.

When Edmund returned, Tilda and Mart had finished their meal and Tilda had gone over to pick up her sleeping baby. Without a word, Edmund extinguished the candle and opened the kitchen door, indicating they were to follow him. The four of them slipped out into the blackness of the night, leaving Fannie in the kitchen. She did not dare relight the candle, fearing it might betray Edmund's return to the house. Instead, she set about putting things to rights, guided by her knowledge of the familiar room. As she worked, the blackness of the room and the shape of her own dark fears merged until there was no separating the two of them. It seemed an eternity before Edmund came back, closed the door after him, and then lighted the candle.

"The rain has stopped," he said, picking up a plate to carry it to the dishpan where she had started washing the dishes.

She did not answer.

"It was good of you to feed them."

"Edmund," she burst out, "we're breaking a law—"

His face darkened.

"Whether we like it or not," she went on stubbornly, "it's still a law."

"Fannie," he told her softly, "look at it this way. If a stray dog came to our door, sick and hungry and followed by boys throwing stones, you'd take him in and protect him. Can you do less for human beings?"

"But that wouldn't mean we'd hide him from his master—"

"Now Fannie!" There was an edge of impatience and even

disapproval in his voice. "Remember how you cried over Eliza's troubles when I read Mrs. Stowe's book aloud? Here is a case even more touching and deserving of your sympathy because these are real people, not characters in a book."

She wanted to tell him that it was one thing to weep over the plight of a woman in a book and quite another to defy the law for the sake of a real person.

"They must stay here all day tomorrow. Then they will be—well, other provisions will be made. Don't do anything out of the way, anything to excite suspicion. When you go to gather the eggs, take food out in the basket. Climb up and set it just at the top of the ladder, inside the loft. That is all you need to do. It is a little thing to ask."

A little thing to ask! To risk their future, the future of their children for the sake of three colored people she had never laid eyes upon until tonight? They said no one had seen them come, but then, Joshua Glover also had felt sure no unfriendly person knew of his whereabouts.

Fannie went to bed, but not to sleep. Several times Arthur stirred in his crib, and she lay listening, her ears intent for any sound of irregular breathing. She tried to shut out from her mind the image of another baby, less strong than Arthur, who was hidden now in a loft. She wondered if Edmund had left enough blankets out there. Men never realized—

Edmund was up and gone early the next morning, before Fannie arose. She went about her work, trying to quiet her uneasiness.

After she had prepared breakfast for herself and the children and washed the dishes, she packed some food in a basket, including a jar of warm milk, and started toward the door.

"Where are you going, Mama?" Lillie asked.

"To gather eggs. I want to bake a cake."

"Let me go with you—"

"No, you stay here and look after Arthur." And, at the dawning protest on the child's face, "That's Mama's big girl—" Since the matter stood in that light, Lillie said no more.

Fannie walked toward the barn, glad to see the sun was shining again and pleased to feel the air warm against her face. She went inside. It seemed to her she could almost hear, in the stillness, the sound of people breathing up in the loft. No other noise or hint of one. How did they keep the baby so quiet? Arthur would never have remained so still. He would have cried or jabbered or wanted to romp about.

She climbed the ladder to the loft, pushing aside the cover at the entrance. Still no sound. Yet, there was a sense of expectancy, so strong she could feel it. She set the basket inside on the floor, replaced the board which covered the opening, and then went down the ladder. She was almost out in the yard once more when she remembered the eggs and turned back to get them. She had nothing to carry them in, having left the basket, so she looped up her apron, hoping no one would notice she had come to the barn carrying a basket and was now going back without it. How quickly fear and caution set a pattern on a person, she thought. Was that how the mother had taught her baby not to make a sound?

Back in the kitchen, Fannie made the cake she had promised and when it was out of the oven, started to work on the little coat for Arthur while the children played on the floor.

A knock came at the front door. Hearing it, Fannie sat, unable to move, a fearful certainty in her heart. The knock came again.

"There's someone knocking, Mama," Lillie said.

Fannie got to her feet, the sewing still in her hand. She made her way toward the door, Lillie and Arthur at her heels. It was only with the greatest difficulty that she put her hand on the knob. The children watched her with wide and questioning eyes.

The knock was repeated a third time, impatiently now, just as she forced herself to open the door. Two men stood before her. Their appearance confirmed her deepest fears; they were not from Milwaukee, and they meant business.

"Good morning, Ma'am," the older one said. They both removed their hats, and the voice of the one who spoke was soft and slurring.

"Good morning," she said, hoping she did not betray her knowledge and her fear.

"We hate to trouble you, but we are looking for a couple of runaway slaves. Three, in fact. The woman has a baby. We have a pretty good idea they came to some house in this neighborhood, and we are checking."

Fannie stood frozen into silence. So here he was—the man who owned Tilda and Mart, or at least, his representatives, and she was left to face them without Edmund to help her, Edmund who had no doubts about the wisdom of hiding escaped slaves.

"Do you mind if we look around your place, Ma'am?" the younger man asked. "Sometimes they'll hide on the premises without the owners knowing they are there."

He treated her with gentleness and consideration, but he was determined nevertheless.

"A man and a woman and a baby—" the older one repeated. "They escaped from their owner in Kentucky—"

And, as if his words had opened up the floodgates of her memory, Lillie cried excitedly, "The black baby, Mama. Where is he?"

"What did she say?" the younger one demanded.

"Mama—" Lillie began again.

In action quicker than thought, Fannie put her hand on the child's head, pushed her behind her own skirts.

"Lillie," she said severely, "you must not interrupt while Mama is talking with visitors." Fannie turned to the man, who looked ready to push past her into the room (and to the barn—oh, he would go there fast enough). "She has a little pickaninny doll," she explained.

"A pickaninny doll—?" His words mirrored his unbelief.

"Many children here do." She turned and there, sure enough, was the doll, lying on the floor. "There it is, Lillie," she said, pointing.

The two men looked, and, apparently, seemed convinced that Lillie was, indeed, asking for her doll. But they were not equally ready to accept the fact that the slaves themselves were not hidden somewhere about the place. The younger one turned to his companion. "Now what are we waiting on?" he said. "Let's search the house first, and then the outbuildings." He turned to Fannie. "If you'll just step aside, Ma'am."

The house first, and then the outbuildings! Most certainly that would include the barn loft. A memory flashed back to her—Joshua Glover, his hands manacled, his hair matted with blood, his face bruised and battered. These men would treat Tilda and Mart—and even the baby—no more gently.

Courage she had never known was hers—or could be hers—came to her. She drew herself to her full height. ("When you get really mad, Fannie," Edmund would sometimes laugh, "you look seven feet tall!") She knew she wore her seven-foot look now, as she said, "Gentlemen, there is no one in the house but my children and myself. However, if you insist, you may come in and see for yourself. I assume you have a search warrant."

It was a long chance she had taken, and perhaps it would not work. The men who had come for Glover did not let the lack of a search warrant stop them.

The men turned now to look uncertainly at each other. They don't have one, Fannie exulted, and they are afraid to come in without it! If I just stand firm—

"Let's go ahead—" the younger said.

"Oh, hell no. I think she's telling the truth."

The younger one did not seem convinced. "We traced them here," he reminded his companion.

"You mean *you* did. I never was so sure. Besides, I ain't got much stomach for barging in on a lone woman and her kids."

"Well—" They stood there a moment longer. Then, moved either by the lack of a warrant or belief in what she had told them, they turned and walked off without even bidding her good-by.

Fannie closed the door and sat down on the first chair she came to. Once there, she began to cry. Was it from relief—or from elation?

When Edmund came home for dinner she told him about the incident.

"All that argument about the law," he said when she had finished, smiling at her with great tenderness on his face.

She couldn't tell him the law had nothing to do with it, or right or wrong or any abstract thing. How could she explain it was mostly tied up with a baby who didn't cry?

"You don't seem a bit surprised," she marveled.

"I'm not," he told her calmly. "I knew you'd act the way you did, if the need arose."

He's pleased with me, Fannie thought. I've measured up. She went to him swiftly; she put her arms around his neck and dropped her head on his shoulder, a sense of exaltation and peace flowing through her. Edmund held her tightly with one arm, while he took her face in his other hand and kissed her warmly, several times.

"Oh, what a wife I married me!" he said proudly.

Fannie leaned against him, wanting to prolong the moment.

"Tonight, after dark, a carriage will come," he said. "We'll put *them*—" he made the briefest of motions toward the barn, "—in it and drive off to the next station."

It was the word "we" that brought her back.

"Oh, no," she protested, "not you. You've done enough for them."

"Fannie—" he said quietly.

5

Fannie sat beside the kitchen window. She had sat there through all the terrible hours of the night, except when it was necessary to replenish the fire or slip in to check on the children. She had not lighted a candle (a light burning all night might occasion questions) so her hands could not have the solace of work. She listened to the clock's slow, measured ticking, and the hollow sound when it struck, and she prayed, silently and in her heart.

This evening after supper—a century away, it seemed now—when she sat sewing the last buttons on Arthur's little coat, Edmund had said, "I'm going now, Fannie."

"Oh, Edmund—" Protest rose to her lips.

"It's all right. Every detail has been carefully worked out. There'll be no slips. Go to bed and don't worry."

Go to bed and don't worry! How like a man to say something that foolish.

He kissed her good-by, as she stood with the coat still in her hands. He turned to go and she ran after him, her hands outstretched. "Here, take this—" she said, thrusting the small garment into his hands.

He kissed her once more, a peculiar expression on his face as he held the little coat.

"Good-by," he told her. "Don't worry. I'll be with Mr. Holton, in his carriage."

She had held to his last words through the night. Things of comfort they were, if one could draw comfort from any part of this whole uncertain business. In Mr. Holton's company, riding in his fine carriage behind his fast team, Edmund was as safe as anyone could be on such a mission. No man in Milwaukee was more respected, more level-headed than Mr. Holton. And yet, Mr. Booth was a man respected and admired! Oh, why did she have to keep on thinking about him and the persecutions which had been his lot since he followed his conscience for the sake of freeing a slave?

Finally, just when she had begun to think it would never happen, Edmund came home. He was inside the house and she was in his arms.

"You're back," she cried. "Thank God."

"Of course I'm back," he told her calmly. "It wasn't so far we went. Someone met us ten miles away. They'll take them on to Waukesha."

"Were they—all right?" she asked.

"They are in safe hands. Tilda sent back her thanks and her blessings for the coat."

They were safe. Edmund was back home. She must hold to those thoughts, not dwell on what might come of the trip. She clung to Edmund as if he had just come back from great danger, as, indeed, he had. Even as she looked at him, he seemed to grow taller.

"Fannie," he said, "I go to work tomorrow."

"Tomorrow!" Joy filled her voice. "Oh, Edmund, where?"

"At the Milwaukee *Sentinel*. William, too."

The *Sentinel!* A larger paper, a better job and, most likely, more pay. Mr. Holton probably had something to do with this. But Edmund would not want her or anyone else to think his new job was a reward for having followed the dictates of his conscience, so she wouldn't even mention the possibility. It was enough to know that he would be working once more and that the winter which had threatened to be such a precarious one would, in reality, turn out to be very good indeed.

III

All for Kansas

1855–1856

THERE WERE times when Fannie Ross wished she would never have to hear the word "Kansas" again.

It sat half a continent away and, for all she could hear, was filled mostly with Indians and wild animals and a few venturesome whites clinging around its edges. Yet apparently nobody in Milwaukee could rest because of what was happening in that far-off territory which none of them had ever seen and few had even heard of until recently.

She said as much to her mother as the two women sat together one February afternoon in Fannie's sitting room. A fire snapped in the grate, the children played on the floor, the kettle bubbled away on the kitchen stove. Presently the two women would put their sewing aside and have tea with the fresh cookies Fannie had made that morning.

"It's all I hear from Edmund or William," she protested.

"It's all we hear from anyone," her mother pointed out.

"It seems to me there's enough going on here in Milwaukee to occupy their minds," Fannie said.

As, indeed, there was. Why couldn't people be satisfied to talk about the newly installed gas lights (Fannie hoped Edmund would agree to having them in their house just as soon as they could afford them); or the telegraph messages which came singing in over a strand of wire; or the Milwaukee and Mississippi Railroad train which chugged in every day from Stoughton, a tremendous seventy miles away, to stop at the depot at the foot of Second Street; or Mr. Holton's bank, which kept piling up deposits because the town was thriving at such a great rate?

"I'm just real proud of Edmund," Ma said, evidently wanting to divert her daughter's mind. "Such a short time on the *Sentinel* and a foreman already."

"Oh, I am, too," Fannie said warmly. She was not only proud, but thankful as she contrasted his present good fortune with that of poor Mr. Booth—in jail and ruined financially because of the Glover case. Edmund, too, had taken part in that rescue and yet he was free, holding down a good job and living in the midst of his family. He had also escaped the consequences for his part in the escape of Tilda and Mart. As far as that went, she herself had not been entirely within the law in the latter episode. Edmund should be grateful for his good fortune, but all he seemed to think about was Kansas.

"Oh, let's have tea and forget about Kansas," Fannie remarked.

It was an easy thing to say, but one more difficult of accomplishment. How could Fannie explain to her mother that Kansas was the nebulous shape of her fear?

Had she been asked to name a specific date for the beginning of her apprehension, she would have said it was the day Edmund came home, greatly upset, to report the passage of the Kansas-Nebraska Bill.

"We're right back where we started from," he said. "The Missouri Compromise very definitely stated that west of the Mississippi, slavery would be lawful only south of 36° 30′ north latitude, except in Missouri. And now Kansas and Nebraska, both north of the line, have been admitted to the Union as territories with the right to decide the matter of slavery for themselves."

"Well," Fannie asked absently, her mind more occupied with whether to bake a pie or a cake for supper, "is that so bad? Why shouldn't free people decide things for themselves?"

"It is very bad," he told her, so gravely she gave up any attempt at meal planning and listened to him intently. "This is an invitation for both sides—proslavery and free-soil people—to rush out to Kansas to vote it their way."

"Why to Kansas rather than to Nebraska?" she wanted to know.

"Because Nebraska is already pretty well filled up with antislave settlers. But Kansas lies next to Missouri, which is, for the most part, proslave. Missourians will be over the line before the free-soil people can make up their minds to start. There'll be trouble in Kansas—you wait and see."

Edmund was right. The passage of the Kansas-Nebraska Bill started a storm which would not be stopped. When President Pierce signed the Kansas-Nebraska Bill on May 30, 1854, there was great rejoicing in Missouri. Senator David R. Atchison told his fellow Missourians to be prepared to rush across the border and hold Kansas Territory for the South. He reminded them of the fifty thousand slaves in Missouri's border counties alone, representing a thirty-million-dollar investment, and pointed out that a free state as a neighbor would be disastrous.

Senator Atchison's *Platte Argus* flashed black type: "Stake out your claims and woe be to the Abolitionist or Mormon who shall intrude upon it or come within the reach of your long and true rifle, or within point blank shot of your revolvers."

Of course, copies of the paper found their way east. Edmund brought one home to Fannie.

"I was right," he reminded her. "See—and they say enough Missourians have responded to settle three proslavery towns along the west bank of the Missouri River—Leavenworth, Kickapoo, and Atchison. Unless the free-soil people get busy, all is lost in Kansas."

Senator William Seward of New York was among the first to reply. "Come on, gentlemen of the slave states," he thundered. "Since there is no escaping your challenge, I accept it, in behalf of freedom. We will engage in competition for the virgin soil of Kansas and God give victory to the side that is stronger in numbers as it is in right."

Fannie could not share William and Edmund's satisfaction in the statement. The implications were entirely too grave. She hoped that people didn't take Mr. Seward seriously. He sounded as if he was just spoiling to start a fight.

Things had gone too far, apparently, for ignoring. The free-soil people were a little slower getting started, but they made up in fervor for that lack. In Massachusetts a man named Eli Thayer started the Emigrant Aid Company to assist free-soil voters in moving to Kansas.

All over the North, people seemed to share Edmund's approval of Mr. Thayer's plan. From his pulpit in the Congregational Church in Brooklyn, Henry Ward Beecher (brother of Harriet Beecher Stowe, author of *Uncle Tom's Cabin*) declared that not only must emigrants be sent to hold Kansas, but boxes of Sharp's rifles should be shipped to these settlers so they could protect themselves against the proslave forces. That in itself seemed bad enough to Fannie—sending arms to a territory already on the verge of fighting—but when he said the rifles were "moral agents greater than the Bible" and people began calling them "Beecher's Bibles" and so labeling the boxes in which they were shipped, she was deeply troubled.

She said as much to Edmund.

"We have to be sensible about it," he told her. "We can't send people into a situation of that sort, unarmed and unprotected. There'll be plenty of need for those guns."

Perhaps he was right. Certainly he had been correct when he said the race for Kansas was on.

The Massachusetts Emigrant Aid Company, whose avowed purpose was to send free-soil men to Kansas, was accused by the very people whose sanction it sought of intending to enrich its founders. The organization floundered and might have failed entirely had not a good man, Amos Lawrence of Boston, advanced funds out of his own pocket to keep it alive. The name was changed to the New England Emigrant Aid Company, and almost immediately emigration started in earnest. One of the towns founded by the new settlers was named Lawrence, for the man who made its establishment possible.

Railroads in the East did their part, offering a twenty-five per cent reduction in fare to St. Louis, as far as the rails went. From there, settlers could go up the Missouri River to land in Kansas.

One of the things which pleased Edmund most in the whole matter was that the Emigrant Aid Company specified there must be newspapers in all the towns established through its aid.

"It's as I've always said," he pointed out, "every place, no matter how small, must have its newspaper. How else can a people get the true picture of a situation and know how to vote wisely? So far, there are no free-soil papers in Kansas Territory, and yet look at the proslave ones that have sprung up, giving only their side of the situation."

Which of course was true. One proslavery editor, so the story went, got out his first edition in Leavenworth under a tree. No roof over his head at all. But he kept on rushing out copies of his paper, filled with proslave pronouncements.

"You see how it is," Edmund said. "Only one side of the question put before the people. The free-state papers of Lawrence were destroyed because they tried to give their side. I tell you, Fannie, when the press in Kansas ceases to be free, freedom everywhere has been diminished."

He spoke so solemnly, he might have been discussing some great personal threat.

Excited as Edmund was about the Kansas situation and the need for newspapers there, how long would it be before he thought he himself should go out and start one?

Such was the shape of Fannie's fear. This, however, she could not bring herself to tell Ma.

The two women sat so long chatting over their tea that Fannie had to finish supper in a great rush. And of course, this would be the evening when Edmund wanted his meal right on the dot.

"I'm going back and work in William's place," he told Fannie, when he got up from the table. "He's going to call on Mary Elizabeth."

Oh dear, Fannie thought—that means I'll be alone another evening. There was a bright prospect to the situation, however. That pretty little Mary Elizabeth Berry would hold William here in Milwaukee, and if he stayed, Edmund might be less anxious to go. The thought put her in such a good frame of mind that she didn't mind preparing the extra meal when William came in, also in a great hurry.

"Well," she said, looking at him, "no need to ask you what has happened. She's a lovely girl."

"Oh, isn't she!" William glowed.

"I hope you buy a house close to us," Fannie said, "so we could be neighbors."

William had a strange, quizzical expression on his face. Slowly Fannie felt the joy in her own heart turn to a chilling foreboding.

"I'm afraid that won't be possible," William told her slowly. "You see—we're going to Kansas, just as soon as we're married. To a town named Topeka. I'm going to start a newspaper there."

2

Fannie's fear became very tangible and real. William's decision to go to Kansas had stirred the other Rosses, as if they had all been waiting for him to make the first announcement. From Janesville came word that Nancy Ross, a younger sister, was going to marry a man named S. P. Wemple and the young couple would join William and Mary Elizabeth in their overland journey to Kansas. Moreover, Father and Mother Ross were planning to go themselves a little later. In the meanwhile, George Ross, not quite sixteen years old, would go with the young couples, driving Father Ross' stock ahead.

Oh, those Rosses! On the move again—father, mother, and all the children. Not quite all. Edmund was still here in Milwaukee. She drew in her breath quickly. How soon would Edmund, too, be convinced that his vote and his skill as a newspaperman were needed in that disputed land?

"I'm certainly glad you don't have any urge to rush out to Kansas," she told Edmund, not caring in the least that she betrayed her own feelings in the matter.

He looked at her strangely. In her panic, it seemed he was making ready to say something which she felt that she, at all costs, must prevent. If ever the words got out into the open—

"We couldn't go if we wanted to," she went on with nervous haste. And, at his questioning look, "I'm going to have a baby."

In due time the Ross caravan reached Topeka, and William's letters came back to tell about the situation there. Kansas Territory was a fertile and lovely country, he reported. Now, in May, the slopes were red with wild strawberries and corn was being planted in soil so rich there was no doubt about a bountiful crop. Topeka was a town slated for big things. A man named Colonel Holliday had laid it out not quite two years ago with a compass watch charm borrowed from one of his associates. Although several towns in the territory were hoping to get the capitol, everybody believed Topeka would win.

Fannie saw Edmund's face grow bright with interest as he read that part aloud to her. But as he went into the next paragraph, his eyes flashed with indignation. The Missourians, William reported, evidently felt the country was well worth fighting for. In the last general territorial election, 6,307 votes had been cast in a region whose census showed a voting population of only 2,095. The extra votes, of course, had come from Missourians who had ridden across the line with guns across their knees and knives in their hands. No wonder thirty-six proslavery men had been elected to only three free-soil ones.

"We'll just have to get more free-soil votes out to Kansas," Edmund declared, a remark which Fannie did not feel required an answer from her. Edmund returned to William's letter, continuing to read aloud.

The Missourians, he said, openly rejoiced in this fraudulent election, defending their conduct by pointing out that the North imported voters, too. About a hundred eastern immigrants, just arrived, had voted Free State in Lawrence, the seat of Free State activities and therefore greatly hated by the Missourians. It was a remarkable town, with remarkable people in it, not the least being the Aid Company agent himself, Charles Robinson, and his wife, Sara. She was always writing back East about the happenings out in Lawrence and had no fear of speaking her mind on any question.

Fannie listened, busy with her own thoughts. In Milwaukee, too, wild strawberries were reddening by now, and flowers bloomed, and the air blowing off Lake Michigan was sweet and fresh. Men did not go about their affairs carrying rifles, and elections were held in an orderly fashion. The more she heard about Kansas, the better she liked Milwaukee.

She was to hear a great deal about Kansas that summer, and with each recital, she liked it less. William's letters came regularly, each containing some new and disturbing note. He told about an organization of Missourians called The Blue Lodge whose avowed purpose was to extend slavery into Kansas. The password was "Sound on the Goose," often abbreviated to "S.G.Q." meaning "Sound on the goose question." Every man suspected of being not sound was termed abolitionist, even though he might be a southerner who wanted no part in rabble rousing. The emblem of the organization was a bit of hemp worn in the buttonhole. The implication was not lost on Fannie. Hemp made nooses for men who had wrong opinions.

Edmund would most certainly be highly unsound on the goose question and, were he in Kansas, would not hesitate to make his position clear. Kansas Territory was no place for Edmund now, if, indeed, it would ever be. Besides, his duty was toward his family, not a strife-torn region beyond the rim of the world.

Fannie wished that William would cease the flow of those letters, all bearing fresh tidings of disaster. But they continued to come. The proslavery men, he said, had worked out a code of laws for Kansas, for the most part using the one already existing for Missouri, bothering only to substitute the words "Kansas Territory" in the proper places. It was against the law to read a free-soil paper (and there William was implying that Edmund should come out so that the two brothers might start one of their own);

a man could lose his vote by refusing to take an oath supporting the Fugitive Slave Law (and how would William—and Edmund if he were there—couch their refusals?); a citizen would lose his property for questioning the right to hold slaves, his life for aiding a slave to escape.

Memory came back to her—Edmund helping to batter down the door to Glover's cell; Edmund, driving with Mr. Holton to Waukesha, Tilda and Mart and their baby in the back seat of the carriage.

Indeed, Kansas was no place for Edmund.

The summer slipped past. Edmund was busy at the *Sentinel* and Fannie, too, was occupied. A woman never rests, she found, with two small children under foot and a third on the way. Except when William's letters came, she was happy enough. He wrote that cornstalks in the bottom lands shot up to three times a man's height and melons and tomatoes, and squash and apples, were thriving. He said you never saw such prosperity and that, evidently, people were so busy tending their crops there was no time for making trouble. And a new territorial governor, Wilson Shannon from Ohio, had arrived and promised to be a good one.

One would think that, in the face of such prosperity, both sides would be content to live happily in this new land of plenty. But the free soilers, apparently, had no notion of accepting the situation for what it was. The matter of the illegal votes cast by Missourians was something they could not accept lightly.

In September, they met in Big Springs and decided to set up their own legislature. They also planned a constitutional convention in Topeka at which the Free State Party would set up a scheme whereby Congress would be asked to admit Kansas as a free state. They said they were not abolitionists, and they wanted no part in fanaticism; that the South was welcome to her institutions, but she must keep them within the borders of her states; and that free-soil squatters, working on their own parcels of land, had neither the money nor the desire to compete with the large landholders who used slave labor.

"There was a very persuasive speaker in the group," William reported. "His name is Lane—James Lane, formerly lieutenant governor of Indiana. They say when he first came out here he was sure Kansas was going to be a slave state until he tried to organize the Democrat Party in Lawrence and met with no success. Anyway, he's a Republican now, or perhaps I had better say, a Free-Soil man, and he proposed the so-called "Black Law," which stipulates that no Negro, either slave or free, is to live in Kansas when she becomes a state. Out of the hundred delegates, ninety-nine voted 'yes' to his proposal."

And, Fannie mused, was this a humane, or even logical, attitude for free-soil men to take toward Negroes?

3

Pitt was born in December of 1855. He was a happy, loving, healthy baby.

"Some children are born to be blessings," his grandmother said. "From the first they show it."

Ma was right. Pitt was Fannie's blessing. He had kept her from the need of refusing to go to Kansas. William had written that things were quiet in that troubled territory now. Maybe the Kansas-Nebraska Bill was not so bad after all; people seemed to be working the slavery question out for themselves in Kansas Territory.

But the next months showed Fannie how great her error had been. New violence broke out, and once more the name of Kansas was on every tongue and in every newspaper. Eastern reporters streamed out to cover the situation; all winter the Milwaukee *Sentinel* was filled with the stories of this sorely beset region. Strange and unfamiliar names rolled off the tongues of the people of Milwaukee—Pottawatomi, Shawnee, and Wakarusa. Lecompton, Pawnee, and Osawatomie. Soft and liquid sounds from which tales of horror and bloodshed emanated. Missourians, lured over into Kansas by the promise of "Free ferry, a dollar a day, and liquor, gentlemen!" came in droves to cast their votes—in favor of slavery. Naturally the free-soil people tried to halt them; and in the conflict of which these voting incidents were only a part, more than two hundred lives and a million dollars in property were lost.

William reported that, in spite of this, the population of Kansas Territory had doubled—a state of affairs which held little comfort for the free soilers since the influx was largely made up of proslave sympathizers. It was scarcely worth while for a free-soil man to go to the polls, since his vote would be cast on the side of the minority—if, indeed, he ever was able to get past the proslave men and their guns in order to cast his vote.

And Mary Elizabeth wrote that they were living in a shake shanty—a small dwelling made of cottonwood poles for sides, with mud-chinked cracks and a thatched roof. The winter was proving to be the coldest one ever seen—thirty degrees below and snow sometimes drifting six inches deep inside the small shack.

Fannie looked about her own snug kitchen, got up and put another stick of wood into the stove and decided to bake cookies. Their fragrance filled the kitchen when Edmund came home for supper. The children rushed to meet him and he bent down to hug and kiss them both. In such an atmosphere of domestic happiness, a man shouldn't give a thought to anything but the delights it offered. But Edmund seemed to regard the cookies, and even the children, absentmindedly.

"Something wrong?" Fannie asked.

"President Pierce blames Emigrant Aid Companies for all the trouble in Kansas. That, in spite of the fact that Amos Lawrence is his cousin. The President maintains that the Free State men have packed as many ballot boxes as have the Missourians."

Fannie wanted to remind him that William himself had indicated as much, but someway she did not wish to mention William now.

"A man as weak-kneed as that has no business being President," Edmund went on. "He's simply inviting people to take matters into their own hands."

She raised her eyes inquiringly to his face, forgetting all about the cookies. She did not like the grave tone of his voice.

"This thing is bigger than Kansas now," he went on. "Already it's brother against brother. The honor and peace of the country are coming to a showdown in this one spot. It's not just a question of whether Kansas will remain free or slave but whether the nation itself will. Kansas is the test case."

"Oh, Edmund," she protested, "it can't be as bad as that."

"It is even worse," he told her solemnly.

Succeeding events to seemed to bear out Edmund's dire prophecy. Lawrence, the town especially hated by the proslave forces, was besieged. People were ill from lack of food and, were it not for the Sharp's rifles sent at Mr. Beecher's instigation, no one could have got through for supplies at all. All up and down the border free-soil homes had been burned and towns laid waste.

On January 24, President Pierce asked Congress to authorize the people of Kansas to frame a constitution, in his message endorsing the proslave Territorial Legislature and condemning the free-soil Topeka government, calling it revolutionary and "an act of treason," since it was formed without a congressional enabling act and in defiance of the elected government.

"And how," Edmund fumed, "was the 'elected government' formed, except by fraud! What sort of constitution will that crowd write—the ones who have elected themselves at gun point? I hope the free-soil people get busy and work out a constitution of their own. That's one thing I'd like a chance at myself—"

"What?" Fannie asked absently. She was sitting in a rocking chair, Pitt in her arms, admiring her fine sturdy child.

"Writing a constitution for Kansas," he told her.

She jerked herself upright so quickly the baby almost slipped from her lap.

"My goodness, Edmund," she said. "That has to be done by the men who live there."

"Oh, of course," he told her. "But I still wish I could give them an idea or two."

"Write an editorial for the *Sentinel,*" she suggested, "and then mail it to William."

He was making ready to answer that when she broke in on him

excitedly. "Edmund—I do believe Pitt smiled at you. Ma says babies don't smile so soon but he is—I know he is!"

Edmund looked down fondly at his son, apparently forgetting such irrelevant things as constitutions for Kansas. "He is a fine little rascal, isn't he?" he observed.

William reported that the Free State legislature had met in Topeka and had drafted a request to Congress asking that Kansas be admitted under the Topeka Constitution. Moreover they had named James H. Lane to take the document to Washington and present it to Congress.

"Isn't he the one who proposed the 'Black Law'?" Fannie asked.

"Yes," Edmund said, looking thoughtful. Lane, evidently, was a man about whom Edmund had not yet made up his mind. "He sounds a bit radical for me. I doubt that he will get anywhere with the Free State Constitution. Still, it's a start."

Edmund's prediction was correct. Although the House approved the document, the Senate did not, tossing it out as "incipient treason."

Mrs. Lathrop, not Edmund, first put into words the matter of going to Kansas. She and Fannie sat drinking coffee together in the kitchen one cold February day.

"What are you going to do when Edmund gets the Kansas fever, too?" Mrs. Lathrop asked suddenly.

Fannie drew back quickly, as if her mother had struck her. "He hasn't said a word—"

"But he's a Ross. It will be just a matter of time until he does."

"He won't," Fannie said, aware that she was speaking too loudly, too defiantly. "All that fighting, and no food unless they can steal it. And the cold. Mary Elizabeth says the snow drifts in across their beds. Edmund wouldn't ask me to take the children into a place like that."

"Spring will come," her mother said, "and they will build new, stout houses out there. Frontiers grow up quickly. I remember Sandusky, when we first came from New York—"

She looked musingly out the window.

"Besides," Fannie told her, "you know as well as I do that the Missourians have blocked all travel on the river, and now nobody can get through there to Kansas."

Which was true. Boats had been turned back on the Missouri River, even after they were almost to Kansas. In several instances lives had been lost; once the whole lot of the people in the boat had been put ashore in a storm and left to make out as best they could.

"You forget," her mother said, "that William and his party went overland."

Go overland! The very prospect was enough to chill the blood. Stories were told of the hapless ones who went out to California and Oregon, only a few years ago. When people got sick there was neither medicine nor doctors. Babies were born and died and small graves were dug beside the trail. Often the graves were larger—the old, the sick, the young mothers. And then there were those terrible dark whispers about the Donner Party. Snowbound they were, and without food, and so, at last—oh, it was too awful to let the mind dwell upon. Even when people were strong and well and prepared for the trip, there were dissentions and fightings within the group. While they quarreled among themselves, like as not the Indians slipped in and finished off the lot of them.

No, Fannie didn't want to follow any overland trail anywhere. Besides, even had traveling been easy, taking three small children to a disputed frontier was unthinkable.

Decision came to her. Here she would take a stand, even before the actual necessity arose. If Edmund felt that his conscience bade him go to Kansas, he could go alone. And when the place was fit for her and the children, they would join him.

She said as much to her mother.

Mrs. Lathrop looked at her curiously, and when she spoke again it was of other things.

4

Only a few days after Fannie's talk with her mother, Edmund came home one afternoon from work to say, "There's a Kansas Aid

Meeting tonight. I'm going, as soon as I've eaten supper." He looked at her with a sideways, appraising glance. "Want to go with me?" he asked. "Everyone will be there."

Certainly a Kansas Aid Meeting was nothing new. People assembled to listen to speakers who told how bad things were out in Kansas and how everyone ought to give as much as he could of money, food, clothing, and guns to those brave people who were already there upholding the cause of freedom. Fannie had no objections to that; after all, the Rosses were well represented in Kansas, and she would be the last one to say the settlers should not be helped.

But no speaker was content with asking for supplies; he also insisted that people pledge themselves to go to Kansas and use the offerings.

"I never want to hear of Kansas again as long as I live," she burst out unexpectedly.

"Well, now, that's just too bad," Edmund said quietly. "Because I'm thinking of going there myself. William writes that he has bought the Lawrence *Tribune* and moved it to Topeka. He calls his paper *The Kansas Tribune.* He wants me to come out and help him publish it."

Then the storm broke. Fannie didn't know exactly what she said; she was aware only of the fact that they had never before quarreled like this. Nor was she sure how long it lasted. But the end of it was clear and definite. Edmund stalked out of the house without his supper. Her first impulse, on hearing the door slam behind him, was to run after him, begging him to come back. She had her hand on the door knob before she brought herself up sharp. Let him go. She had wanted to make her position clear about Kansas, and she had succeeded. Having made the decision, she sat down by the kitchen window and cried until no more tears would come. Then she became aware of Lillie and Arthur standing beside her, tugging at her dress, half-crying themselves.

From his crib Pitt joined the general clamor, his fat legs and arms flailing about as he cried out. Fannie ran to him and snatched him into her arms. His mouth spread into a wide, toothless grin.

She sank into a chair, holding him hungrily to her heart. She reached out to embrace Lillie and Arthur, who were still regarding her with puzzled curiosity.

"I'm all right," she told them.

And so she was. Right and confident. She *should* have stood up to Edmund. Only a foolish mother would consent to take young children across the plains to Kansas.

She fed the children and put them to bed early. This done, she went back to the kitchen, thinking to wash the dishes and make things tidy. Then she would sew. Or read. Or maybe bake a cake. No, not that. A cake would look like an apology to Edmund, when he finally came home from the meeting.

If he did come home!

What a foolish thing to think. He would come home, and he would put his arms around her and tell her he was sorry he had said the things he had. That he could see now she was right—going to Kansas was foolish and unnecessary. That was an enterprise for young, unencumbered men. Family men should stay at home. There was work to be done here in Milwaukee, as well as in Kansas. Good and necessary work.

The clock on the mantle ticked away, slowly, with great dignity. Strange, she so seldom heard the clock tick. Now it seemed to speak. "He won't go to Kansas," it said, distinctly as if the words had been voiced. "*He won't; he won't, he won't.*"

She couldn't stand it another moment. Jumping from her chair she went to the closet and got out a coat. She threw open the back door and suddenly she was running the short distance which separated her from her mother's house. Once there, she flung open the door, calling as she did so, "Ma—Ma—"

"What's wrong, Fannie?" Mrs. Lathrop cried. "The children—Edmund—"

"They're all right," she said breathlessly. "But—well, I just wondered if you would—if you would stay with the children for a little while."

"Why, of course, Fannie. You know I will. You and Edmund going somewhere?"

A perfectly logical question, a normal one. And yet, she found it hard to answer.

"Yes—I mean no—" She hesitated, then went on. "Edmund has already gone to a—a meeting. I thought I'd go, too."

Mrs. Lathrop looked at her keenly.

"The Kansas Aid Meeting?" she asked.

"Yes," Fannie told her, almost in a whisper.

Ma knew; she knew good and well why Fannie must be there, too. If she sat in the audience, plain for Edmund to see, he wouldn't dare volunteer to go to Kansas. Not after she had told him so plainly how she felt about the matter. Ma didn't know about the quarrel, but she was aware of the urgency of the situation.

"Wait till I get my wraps," Mrs. Lathrop said.

She was back in a moment.

"Go on to your meeting, Fannie," she said quietly. "But don't be so sure ahead of time what you'll do, once you're there."

The meeting had already started when Fannie slipped into the room. In the gas light she could see a number of familiar faces, for, as Edmund had prophesied, almost everyone was here. Mr. Holton, to be sure, and nearly all of the *Sentinel* staff, and friends and neighbors. There were, as well, people unknown to Fannie, ones who had probably come from the surrounding towns. Mr. Edward Holton was presiding, which was only natural. He was speaking when Fannie entered, so she sat down quietly, being careful to put herself in such a position that Edmund must see her if he so much as raised his eyes. She was close enough to catch the slight lift of his head, the involuntary flick of his nostrils, indicating his awareness of her entrance.

There had evidently been a great upsurge of enthusiasm just before she came in, so much, in fact, that Mr. Holton was having some difficulty in getting the meeting back to order. He rapped on the table before him, and called, "The chair recognizes Mr. Dawes, from Waukesha."

They would be here in full force, Fannie thought. All that crowd from Waukesha. The man so recognized began to speak, and gradually the group quieted down to hear him. He said it was fine to get worked up about Kansas, but now practical evidence of sympathy was in order. Who would volunteer to go himself? Failing that, who would help others to go? Would the chairman set the audience an example?

"I have no desire to dodge," Mr. Holton told him. "If five hundred dollars would help, it is at their service."

A round of applause broke out, while the secretary made note of the offer. Of course no one could match Mr. Holton's gift, but all over the room people began springing to their feet, announcing their own contributions. Offers of money and rifles poured in so fast the secretary had difficulty in taking them down. Then Mr. Spicer from Milton guaranteed five to eight young men for Kansas. (And who was he to settle their destiny, probably without asking them in advance, Fannie thought rebelliously.) His speech started a series of people rising to volunteer to go.

Fannie never took her eyes off Edmund. So it was that she knew the exact second when he made up his mind. As if he had called out the information to her, she knew it. He was going to take her at her word and go to Kansas alone. He had given her a chance and she had refused. She had come to this meeting to prevent him from volunteering; now, she would be forced to sit and watch helplessly while he offered himself on the altar of Kansas' need. What she should do this moment was to stand up before all these people and forbid him to do this thing. A wife had some rights; a wife had *every* right when there were little children asleep at home.

For one wild awful moment she let herself think what it would be like if she acted on her impulse. Then the madness left her, a strange sick dizziness replacing it. When she could see again, Edmund was getting to his feet. Slowly, as if the movement was costing him great effort, but rising, nevertheless.

He was going to volunteer to go to Kansas. It was a need which went beyond family or personal comfort, touching rather the deepest core of his own integrity. If he stayed here he would come in time not only to despise her but himself as well.

Suddenly Fannie realized she could not let Edmund go to Kansas without her. She—and, yes, the children—would take their chances along with him. Better to face dangers together than to stay here, safe and secure, and alone. But how could she tell Edmund of her decision, now, before he said the words so obviously on his tongue?

As if sensing her agitation, Edmund looked in her direction. Now was the time to tell him, as best she could, that she was willing to go wherever he went. To Kansas. To the ends of the earth, and beyond. Ma said that people married a long time did not need words to communicate their thoughts to each other. Had she and Edmund been married long enough for that wordless sort of message to pass between them? Not quite eight years. And they were both young. Neither one yet thirty. What had time built into them to help bridge this chasm?

Edmund! Her heart cried out to him, wordlessly, as his own would speak. *I didn't mean what I said. We'll go with you—the children and I.* For one awful moment he continued to look at her as a stranger might do. And then he smiled, his eyes signaling to her that he understood. She leaned weakly back against the chair, knowing whatever he said now was all right, because he was speaking for both of them.

"Mr. Edmund Ross—" Mr. Holton said. "The chair recognizes Mr. Ross."

Edmund began to speak, his voice unhurried, deep, assured.

"I give myself," he said simply. There was the briefest hesitation, and then he looked at Fannie. She nodded, quickly, brightly. "I give myself, my wife, and my three small children to Kansas," he finished. And sat down.

Three times Mr. Holton tried to accept the gift, but each time his words were drowned out by the cheering. Finally when the crowd was quiet, he said, "Mr. Ross' gift is the most valuable of all." And then the cheering broke loose again.

Fannie and Edmund walked home together, arm in arm, after the meeting was over. They did not talk much—that would come later when they could discuss the matter quietly. Now she was so filled with excitement and joy that she couldn't have said much had she tried. And a peace and contentment such as she had never known before.

Mrs. Lathrop looked up quickly as they entered the house, a question in her eyes.

"Oh, Ma," Fannie cried. "Guess what? We're going to Kansas."

"Of course," the woman said quietly. "I've known that all along. I was just sitting here thinking about it this evening, and I've decided I'll go, too."

IV

The Lane Trail

Summer 1856

FOUR AND a half miles out on the Janesville Plank Road the caravan had halted for the night. Although the distance was short compared with what was hoped would be the customary pace once the group was well on the road, this was deemed far enough for the first day.

Besides, half the population of Milwaukee was trailing the group. Not since the escape of the slave, Joshua Glover, had so large a crowd of people accompanied anyone out of town. Certainly, this occasion resembled the other only very slightly, in that although it had been undertaken in the same general cause, it was a happy one. Milwaukee was sending off, on this historic day, May 20, 1856, a group of emigrants to Kansas.

Mr. Holton, apparently considering the whole expedition his special charge, was everywhere, complimenting, exhorting, encouraging. He reined in his fine team next to the Ross wagon.

"How do you do, Mrs. Ross," he said, lifting his hat. He looked at her seriously. "As a woman, you must have some qualms about this venture."

"As a woman—and a mother—I have many qualms," Fannie admitted honestly.

"I can understand. But you must feel proud that your husband should want to help."

Fannie let that pass.

"Kansas is without settled government. They can't decide among themselves who is to rule. Edmund is a man of decision and strength, as are all these people in your party. Once they arrive they'll help put things back in order."

Fannie felt the need to murmur her thanks.

"I have the utmost confidence in Edmund," he went on. "You may know I offered to pay the expenses of his trip. But he refused."

"It was very good of you," she said, "but he felt he would rather do it himself."

That was Edmund's way. Going to Kansas was a matter of conscience to him, so he would finance the method of his going. A man did not sell his conscience.

"Of course, you know the group thinks so highly of your husband that they have elected him as their leader."

Fannie nodded and waited. These are not the things Mr. Holton really wants to say to me, she thought. He is unsure about me, even yet. He would like to feel confident that I will not hold Edmund back, even in spirit. Mr. Holton and Mr. Beecher and Mr. Booth—they are all of a piece. To them, the Cause is more important than the people who carry it out.

"Such leadership will entail great responsibility," Mr. Holton said. "I trust you are prepared for that fact. You can do much—"

"Mr. Holton," she interrupted him with dignity, "as a woman and a mother I cannot deny those qualms I confessed a moment ago. But as a wife, I will follow my husband wherever he feels the need to go, and furnish him with all the help and encouragement that is in my power to give."

Mr. Holton looked at her, a strange expression on his face. For a moment he was silent, then he bowed low as he said, "You are a wise and brave woman, Mrs. Ross. I must congratulate Edmund on having such a wife. I think the rifle given him by his fellow workers might well have been inscribed to you also. Good day, Ma'am, and good luck."

"Well," Ma said, watching him as he rode away, "that was real nice of him. Especially that part about the rifle."

Of course Ma knew about the rifle, just as did everyone in Milwaukee. Edmund's fellow workers at the *Sentinel* had given it to him, a full account of the ceremony appearing in the paper. Fannie had clipped it to put away with her keepsakes, but not before she had read and reread it often enough so she could almost repeat it from memory.

Rifle Presentation

There was quite a gathering of the Craft in the *Sentinel* Counting Room Saturday evening to witness the presentation of a Milwaukee rifle to Mr. E. G. Ross, Foreman in the Job Office, who intends starting for Kansas in the coming month of May. The rifle is a capital one; in point of efficiency will, we think, be found equal to any Sharpe's. A silver plate on the stock of the rifle contains the following inscription: "Presented to E. G. Ross by his comrades in the Milwaukee *Sentinel* Office as a mark of their personal regard and as earnest of their good wishes for FREEDOM IN KANSAS. Milwaukee, April 5th, 1856."

"Yes," Fannie said, pleased to have the stamp of approval put upon her by a man as substantial as Mr. Holton. "He's a good man. And now let's go join the others."

The celebration was in full swing, like the Fourth of July, or the opening of a fair. Basket lunches were carried from buggies and wagons. Women set out food, calling everyone to come share it, while their children raced about, wild with delight.

Once the meal was over, targets were set up and everyone took his turn at shooting. They made a game of it, and Fannie tried not to think that perhaps at the end of the journey those same rifles would be used for sterner needs.

"Edmund's going to shoot at the target," Ma said. "Look—"

Fannie watched as Edmund lifted the gift rifle to his shoulder, his eyes shining with pride. He took steady aim, and then the bullet flew, straight and true, toward the mark. A great cheer went up from the crowd.

2

The caravan plodded on, the goal ten miles a day. Ten steady miles, sure and dependable as the oxen which drew the wagons. The wagons themselves were of the best—six of them, all exactly alike, well made and well equipped, each bearing a family both responsible and dedicated. Walking beside every wagon was a young unmarried man whose duty it was to act as helper to the family he accompanied. Young John Rastell, sixteen years old and formerly an apprentice at the *Sentinel*, had been chosen by Edmund to accompany the Ross wagon.

There were fifty people, all told, in the party. Fannie was proud of the caliber of the group, knowing much of the high quality was due to Edmund's insistence that only the truly qualified be allowed to join. Here was no ragtag and bobtail bunch of failures, escaping a home town where they were unable to make good.

Almost due west they went, the noses of the oxen pointed toward Janesville, one hundred-odd miles away, where Edmund's parents and their younger children were to join the group. From there they planned to follow a route which would take them across Iowa to Nebraska City, and thence south to Topeka. It was a longer road than the one taken by most of the earlier immigrants—cutting diagonally across Illinois to St. Louis and then to Kansas by way of the Missouri River. This shorter, easier route had been closed by proslave Missourians, unwilling to allow free-soil voters to pass through.

Edmund, apparently, felt no regret that the shorter route was closed to them.

"We're following the Lane Trail," he told her.

"Is he the man William told us about?" she asked.

"The very one. He saw what was happening to the emigrants who tried the old route, and he started agitation to open this road across Iowa and Nebraska. It may be longer, but it's more sure."

Lane—he of the "Black Law" and the other uncertain behavior. How could anyone be sure it was safer to follow a route he had planned?

"We're among the first to follow the Lane Trail," Edmund told her. "In a way, we're making history. There'll be hundreds coming after us. Wait and see."

Three days out they camped near a small town, and there were able to collect news and see papers. The things they heard were highly disquieting. Lawrence, always the target for the hatred of the Missourians, had been sacked by Sam Jones, a United States marshal who had moved in on the town with warrants for the arrest of certain Free State men, among them Jim Lane and Charles Robinson. Lane had already escaped into Iowa, but Robinson, also on his way back east, was taken off the boat at Lexington, Missouri (although his wife, Sara, was allowed to proceed). Finding most of their intended victims gone, the posse turned into a mob, looting Lawrence at will. The presses of *The Kansas Free State* were seized and type thrown into the river; the torch was set to the Free State Hotel. The Robinson house, high on Mt. Oread, was also destroyed.

Edmund shook his head gravely as he read the accounts.

"It's as I said," he told Fannie. "This matter of slavery is coming to a head in Kansas, not in the South where it actually exists."

The next bit of news was even more grave.

A man had drifted in from Connecticut to join his five sons, already settled in Kansas. He came not to make a home for himself, nor yet to help his sons in their struggle to tame the pioneer land but, in his own words, "to let a little blood." Something rare to Kansas, an abolitionist, he wanted the slaves freed at any cost. He had no patience with anyone who did not believe as he did, that the only way to free Kansas was to run out all the proslave settlers. When he heard about the sacking of Lawrence, he went berserk. Gathering a small band of men together—seven or eight, all told, including four of his sons—he slipped down Pottawatomie Creek under cover of night to a proslavery settlement whose residents were in no way connected with the Lawrence affair. Once there, he called five settlers out of their cabins, shooting them as they emerged.

The name of the man at the head of the expedition was John Brown.

"It's the deed of a fanatic," Edmund said, a pronouncement in which Fannie heartily agreed.

"It's the worst thing I've ever heard of," she declared, looking around her, half-fearing that out of nowhere would come some danger, some menace, to threaten them before they were even well started to Kansas. Edmund must have sensed her uneasiness, although he made no move to comfort her or deny her fears. Perhaps he felt that the best way to meet these uncertainties was by ignoring them altogether.

The established routine along the trail became as natural as the way one lived back home. In fact, the trip took on the nature of a family outing when, at Janesville, Edmund's parents joined the party, riding in a surrey drawn by two stout horses. Each day they drove ahead in order to locate a good camping spot for the night. Edmund's two younger brothers, Charles and Walter, fourteen and ten years old respectively, drove a low covered farm wagon which a horse and cow trailed. Their feeling of importance knew no bounds. It irked them a little to have John Rastell, from the eminence of his sixteen years, take charge of them with an air of responsibility. This the boys would not have endured for a minute had he not proved a fine companion.

As the caravan came to Dubuque on the Mississippi River, they could see a group of horsemen waiting for them on the Iowa side. All the stories Fannie had heard about disputed passage to Kansas came back to her now. She glanced quickly at the rifle hanging conveniently inside the wagon. If they must stand and fight, almost before they were well started, what on earth would she do with the children? Push them under the featherbed? She looked at them, playing in the back of the wagon while Ma napped, and then at Edmund, who was watching the waiting horsemen narrowly, trying to gauge their intent. He must be thinking, as she was, that here could well be their first challengers of the road.

As the Ross wagon, first in line, reached the Iowa bank, a man detached himself from the waiting group. Fannie saw Edmund's hands tighten on the reins.

"Good afternoon," the man said. "Are you the Milwaukee party?"

"Yes," Edmund said, still alert and watching. "My name is Ross —Edmund Ross."

"Mr. Holton sent word to expect you. We'd like to invite your group to a banquet given in your honor this evening."

Fannie leaned weakly against the back of the seat. She was both ashamed and embarrassed, as well as greatly relieved, that it was Edmund who had to accept the invitation.

The banquet could not have honored them more had they been real dignitaries. Since Edmund was the leader of the group, he and Fannie had the place of honor at the table with the mayor and his wife. Ma with the children in her care sat at another table.

The mayor and Edmund had much to discuss. There was the matter of the recent organization of the Republican Party in Illinois, held in Bloomington. A most remarkable woman from Kansas, Sara Robinson, had made a fine speech on the situation there.

"My brother William knows both her and her husband," Edmund said. "Mr. Robinson is in prison and could not be present."

"Yes, so we were told."

And an Illinois lawyer, Abraham Lincoln, who had finally been persuaded to leave the Whig party and throw in with the Republicans, had delivered such a fiery speech that the newspaper reporters threw down their pencils and forgot to take notes.

"All agree it was the most stirring thing they had ever heard, yet nobody could remember exactly what he said, except that it concerned Kansas," the mayor explained.

"Everyone is talking about Kansas now," Edmund remarked. "It is all tied up with slavery, which must expand or die. The South got to Kansas first, and naturally voted in favor of the institution. Now we and our fellow free-soil people are rushing out to establish at the gateway to the Great Plains—and to the lands farther west—a deadline at which slavery shall be forever barred."

The mayor nodded in understanding.

"The struggle in Kansas," Edmund went on, "is, in the highest possible sense, a question of politics. On its solution hangs the gravest, grandest problem that has ever confronted the philosopher or the statesman—whether this great republic shall henceforth be the citadel of freedom or the kennel of the slave."

All conversation had ceased while everyone listened to Edmund. It was as if he were making a speech, announcing the beliefs of the Milwaukee party.

"It is on the plains of Kansas," he finished quietly, "that this issue, one of the greatest ever to vex the world, will be fought to a finish."

3

Dubuque was a pleasant memory when the caravan, now headed southwest, drew close to Iowa City. As they made camp and were going about the usual preparations for the evening, a man came up to talk. This was nothing unusual—visitors were always dropping by.

"My name's Jenkins," the newcomer said, regarding the Ross wagon with frank curiosity.

"Mine's Ross."

"You folks going to Kansas?"

"How did you know?" Edmund asked.

"Oh, you have the look."

Edmund seemed ready to ask for amplification of the statement and then apparently discarded the idea to ask instead, "Where are you from?"

"Over Hannibal way," Jenkins told him. "Been up here visiting some cousins."

"Hannibal—" Edmund said. "That's in Missouri, isn't it?"

"Sure is, Mister," the man said, speaking in a relaxed easy manner.

"Then you—" Edmund hesitated.

"If you mean I'm one of those Missourians who wouldn't let you and your bunch go through my state, you're right," the man told him, still speaking with no rancor. "We just happen to think you have no call rushing out to Kansas. Oh—" as Edmund looked ready to protest, "—it's not your doings. It's that bunch of abolitionists up in New England that has everybody stirred up. It's none of their never-mind what Kansas does. Missourians believe every state and every territory's got the right to decide things for themselves—about slavery and anything else that comes up."

"But that's the trouble," Edmund told him. "The proslavery people keep rushing in, so we have to go, too, in order to help keep a balance."

"As far as I'm concerned," the visitor continued, "I don't hold with slaves. I have a little farm back in Missouri, and I wouldn't have a slave on it if you gave me one. I hear they're lazy, and have to be watched over like children. I'd rather hire me a hand and pay him. If the wife is sick or gets behind in her work or has a baby, I hire her a good girl. But no slaves—they cost more than they're worth."

"It isn't just a question of economics," Edmund broke in.

"Don't you go saying that to the folks living along The River," Jenkins admonished him. "They have regular plantations there, with fine big houses and thousands of acres of land, and all that. It's a mighty pretty sight, up and down The River, from Boonville to Independence. Those folks couldn't keep their places going without slaves."

"No matter how much they need the slaves," Edmund said, "they have no right to keep them—no moral right."

"All depends on the way you look at things," Jenkins said. "They have big money tied up in these slaves, and I bet they figure that gives them all sorts of rights—legal, and moral, maybe, too, if you want to put it that way." And then, as if he had exhausted that subject, he looked at Edmund's rifle.

"That's a mighty fine gun you have there," he remarked.

"It was given to me by my fellow workers, before I left Milwaukee," Edmund explained proudly.

"That's another thing," the man continued. "It's no skin off my nose, but I can't see why you Yankees keep sending all those rifles out to Kansas. It just makes strife and bloodshed. And they tell me they ship them through in boxes labeled 'Bibles.' That don't make sense to me, besides being a downright lie."

Edmund smiled a little as he spoke, "They have to defend themselves against you Missourians!"

"It's a two-way road, between Kansas and Missouri," the man went on. "The Kansans come over and raid and kill, without any reason for it. That man Lane himself, the one they named this road for, is the worst of the lot. Thinks he's God Almighty himself, set out to avenge the slaves. Every bit as bad as that old madman John Brown, if you ask me."

"There is bound to be wrong on both sides," Edmund agreed, "but we must look for the larger good."

"It seems to me," Jenkins answered, "that the larger good, as you put it, would be to let the people of any region have the right to go about their own business. Quiet, and undisturbed. Now out there on my little farm, I've come through a lot of things—drought, and floods, and bugs eating the crops. But I've just about got it paid for, in spite of everything. All I ask for now is a chance to work it in peace. And do you know what can happen if you fire-eaters rush out to Kansas and begin some real fighting? You're going to start us a war, that's what you are going to do. You'll keep on fighting amongst yourselves, and the first thing you know, you'll have the whole country mixed up in it. All on account of some blacks. I ain't got anything against them, personally, but I don't want to start a war over them."

Edmund opened his mouth to protest, but the man interrupted him.

"Just don't start your arguing, Mister. I already know all the things you are going to say. Part of some of them I believe. But there are two sides to this slavery question, just as there are two sides to the Missouri-Kansas mess." He paused, as if he meant to say more, but then thought better of it. Instead, he turned to walk off. He took a few steps, then paused, and again faced Edmund.

"Good-by, Mr. Ross," he said, "and good luck. But let me tell you this. Once you get to Kansas, you stay there. Hear me? Don't come over to Missouri and start any fusses, or do any raiding."

"I have no intention of bothering you," Edmund told him. "I simply don't like the institution of slavery and mean to see it gets no foothold in Kansas."

"If I remember my history right," Jenkins said, "you Yanks thought slaves were a fine idea—long as you were bringing in ships full of them to sell. Then when you turned to manufacturing up there, work the Negroes couldn't do, you suddenly discovered slavery was all wrong. From what I hear, slaves in the South have things mighty good compared with your factory workers in the North."

It was the classic response of the Southerner, one with which the North was thoroughly familiar and which, Fannie sometimes suspected, was difficult to answer. The man must have known this, for he walked away quickly before Edmund could reply.

Fannie looked at Edmund curiously. How had he taken this straight talk from the Missouri farmer? Edmund said nothing. Was he considering the man's words, as she herself was; was he wondering, as she was, whether truth was always a coin with two faces? Or, as far as that went, were truth and right and justice—all those beautiful abstractions for which men gladly risked their lives and honor—questions which might have more than one side?

4

Late July and the rains had set in. Fannie listened to the beat of them on the canvastop of the wagon, watched the rivulets stream off the backs of the oxen as they moved along. Sometimes she drove, and sometimes John Rastell did. Rarely did Edmund stay in the wagon when a rain was falling, preferring to walk beside it, bareheaded, through the storm. For him, the rain seemed to hold a great fascination.

"You'll take cold," she had protested, the first time he did this. He merely smiled at her, that curiously sweet and warm smile which he often used to allay her worry or concern. Oh, she would worry, as a woman naturally would, or be depressed, but if Edmund ever did either he kept it to himself.

They came to a stream which was swollen by the rains. Here the wagons, with the Ross outfit in the lead, paused.

"No bridge," Edmund said, looking at the muddy stream running up to the very banks. "We'll have to ford it."

"Yes, Mr. Ross," John Rastell said. If the man had said, "We will have to walk into a fire," doubtless the boy would have answered, "Yes, Mr. Ross."

Edmund made his way toward the water.

"Oh, no!" Fannie protested, seeing what he meant to do.

He did not appear to hear her. Walking down to the bank he took a few steps in each direction, finally returning to the spot from which he had started. He looked at the water appraisingly, and then turned back to the wagon.

"I'll walk across," he told John. "You watch carefully. As soon as I'm on the other side, drive the wagon through along the path I take. Understand? The other wagons will follow you. Pass the word along."

Fannie couldn't decide which was the more fearful prospect—Edmund, forging ahead into the unknown dangers of the stream, or his family being driven through it by a sixteen-year-old boy. Edmund stepped into the dark, coffee-colored water. He moved forward. The water was up to his knees. He went on. Now it came to his waist. He went on . . . it was to his armpits. He could swim, of course, but there might be unexpected sink holes; there might be undercurrents that would catch him up, pull him under. Fannie held her breath. Then, even as she watched, she saw that he had come through the deepest water. It was only up to his knees now . . . it was around his ankles. He turned and motioned to John.

The boy headed the oxen down the bank, into the water. Behind him the other wagons began to move forward. They were in the water now, the oxen pulling their cargo with strong, unfailing ease, their noses pointed toward Edmund, standing on the other bank, imperturbable and confident. He had led the way here, as he had done all along the trip. No wonder the people in the caravan respected him.

The rains stopped, the sun shone once more, and all was well again. It was good to set one's feet on the ground after a day of riding. It was good to rest while John Rastell made the fire and helped with the chores. The children rushed eagerly to join their grandparents; they played tag or games of their own devising. Pitt did not like to stay on the quilt Fannie spread for him on the grass, protesting loudly at being left while the others ran off to play. One evening while Fannie was cooking supper, she heard Lillie crying, "Look, Mama! Look at Pitt—"

Fannie turned and saw Pitt scrambling off the quilt which had formed his prison, intent on joining the others.

"Pitt's crawling, Mama," Lillie said, delighted with the exploits of her younger brother. "He's headed straight to Kansas."

"And so he is," Fannie told her. "We'll tell him, when he is bigger, how he crept to Kansas."

She watched the slow, ponderous oxen being corralled for the night by John Rastell. She glanced at the road they had come over, indented by the tracks they had made—tracks, so Edmund said, which others would follow in increasing numbers as the summer went on. She looked ahead, at the almost unmarked road. In this direction Pitt was taking his clumsy, uncertain way now. It was only accident, of course, that he was headed in the direction of Kansas.

Or was it? Perhaps in Pitt's blood was the instinct, the one that ran so strong in all the Ross family, to be out and away, west—always west—headed toward new adventures.

"That's what we're all doing," she laughed. "We're all creeping to Kansas, right along with Pitt."

At almost every camping place, families joined the party. "We thought we'd just travel along to Kansas with your outfit, if you don't mind. We have our wagon and gear ready—"

Always they addressed their request to Edmund, whom everyone recognized as the leader. He talked with the inquirers and, once he had assured himself of their fitness, he gave them permission to fall in line. These newcomers usually had a great deal of information to pass along—news of what was going on out in the world.

The Anti-Slavery section of the Know-Nothing Party had met in New York and nominated Frémont for the Presidency. The group, however, was having trouble within its own ranks, and it looked as if the party itself might dissolve. Edmund said this was not surprising—it had been founded with the avowed purpose of preventing Catholics and foreign-born citizens from holding office. A few weeks later the Republican Party, meeting in Philadelphia, also nominated Frémont for President. Fannie thought of Jessie Frémont, and how proud she must be. The Republicans tried to nominate Abraham Lincoln for vice-president, but in spite of the fine speech he had made at Bloomington, he lost out to William Dayton of New Jersey.

But for the most part, everyone in the party talked about Kansas.

"People are coming in from every which-way," the newcomers invariably reported. "They all have plenty of arms, but not many women or plows. Not like the usual bunch going West. Lots of them aren't looking for homes; they just figure they'll settle down long enough to vote and maybe do a little fighting."

"We're going out to settle," Edmund said. "My brother William is already in Topeka. He is printing a newspaper and I plan to join him."

"Don't you bank on starting anything, anywhere, in Kansas. Topeka is not quite as upset as Lawrence, but things aren't all a picnic there, either. Way we hear it, they've organized a militia company in Topeka—Company B, Second Regiment—to protect supply trains from attacks of proslavery people. Seems like the folks in Kansas can't be sure of a bite of food. The Missourians won't let them get through with supplies, and they won't let them have any peace so they can raise their own. Maybe you just think you're going to be a newspaperman in Topeka. You may have more use for that good rifle of yours than for a printing press."

"I know how to use both," Edmund smiled.

Fannie remembered the Missouri farmer who had said the road between Kansas and Missouri ran two ways. What sort of country was Edmund taking his family to? Perhaps, as the Missourian had said, the best thing for them might have been to stay home and mind their own business. But it was a sentiment which Edmund did not share. The Kansas venture was a clear and bright necessity for him, one about whose wisdom, apparently, he had no doubts. Or if he had them, he kept them to himself. Fannie wished she had her husband's ability to cut straight through a situation and see what he believed to be the right of it. More than that—she wished she had his singleness of purpose, his unwavering courage to pursue the right once he had found it.

He never seemed to be discouraged or upset. If the day had been an especially hard one, instead of saying he needed to go to bed early and rest, he would suggest that the whole group meet around the campfires for games and music. At such times, he would be the one to start the singing. Once or twice she found Edmund and herself singing alone, the others listening. It pleased her to find they could still recapture the old magic, as they had done in Sandusky and again in Milwaukee.

"Come where my love lies dreaming," she and Edmund sang together, their voices ringing out across the flat level stretches of Iowa cornfields. And she thought as they sang—Edmund is no dreamer. He is practical and efficient. He was elected captain of the train; he has kept peace and order. He has never faltered. She, too, must trust him and the country toward which he was taking her.

The days and nights of their journey were full and satisfying. This, Fannie realized, was an interlude in their lives. They found time to have leisurely talks—Edmund did not have to rush to the office or attend meetings or write editorials. He was much at her side. It was as if she were getting reacquainted with her husband. She felt she would like some tangible reminder of this journey, and so brought out the quilt which she had started in Milwaukee. There was plenty of time to work as the oxen plodded slowly on. She sewed a piece of Pitt's dress into a block, binding it together with squares from her wedding petticoat. She made another from the left-over scraps of the bonnet she was wearing to Kansas and still another from pieces of Edmund's shirt. She put them together with small neat stitches, thinking as she did so that she was fashioning a pattern from the various lives they had led, linking Ohio with Wisconsin and Wisconsin with the road to Kansas, and planning, in her mind, other blocks she would add at journey's end, in Kansas itself. She was bound to these places she had left; a bit of herself in each place. A bit gained; a bit given. Each block would bring back its own memory.

"You'll pretty well have a record of your married life sewed into that quilt," Ma remarked.

And Ma was right.

They came to the Missouri River. No bridge was here, so the crossing was accomplished by the use of a flatboat propelled by oars. They loaded one wagon at a time on the boat, which was then turned upstream and forced against the rapid current by means of a rope in the hands of men on the bank, while other men worked with poles on the boat itself. It was necessary to go about a quarter of a mile upstream. The craft was then cast adrift and, by vigorous rowing with the boat headed upstream, a landing on the west bank, opposite the starting point, was accomplished.

Edmund directed the operation skillfully, checking each wagon as it went across, watching as the flatboat came back for the next one in line. It was slow and desperately hard work. Once across, however, they had their reward. They were on Nebraska soil. No more deep rivers to cross. Straight south they would travel now until they came to Topeka. The end was in sight.

5

They arrived at Nebraska City the first week in August. By this time, the Milwaukee party had become accustomed to families joining them at almost every stop. Even so, they were not prepared for the crowd camped at Nebraska City which apparently had every intention of falling in with the party on its way to Kansas.

Many of them were in a sorry condition, their wagons barely

holding together, their teams emaciated, their supplies low. It looked doubtful whether they would hold out until they reached Topeka, even though the town was not so many miles away now. One had only to take the most superficial look to be able to distinguish the Milwaukee party from these ragged new recruits. Once again Fannie felt pride in Edmund, whose judgment and foresight were, in a large measure, responsible for their group's well-being. The people from Milwaukee knew why they were going to Kansas. No dream of sudden wealth was theirs; no illusions about what the future had to offer in this new country. Rather, there was a sober realization of all that lay ahead, and a simple determination to face it.

"Funny looking bunch, aren't they?" asked Mrs. Conklin, whose wagon was parked next to the Rosses'.

"They certainly are," Fannie agreed. She was busy seeing that the children donned fresh clothes. No reason to let them go like ragamuffins just because they were on the road.

"If that's a sample of what's going to Kansas from here on," Mrs. Conklin said complacently, "I think I'd as leave go in some other direction."

"I imagine we'll be pretty much of every kind in Kansas," Fannie remarked as she buttoned Lillie's pinafore. "Just as we were in Milwaukee." Or, she added in her mind, in Sandusky, or in all the world. No reason to feel that ever, anywhere, one would find a place where all the perfect people dwelt. For the most part, it seemed to her, women realized this. It was the men who pushed on, thinking to find perfection somewhere around the turn of the road or the bend of a river—forever exploring new country, hoping it would hold the image of their dreams. The women went along because they loved the men and so, somewhere beyond the last frontier, a new place got started. Fannie supposed it would go on like this until all the remote corners of the earth were settled and then, like as not, men (at last made to realize the earth could never be as bright as their hopes for it) would set their hearts on starting anew on the moon or some of the planets.

She gave Lillie a last pat and sent the child on her way.

•

"I wish you'd look," Mrs. Conklin went on, her attention diverted to a small group of men riding in their direction. "I hope *they* aren't wanting to throw in with us!"

The men approaching were, indeed, a strange-looking set of individuals, even in the motley crowd camped here at Nebraska City. The leader—he must have been that, for he rode slightly ahead on a fine dun horse—was thin and wiry. He wore homespun breeches, buffalo-hide boots and a cowhide vest with the hide side out. His red, untidy hair shone in the sun; his sad, deep-set eyes looked on the world as if he expected the worst of it. But as a pretty young woman started walking across the road, his glance followed her swinging skirts. Not until she had moved out of sight did he ride on to the Ross wagon.

"I'd like to see the captain of the train," he said.

Fannie was instantly on the alert. What sort of man was this, anyway, demanding to see Edmund? Various emotions seemed to be churning inside him—ambition, resolve and uncertainty, making his face almost sinister. His companions did not inspire any more confidence in her than did the leader. The man riding directly behind him was enough to set her shivering. Tall, gaunt, grizzled, old, he had the eyes of a zealot and a mouth like a bear trap.

"Mr. Ross is our captain," Mrs. Conklin said proudly as Fannie hesitated. "Here is our group." She indicated the clean orderly camp of the Milwaukee group, so much in contrast to the squalor of the others. "And this is Mrs. Ross," she continued.

The man on the dun horse swept off his hat and bowed to Fannie. She could feel the magnetism in his eyes as he looked at her, but did not like or trust him any more for all that.

"I am indeed glad to meet you," he told her, his voice and manner changing. He could have been bowing in a ballroom; even his clothes seemed to take on the appearance of formal attire. The old man behind him did not change one iota; his smouldering eyes continued staring at a point just over her head.

"My name is Lane," the leader told her. "James H. Lane."

"Lane?" Fannie looked at him in amazement. "Then you—it was you—"

"You are right, Ma'am," he told her. "You've been following the trail bearing my name."

"How do you do, Mr. Lane—" she found herself stuttering a little in her astonishment. James Lane, who had mapped out the trail the Milwaukee party was following to Kansas. Surely her first impression of him had been wrong. But then she remembered the words of the Missouri farmer, "Worse than old John Brown," and she wasn't too sure.

"Mr. Ross is right over there," she told him, pointing toward the spot where Edmund stood talking with several other men. "See—the one with the beard."

"Thank you, Mrs. Ross," Lane said politely, turning his dun horse and riding off. The wild-eyed old man, astride his motheaten nag, followed close behind him, the others in the group trailing along.

Fannie tried to go back to her work, but could not keep her mind on what she was doing.

"So that was Lane," Ma, who had remained in the wagon, said.

"Yes—and I'd give a good deal to know what he wants with Edmund," Fannie told her.

"Don't worry," her mother said soothingly. "It's no more than natural that he should meet the group that is traveling the road named for him."

"Yes—" Fannie agreed. But she was still uneasy.

Her concern grew as the hours went by. A great deal of talk was going on in camp, Lane and his companions always in the center of it. It was easily apparent that Lane, from the back of his horse, was urging some sort of action. At times Fannie could hear his voice as it rose and then, before she could catch what he was saying, it would die to a hoarse whisper.

Fannie prepared the midday meal, and still the men talked on. She fed the children and, at Ma's urging, tried to eat something herself. The food was cold when the group finally broke up and Edmund came back to the wagon.

"What did James Lane want?" she burst out.

Edmund looked at her quickly. "How did you know him?" he asked.

"He came here first," she explained, "asking for the leader of the train."

"He has some notion that we should enter Kansas as an army," Edmund told her. "Lane's Army. He says there's a real border war going on now, with the Missourians coming over to rob and loot and kill. He says if we went in as an army, we would scare them off."

Again Fannie remembered the Missouri farmer and his advice that, once the Milwaukee party got to Kansas, best they stay there and not start any fighting.

"I thought you were going to Topeka to work on a newspaper," she said. "I didn't know you had any idea of getting into an army."

But even as she spoke, she remembered the rifle.

"Of course I plan to work on a newspaper and to make a home for my family. But a man can't settle down with outlaws on his front porch. He can't publish a paper under those conditions, either. If we are to have anything like a good life in Kansas, we must take a firm stand, once we get there. Perhaps even before we arrive."

"And that means—"

Edmund did not answer her directly. "I told him I'd think it over," he said.

In a way that *was* an answer—one whose import she feared.

"I also told him I wanted to discuss it with my group," Edmund continued.

Fannie realized she must be satisfied with that, at least for the time being. All the same, she didn't like, or even trust, Lane. She didn't like his companions, either. Especially—

"Edmund," she asked, "who was that old man with him?"

He hesitated, looking at her obliquely. "Oh, that one," he finally said. "That was John Brown."

Fannie was clearing away the remains of breakfast while Edmund worked at checking the condition of the wagon and the harness. Even without looking at him, she knew he was not at ease about the turn affairs in camp had taken. The men in the Milwaukee group were divided among themselves as to whether they should throw in with Lane's idea or pursue their original plan of going to Kansas as a peaceful group of settlers. Among the ragged, disreputable recruits newly added to the band, however, there seemed to be almost a unanimous agreement that they should follow Lane. Unarmed, underprovisioned, poorly equipped they were, yet they still were confident that, under Lane, they could sweep into Kansas, conquering everything in their path. Fannie considered this idea ridiculous, if not downright dangerous. Why couldn't Edmund say "no" to it immediately, since the Milwaukee group still looked upon him as their leader, in spite of the way Lane had gone about the camp assuming charge? You'd think that Lane and Lane alone had recruited these people, yet all he had done was to join them yesterday here at Nebraska City. Now he had brought about a situation of near-mutiny within the encampment with his haranguing. If he kept on, the men might get out of hand entirely and rush down the rest of the way to Kansas, shooting and looting in the name of freedom.

She wanted to tell Edmund this, but refrained. How well she knew that her husband had a stubborn streak in him; there were times, much as she hated to admit it, when he seemed to be set on an idea he didn't like too well himself simply because someone opposed him. She had a hunch he didn't want any part of Lane's proposal; certainly she did not want to be the one who pushed him into an unwise decision with her own protests. While she hesitated, she saw two horsemen approaching.

"We were told we would find Mr. Ross here," one of them said, reining in by the wagon.

"I am Edmund Ross," Edmund said to them. "Good morning. What can I do for you?"

"Ah, good morning, Mr. Ross. I am Thaddaeus Hyatt and this is Dr. S. G. Howe. We are representatives from the National Kansas Committee. We come, actually, at the request of Governor Shannon to get some information about the purposes of this group of emigrants. We were told, when we arrived, that you are the leader."

"Of the Milwaukee group only," Edmund corrected him. "I was elected before we left."

He's no prouder of this motley bunch who joined us here, nor of their plan, than I am, Fannie exulted to herself.

"We have heard some—well, some most disquieting reports," Mr. Hyatt went on. "We have been told that this entire group forms Lane's Northern Army. Governor Shannon urged General Smith to meet your band with all disposable forces at his command. General Smith has declined to do this on the grounds that the information about your intentions might be inaccurate. We have come to check. Is it true that you are part of Lane's Army?"

"The Milwaukee party has had no such intentions," Edmund told him. "I, for one, am going to Topeka to join my brother in publishing a newspaper there. True, we are free-soil men. But we are not an army."

"In that case, I will tell you that we carry papers for Lane's arrest. The situation is very trying now. President Pierce has issued a proclamation against the Kansas Free State government. He dissolved the Topeka Legislature by sending Federal troops. Kansas is prostrate; her leading men with Free State convictions are in jail. We feel Lane cannot be trusted in this emergency. We have confidence in neither his discretion nor his self-control."

Edmund was silent. He must have felt there was more to come, and indeed there was.

"We realize that some hasty or ill-timed action on his part could defeat the purpose of your expedition. So we have been authorized to say, on behalf of the Committee, that if you persist in holding with Lane's plan, all supplies will be cut off from you. We cannot assume responsibility for what will happen if you do not sever all connections with him."

"I have had no wish to follow him," Edmund said. "On the other hand, I could not prevent the others—those not of our party—from acting as they wish."

"I am glad to hear that," Dr. Howe told him. "I think now the man we must see is Lane himself."

They bid Edmund farewell and went to find Lane.

When Hyatt and Dr. Howe gave their ultimatum to Lane, he took it hard. "If the people of Kansas don't want me," he cried, "I'll cut my throat today."

But he did nothing so drastic. Instead, he rode off, Old John Brown at his heels and the others of his party straggling after. Lane's face was sullen and mutinous. Watching him, Fannie had the uneasy feeling that neither this group nor Kansas had seen the last of the man. But she had little time to brood over the thought. Edmund came to announce that the train would start moving and they could get things ready. It suited her fine. As far as she was concerned, they couldn't get away from this place fast enough.

With Lane gone, peace settled over the camp once more as travel was resumed. Another week would bring them to Topeka, Edmund told her. The Milwaukee group drew closer together in the last stage of the journey. Some of the newcomers stopped to found a town of their own, named Holton at Edmund's suggestion. Fannie got out the quilt, put aside during those trying days at Nebraska City. She wanted to stitch in this last stage of the trip.

"We should make Topeka by night," Edmund told her one morning.

On the trail, dates hadn't mattered much. One day melted into another. But now, with the end in sight—with a permanent home in a new land—suddenly the day seemed important.

"What's today?" she asked.

"August 11," Edmund told her. "August 11, 1856."

Sure enough, that afternoon they came to Topeka. They had driven through rows of sunflowers as high as the oxens' heads, and over grass up to their shoulders. Heat was lifting up from the flat expanse of prairie land and pouring down from the bright, rimless sky. It squeezed Fannie between, making her feel she could not bear it, now or ever. Beyond them, in the direction they traveled, she saw a stretch of blue water—the Kaw River, Edmund said—and clinging to its banks, as a barnacle clings to a ship's hull, the small wavering cluster of huts and buildings which made up the town. For this, she was thinking, they had driven hundreds of miles across muddy roads and treacherous streams. For this, they had given up the safe comfort of Milwaukee.

Fannie glanced at Edmund. His face held the bright happy look of one who at last beholds the structure of a dream. But his dream was not for this little village hanging precariously to the side of the river. It was for something larger, finer, than any visible thing.

"There it is," he said, deep excitement in his voice. "There's Topeka."

"Yes—" she echoed.

If she failed to get the enthusiasm into her voice which the occasion warranted for him, he had not seemed to notice.

PART TWO

BLEEDING KANSAS

V

Topeka

1856–1858

FANNIE HAD only to look out the window to see Kansas Avenue, broad as two streets needed to be, running up the hill and sloping off to both sides. Already she knew the buildings facing it—Mr. Walter Oakley's Topeka House, its frame hewn from cottonwood, its walls plastered over concrete; three houses made from brick kilned here in Topeka; shake shanties, their sides huge poles with oak weather boarding; the Methodist and Congregational churches under construction; Mr. Willets' store. And Constitution Hall in whose basement William had set up his printing office when he first arrived. In the principal room of this hall the Free State Convention had been formed last October; here, too, the first Free State Legislature had met in July, only to be dissolved by Colonel Sumner at the orders of President Pierce. Now William's basement office had been replaced by a depot established to house the commodities—food, clothing, various necessary provisions —which Colonel John Ritchie had captured during his raid on the little proslave town of Oskaloosa and brought back to distribute to the needy in Topeka.

"It's just another word for stealing," Fannie burst out hotly to Edmund.

They were trying to fit their possessions into the small house William had helped them find (thank heavens, it was no shake shanty, as she had half feared it might be). The August heat bore down on them from a burnished sky and the dust lay thick on everything. Ma had taken the children to the river, a quarter of a mile away, to bring back water, and Fannie thought of the tight sturdy house in Milwaukee with a breeze blowing off Lake Michigan, and with its cistern on the back porch.

"If you look at things in one way, yes," Edmund agreed. "But remember—wagon trains loaded with goods bought and paid for by the citizens of Topeka have been stopped repeatedly by the Missourians and the contents confiscated. People were without food here. I grant you this was a poor way to get it, but even so, people cannot starve."

"The whole border has gone mad," she said.

Three days of Topeka and already she could make that statement with confidence. Each day brought in its own stories of killing, looting and imprisonment. Personally, she couldn't decide who was more at fault, the proslavery people or the free-soil ones. No wonder Governor Shannon had sent a letter of resignation to the President and declared a man "might as well try to govern the devil in Hell as to govern Kansas Territory these days." Once the letter was mailed, he had left the Territory.

"I wouldn't touch a bit of that—that loot—if I were starving," Fannie said.

"I wouldn't want you to," Edmund assured her.

"But Edmund," she asked, realizing quite well she was arguing on the other side now, "if the supply trains are blocked, how are we going to get food? Without a governor, we can't hope for things to get better, either."

"No, we can't. That's why I'm going with the Free State troops."

"Going with the Free State troops—" She got to her feet so hastily a cup she was unpacking fell to the floor. She watched the broken pieces roll off into the corner of the room and felt no sense of regret, even though it was one from her best set of dishes. "The army—"

"Fannie," he told her patiently, "I have no choice. The President has appointed John Geary of Pennsylvania to take Shannon's place, but it will be several weeks before he can get here. In the interim, Daniel Woodson has taken over. And you know what that means."

"Not exactly—only that he's secretary of state in the Territory."

"He is. But he's also a proslavery man. He's taken advantage of Shannon's leaving to declare that a state of rebellion and insurrection exists among the free soil people, and to urge the Missourians to prepare to advance on Kansas in order to secure it for the Union. The Union, indeed! It is up to us free-soil people to hold the Territory until Geary arrives. If we don't make an organized resistance, the proslave group will have taken over before the new governor arrives, and the only way we'll have to get supplies at all will be by raiding, as Ritchie did."

She was still not convinced.

"Right now, a thousand men, commanded by Senator Atchison of Missouri—mostly Missourians and all proslave—are camped on the Little Santa Fe, on the border, ready to march."

"All right," she said wearily. "When must you go?"

"In the morning." He walked across the room and lifted the Milwaukee rifle from its place above the door. He took a piece of cloth and began to polish it carefully. Then he raised it and squinted down the burnished barrel. "It certainly is a good rifle," he said with satisfaction.

It was all Fannie could do to prevent herself from running to him and pleading, "Don't go, Edmund. Please, please don't go. This is no mild skirmish you're headed for. Those groups have met before, and never without—"

Even in her mind she would not let herself finish the sentence.

2

In the two weeks Edmund had been gone, Fannie found work her refuge. Fortunately, of this there was no lack, what with getting settled in a new house in a strange town. But the thing she found hardest to accept was the fact that because of the uncertain times, there would be no school this fall. And here was Lillie, almost six years old, and of an age to begin. She looked out the window to see the Kaw threading its blue way through a narrow fringe of trees at the bottom of the hill, and once more she thought of other waters she had lived near—Put-in Bay and the vast expanse of Lake Michigan. She yearned for both of them.

"Anybody home?" Mary Elizabeth called, opening the kitchen door as she did so.

"Oh, come on in," Fannie urged.

The young woman walked in carefully, as if she were treading on eggs, after the manner of women in their first pregnancy.

"I'm glad to see you," Fannie said. She liked William's wife.

"I came over to see if I could help you," Mary Elizabeth said.

"I'm about finished," Fannie told her. "Let's sit down and have a cup of coffee."

"That would be nice. We've been out for a couple of days; you know—the Border Ruffians held up a freight wagon out of Westport. And William wouldn't let me get any from the supplies Colonel Ritchie brought in."

"I should think not," Fannie said with decision. "Thank goodness Edmund felt the same way. That raid was stealing, and nothing else—"

"It was a military necessity," Mary Elizabeth corrected her. "Whether we like it or not, the situation demands a military approach. That's why William and Edmund had to join the Free State Army—" Mary Elizabeth had become like the other Rosses. They counted no hardship too great if undertaken for freedom's sake.

"I can't quite reconcile myself to seeing the men form an army," Fannie said. "It looks as if they were taking the law into their own hands—"

"They have to stop Atchison's men," Mary Elizabeth pointed out. "You know that. They must hold the Territory until Geary arrives. Everyone says he's a good man; he'll keep the peace. But that Woodson—he's a real villain."

"Then why don't the Federal troops come in?" Fannie asked. "They're stationed at Leavenworth and that's not far at all."

"The Federal troops," Mary Elizabeth said, "are controlled by President Pierce, and by Jefferson Davis, the Secretary of War. Do you think those two Democrats are going to take a step—a single step—to help out the free-soil people?"

"I still can't see why we should take the law into our own hands," Fannie argued.

"My goodness, Fannie, you just don't seem to understand," the young woman protested. She was flushed and excited, and in her condition—

"Some more coffee?" Fannie asked her, changing the subject tactfully.

"No—I think maybe too much of it isn't good for me." She stood, and Fannie stood with her. Oh, they had much in common, Fannie thought. She and Mary Elizabeth—both bearing the same last name, both married to men who had that same passion for justice and right, and both either the mother of babies or expecting one, who would, in time, carry on the name of Ross and, doubtless, the tradition.

"I haven't felt so well the last few days," Mary Elizabeth confessed uncertainly. "And with William gone—" her voice trailed off.

Fannie reached out to pat her hand. "Don't worry," she said. "Things will work out. William will be here before long—you said yourself he would be back as soon as the new governor arrived. If you need me, just say so."

Fannie smiled a little, thinking how strange this must sound from her who, only a few minutes before, had been expressing her fears with abandon.

She might reassure Mary Elizabeth, but she was still far from being at ease herself. Young John Rastell, afire to be out doing battle himself, kept her informed of all the rumors that came back to Topeka. A group of Missourians under General John Reid swooped down on Osawatomie (especially hated as the home of Old John Brown), drove off the people who lived there and set fire to the town. Only four houses had escaped burning. At Lecompton, territorial capital, the proslave citizens burned the homes of the seven Northern families. In the midst of these difficulties, James Lane came in from Nebraska, gathered a force of three hundred men, and marched toward Atchison's camp on the Little Santa Fe.

"Oh, why does he want to do that?" Fannie cried. "He'll only bring down retaliation on all of us. Besides, what can he do—three hundred against a thousand!"

"He can do a lot of jayhawking," John told her.

"Jayhawking—?"

"Yes, Ma'am. They say in Ireland there's a bird called the jayhawk that worries its prey. Lane and his bunch can worry those Atchison boys a lot. We all can."

"Now, John," Fannie protested, "don't you get any ideas about mixing up in this fight. You're much too young."

She knew she had said the wrong thing as soon as the words passed her lips.

"Mrs. Ross," he told her with great dignity, "I've already joined the Free State militia. I mean to get in on that jayhawking business myself."

He was gone, walking very straight, every inch a soldier. Fannie, watching him, was both proud and sad.

A few days later, on September 10, Governor Geary arrived on Kansas soil. What he saw could certainly have given him no reassurance. He rode through a land filled with evidence of violence. Almost every house along his route had been destroyed, either by proslave or Free State forces, leaving only bleak and lonely chimneys where once homes had been. Lane's men had only recently marched away from one small settlement, after pillaging the two stores and leaving whiskey barrels, heads broken in, flung along the path of their retreat. It was no wonder the new

Governor said, "The condition of Kansas Territory could be no worse. But," he added, "I mean to establish peace and quiet."

It was on this hopeful note that Edmund returned several days later.

"Well, I'm home," he said needlessly, grabbing her in his arms and kissing her with youthful exuberance. His clothes were dusty and wrinkled, not at all like his usual careful grooming. But she clung to him, not minding. He was home from the wars and safe. And, she thought, looking as if he thrived on fighting.

"What are you grinning about?" he asked, holding her at arm's length.

"Oh—nothing much. I'm just glad you're home."

"You know," he said, regarding her solemnly, "you're a twinkling sort of girl. I think that's why I fell in love with you."

She said, "Oh, my goodness, Edmund," flushing with pleasure. A twinkling sort of girl, indeed! Edmund was at home and had it in his heart to say pretty things to her. Kansas suddenly looked better than it had at any time since her arrival. She might as well realize she was married to a man who loved a good fight for its own sake. She, who did not like a fight under any circumstances!

"We Topeka men helped to hold the Territory until the new Governor got here. That's something our children can tell their children, and be proud."

"That's a relief," Fannie remarked dryly. "At least, you won't have to take matters into your own hands again."

"I hope not," he said. "But in a territory, citizens can never be absolutely certain. Governors, and as far as that goes, all top officials, are appointed by the President, confirmed by the Senate. Residents have nothing to say in the matter. Kansas has had a lot of weak, even vicious appointees. If it happens again—and it could—we'll have to take up arms once more. Like the Minute Men."

"In the meanwhile, what will you be doing?" she asked.

"William and I will publish the *Tribune*."

He'd have a Free State paper. He had been a member of the Free State Army. He could not, by any stretch of imagining, be called "Sound on the Goose." If only he did not feel it necessary to express himself so freely! Was he going to be any safer running a newspaper than he would have been had he continued to carry a gun?

3

She did not have long to wonder. The paper was no more than well started when Edmund came in one afternoon, rushing past her, scarcely noticing either her or the children. He made his way immediately to the bedroom, closing the door after him. She heard the sound of water being poured from the pitcher into the bowl, the hasty thud of china against the marble top of the washstand. It was unusual enough for him to be home at this hour, without explanation, but to be washing up now, even as careful as he was about his appearance, did not make sense. She went to the bedroom and opened the door.

He was standing before the mirror, his face white with lather, while he drew his razor carefully, although hastily, across his cheek. She couldn't believe what she saw. He was shaving off his beard!

She remembered how proud he had been when he had first started it, back in Milwaukee, and how, with girlish giggles, she had told him he couldn't kiss her unless he got rid of that old scratchy beard and he had said oh, if that was the way she felt about it he wouldn't kiss her at all and she, a mother of two children, had run to him crying with girl-like ardor, "I didn't mean it—"

And now, he was getting rid of it. Swipe—a long clean line across his cheek. Swish—another space of bare skin.

"What on earth are you doing?" she asked.

"I'll tell you later," he said. The shaving was finished, and he was bringing from the wardrobe a black broadcloth suit, usually reserved for Sundays, and a silk hat. He donned these with haste and started to leave the room.

"Edmund," she demanded. "Tell me—"

He bent to kiss her, the smell of shaving soap strong on his still damp skin, the feel of his cheek smooth and strange against her face.

"After a while," he said, and left the house, walking rapidly in the direction of Constitution Hall.

It was much later when he came back. She had put the children to bed and had brought out the quilt, thinking to quiet her nervousness with work. There was no manner of evil she could not imagine because, for the first time, she had no idea of the sort of danger which Edmund now faced. Concern was also intermingled with anger. He was, quite obviously, in a hurry, but still, he could have told her!

Finally he came home. She looked up to see him there—a smooth-shaven stranger, dressed in his best. And, she had to admit, looking very complacent.

"Well?" she asked quietly, an upward inflection in her voice.

He came over to kiss her, and in spite of herself she drew back a little.

"I remember," he said, smiling at her, "once when you wouldn't let me kiss you *because* I had a beard."

"All right," she said. "Go ahead and tell me—"

"They were looking for me," he began.

"Who?"

"United States Marshal Donalson and a company of soldiers from Fort Riley. They were rounding up all the members of the Topeka Volunteers. They said they wanted me especially because I also wrote Free State editorials. They were asking people if they knew me."

"Whom did they ask?" Fannie asked curiously.

"Well, me for one."

"You—"

"Yes. As soon as I got back after—well, after I changed my clothes—one of the soldiers came up to me and asked if I knew the boss of the *Tribune.* I said yes—he was a man with sandy hair and a beard, who always wore a brown plush cap and a brown suit."

Fannie began to laugh. She laughed until the tears rolled down her cheeks and then, unthinkingly, she wiped them off with the quilt block she had been sewing.

"Don't laugh," he told her soberly. "They've arrested a hundred men or more, and have taken them to Lecompton and thrown them into jail. Without warrants for their arrest, or indictments."

"How dreadful," she said, thinking how easily Edmund might have been among them.

"Yes," he said. "It is. One of them was John Rastell."

"Oh, no," Fannie protested. She remembered how the boy had helped her all the way over the Lane Trail; and how he had come to her to announce his enlistment in the forces, when she pronounced him too young.

Too young, perhaps, to be a soldier, but not too young to be thrown into jail as a traitor to his country. Kansas Territory was, indeed, in a terrible condition. She could only hope that Governor Geary would be as good as his word and bring peace and quiet.

4

It seemed to Fannie Ross, looking out toward Webster Peak on a bright October afternoon, that the Governor had succeeded. A peace of sorts had settled over Kansas Territory. True, there were rumors from time to time that men on both sides had been threatened, robbed or molested; that horses or supplies had been stolen. But in Topeka, fortunately, these stories remained only rumors. In Topeka, grapes grew purple on vines along the bluffs; corn shocks stood straight and proud with yellow pumpkins at their bases; nights were crisp and exhilarating, and in the daytime the sun shone brightly in a lacquer blue sky, while the trees along the Kaw were bright with swatches of color. And, on Kansas Avenue the presses of the *Tribune* were humming.

The weather couldn't last much longer; she and the children ought to be outside taking advantage of it. "Come on," Fannie called brightly to them, "let's walk down and see Papa."

"Pa-pa—" Pitt echoed. He had pulled himself up from the

chair to undertake a few experimental steps. Finding it impossible to master both skills, speech and motion, simultaneously, he let loose and plunked to the floor, his fat little bottom making a dull thump when he landed. He was ready to cry with the shock of his fall and the laughter which greeted his mishap when Lillie cried delightedly, "Did you hear, Mama? He said 'Papa'!"

"Well, he tried," Fannie agreed cautiously. "Come on, now, let's make ourselves tidy, so Papa will be proud of us."

In a short time they were walking down Kansas Avenue, all of them very neat and clean. No easy feat, this, with water so scarce. Edmund declared it was just a matter of time until the town would have wells, but then Edmund was sure that eventually all good things would come to Topeka.

"Here we are," Lillie said, darting inside the building, and then leading the way to where the presses, quiet now, were located. Edmund stood in the room, wearing his apron, his green eyeshade pushed up on his head, as an old woman would wear her glasses. His back was toward the door, while he engaged in earnest conversation with a visitor. Seeing it was Colonel Holliday, Fannie was half-ready to retreat, but the visitor himself said, "Good afternoon, Mrs. Ross," and at his words, Edmund turned to face the family.

"Good afternoon, Colonel," Fannie said, matching the man's dignity with her own.

Everyone treated Colonel Holliday with respect. It was impossible to think of Topeka apart from him. He had been among the first to arrive. Only a few men were there at the time—mostly traders, living in huts of buffalo hide, at a spot called Pappan's Ferry. From the moment he helped lay out the town—as William had said, with twine and a small watch-charm compass—he had never doubted its destiny. Topeka was going to be the capital, once the Territory became a state, and it was going to have a railroad running through it and beyond.

Like Edmund, he had been a member of the Free State Army and, like him, had escaped arrest when Donalson came to town. The two men were evidently deep in a discussion of some phase of the fighting when she came in, for Colonel Holliday turned to her to explain, "I was just reminding your husband of the special edition of the *Herald of Freedom* which he helped put out."

The *Herald of Freedom*, she knew, had been the Free State paper in Lawrence, captured when the town was raided, its presses thrown into the river.

"We raised the type from the river," Colonel Holliday explained, "melted it into bullets, 'reissued' it to our proslave friends, and told them we were sending back a second edition!"

Lillie moved to her father's side with Arthur close behind her. Pitt, wanting to be a part of things, started his excited jabbering once more, flailing his arms. Edmund reached out to take the child. It was perhaps this scene of tranquility which reminded Colonel Holliday that Edmund was, first of all, a family man, with a great stake in the future peace and stability of the Territory.

"Well," the Colonel said thoughtfully, "I suppose it's high time we started talking railroad again."

Railroads, indeed, Fannie thought. With the national government wrangling and nobody thinking Frémont was going to be elected President (and how would Jessie feel about that, after she had cherished such great hopes for him?) and Pierce just sitting in his office, waiting for Buchanan to take his place. Almost everyone was sure Buchanan would go in, and there would be another Democrat who didn't care much what happened to Kansas so long as it didn't make trouble for the rest of the country. And out West, where Holliday proposed to push the railroad, were Indians threatening every minute to go on the warpath. What did the country need with a railroad leading into that sort of region?

"Yes," Edmund agreed, apparently ignoring any of the difficulties which had occurred to Fannie. "It's time for railroad talk again."

"We'll never get one until we become a state," the Colonel said.

"That won't be possible so long as we have a Democrat for President," Edmund reminded him. "He would never listen to a Free State party, or any of their propositions. Remember how it was with the Topeka Constitution—"

"Our only hope is to band together and form a constitution which will be accepted in Washington, one which represents the true convictions of the Free State people who now form the bulk of our settlers. If we are allowed to proceed without fear or intimidation, we can do it."

"First," Colonel Holliday remarked, "we must have a strong and just governor to protect our rights."

"Perhaps Geary will be our answer," Edmund told him.

"We can hope," the Colonel continued. "The difficulty is that the people who live here have little or no say about who will govern them. They are citizens of the United States, living outside its limits. Government without the consent of the governed. That's why we fought the Revolution."

What a way to talk, Fannie thought. Revolution, indeed!

"We must have a constitution on which we can agree, and railroads connecting us with the rest of the country. I plan to start a series of editorials on those subjects," Edmund went on.

"You are a real addition to the Territory, Ross. We need more men like you if we are to accomplish anything here."

"Give us time," Edmund told him. "Less than four years ago Kansas was nothing more than a name. A state can't be built in a minute."

Fall turned cold and rainy, promising a winter not as severe as last year's, about which Mary Elizabeth had given such graphic details, but cold nonetheless. The first days of November brought temperatures so low that wild turkeys, numbed by it, could be shot with pistols. A big snow, the season's first, fell on the day when the citizens of the United States went to the polls, with Kansas as their rallying cry. The Republicans said that in this strife-torn territory lay the struggle between slavery and freedom, quoting liberally from *Uncle Tom's Cabin* the while; the Democrats said they believed in freedom, too—freedom of choice which gave the people of Kansas the right to choose for themselves. The Democrats said the Republicans were challenging the South to secede, which it would do if the Republicans won.

Edmund remarked that on such a basis anyone could be sure which way the election would go—the people would not be willing to vote for dividing the Union. He was right. James Buchanan was elected.

Even though Edmund had prophesied the outcome, he took the election hard.

"Any constitution we would draw up for Kansas now, short of a proslave one, is doomed," he said.

He found no hope in the news that a census would be taken in preparation for a June election, set in order to elect delegates to a constitutional convention.

"The Territory is predominantly Free State now," Fannie pointed out. "Surely that will mean they will have their say."

But when he reminded her that the census takers and election judges would be proslavery men, even she could see this act would bring no great gain to the Free State hopes.

Governor Geary, apparently doing his best to be fair to both sides, felt he was getting scant backing from the party which appointed him and resigned in disgust, once more leaving Kansas Territory without a governor.

"It looks as if we do better without a governor than with one," Edmund said thoughtfully.

For more than a month there was not even an acting governor, a period which had been remarkably quiet. Then a new secretary of state, Fredrick Stanton, arrived to assume the position of acting governor, pending the arrival of a new appointee. Stanton had scarcely arrived before he drew down the anger of all the free-soil people by announcing the apportionment of delegates to the constitutional convention on the basis of the census just completed.

"And what will we have?" Edmund fumed. "A whole bunch of proslave people, rigged up by those proslave census takers."

"What can you do?" Fannie asked.

"The free-soil voters will stay away from the polls," Edmund foretold. "It is not a legal election. We will not even vote on delegates appointed by fraud."

His prophecy was correct. Few of the free-soil voters bothered to vote.

"It seems to me you Free State people played right into the hands of the proslavery ones," Fannie said. "You should have voted, even though you know it wouldn't count. That's the only way you had to protest. Besides, it was your right as a citizen."

But the Free State people—and Edmund with them—did not agree. A vote cast under such circumstances was simply recognizing the election as legal, which it was far from being. Better to ignore it entirely than to give it status by casting even a protest vote.

5

The children were already in bed that evening and Fannie and Edmund were sitting together in the living room, he reading, she occupied with the everlasting mending necessary to keep three small children clad, when a knock came at the door. Almost simultaneously with the knock, the door was flung open, and a boy catapulted himself into the room. Before he was well inside, he had closed the door and then stood, his back against it, breathing fast. In spite of his unkempt appearance—his coat hanging off him, his trousers torn, his shirt ragged and dirty—Fannie recognized him. She and Edmund spoke together.

"John—"

And Edmund said, "What on earth are you doing here?"

"I escaped," John Rastell explained. "I came here, because I didn't know where else to go. Let me stay."

Fannie's heart yearned over the boy, so thin, so ill-clad, so frightened and desperate. Her mind went back to John as he had been along the Lane Trail—manfully proud of his responsibility, confident great things awaited him at the end of the road. Was this the way Kansas rewarded those who had come out with high hopes and willing hearts and guns to back them up?

"Sit down, John," Edmund told him. "Fannie, get him something to eat."

The command was not necessary. Already she had moved to the safe and was bringing out food.

"You'll let me stay, won't you?" John begged. "You'll hide me?"

"Go wash your face and hands," Edmund told him, gently as if he were talking to young Arthur. "Then come back and eat the food Mrs. Ross will have ready. We'll talk things over while you eat."

The boy went to the basin sitting on the little stand. He washed carefully, and then combed his hair. By the time he came to the table he was calmer, and could begin eating.

"I was lucky, managing to escape," John said, talking as he ate. "A hundred men are still there in jail, penned up like animals. No use thinking the law will come to their rescue—the law is proslave, and it won't give them any hope of getting out."

"In time, something will be done," Edmund said. "It must. Men can't be kept in prison forever, without warrant for arrest or any sort of indictment. It's against all the rights the Constitution of the United States confers upon us."

"If you ask me," John said, "the Constitution isn't giving us much of anything. We sort of have to take things in our own hands. That's why I slipped off when I had a chance. You'll let me stay here, won't you, Mr. Ross? I can find some place to hang out—sleep days, work nights, until I can get back into the Free State Army again."

Edmund was silent. The boy put down his fork, looked at the older man fearfully.

"You won't turn me in, will you?"

"No, John, I won't do that," Edmund promised. "But on the other hand, I'm not going to encourage you to stay here."

"Now, Mr. Ross," the boy burst out, "you aren't going to make me go back to Milwaukee, are you?"

"No. You're a man now, with a record of courage behind you. But I'm going to tell you I think you should go."

The boy looked at him, hurt, rebellion, disillusionment in his young face. Now that he was among friends, washed, rested and fed, he looked younger and, strangely enough, even more vulnerable than he had seemed in fear and flight.

"But that would be running out on a bargain," he protested. "I said I was coming to Kansas to settle, and I meant it. *You* aren't giving up and going back, like a—like a coward—"

"I was not caught and thrown into prison," Edmund pointed out. "I am not an escapee, as you are. You must realize that the Federal officers will be looking for you now, and, when you are caught—and you will be, if you stay here—your sentence will be even greater because you have escaped. Under the circumstances, you can't do much good for Kansas. Go back to Milwaukee. There you can bide your time and, once this thing is settled, come back . . ."

"But Mr. Ross—"

"Eat your supper and go to bed. Then, when you have rested a little, slip out and make your way northward, toward Nebraska City, and then across the Lane Trail, to Milwaukee. You know the way—it won't be easy, but you can do it."

John was not convinced, but he went off to bed at last and Edmund followed him for one more talk with the boy.

Fannie cleared up the remains of the meal, thinking of how Edmund had escaped John's fate. Again he had been fortunate, as he had been when he avoided the consequences of his part in helping Joshua Glover and, later, Mart and Tilda. Did he, indeed, lead a charmed life?

She wondered what he would have done had he, like John, been captured and thrown into jail at Lecompton. Would he have tried to escape as the boy had done? And, once he had succeeded, would he have acted as he now urged John to act? Would he have gone back to Milwaukee? She doubted it. And yet, she could see that retreat was the wise thing for John, even though for Edmund such a course was impossible. She smiled a little, remembering his rushing home to shave off his beard and change clothes. The beard was almost back to its old luxurious state now, and Edmund looked more like himself. Edmund and John Rastell were two different people, she thought. Edmund was a clever, resourceful man, able to take care of himself. None but the best could stay here now. Edmund was a man, and he would stay. John was a boy, and he would go.

But what if Edmund had been caught and, as a result, she and the children had been forced to go back to Milwaukee? Would she have welcomed the chance to be out of this fighting and uncertainty?

Her mind put the question to her heart. And, although she could scarcely believe the answer she got, she knew she would have gone unwillingly, had the move been forced upon them. Her stay in Kansas had taught her something. She wasn't the one for retreating, any more than Edmund was.

6

Sometimes it seemed to Fannie that the procession of governors in Kansas Territory was like a game of musical chairs. Robert Walker arrived in mid-May, "a little whippet of a man," Edmund called him. He tried hard enough to please everyone with the inevitable result that at times he pleased no one.

When the Free State Legislature met in Topeka in early June, Walker journeyed over to talk with individual members, reminding them that since the Legislature was not really legalized by the voters, anything it did would be unacceptable by the national government. Instead, he said, their one recourse was to get out and vote on the constitution which the Lecompton delegates would shortly prepare.

"As if any free-soil man would vote on a constitution formed by delegates illegally elected," Edmund said bitterly.

"Maybe that's where you're making a mistake," Fannie pointed out. "If you don't vote, the constitution formed there will be by those who do vote, and then what sort of objections can you raise? You had a chance to protest, and didn't make use of it."

He looked at her thoughtfully. "You just might be right," he told her finally.

Walker proved to be a man of principle and decision. When

the election came up in October, he kept his word and posted Federal troops in the fourteen precincts where Missourians might be most likely to slip over the line to cast their illegal votes in order to keep Kansas proslave, overlooking, however, two small counties, McGee with only a handful of white settlers and Oxford containing only eleven buildings, including stores and barns.

The returns, when counted, startled everyone. McGee showed a total of 1,226 votes, against the 14 at the previous election, and Oxford had 1,628. No one, least of all Governor Walker, could ignore the facts. He threw out the votes. And then, in spite of proslavery protests, he announced that the next Territorial Legislature would consist of nine free-soil councilmen and four proslave; twenty-four free-soil representatives and fifteen proslave.

"It's evident to him, as to everyone else by now," Edmund said with satisfaction, "that Kansas is predominantly free soil in its sentiments, and is bound to come into the Union as a Free State."

However true that fact might be, the Lecompton Constitution, drawn up by proslavery delegates was rigged in such a tricky way that any vote cast against it would be meaningless. The free-soil voters again stayed away from the polls. President Buchanan, doubtless taking notice of this fact, urged Congress to admit Kansas into the Union under the Lecompton Constitution. When news of the President's stand came to Governor Walker, he resigned in protest, and once more Kansas Territory had only an acting governor, Secretary of State Stanton.

There was one gain. The Kansas Legislature, meeting in special session at Lecompton after having overcome the reluctance of Acting Governor Stanton, was predominantly free soil. Of course, this body denounced the proslave Lecompton Constitution. But Fannie thought they showed a lamentable lack of judgment by making the Free State Militia, with Lane as commander, the official military force of Kansas Territory. To give him power of this kind would only license him to engage in further looting, of which there had already been too much.

As always, any event in Kansas was ballyhooed in Washington and converted into political issues. The Senate approved the admission of Kansas under the Lecompton Constitution, but the House turned the measure down. In the midst of it all, Hughes of Indiana stood on the Senate floor and, in discussing the matter of the troubled Territory, coined the phrase, "Bleeding Kansas."

There was no doubt of the issue now. The word Kansas was on every lip.

In Kansas Territory itself nothing happened to allay the national concern over her destiny. James Lane killed a proslave man, Gaius Jenkins, over a land dispute; feuds and factions in both groups, the members fighting among themselves, jockeyed for power and position; jayhawking continued, with a new face appearing on the scene, that of a free soldier named James Montgomery who held with John Brown that all proslave settlers should be driven out of the Territory. He and his men fired on a small group of Federal dragoons, killing several. In a retaliation not to be wondered at, the proslave forces lined up a group of those implicated in the massacre and executed them at a small place called Marias des Cygnes. Newspaper headlines flashed huge and black once more, and up in Massachusetts Mr. Whittier took pen in hand in order to compose a rousing poem describing the return of the victims' bodies "yet warm with their lives," and to declare to the world that "on the lintels of Kansas the blood shall not dry."

As if, Fannie thought, there wasn't enough emotionalism in Kansas already.

Scarcely noticed in the turmoil, the new governor, James Denver, arrived. And then something happened which shifted the national interest away from the activities of proslave and free-soil groups. Gold was discovered in western Kansas. Once more talk of railroads started; people wanted a quick, sure way of getting to the precious stuff.

Fannie hoped the situation would settle down. But Abraham Lincoln started the whole thing rolling again. Up in Springfield in June of 1858 he told a convention of Republicans that "a house divided against itself cannot stand. . . . America cannot endure half slave and half free." He maintained the agitation about slavery had not ceased but, on the contrary, was growing greater.

Fannie, reading the account of his speech, was divided between exasperation at his having laid down so clear an ultimatum and a knowledge that he was right. The Rosses had been in Kansas two years now, and nothing had changed for the better. No constitution, no railroads, no admission to the Union, no peace. None of the goals Edmund had hoped to help achieve when he decided to come. And, might as well admit it, the roots of the failure lay in the fact that the nation couldn't decide for itself whether or not it wanted slavery. Disturbing as Mr. Lincoln's words might be, she could still see the element of truth in them.

7

In spite of the uncertain conditions, however, Topeka was prospering. A boom had started with town lots selling at fantastic prices. Merchants were rolling in cash, selling supplies to the prospectors rushing out to the gold fields. Thirteen business houses now served a population of better than 1,200. Four-horse coaches traveling between Kansas City and Fort Riley crossed the river at Topeka, thus furnishing a regular and dependable mail service. Nor was culture neglected. Lillie and Arthur attended the new school, a proud eighteen by twenty-four feet in size and boasting two stories. The Kansas Philomathic Institute busied itself with "self-improvement, literary contributions, public readings and music." The group sponsored a small library, and recently had even given a passable local talent presentation of *The Drunkard.*

Fannie and Edmund were walking home from a meeting of the Institute one July evening. A great golden moon hung in the sky, so low it seemed almost on their shoulders. Fannie was recalling with pleasure the program, finding it difficult to reconcile it with the raw frontier where it was being held. The speakers were cultivated, well-informed people who would have appeared with credit in Milwaukee. Either by accident or intent, nothing was said of politics, burning though the issue might be.

"I certainly enjoyed the program," she told Edmund.

"Yes—" he answered absently. "By the way, Fannie, a man is coming tomorrow to talk business with me. He is bringing his family with him. Do you think you could have them for dinner?"

"Oh, Edmund . . . Who are they? How many—?" Perfectly natural questions of a hostess in a place where food was neither varied nor easy to come by. (And so short a time to prepare—with three children underfoot at that!)

"His name's Robert Ream," Edmund told her. "He and his family moved to Leavenworth three years ago, as soon as the territory opened to settlers. He is chief clerk to Surveyor-General Calhoun."

"How many?" she repeated.

"Oh—he and his wife and three children. Two girls and a boy. Their youngest girl must be ten or so. The others are older." He turned to Fannie once more. "How about it?" he asked.

"Bring them on," she said. "I'll work out something."

"I knew you would," he told her calmly.

She looked at him keenly, but his face was as bland as milk. Good and well she knew that, manlike, he had already asked the Ream family to dine with them.

"They're from Wisconsin," Edmund told her. "Madison—"

Instantly Fannie was alert. She could almost see Lake Michigan, gleaming blue and restless against the sky, and the streets of Milwaukee, and all the dear familiar things she had known there. It was going to be good to talk with someone who shared these memories.

Fannie liked the Ream family on sight. Mr. Ream was frail and certainly did not seem the type to lead the active life of a surveyor. Mrs. Ream was brisk and capable and well-bred: a very charming woman. Their son, Bob, had not come, but the two daughters were with them. Mary, perhaps sixteen, and thin like her father, was a quiet, mannerly girl. But it was the youngest one, Vinnie, to whom Fannie felt particularly drawn.

Vinnie was a dark, plump little girl with an eager vitality about her. She was shy, but not painfully so. She had, too, a merry little way which served to attract people to her instantly.

Once the introductions and greetings were taken care of, Vinnie turned to Lillie. "Come on, let's go play in the yard," she suggested.

"Oh, yes—" Lillie cried rapturously. "Me, too," Arthur and Pitt echoed. The four made their way to the door, while Mary, doubtless feeling herself quite adult, stayed with the women.

"Do be careful, Vinnie," her mother called after her. "Don't get your dress dirty." Once the children were outside, she turned to Fannie. "She's forever wanting to get her hands in mud or clay or sand. Always making things—"

"Well," Fannie said, "if it keeps her happy—"

"I don't know about the happy part," Mrs. Ream declared. "But I do know it keeps her dirty—"

Fannie began setting the table, getting out the good cloth and the dishes and silver she had brought from Wisconsin. All the time she worked, the women talked. Mrs. Ream spoke with a voice from home; yet unhappily for Fannie, she wanted more information than her visitor could give.

"We've been here three years," Mrs. Ream reminded her hostess. "Here—let me help you." And, at Fannie's polite reluctance, "Oh, my goodness. I don't count helping you as work. We've been running the old Inn at Shawnee, and I've learned to cook a meal for a big crowd without giving it a thought. Of course, Mary is a big help."

An amazing woman, Mrs. Ream.

"I think it's ready," Fannie said at last. "Call the children—"

The children, with Vinnie leading the way and the others at her heels, came into the house.

"See, Mama—" Lillie cried. "See what Vinnie made for me."

The child held up a small head that had been shaped from clay. "It's me, Mama."

"It does look like you!" Fannie was amazed.

"And Mama—Vinnie says that when they moved from Shawnee to Wyandotte, she walked and drove the cow herself, every step of the way."

Fannie waited for Mrs. Ream to confirm this.

"Indeed she did," the woman said. "I wanted her to ride, but she thought walking was fun."

"Mama," Lillie begged, "may I put this little doll that is me on the clock shelf?"

"Of course you may," she said. "It is a very good likeness, and you'll want to keep it."

"Oh, dear Mrs. Ross, do you *really* think so?" Vinnie cried.

"I do indeed," Fannie assured her.

The child's eyes glowed, her face alight with a quality that went beyond happiness.

Fannie was to find out, after the Reams were gone, that the family itself was not so amazing as was the effect it had upon the Ross way of life. Mr. Ream had persuaded Edmund to file on a section of land.

"Oh, my goodness, Edmund!" Fannie exclaimed, aghast at the announcement he had just made to her. "What on earth? You are no farmer."

"Land is going to be worth a great deal out here as soon as the Territory becomes a state," he told her.

"Then why not buy here in Topeka?"

"You know well enough why I don't. Speculators have the lots tied up—and even if one were available, the price would be exorbitant."

Yes, she knew that. Men went around dazed and glassy-eyed, buying and selling. All sane valuations were gone. If Edmund were to invest in land, it must be a claim, not town lots.

"Where is it?" she asked.

"Not far. In Wabaunsee County, next to Ma and Pa. Ream says it's good land and he knows, because he surveyed it."

Involuntarily she glanced around her, checking the details of the room in which they sat. Almost it was as if she were reliving a past experience. Just in this way she had looked at a room in Sandusky and another one in Milwaukee. As with a kaleidoscope, the pattern she saw would never come back again exactly as it was at this moment.

"When?" she asked.

"Soon."

"You plan to walk off and leave William to run the *Tribune* alone?" she burst out. "Your editorials have been the strongest power on the paper, and you know it."

"William is filing on a claim nearby," he told her. "He knows as well as I do that we need homesteaders to fill up the land if we are ever to make a state out of Kansas Territory."

There was no use arguing with him when his mind was made up as certainly as it seemed to be now.

"I knew you'd see it my way," he said with what, to her, was infuriating calm.

VI

The Gathering Storm

1858–1861

FALL IN KANSAS, glowing and golden. No skies could be so blue as these, Fannie thought; no sun overhead so bright; no air so clear and winelike. Quail whistled in the meadow, and trees were dark with migratory birds resting briefly on their long flight south. Edmund, sowing wheat for next year's harvest, building fences, caring for stock, doing all the work necessary on land claimed for the first time, did not seem to have time or energy enough left over to worry overmuch about the slavery issue. Fannie, watching him, thought she should be entirely satisfied.

As a matter of fact, she could feel little except extreme lassitude. It was a state of affairs she could not understand; she had never felt like this in her other pregnancies. Mother Ross came over from their claim nearby to give Fannie reassurance based on her own fourteen pregnancies, and Mary Elizabeth, from William's adjoining claim also came, feeling her one child qualified her to speak.

"Moving has worn you out," they both told her.

"Ma helped me," Fannie said. "It wasn't too hard."

"Besides," Mother Ross maintained, "it's been a hot summer. And Pitt and Arthur are of an age to make a lot of work."

If only Ma were with her now; but the house was too small to hold another person, so naturally Ma stayed in her own home in Topeka.

"Just keep the boys busy," Mother Ross advised.

That was good enough council. Sometimes Fannie thought, with amusement, the advice held good for men as well as boys. Keep them busy and maybe they wouldn't be off trying to start wars. Perhaps if Mr. Lincoln had a better law practice he wouldn't keep stirring up the slavery question, making speeches about the inability of a half-free, half-slave nation to endure and letting it be known he was referring especially to the danger Kansas Territory represented. She wished he'd mind his own business and let Kansas alone.

"Once the baby comes, you'll feel better," Mother Ross told her sagely.

Flint Ross was born November 15, 1858. Mother Ross left her own place to come and take over, tremendously proud that the new baby should bear the middle name of Father Ross. Mary Elizabeth spent every possible minute there as well.

"A fine baby," they both assured Fannie.

A strange timidity prevented Fannie from asking the two women if they didn't think this baby seemed—well, not quite as strong as the others.

Mother Ross, seeming to sense Fannie's thoughts, went on briskly, "He's a little small, but some babies are just naturally huskier than others to start out with. Now Edmund, when he was born—" And she went on to recount once more the long-familiar story about the little face which had been no bigger than a teacup.

Fannie hugged Flint to her heart, feeling relief from some threat she hadn't been quite able to analyze. She herself could see how strong Edmund had become.

"Mama," Lillie begged, "may I hold my little brother?"

"Yes—" Fannie hesitated only briefly. "I'm sure it will be all right."

"You know I'll be careful," Lillie told her, looking slightly aggrieved. "I held Pitt, didn't I, and I was *much* littler then."

How could Fannie tell her Flint was not like Pitt?

Autumn slipped into winter and Fannie felt stronger, as Mother Ross had prophesied. She could look around her and take stock of her blessings, not inconsiderable. Edmund had gathered in the harvest—small, since he had not arrived at the claim in time to do much planting, but a harvest nonetheless. Something tangible and real. That was one of the rewards of a farmer, Fannie thought—you could see the results of your labor. Different from running a newspaper where you couldn't be sure people would read what you wrote or, reading, do anything about it.

The children were as active as little eels, busy every moment, full of energy and vitality. Except—perhaps she had forgotten about her other children as babies. Perhaps they, too, lay quietly in their cribs, making few demands and sleeping a great deal, as Flint now did.

For Kansas Territory, too, things went reasonably well. Mr. Horace Greeley, who for some years now had been urging all young men to go West, came out to look things over. He liked the country itself, but was greatly taken aback at its lack of conveniences. There were no baths, or barbers, or bootblacks, he complained. Men laughed slyly at him, and said they got along all right without these things, so perhaps, if Mr. Greeley missed them, he had best stay in the East, where they were present in abundance.

About this time John Brown chose to come from wherever he had been keeping himself since the border warfare had settled into a lull. As if he hadn't given Kansas Territory enough trouble already, he now announced another proposition to the Free State men. "You wanted Kansas to be a free state. That is why you came here. Everyone agrees you are succeeding and that when Kansas becomes a state she will be free. But I have another plan. I want to strike a blow at the institution itself. Nothing but war can extinguish slavery. The sooner it is inaugurated, the better." He was going to free the slaves, starting here. By violence, if necessary. Once they were free, he would set up a refuge for them in Canada.

That evil, mad old man! Fannie thought. Unless he is checked, he will bring ruin on us all. In Kansas, where he evidently meant to start his campaign, there were practically no slaves at all. People said that even the South was finding them a drag on the economy. If everyone would just keep cool and quiet, slavery might die out of itself. She said as much to Edmund.

"With things relatively quiet now," she protested, "I don't see why anyone would want to risk stirring up trouble. I can't see how it's any concern of John Brown's."

"I remember once when you risked a great deal for the sake of some slaves who were of no concern to you," Edmund reminded her quietly.

"Oh, that was different—they were in our own house. You were helping them—I couldn't let you down."

"That's what Mr. Lincoln means by a house divided," Edmund said. "The country has to stand together on this question. In a larger sense the issue of slavery is with us in our house. On our conscience."

She was silent. It was always difficult to answer Edmund when he talked like this. But she was still disturbed. Old John Brown and Mr. Lincoln—they were both saying upsetting things, and if they didn't watch out they'd get the country into war yet.

John Brown's proposition was the signal for more unrest. Jayhawking expeditions, led by James Montgomery, broke out, the avowed aim being to drive all Southern settlers out of Kansas. Governor Denver, evidently thinking he had had enough, followed the example of several of his predecessors, and resigned and left, not even waiting for his successor, Samuel Medary, to arrive. Once more, the Territory was left in the hands of a secretary of state.

"It doesn't look very good to the rest of the nation," Fannie told Edmund, "if we act in such a way that no governor is willing to stay with us."

"Perhaps Medary will have better luck," Edmund reassured her. "Certainly he'll have the people of the Territory behind him, if he really tries to work things out."

2

Whatever bright hopes the people of Kansas might have had for peace were doomed by John Brown, just as Fannie had feared they would be. Two days before Christmas, a time when men should certainly have been without hatred in their hearts, he marched a group of his followers to the Little Osage Creek in Missouri. Dividing his forces into two squads, he ordered them to move forward, destroying as they went. The raid finished, the two groups whipped back across the Kansas line, bringing with them eleven slaves and all the movable possessions of two Missouri families. Behind them they left one person dead—David Cruise, who, according to his neighbors, was a good man who had never so much as harmed a fly in all his life.

Free-soil men were indignant, as well they might be. They did not hesitate to express their disapproval of the old man's actions, a sentiment which Fannie shared.

"Murder and robbery—that's what it is," she cried, all her distrust and fear of the old madman rising up once more.

Edmund agreed with her. "I'm going over to Topeka," he said, "and add my protest to the others."

He came back to make a report to Fannie concerning the meeting.

"We let him have it," he said. "Straight, and with no hedging. We reminded him that he wasn't a settler, and so could slip away and avoid the consequences that would come of his act, while we would have to stay here and pay for his crime."

"How did he take it?" Fannie asked. She really wanted to know, of course, whether he would get out of Kansas. How could anyone in the Territory draw an easy breath so long as that fanatical old man was lurking around in the bushes, ready to pounce out on proslave people, or those he believed were proslave, every time his half-crazed fancy dictated?

"He was hurt. He said he did it for the sake of the Free State people, and asked if they thought he was getting any pleasure out of exposing his life. When they wanted to know why he went on with it then, he told them that if they no longer wanted or needed him, he'd be glad to go."

"I hope you didn't—" she began.

"Nobody asked him to stay, so he's started off—they say he's camped on Sugar Creek now."

"And the slaves?" Fannie asked.

"He has them with him," Edmund told her.

"The Missourians surely aren't going to let him get by with that!" Fannie cried.

"I'd hardly think so," Edmund told her.

It was a prediction in which they were both entirely correct. Missouri's Governor Stewart sent an appeal directly to President Buchanan asking for action, while the Missouri Legislature framed an act enabling the state to raise a militia in order to dispose of the outlaws in Kansas Territory. The new governor of Kansas Territory, Medary, also telegraphed the President, trying to explain that the raid was not sanctioned by the Territory itself. On both sides of the border responsible people were grave and concerned, realizing that if the Missouri miltia marched on Kansas it would be met by one from the Territory. And there would be brother facing brother, neighbor fighting neighbor. What could come of that but civil war?

Governor Medary publicly laid the blame for the border troubles on Kansas.

Edmund was indignant. "Downright weak-kneed of him," he protested. "Both sides are at fault, of course."

Missouri, not the least mollified by Medary's confession, offered a three-thousand-dollar reward for John Brown. Governor Medary, doubtless realizing he could not get by with a simple declaration of fault, sent word to Colonel Edwin Sumner, stationed at Fort Leavenworth, to send troops after Brown. They almost caught him once but the crafty old rascal escaped. He and his party, still with the eleven slaves, eluded the detachment and slipped over the Nebraska line, where they were safe. Brown himself took the slaves straight to Canada through the Underground Railway. Once there, he wrote back and bragged about his success.

"Anyway," Fannie said when the news came, "we're rid of him at last."

"Perhaps—" Edmund said. He didn't sound too sure. But Fannie ceased to worry. Canada was a long way off. She felt safer than she had for a long time.

3

Winter gave way to spring, and spring, in turn, to summer. By June the grass waved green and lush in the prairie wind and wild roses flaunted their fragrance in every fence row. Verbenas and other brightly colored wildflowers dotted the ground, and already the first sunflowers were beginning to bloom. The garden was thriving; and Edmund's wheat, planted so hopefully, was a thing to delight the heart.

In early June, a storm came up, starting with a hard steady blow from the south, and for three days increasing in velocity. Toward the close of the third day clouds banked up in the northwest. Twilight, usually long and pleasant, had an eery hue which, even after the sun was gone, lighted up the clouds. Then there was calm, and lightning threaded through the dark clouds.

"We certainly can use the rain," Edmund said. "But just let's hope it isn't too much, with the wheat at the stage it is now."

Less than a year on a farm had taught Fannie that the farmer was as dependent on the weather as a sailing vessel on wind. Too much rain—too little rain; sun hiding behind clouds, sun blistering down with no clouds to break its force; too much snow, too little snow. There didn't seem to be any time when a farmer could relax and feel he had things to his liking.

"I hope we don't have a cyclone—" Fannie worried.

Neither heavy rain nor cyclone materialized. The wind died down and the storm blew over, leaving only a light sprinkle to show for all the fuss it had made.

Normally a disturbance of such magnitude would have left the weather cooler; but the days grew hotter than before. The crops themselves, either puzzled or disheartened, began to droop visibly. Fannie wondered how long it would be before Edmund would show concern.

Before he had time to start worrying in earnest, another event took his mind off the crops and their need of rain. A new constitutional convention was called.

"It will be at Wyandotte," he told her. "I'm the delegate from Wabaunsee. Perhaps this time we'll have some success."

"Now that they have a smart man helping out," she said, feeling proud and pleased and wanting him to know it, "they'll be sure to work out one Kansas and Congress will both accept."

"We'll see," he said hopefully.

Fannie sprinkled clothes for tomorrow's ironing, one eye fixed on Lillie, Arthur and Pitt playing in the yard. She hoped they weren't exhausting themselves. Even now, at twilight, the heat was well-nigh unbearable. Everyone said this was the hottest summer they had ever seen in Kansas. Perhaps it was the heat which made Flint seem more listless with each passing day.

She wished Edmund was here. He had been gone for so long! The convention had opened the day after the Fourth of July, and here the month was almost gone. It sounded mighty fine to say he was off at the Wyandotte Constitutional Convention, but the fact of it wasn't all pleasure. When evening came and she lighted the candles, a desperate sort of loneliness settled over her. Oh, she was busy, when she fed the children and saw them to bed. But once that was done, she was alone, with a clock that ticked in the great stillness of the house.

It was no small thing in which Edmund had a part. She should concentrate on that thought rather than on Wisconsin and its green coolness in contrast to this heat-seared prairie. Perhaps Flint —she made herself face this fact—wouldn't have been any better had the family lived in Milwaukee. And yet, there were times when she wondered, fleetingly, how much a woman owed her husband, how much her children. If the climate here was bad for baby Flint

—oh, there was no use thinking of such things. Edmund had wanted to come to Kansas and she had wanted to come with him. He was doing good work; the least she could contribute was a willingness to hold the home together while he was away.

"There comes Papa!" she heard Arthur cry from the yard. Disbelieving, she looked out the door. Sure enough, Edmund was riding up to the gate.

She was the first to reach his side. No child could run as fast as she did. He swung down off his horse, and she was in his arms. The children crowded close for their share of the greetings.

She put together a hasty meal, talking so fast it was a wonder she got anything cooked. Pure joy, she found, could be as unnerving as sorrow. And when they finally sat down she could not eat at all.

"You're thin, Fannie," Edmund told her, laying down his fork. "And no wonder—you aren't eating a thing."

She couldn't tell him that she had been unable to eat from sadness; and now joy kept her from wanting food. This was the longest time they had been separated since their marriage, more than ten years ago.

"I'll eat now," she told him. "Now that you are home—"

Across the heads of the children they looked at each other. And for a moment, those children might as well not have existed.

"Did you get your constitution, Papa?" Lillie asked, unwilling to be ignored.

"Yes," he told her, "we wrote one."

"Oh, that is good," she said with quaint dignity. She knew the matter was important, and that she must treat it with grave respect. "What does it say?"

Another father might have laughed at this, but not Edmund. He must have realized that here was an occasion which should remain in the child's mind forever as something wonderful and significant.

"It says that Kansas is never to have slaves," he told her. He turned to each child in turn. "Remember that. No slaves, ever, in Kansas."

He paused a moment, and then he went on, "We will be admitted to the Union this time. This Constitution is going to do it."

"What's a consti—a constitu—what is it, Papa?" Arthur asked.

"It's a piece of paper—a long one—and on it is written all the things the Territory of Kansas wants and believes in. The things it will abide by, once it is a state. And at the end, the men's names are signed—the men who wrote it."

"Is your name there?" Lillie asked quickly.

"Yes, it's there. Down at the bottom."

"You should have signed first," Arthur told him jealously.

Edmund seemed pleased at his son's words. "We signed in alphabetical order," he said.

"Oh—" Arthur wasn't sure what he meant, although he wouldn't say so.

"You know," Lillie pointed out smugly, " 'Ross' starts with an 'R' and that's way down at the end of the alphabet. After 'Q' and a lot of others—"

"Can I see it sometime, Papa?" Arthur cried excitedly.

"Of course," Edmund told him.

Fannie sat thinking. The Territory would become a state—this time. And down through the years that come and go, Edmund's name would be on the constitution which had made it possible. There for Arthur, and everyone else, to see.

"We'll be a state," Edmund said with proud assurance. "Now, maybe we can get the railroads built."

"Of course we will," Fannie agreed.

Edmund was silent a moment, and then he turned to face her. "Fannie," he asked, "how would you like to move back to Topeka?"

"To Topeka—" she could only echo his words.

"Yes. I think now we must keep hammering away at people about the need for railroads. That can be done best through a newspaper."

"But you sold your paper," Fannie reminded him.

"I know—" As always he was a little impatient at any hint of doubt. "I've talked this matter over with William. We're newspapermen, not farmers. We've decided to go back to Topeka and start another paper."

4

It was good to be back in Topeka, Fannie thought, although the town was no greener, no more flourishing than the farm had been. But here, one did not have to depend solely on the vagaries of the weather. Fannie busied herself with setting the house in order, pleased to have a new one, larger than the one in which they had lived when they first came to Topeka, and certainly more roomy than the one on the claim. From the window she could see that the trees which the newly organized city government had ordered planted on the east side of Kansas Avenue between Fifth and Sixth Avenues were taking root and growing; she hoped they could withstand the lack of rain. She could see other signs of progress—the Ritchie Block, proudly boasting it would be the first all-brick block in the town, did indeed have some additional buildings; and the Chase Hotel was finished.

Edmund seemed happy, too, at being once more the editor of a newspaper. He and William planned to issue the Topeka *Record* weekly until the paper was well established, and then begin a daily. His lead editorial left no doubt as to what stand he was going to take.

"We will be on the side of Republicans," he said, "but under no circumstances will we suffer ourselves to become the medium for the promotion of merely partisan or personal ends."

How like him, Fannie thought.

"The responsibilities of public journalism," she read on, "are of so great a character as to forbid any motive save that of the most exalted patriotism to sway in the advocacy of public measures."

Fannie went to find a pair of scissors. She clipped the editorial carefully and put it away with her keepsakes. This was a declaration of purpose and faith which should be preserved for the children, as one would put away treasures of great worth.

The major part of the paper, however, was devoted to a discussion of the needs facing Kansas Territory now—railroads, and the acceptance of the new constitution.

When the voters approved the Wyandotte Constitution in October, Fannie chose to believe that no small part of this approval was due to Edmund for his work in helping to draft the document as well as for the fact that he kept the issues well defined before the people. Now, if only Congress would approve the admission of Kansas. Once that was achieved, railroads would come.

But in the midst of this mood of confidence, John Brown broke loose again. This time it was at Harpers Ferry in Virginia. With a group of well-trained followers, he attempted to start an insurrection of slaves against their masters. His plot was foiled by a detachment of marines under command of Colonel Robert E. Lee and Lieutenant Jeb Stuart. Stuart had known Brown in Kansas, and accused him of having been sent by the abolitionists of that region, abetted by the New England Emigrant Aid Company. This the old man denied, but even so, in the eyes of many people, Kansas was to blame.

"We'll never get to be a state now," Fannie said to Edmund.

"Now don't say that," Edmund reproved her sharply. But he was worried, too, as any thinking man would be. Fannie remembered the first time she had seen John Brown, the day he came riding up with James Lane to meet the Milwaukee Company at Nebraska City. Even then she had known he was a fanatic and had feared him. She remembered also that she had felt no less fear and apprehension concerning Lane himself. It was no surprise to hear that Lane was publicly condoning Brown and his infamous act at Harpers Ferry.

"Whether we like it or not," Fannie pointed out, "John Brown's name is linked with Kansas. And," she added, "with the Republican Party. The Democrats are going to be glad for this excuse to keep Kansas out of the Union. They'll win again, just reminding people of John Brown and Kansas."

"I wouldn't be at all sure about that," Edmund told her, with the lofty implication that a woman talking politics is quite out of her element. "I have my eye on Abraham Lincoln."

"Abraham Lincoln—" Fannie couldn't share her husband's enthusiasm. She was still vaguely uneasy about that "half-slave, half-free" speech. Lincoln was only a prairie lawyer. What did he know about the problems he discussed so freely? The very fact of his obscurity would prevent him from being considered seriously.

In this thought she was mistaken, however. Lincoln's name was increasingly on the lips of people and in the newspapers. Fannie was thinking about this one day when Edmund came home, a look of suppressed excitement on his face. "Abraham Lincoln's coming to Kansas," he announced.

It wasn't even safe to think about the man! It was as if she had conjured him out of the air.

"His wife's cousin, Mark Delahay of Leavenworth, is bringing him. He'll be here the first few days of December. He'll be talking in two or three places. I want to hear him."

"So do I," Fannie said firmly. Once and for all she wanted to settle in her mind what this man was like.

"There's no reason you shouldn't," Edmund told her. "I imagine everyone will go."

The Leavenworth *Times* reported the arrival of "Hon. Abe. Lincoln" at St. Joseph, Missouri, on December 1, 1859, together with the fact that he was met by his kinsman. He went to Elwood to speak and then worked his way down to Atchison, and from there to Leavenworth, where Edmund and Fannie went to hear him.

Fannie especially wanted to hear what, if anything, Lincoln would have to say about John Brown, executed only the day before for the affair at Harpers Ferry. Would he ignore the matter entirely, or condemn, or justify?

Her first sight of him was both shock and disappointment. He sat on the platform, a tall, thin, gaunt man with a deeply furrowed face, ugly almost to the point of being a caricature. His long body was folded up like a giant grasshopper making ready for flight, so that he looked awkward and uncomfortable in his wooden chair. Each black hair on his head seemed to have a will of its own and stood every which way. Surely nothing about him could capture the imagination of the voters. Or inspire their confidence, either. Fannie began to feel a little sorry for poor Mr. Lincoln.

Finally Lincoln was introduced. Toward the speaker's rostrum he shambled, his rusty black suit untidy and poorly fitting. In spite of his appearance, a great deal of applause greeted him. When it subsided, he raised his hand in a stiff self-conscious gesture. The crowd quieted down and he began.

"Mr. Cheerman—" he said.

The man couldn't even talk correctly, and he a lawyer! His voice was thin and high, not too pleasant. He seemed ill at ease. Raising one of his huge hands in emphasis of a point he meant to make, he threw back his head, while the black mane spread out.

Fannie couldn't tell how it happened—whether his own confidence came to him, or whether the crowd sensed what sort of man this was—but suddenly he caught fire from within and began talking as she had never heard anyone speak before. He did not seem homely now, or unsure of himself. He was transfigured. Even the quality of his voice changed; when he spoke softly, you could hear the man next to you breathing. Then, his voice rang out and you were aware of nothing but deep sincerity and a compelling passion for justice and right.

Lincoln did not evade the John Brown subject. He did, however, disclaim any connection with it, although, he said, people were accusing him of being in sympathy with the raid. He said it was an awful thing, the deed of a madman. A man who had brooded so long over an injustice to a people that he felt he could, single-handed, wipe out the bad thing he deplored. It was the same impulse which had always set men to killing their rulers, not realizing this was no way to right a wrong.

He spoke with logic and with power. Fannie apologized, in her heart, for ever linking him, even in her thoughts, with John Brown. This was no fanatic. This was a man of great singleness of purpose and steadfast beliefs. In some ways he reminded her of Edmund. Once either one of them made up his mind about the rightness of a course, nothing could change him. Lincoln apparently had made up his mind on the slavery question. He thought Kansas was the pivot of it. Long ago Edmund had said this; that was why he had decided to come here in the first place. . . . Once more Fannie felt a chill of fear. Maybe, after all, Mr. Lincoln would bring them into war with his no-half-measure pronouncements.

But a strange thing had happened. Suddenly Fannie Ross felt that she would follow him—even there, if need be.

5

Flint was past a year old now, yet he had not grown stronger, as Mother Ross had predicted he would. Still small, he did not gain weight, seeming content to lie in his cradle or in Fannie's arms. He smiled gently when anyone looked at him, but he did not wave his arms and legs and gurgle and make a great fuss to be let down so he could be on his own. There were times when Fannie saw another child, a dark-skinned one, lying in his mother's arms, making no sound. Always she pushed the thought from her. When she caught her mother's eyes on the child, Fannie hastily changed the subject. It was almost as if she feared to voice her thoughts lest they become realities just from having been put into words. She consoled herself by thinking that perhaps when spring came, Flint would grow stronger.

Spring came, bringing neither courage nor health nor hope for anyone. The drought, started last June, continued. By summer, the situation was critical. The wind blew a fiery blast, parching the already dried-out soil. There was no relief by day from clouds over the sun; nor at night, with the stifling heat hanging over the earth. Dust rose from the dead grass; great cracks opened in the ground, making it dangerous to drive a carriage or wagon over them lest the narrow wheels fall in. The wheat was long since ruined.

"I hear it's not so bad in Shawnee," Edmund said, trying to make a little joke. "They're getting an eighth of a bushel to the acre."

Fannie could not bring herself to laugh. The children were playing listlessly in the yard. There was no merciful shade to protect them unless they went to the side of the house. Leaves had fallen before August was ended.

And as if one's own difficulties were not enough, there was the sight of those who had given up, daily trailing through town. Families in covered wagons were headed East. Sometimes the men said they were "going back for a little visit with the wife's folks." Sometimes they frankly admitted their plight by writing across the canvas of their wagon, "In Kansas we trusted, in Kansas we busted." And whether they said so or not, they wanted no more of the place. August gave way to a blazing September, and still no rain nor promise of any. Fannie wondered how Edmund could still dream and talk of bringing a railroad to this drought-ridden land.

"We need to get the idea into the minds of the nation," he told her. "This drought makes it all the more necessary. People are feeling sorry for us now, all over the country. But we don't want pity. This is the best time to let everyone see that we have courage and spirit. Now's the time to talk railroads for Kansas."

Railroads! Was that all Edmund could think about?

He was not alone in his obsession. No matter how much he planned for them, Colonel Holliday's enthusiasm outreached him. The Colonel fell into the habit of dropping by the house on the evenings when Edmund was home. The talk went on and on, forever on the same topic: how best to get the railroad. Fannie would sit listening to them, her sewing in her hands. (Such a lot of sewing for four children!)

"I suppose you are disappointed that the government turned down the idea of a railroad grant for Kansas," Holliday said.

"Disappointed, but not surprised," Edmund told him. "So long as each man goes out from Kansas as a committee of one to see that the railroad follows the route he wants, we'll never have one. First we must get together ourselves."

"If only Congress would admit us to the Union. Then our senators could speak for us."

"If we manage to select the right ones, yes. Right now it looks as if Lane can talk himself into the place."

"An amazing man, Lane," Colonel Holliday asserted. "He does have a certain power over men. I've seen it demonstrated time and time again. He'll go as our first senator, mind you. He and Pomeroy. We'll turn them loose on this railroad question, once they arrive in Washington."

"We don't have to wait for that," Edmund told him. "We must first agree among ourselves, as I told you. I'm in favor of a railroad convention to discuss the matter."

Colonel Holliday looked doubtful. "Now, with the drought? People won't have much heart for it."

"This is a good time," Edmund told him firmly. "Let them see what railroads mean. Already drought supplies are coming in from outside."

"I am glad you were asked to administer those relief supplies."

"I'm doing the best I can with them. But think how much better it would be if they could come by railroad instead of the freight wagons. Then, too, if the people here could see that the building of a railroad makes work and puts money in their pockets so they won't have to rely solely on the products from their burnt-out fields."

"You're entirely right," Colonel Holliday told him. "We'll get the railroad, if only we persist enough. First, of course, we must be admitted to the Union."

"That will come, too," Edmund assured him. "It shouldn't take too long. At least we have a constitution on which the voters of the Territory have agreed. We've come a long way."

Things did not move as rapidly as Edmund believed they would or, at least, professed to believe. In February the Wyandotte Constitution was introduced in the Senate, reported out by the Committee on Territories in March with a recommendation that Kansas be admitted to the Union. Admission, however, did not come. The very word "Kansas" seemed to have an explosive quality, setting off talks, accusations, and countercharges.

Mr. Lincoln went to Cooper Union in New York and there made a speech. Fannie read the accounts of it, feeling as if she were hearing an echo. He disclaimed all connection with John Brown, for both himself and the Republican Party before he said: "An enthusiast broods over the oppression of a people until he fancies himself commissioned by heaven to liberate them. He ventures into the attempt which ends in little else but his own execution."

Weren't those the exact words he had used in Leavenworth, back in December? Again Fannie could see the tall, awkward figure shambling toward the rostrum; she could hear the hesitant, high-pitched, nasal voice beginning the speech; she could feel the spell being cast over the audience. She was not surprised to read that, at the end of the speech, the audience had sprung to their feet, yelling like Indians.

Nor was she surprised when the Republicans, meeting in Chicago in May, nominated Abraham Lincoln as their candidate for the Presidency.

Edmund, although pleased at this turn of events, was also interested in another matter—a convention to agree upon a site for, and details of, a railroad in Kansas, to be held in Topeka in October. He enthusiastically started a series of articles and editorials in the *Record* concerning the proposed railroad.

6

The Railroad Convention met in Topeka on October 17. For two days, Fannie scarcely saw Edmund. The meeting had elected him as its temporary president, and as such, he had a great many duties to perform.

Certainly not all that went on at the meetings was agreement. Edmund came home for brief intervals to rest and to change clothes, and from him Fannie hastily gleaned bits of information, flung at her over his shoulder. Yes, things were going as well as could be expected. No, not everyone was in accord with everything. The delegates from several counties, Leavenworth and Wabaunsee, to name two, had withdrawn because they did not agree with what was going on. But plenty were staying. Yes—things were going fine.

At the end of the second day, Edmund came home, exhausted but elated.

"We've come to some agreements," he told her. "There are five suggested routes, and we are going to send the report to Congress."

No need to remind him that Congress was not given to accepting recommendations coming from Kansas. Instead, she busied herself with preparing something to eat.

"What is your part?" she asked as she worked.

"First of all, I must continue to keep the matter before the people by writing about it in the paper. Then, I am also on the executive board of the railroad we mean to name the Atchison, Topeka and Santa Fe."

"Well, it certainly has a long enough name," she said, smiling at him. Bless his heart, he was as excited as a child with a new toy. "Come on now—supper's ready."

"It will be a long railroad," he told her. "We've made history here in Topeka these two days. People are going to remember this, long after we are gone."

"Eat your supper," she told him. "The railroad will never begrudge you the time."

He looked at her, as if just now he was realizing she was in the room with him. He smiled. "Same old twinkling girl," he said. "I haven't been any good around this place in the last few weeks, have I?"

"Oh, I've managed," she told him.

How could she expect him to be much help, with all the big things he was trying to work out? Perhaps she shouldn't even bother him with discussions about Flint's persistent colds and the fact that Lillie needed new shoes.

He stood up, yawning. "I think I'll turn in," he said. "Haven't had much rest the last week or so."

As if he needed to tell her that!

"Well, you can take things easy for a while," she said, beginning to clear away the remains of the meal. "Nothing much to write about now."

"With the election coming up," he chided her, "how can you say that?"

"For the moment I had forgotten," she said. And then, curiously, "Who do you think will be elected?"

"Lincoln, of course. Who else?"

Abraham Lincoln it was. Fannie saw once more the gawky figure, the earnest and rugged features of the man who had talked to them at Leavenworth. Everywhere he went he must have made the people feel as she had felt.

Lincoln had disclaimed any part in the John Brown episode, and yet his name continued to be linked with it which did him no harm in the North. Where before the war cry had been "Kansas," now it was "John Brown." Once the spirit had been a region, now it was a man. Perhaps it was easier for people to cope with things that way.

Not without protest would the South accept Lincoln's election. The day after, South Carolina took steps to call a secession convention, and on December 20, the state announced it was no longer a part of the Union. By February 1861, Mississippi, Florida, Alabama, Louisiana, Georgia and Texas were also out. Together these states banded to form the Confederate States of America, elected Jefferson Davis for their President, and began preparations for war.

On January 29, 1861, President Buchanan signed the paper which made Kansas a state, with the Wyandotte Constitution as the guide for its statehood.

7

As Edmund and Colonel Holliday had foreseen, Jim Lane made a try for the senatorship of Kansas. The first legislature would elect the first senators, so Lane rushed home from the East to campaign for the men who would support him.

"Lane is a persistent man," Edmund said. "He usually gets what he wants."

Day and night Lane walked the streets, talking with the solons on their way to assemblies. He stopped them in vestibules, in dining rooms, washrooms. He gave them no rest. Some of the assemblymen took to the hazel thickets along the river in order to escape him, and others slipped off to hay lofts, hoping to find a night of peace and rest. Their hopes were in vain. Lane found them all.

In one way or another, Lane was associated with all the legislatures which had met in the state, legitimate and otherwise. His name was the best known in Kansas, and what did it matter if to some it was a hated word? At least it was known. Hadn't he even challenged Stephen Douglas to a duel? Something about the man appealed to the imagination of this frontier region. Fannie could see why people would, perhaps even grudgingly, admire him.

Finally, perhaps more for the sake of ridding themselves of him than for any valid reason, the legislature elected him as one of the two senators from the new state of Kansas. And as Edmund and Colonel Holliday had predicted, the other one was Pomeroy. Dr. Charles Robinson of Lawrence, a man prominent in the history of the Territory, went in as governor.

Lane laid aside the calfskin vest and the sealskin coat which had been his uniform in Kansas, boarded up the little slab-sided cabin he had called home, borrowed money for a broadcloth suit, and made ready to go to Washington.

As if he felt the need to replace Lane, James Montgomery, the little black-bearded Campbellite preacher, now broke out again, raiding the proslave settlements, stealing, burning, killing. Missouri headlines screamed at each new atrocity, SOME OF MONTGOMERY'S WORK, although there was doubt at times whether he was really responsible. It was only natural to blame him for the foray against the plantation of wealthy Morgan Walker who lived just out of Independence, Missouri, on his two thousand acres of land, stocked with hundreds of horses and mules and thirty slaves. This raid, however, did not follow completely the pattern of the others. For one thing, the attackers were repulsed and forced to flee in the very wagon they had brought for the purpose of carting the slaves away with them. In the flight, several raiders were killed.

MONTGOMERY OUTRAGE, Missouri papers shrilled.

Only, it wasn't Montgomery this time. It was a young man who called himself Harte.

"You know," Edmund said thoughtfully, "I think I've seen that lad. He's been in Lawrence, and even in Topeka. In Kansas, he poses as a free soiler; when he goes to Missouri, he's proslavery, to hear him tell it."

"He's worse than Jim Lane," she said.

"Harte's a gambler and a loafer," Edmund went on. "He picks up a dollar now and then betting on a horse or a foot race. They say he followed the wagon trains to Pike's Peak, picking up many an easy dollar gambling."

"It's awful," Fannie told him. "I feel so sorry for those unfortunate Quakers he persuaded to join the raid. They thought they were doing a great deed, trying to free the slaves. And then they were all killed."

"It comes out now that he double-crossed them," Edmund said. "He sent word ahead to the Missourians. That way, he's in solid with the slavery group."

"I never heard of such a thing," Fannie burst out.

"And do you know, it just comes to me—Harte isn't his real name at all."

"What is it?" Fannie asked. Not that it mattered—the deed was the thing.

Edmund frowned in concentration. At last his face lighted up. "I have it," he said. "His name is really Quantrill. He used to teach school. I remember—it's William Clarke Quantrill."

Abraham Lincoln and his family left Springfield in February for Washington, according to the papers. They said he went to the rear platform to bid his friends and townsmen farewell—at least a thousand of them had flocked down to the station. The accounts sounded mournful and serious. The threatening cold of that rainy morning; the people silent and sad, some of them weeping.

She could almost hear that mournful voice speaking the words reported by the papers: "Here I have lived for a quarter of a century—here my children have been born, and here one is buried—trusting in Him who can go with me, and remain with you, and be everywhere for good—to His care commending you, as I hope in your prayers you will commend me—I bid you affectionate farewell."

"He sounds as if he thought he'd never come back," Fannie said to Edmund. "So troubled and serious—"

"These are troubled and serious times," Edmund reminded her.

Indeed they were. There were threats of assassination before the new President even took office. Hearing these, Jim Lane sent word that he would be glad to bring his Kansas boys out to act as bodyguards to the President, a kindness which Lincoln rejected.

En route to Washington, D. C., Lincoln stopped at Philadelphia on Washington's Birthday, and there made a speech as the first flag containing the new Kansas star was raised over Independence Hall. How proud the Kansans felt when they heard about it!

On March 4, 1861, Lincoln took the oath of office. "In your hands, my dissatisfied countrymen," he told the nation, "and not in mine, is the momentous issue of civil war."

And he was right. The matter was out of his hands. On April 12, the Confederate forces bombarded Fort Sumter in Charleston harbor. On April 15, Lincoln called for 75,000 volunteers.

One of the first groups to respond was Jim Lane's hastily organized Kansas Frontier Guards. Armed with Sharp's rifles and cutlasses, they marched to the White House and established themselves in the East Room. When Lincoln and his Secretary of War appeared in the door, Lane stepped forward and saluted, offering the services of his group.

All this, of course, was reported in Topeka, as it was all over the country. Fannie listened, her face pale.

"This means war has begun," she said to Edmund, almost in a whisper.

Edmund regarded her gravely. How else could you look at anyone these days?

"In Kansas," he said slowly, "it is nothing new. For us, it started seven years ago."

VII

House Divided

1861–1863

"MAMA . . ." Pitt was at her side, anxious and troubled. "What is war?"

"It is—" Fannie hesitated for words, "—it's men fighting."

"But you tell us not to fight."

"So I do. And I mean it."

How to tell children that what is wrong for them is sometimes an inescapable necessity for their elders?

"As Papa has told you," she said firmly, "they are fighting to save the nation—and that is all right."

Or was it? Was war right, for any reason? If women ever made these decisions, would there be any wars, even for just causes? Surely there must be some other way.

"And so there'll be no slaves," Lillie put in smugly. Past twelve now, she had been brought up on talk of slavery, and preserving the nation, and the need to follow one's conscience. "Papa will probably get his gun and go fighting again, the way he did when we first came to Kansas."

"No!" Fannie told her hastily. "No—this is different from that other time."

The children, apparently satisfied, went off to play, leaving her to her thoughts. Were things different, now in the early summer of 1862 from the way they had been when Edmund first arrived in Topeka, almost six years ago, and felt he must shoulder a gun and be off with the Free State Army immediately? Then people called the trouble "border scrimmages"; now the name was Civil War.

The situation differed little except in scope. Forces still fought up and down the border, except the present struggle was over Missouri, not Kansas. But the purpose was the same—to determine whether the state would go with the Confederacy or the Union. Fighting raged from Wilson Creek up to the rich, aristocratic little county-seat town of Lexington, proslavery in its sentiments, and back again. Claib Jackson, Missouri's governor, was determined that Missouri should go with the South, and dashing Jo Shelby and Sterling Price had gathered an army of surprising strength and force to back him up. Frémont, in St. Louis, had dillydallied until Lincoln threatened to remove him, whereupon Jessie had journeyed to Washington to plead with the President in her husband's behalf. And had got nowhere. (Imagine begging that your husband be retained in a position of danger!)

The border war and the looting—these went on, too. Lane had collected an army around him, a half-armed, mutinous rabble made up of whites, Indians, and Negroes who took votes to see if they wanted to obey unpleasant orders. In spite of Lane's commands not to plunder, they did not hesitate to do so if the spirit moved them. And Young Quantrill, who had once called himself Harte, had also gathered his own group—slant-eyed young fighters in shirts patterned after Western plainsmen's, cut low in front, the slit narrowing to a point above the belt and ending in a rosette. Made by sweethearts and wives, these garments ranged from brilliant red to homespun butternut. The men wore wide-brimmed slouch hats, rode the finest horses in western Missouri, carried Colt revolvers, anywhere from two to eight each, and fancied themselves the wildest of the wild, even though many of them were still too young to have a beard. Their exploits, however, bore out their boasts. Tales of their looting and murders filling the border. They had broken loose from Price's men because that meant too much discipline and were waging a bushwhacking war of their own.

And in the confusion now, as before, one often found it hard to distinguish friend from foe. Young Bill Hickok, wearing the gaudy clothes he loved and sporting the handle-bar moustache of which he was so proud, went back and forth, first posing successfully as a Confederate, and then darting back to General Curtis, in command of the Federal troops, to give him information concerning the real situation.

In the fourteen months since the Civil War had started, things had not been greatly changed. But for herself . . .

Why must she think so much of Flint? Always, from the moment of his birth, she had known he was the frail one. She had never really believed Mother Ross' assurance that he would grow up to be as strong as the other children. But there was the little grave in the cemetery, with its small headstone and the rosebush she had planted. She knew every detail concerning it. And the wording on the burial certificate:

> Flint Ross; date of birth, November 15, 1858; place of birth, Wabaunsee County; date of decease, March 7, 1862; late residence, 162 East 6th Street; date of interment, March 8, 1862; cause of death, heart disease; relatives, Edmund G. and Fannie Ross.

Yet her heart had refused to accept Flint's absence. That was the real reason why she had named the new baby, a girl born a few months after Flint's death, Eddie. As if she had half-expected to replace one small male child by giving a boy's name to the new one.

"Three boys," Edmund had smiled, when the name was suggested, "and yet we call a girl after me."

Eddie was strong and healthy, like all her babies. Except—oh, there she went again, forgetting, for the moment, to think of the living rather than the dead. But was this not the way of parents? She remembered Mr. Lincoln's words as he left Springfield—"here I have lived—here my children were born—here one of them lies buried."

Fannie Ross had lived in Topeka. Two children had been born

in this town and here one lay buried. She thought of Mary Lincoln, whose mind must turn to Springfield, away from the three children who lived, back to the one they had left there. Did she, too, find it more natural to dwell on her own problems than to think of national affairs?

Besides, there was no making sense out of the way things happened. Lane, it was said, went to President Lincoln with a plan to enlist free Negroes and Indians into a fighting force for the Union. The President, unwilling to put either group to fighting the South, refused to go along with him, proposing, instead, that they be trained to protect themselves against invasion.

Then, stirred up by Albert Pike, the Indians began to secede from the Union—Choctaw, Chickasaw, Creek, Seminole and, finally, the powerful Cherokee. With Stand Watie as their leader, they went into war on the side of the Confederacy. There were reports—repeated and undeniable—of scalping in battles and of other indignities to the bodies of the Union dead, stories too awful even to think about.

"Oh, surely—surely, there must be something that can be done to stop this," Fannie cried. "War is bad enough—that is barbarism."

"Lane set his men to get revenge," Edmund told her. "He has sent them sweeping northward through Missouri, with orders to 'shoot everything disloyal from a Shanghai rooster to a Durham cow.' They seem to be doing more than that. At last reports they've gathered up everything—horses, mules, lead, kegs of powder, food and, of course, whiskey. Lane himself got a fine team and carriage and sent them to his home in Lawrence."

"The Bushwhackers will be over here because of that," Fannie said.

"They'd probably have come without an excuse," Edmund told her. "Always there are men waiting on the fringe of war, ready for plundering."

"Things are bad, aren't they, Edmund?" she asked seriously.

"Very bad. The Seven Days battles in Virginia were distressing for the Union. Lincoln has asked for three hundred thousand additional men. The border will have to send its quota."

She lifted her head quickly, an instinctive gesture of fear and premonition.

"And that means—"

"With so many Union men gone, Confederate guerrillas will take Missouri. Quantrill has already been commissioned a captain in the Confederate Army. He will welcome the chance to strike."

Neither spoke. Outside, in the twilight of a Kansas July evening, the children's voices sounded shrill and clear as they played hide-and-seek. "All that's not ready—" Arthur chanted the age-old ultimatum. Oh, I am not ready—I am not ready for what Edmund is going to say to me, Fannie thought frantically. She got up restlessly, went over to pick up Eddie, who lay gurgling in her crib. Fannie held the child close to her as she went back to sit in the chair.

"Fannie," he said softly, "I feel that I must volunteer."

Outside Arthur cried the warning, "All eyes open—here I come—"

Oh, she might have known. She had known. But she had closed her eyes, refusing to face the fact.

"Fannie—" he said again, and urgent note in his voice, "—did you understand what I said?"

"Yes," she spoke, scarcely above a whisper.

"There is nothing else I can do," he told her simply.

That statement she could believe. Being Edmund, there was no other alternative for him. Just as there had been none when he decided to come to Kansas; or, once arrived, that he should enlist in the Free State Army.

"How about the paper?" she asked.

"I can sell the paper," he told her. "McDonald and Adams are wanting to buy. I'll make the arrangements and then—I'll recruit my own company."

That was like him.

"We'll help patrol the border, as I understand it," he explained. "Protect our homes."

The way things were going, this made sense.

"But it isn't just for us, for Kansas," he went on. "It's to preserve the nation."

He would feel this was necessary, although it was a sentiment not shared by all. Daily the covered wagons went through now, bearing settlers bound for the West. They felt no need to stay and help save the nation.

"Will it be too large a burden for you?" he asked. "Leaving you with everything, as I'll be doing?"

Leaving her with four children, the last one only an infant. And with almost no money, save what he could send back to her. Leaving her to manage the work, with the two oldest children scarcely of an age to be of any help at all. Oh, it was not a light thing.

He put his arm around her and she leaned against him. She could have wept and urged him to stay; she could have pointed out that a man owed some obligation to his family. Perhaps his first obligation, his foremost loyalty should go to them. Edmund had already done his part—more than his part—for Kansas, for the nation. Besides, could not great work be done in the newspaper, telling people the truth about this whole confused situation?

"You mind very much," he said softly.

"Of course I mind," she told him honestly. "No woman ever wanted her husband to go to war. No wife ever wanted the father of her children to go into battle."

"But you still know I must go, don't you?"

"Yes—"

She realized she could not hold him back if she tried; would not hold him if she could. He did not go because he loved his family too little, or because he was restless for change and excitement. He went because to remain here would have made him only a shell of a man, unworthy ever again to speak out on the side of right.

He must have sensed her thoughts, for he patted her shoulder tenderly. She linked her arms around his neck and they stood so, in the attitude of lovers. She knew what she looked like—a woman past thirty, a little tired, a little worn. But the old magic was still there.

"I hate to leave you," he said, almost in a whisper.

"Yes, I know," she told him. "Now don't worry about me. I'll manage."

He looked at her keenly. Then his arms tightened around her and he kissed her.

"I love you very much, Fannie," he said softly. "Never forget that."

"I never do," she told him steadily. "I never will."

A week later he came home with a paper, his eyes shining with suppressed excitement.

"Here," he said. "Take a look at this."

It was not necessary for her to read the document to know its substance, but her eyes ran down the page anyway.

> Fort Leavenworth
> August 12, 1862
> Hd. 2nd. Dep. Kansas
> (Muster Office)
>
> I certify that I have this day mustered into the service of the United States for three years or the duration of the War, Edmond G. Ross as Recruiting Officer with the rank of 2nd Lt.
>
> 2nd. Lt. Lewis Thompson

Her first reaction was one entirely irrelevant.

"Oh, Edmund," she cried, "he's misspelled your name!"

"I'm still signed up hard and fast," he told her, smiling a little. "Is that all you have to say?"

She had much to say, but this was no time for saying it. She went to him and put her arms around him. She kissed him soundly, several times.

"I'm very proud of you, Lieutenant Ross," she said, and standing back, she saluted him smartly.

"Now that's my twinkling girl again," Edmund told her.

"When do you leave?"

"As soon as things can be organized. Probably in a week or two."

2

For women, war is waiting: this Fannie Lathrop Ross soon discovered. It was waiting and longing and praying, intermingled with the ordinary everyday things one must do.

Edmund recruited his own group, Company E, Eleventh Kansas Regiment. Several young men from the *Record* office joined up.

"Young Henry Lindsey is going," Edmund told her.

"How can he?" Fannie protested. "He's just a baby."

"He can't go as a soldier, but we're taking him along as a drummer boy."

"What does his mother say?"

"She doesn't mind—"

Oh, was the woman made of stone?

Once the group was formed, Edmund marched them over to Leavenworth to join the regiment commanded by Colonel Samuel Crawford. Here they were issued their equipment—long heavy rifles made in the early 1800s, loaded with three buckshot and a .72 caliber ball.

Early in October the Eleventh Regiment, still carrying its ancient equipment, was ordered south to assist in repelling the Confederate advances into Missouri and Kansas. They marched into fighting, encounters of a nature to try seasoned veterans. All Topeka waited for news of its own, knowing immense pride at the courage the regiment displayed. Fannie listened to every report, every rumor that came in, allaying the fear of the children when it was bad, trying not to show her own concern as she did so.

Edmund's letters arrived with surprising frequency, considering the lack of regular mail service. Each letter was a precious thing, to be read and reread. Then it was filed away with its predecessors and, at intervals, brought out once more. Reading them gave Fannie the feeling that she marched along with him in body as she always did in spirit, knowing the details of the days he faced, feeling weariness and cold and loneliness along with him.

The one from Fort Scott, for instance, dated September 10, 1863, gave her a special sense of his nearness.

> My dear Wife,
>
> I arrived here with the commander at 1 o'clock today, after a march of 130 miles through dust, rain, and mud—20 miles yesterday through a terribly cold driving rain and such a depth of mud as I have never before seen anywhere in Kansas and at night lay down and slept like beavers in our wet blankets on the wet, muddy ground.

He slept on the wet, cold ground, which he thought a sort of lark. Why should she complain of anything that happened to her here, safe and warm and sheltered?

> We are ordered to leave here in Sunday next for Missouri. There is fighting going on about 50 miles from here with success on our side so far. It may all be over before we get there, but both sides are concentrating heavy forces, so there is a prospect of warm work before many days. We shall whip them, of course, for Hell itself couldn't stand before such men as we have here. Everything is going on smoothly in the Company and I have reason to believe the "boys" take a good deal of stock in their captain.

And well they might, she thought proudly. The men in the printing office, back in Milwaukee took great stock in him, as did the men of the Milwaukee Company, and the members of the Wyandotte Convention, and the delegates to the Railroad Convention. Men liked and trusted Edmund. Her eyes skimmed down the closely written pages. It was all fine to hear the attitude of his soldiers, but there were other assurances she wanted from the letter. She found them, as she knew she would.

> I shall be glad indeed when it is all over and we can all go home again. I do not think I shall ever have occasion again to leave you and the little ones. My fireside has too many attractions to me to ever again leave it, except upon the most urgent necessity. This time I felt that the necessity of the

country demanded the sacrifice from every man that could possibly make it and when it is over I know I shall feel much better satisfied and you and the children will feel a thousand times more proud of me for having done what I have done.

I was proud of you anyway, she cried out in her heart. I did not need this to make me so.

If we should remain here during the winter and the enemy should retire so that there will be no more danger of fighting before I could return, I will try to come home for a few days. It would necessarily be a short visit as it would take so long to go and come, not less than ten days each way and through cold weather and very bad roads. But even a short visit would be very great satisfaction to me as I know it would to you all and I would cheerfully endure all the privations incident to the trip for the sweet pleasure of clasping you all to my heart once more and feeling your sweet kisses on my lips.

She went back and read the last part once more. This was what she had wanted, above all, from the letter. Across the miles his words came to her, beautiful and comforting, holding them together. It had been like this all those months before their marriage, when his letters had come to her from all those towns whose names became real to her only because he had been there. She still had the letters packed away in a box. They would go with her wherever she went, for they were a part of both of them. Suddenly she had a great wish to reread those letters. She went to the trunk where she kept them stored, alongside a box labeled "Quilt Pieces." Here was another memory—she had put the quilt away in these past busy years, forgetting all about it.

For a while she sat on the floor beside the trunk, touching each quilt block, letting the memories it evoked take over. She got to her feet. She would finish the quilt. This must be special and beautifully done, a creation which would have meaning for her all her life as well as for her children and grandchildren after she was gone.

She had felt the work on the quilt would keep her occupied, but she had not realized the extent to which it would help. Now, as she stitched a block from left-over scraps of Flint's little blouse, she could let herself think about him. Almost it was as if, in this simple action, she faced the fact of his death. She would have him in her heart, and here, in this block, and that was something. She had four living children, all of them strong and healthy and good. She had a husband who, though absent from her, could still, after almost fourteen years of marriage, write the same things he had written in love letters before their marriage. Reading his words, she could feel a rush of love even greater than she had felt as a girl.

Many women had less.

So Fannie kept on making the familiar motions of life. From force of habit, or necessity. Each morning she sent Lillie and Arthur and Pitt off to school. ("See that the children attend school regularly," Edmund urged in his letters.) Wasn't it strange, she thought, that when they had first come to Kansas, in '56, everyone had thought the times too troubled to establish schools? And now, when war beset the whole nation, school went on without interruption. By this time people seemed to have accepted the ways of war. Perhaps they even thought it would go on forever and they might as well get used to it.

When the three older children were away, Fannie turned her attention to Eddie, who by now was beginning to jabber sounds which Lillie fondly interpreted as words. ("When she does begin to talk, teach her to say my name," Edmund had written. Poor little baby—though named after him, she must grow up a stranger to her father. The others could talk about him, remembering.)

As Fannie worked to make the house tidy, she could look out the window and see the *Record* office, owned by others now. And, in the other direction—no, she must not look too much toward the cemetery, she must concentrate rather on life and the ones who lived. There were meals to plan—the children were always hungry. There were the everlasting mending and sewing and washing and ironing. Children were so hard on clothes. Evenings, she sat with them while they did their lessons. And, as a treat to make them hurry, she promised to read from Papa's letters, once they had finished. She read each one again and again, until it was, in turn, replaced by a new one.

> I have marched 275 miles in fifteen days. I have not ridden a step of the way except about an hour when I was officer of the day. I would not want to ride while the men who are just as tired as I was and had just as good a right to ride were trudging along on foot.

A sob from Lillie broke into the reading.

"Poor Papa," she cried. "He shouldn't—oh, he mustn't get so tired. All that long way—and it was cold, and raining—"

"Papa is a soldier. Soldiers have to march," Arthur told her loftily.

Fannie wanted nothing more than to join in Lillie's tears, but she must also remember that she had sons and try to see the situation through their eyes. How did women manage, she wondered, when they were left alone with the children while husbands went to war? How did they build a man's courage into their sons when all they really wanted to do was to give way to their own womanly fears?

He had written from Pea Ridge, the battlefield where, last year, Federal troops had been so horrified to discover that Indians on the Confederate side had resorted to their own barbarian past and scalped their victims. Thank God the Indians were no longer there. She put behind her the remembrances of other tales of horror, mutilations even worse than the scalpings.

"I am captain now," Edmund wrote. "I was appointed by order of Jim Lane."

Fannie was divided between pride in his promotion and distrust of the man who was responsible for it. Lane had long been trying to take over the army in Kansas. Governor Carney, who had followed Charles Robinson, had no such power as Lane wielded, a fact which the Governor had gone to Washington to protest. When he talked with Lincoln, the President apologized for allowing Lane to gain so much influence, explaining the situation by saying, "He knocks at my door every morning. You know he is a most persistent fellow and hard to put off. I don't see you very often and have to pay attention to him."

"Papa's a captain," Arthur said proudly. "Captain Edmund Ross."

"What's a captain?" Pitt asked.

"He has to lead his troops," Arthur explained tolerantly. "He has to go first, always . . ."

Fannie went back to the letter, although what she read there was little comfort.

> I think I shall do about as good fighting as the bravest of them. At any rate, my Topeka friends shall never hear it said of me that I have not performed my whole duty in the field or exposed my men to any danger that I did not have to meet myself. I know I shall have your prayers that mine and my children's name shall never be sullied by any act of cowardice on my part, cost what it will. Knowing this, I shall go into the fight doubly armed. If I fall, it will be a consolation to you, and a matter of pride to them, to wear a name of which they will be proud as having contributed something toward the success of this glorious cause. But we must not anticipate any such calamity, but look forward to the end of these troubles when we can muster our little flock in peaceful happiness.

When the children were in bed, she reread the letter. It was almost as if he were with her, there in the stillness of the room. Edmund had a way of reaching out through the written word, of putting his personality into his letters. She read it all again slowly, carefully, dwelling on every word until she came to the end.

"Good night my dear wife. Pray for me."

As if she needed to be told!

His letters arrived by all sorts of means—young men coming through the lines, farmers who had been near the encampment and were entrusted to pass letters on. Occasionally he sent money—twenty dollars, thirty, sometimes more. Now and then there was information touching on military matters.

"At least the infamous Quantrill is here fighting us," Edmund wrote from Cane Hill, "and not in Kansas. We drove him with the rebel army over the Boston Mountains on Friday, last, so he will not trouble Kansas any more very soon."

Fannie wondered about this. Quantrill did not seem to be the sort of man who would stay long with any army, especially one which was retreating.

Sometimes the details of the letters were homey and reassuring. He wrote that he and his comrades had found a discarded printing press in the street at Cane Hill, Arkansas. It had been used to print a missionary paper called *The Cherokee Messenger*, so part of the type was in that language. A little difficulty of that nature would not stop a newspaperman, he assured her. He and a group of men planned to put out a newspaper which they would call *Buck and Ball*. He promised to send her a copy.

When the paper came, it did nothing to quiet her concern for him.

Printed on ruled foolscap, the front sheets bore an account of the Battle of Prairie Grove. An inside paragraph said, "The outside of this paper was printed on the 6th Inst. [December, 1862] but owing to the great battle on the 7th it was impossible for us to issue our paper before the 15th."

Well, at least the battle was over; he had come through safely and had written and printed the story of it. From such small things she must draw comfort.

3

One morning young Henry Lindsey appeared at Fannie's door. He wore a Federal uniform, and no longer looked like a baby.

"Why hello, Henry," she greeted him warmly. "My goodness—you're not a drummer boy any more!"

"No, Ma'am," he preened himself, wanting to show off the blue uniform. "I'm a real soldier now. And say, I got something for you. Captain Ross sent you a letter."

She reached out to take it, hoping she did not seem to be snatching.

"How—how is he?" she asked.

"He's fine—he's just mighty fine. He said to tell you not to worry about him."

The boy put the letter into her hands.

"It's got money in it," he said proudly, plainly feeling it no small thing to have been entrusted with the errand.

"Oh, thank you—"

Why didn't he go? Why didn't he leave her to read the letter?

"You ought to be real proud of your husband," the boy went on. "I was scared to death at Prairie Grove, I don't mind telling you. But he just kept us all going, and never seemed to have a thought for himself. Colonel Crawford himself said he had never seen anything like it. . . . Well, Ma'am, I must be getting along."

He was gone before she remembered that she had not so much as offered him a cup of coffee.

She ripped the letter open, tearing off a small corner of it in her haste. Her eyes skimmed down the lines, so closely and firmly written. She found, very early, the lines which made this letter better than any she had received so far.

The regiment was being ordered back to Kansas City, where it would be reorganized as a cavalry unit and, by order of Governor Carney, Edmund would be made a major. Their old muskets would be replaced by sabers and carbines. Fannie's thoughts raced ahead to all the benefits this new arrangement offered. Edmund would no longer need to walk. He would be well armed. He would be a major.

And, then another thought came to her. Governor Carney, not Jim Lane, was conferring his promotion upon him. At long last, the Governor had evidently succeeded in making President Lincoln understand what sort of a person Lane really was.

Lane was not to be so easily pushed into the background. Rumors came back of his activities. He had his own army of somewhere between 2,500 and 3,000 men. They boasted of their plunderings, all in the name of the Federal Army, and offered to sell Rebel caps at ten cents apiece. Fall Leaf, the Indian from the reservation near Lawrence, with fifty-four of his men, was reported to have joined Lane. Thirty Wyandottes also were in the group, as well as many Negroes. They burned and pillaged and killed; anything they came upon was theirs if they wanted to take it and were able to do so, their depredations amounting to millions of dollars worth of property. Lane himself rode at the head of them, in civilian pants and a soldier's blouse and a dilapidated white hat. From under his dark brows his piercing eyes surveyed the havoc, and all the time he shrieked that the Indians should rise up, with tomahawk and fire, to destroy the South.

As if waiting for just such an inspiration, Jennison's Red Legs were organized. This group took its name from the red morocco leggings worn by the members of the group, men between twenty-five and fifty years of age who were apparently dedicated to the business of horse stealing, but who did not mind picking up cattle and other property or, if the occasion arose, branching out into assorted crime. Gangs would ride over into Missouri, then dash back to Lawrence with their booty, bragging about their exploits. Everyone knew that Lawrence livery stables were filled with stolen horses and yet the people were either unable to stop them or thought whatever happened to the Missourians was all right. A natural hesitancy might have come from the fact that Jennison's men did not hesitate to shoot down anyone who questioned them or gave them trouble.

All this, Fannie knew, would serve only to give the Missourians, especially Quantrill and his followers, an excuse to raid Lawrence once more. She was not surprised when Edmund sent word that General Ewing had detailed Edmund and his own Company E to Lawrence in order to protect the town against possible reprisals.

4

Edmund and his company were transferred to Lawrence in early spring of 1863. For the first time since he had gone into the army, he was able to come home frequently.

"And a good thing," Fannie declared when Eddie, seeing her father on the first of these visits, hid her face in her mother's shoulder. "She hasn't had a chance to know her own father."

"We'll get acquainted quickly," Edmund said. "Come here to Papa, darling."

Eddie looked at him shyly and then, apparently deciding she liked this visitor, smiled at him. Edmund reached out to take her from Fannie.

"I feel almost a stranger to you myself," she said. "In those few furloughs home, you no sooner got here than you had to leave once more."

"That's war—" Edmund reminded her. "But now, I'm closer and we can be together more."

Actually, the situation, although better, was not entirely satisfactory. "It is hard to be so close," he said on one of his trips home, "and yet separated. Every day I miss you more. I am going to try to find a place for you to stay in Lawrence. Would you like that?"

"Why, Edmund," she cried, "what a thing to ask!"

Soon after that, he wrote that he had the loan of a small house for the month of August (the owners having left for a trip to Washington on business) and now she and the children could come to Lawrence.

The Lawrence house, when she first saw it, looked small but adequate. It seemed all the smaller because the one next door to it was on the imposing side, with formal gardens laid out in the back and flowers blooming in a rather delightful confusion in the front. Edmund caught her eyes on it.

"Mrs. Carter's," he said. "She's a widow. You probably won't see her much. She's a fine, intelligent woman, but she spends most of her time reading and looking after her flowers."

"Oh, I won't mind," Fannie told him. "I'll look at her flowers and not expect to neighbor. And I'll have you—"

Edmund came home almost every day and sometimes stayed all night. On such occasions, the family could eat together and become acquainted once more. Eddie quite forgot her shyness.

The children quickly made friends with everyone in the neighborhood. One day Arthur and Pitt came home, each carrying a small Union flag.

"Menzie Kemp gave them to us," they explained earnestly. "She wants us to carry them everywhere we go, so people will know she has them to sell."

It was a fact Menzie herself confirmed the first time Fannie saw her. And Arthur and Pitt marched around town giving, Fannie hoped, a big boost to the sale of flags.

They found playmates their own age, but liked best of all to tag after the big boys. Most of the older ones were not too happy with their small satellites, but one, a twelve-year-old named Bobby Martin, was kinder than the others. His mother had cut down one of his father's Union Army uniforms to make a suit for him. Bobby wore it constantly; Fannie suspected he even slept in it. His innocent boyish face wore such a look of pride in his costume as to be almost ridiculous.

"Mama," Arthur begged, "please make me a suit out of Papa's!"

"We'll see," Fannie temporized.

The children played in the yard in the long August twilights and she and Edmund sat watching them, talking, talking, talking. Mrs. Carter, next door, worked among her flowers. She nodded to Fannie, but beyond that their conversation was made up of the briefest remarks. A small, prim woman who worked in gloves and garden hat, Mrs. Carter disdained the sunbonnet which most Lawrence women considered part of the normal wardrobe. Fannie was always firm in her instructions to the children—they were not, under any circumstances, to go near Mrs. Carter's flowers.

Those nights Edmund could stay at home were the best, of course. Once the children had gone to bed, she and Edmund would go on with the talking, far into the night. There was so much to catch up on, so many many things she had kept stored in her heart.

Fannie knew Edmund was troubled about something, as soon as he opened the door that evening. The children rushed to meet him and he kissed the girls and patted the boys' heads absently.

The minute the children were in bed, she asked, "What's wrong?"

"Have you—well, heard any complaints about the soldiers?"

"Complaints—no, of course not. I should think it would be

foolish for the people of Lawrence to complain, knowing why the soldiers are here."

"Nevertheless, there have been complaints. They'll get to you in time."

"What about?"

"It seems some residents dislike having the soldiers come to their wells for water. How else would they get water? There is no town well. They say the soldiers talk and sing too loud in the evening. Of course they do. Listen—"

Sure enough, the voices of the young soldiers could be heard now, raised in song, carrying across the distance between camp and town. To Fannie, it sounded reassuring. Only the disgruntled could complain.

"Some people must have something to fuss about," Fannie said. "Don't worry—most of Lawrence very much wants you here."

"Perhaps," Edmund said, and went on to talk of other things.

He was scarcely gone the next morning when Fannie had a caller.

"I'm Mrs. Bishop," she said. "I live a few blocks down from you. I hope I'm not upsetting your work," she added, looking at the unwashed dishes and unmade beds.

"My husband was home last night," Fannie explained, "and I'm later getting started. I'm sorry the place is in such a mess."

"Oh, that's all right. I'm slow myself. I couldn't sleep last night. The way those soldiers yelled and carried on, half the night—"

Fannie braced herself. "Oh, they're just a group of young men—boys, really. They don't mean any harm."

"Mean any harm or not, I haven't had any sleep since they came. It's got so I hate to let the children play in the yard. Those soldiers come for water from my well, and the way they talk—it's not fit for children to hear."

Fannie wanted to remind her that frontier children were accustomed to hearing talk which might send effete eastern offspring into fits of vapors.

"Everyone's complaining."

"Everyone?" Fannie raised her eyebrows.

"Well, just about everyone—" the woman hedged.

"But don't they know—can't they see what the presence of the soldiers does for us? With Quantrill just over the line, ready to strike—"

"Jim Lane will save us from Quantrill; he'll stop that bunch from coming here."

"Jim Lane, indeed," Fannie snapped. "He's the reason we need protection. He and Jennison. You know as well as I do about all those stolen horses in the livery stables here. You know that carriage Mrs. Lane drives and the team hitched to it were both stolen by Lane from Missourians. That's all the excuse Quantrill needs—if he does need one at all."

The woman stood up, her eyes small sharp points of malice and anger.

"You talk mighty fast and blunt, Mrs. Ross," she said, "and don't think I don't know why. If my husband was at home living off the town, instead of out fighting a war, I'd talk different, too."

Fannie stood up. She knew she had her seven-foot-tall look, just as she knew that, seldom in all her life, had she been this angry. Mrs. Bishop backed toward the door, never taking her eyes off Fannie. My goodness, Fannie thought, she looks as if she's afraid I'm going to strike her. Once at the door, the visitor put her hand on the knob, opened it, and scuttled out.

When Edmund came home that evening, she did not need to ask him the reason for his preoccupation.

"Don't bother to keep it from me," she said, almost as soon as he walked into the house. "You've had news."

"So they've come to you, have they?" he said, making no effort to deny anything.

"Not they—just one woman. A Mrs. Bishop. And did I ever tell her a few things. She was pretty surprised, I can guarantee."

"That I don't in the least doubt. I've been surprised myself, upon occasion. How anyone who looks so mild, and is such a bit of a thing can rise up—I know Mrs. Bishop, all right. She has a big lubberly boy of fourteen or so who has taught the soldiers some words they'd never even heard of."

"As if she doesn't know that, but for you, Quantrill would be right over here."

"Maybe," he agreed, "but there's no sense in quartering troops where people don't want them, even for their protection. We listed that in the Declaration of Independence."

Oh, why did he always have to be so logical and so legal about things?

"You aren't going to pick up and leave, are you, just because a few women complain?"

"I have no choice," he told her. "A petition has been sent General Ewing asking him to remove my troops. We leave tomorrow."

5

Fannie sat out in the yard of the Lawrence house, the heat of late August closing down on her. The children played in the gathering dusk, chasing the fireflies. Once they caught their prize, they put it into a bottle and watched with delight the glow that came and went. She supposed she ought to forbid it . . .

The night was very quiet. No soldiers came to the wells for water; no sounds of songs and laughter filled the air. Edmund and his men were off, marching to join the other Federal troops fighting all up and down Missouri.

Until the last moment Fannie had hoped vainly that something would happen to rescind the order—some last-minute retraction by the people of Lawrence, realizing what his presence meant, or some second thought by General Ewing. It was not until Edmund came to tell her good-by that she made herself accept the fact that he must really leave.

"Good-by," he said, taking her into his arms.

It was the same thing he used to say when he left each morning to go to the newspaper; it was no different from his farewell those mornings here in Lawrence after he had spent the night with his family. Wasn't it strange there should be no difference in the word one used to say good-by for a few hours and the one you used for an absence which might stretch for months or days or maybe even forever? Your lips said the same word; it was in your heart you knew the difference. She stood wordlessly in his arms, not even trying to speak.

He kissed her, and then turned to bid the children good-by. "Be good children," he said, "and take care of your mama."

He came back to her once more. A quick kiss and he was gone, off to the fighting which was daily growing hotter and more frenzied. The big battles might be fought in the East, but on the western border men were fighting and dying, many of them, every day.

Tomorrow she must pack and return to Topeka. With Edmund gone, there was no reason to remain here. Today was—let's see, she had lost count of time. Yes, it was the twentieth of August, and soon the children must be starting back to school. She herself would face another year of being father and mother to the family, of making decisions for both of them. The prospect seemed all the more lonely after the satisfaction of having had Edmund with her these past weeks.

Lillie, always sensitive to her mother's moods, slipped to her side. "Don't worry, Mama. Papa will be all right."

"Of course, honey," Fannie agreed. "Now—it's time you children went to bed."

They trooped inside and Fannie went through familiar motions, seeing that they washed the dust of the day off their feet, donned nightgowns, and said prayers.

"God bless Papa," they said.

"Papa—Papa—" Eddie prattled.

Well, at least Papa was no longer a mere name to her. That much the Lawrence visit had done.

At last they were in bed (Arthur and Pitt with their cherished flags pinned to their pillows) and Fannie was free to sit by the open window, trying to catch a breath of air and cool off before she, too, joined them. She could see a light burning in the window of the Lane house (one of those fancy new kerosene lamps which, rumor said, he had brought home from a raid in Missouri) and knew, by the look of festivity about the place that Lane must be home tonight. No doubt Mrs. Bishop would sleep more soundly, knowing this. Dimly visible on the ridge west of town where Edmund's forces had camped stood the tents of the dozen or so raw young Federal recruits, the sole force guarding the town. Two thousand people—men, women, and children—left with only untrained boys for protection!

And somewhere in the night, eastward, in the direction of Missouri, Edmund slept. Soon he would be joining Blunt's forces, fighting Sterling Price.

There was no use trying to go back to sleep, even if her mind had been at rest. The relentless, simmering heat bore down upon her. Her gown, her hair, the pillow were all wet with perspiration. Beside her, little Eddie stirred restlessly, and Fannie reached out a hand to soothe her. Poor little thing—hot weather was hard on children. And this was her second summer, too, the time so feared and dreaded by all mothers. Fannie slipped out of bed, got a wash cloth and dipped it in tepid water, and went to sponge off the child's body.

It was almost morning; she could see light pushing across the sky to the east. She went to the window and sat there in her nightgown, wondering how many women, all over the land, sat as she did now in Lawrence. Women left at home to watch over families while the men fought the war. And she wondered, here in the breathless heat of a Kansas dawn, whether the result would justify all the fighting and killing and dying that went on.

It wasn't good to sit thinking. She might as well dress and make a pot of coffee. If she were returning to Topeka, this day would be filled with countless errands.

Fannie was drinking her coffee when she heard the sound of shooting. She listened, the cup halfway to her lips. Perhaps she was mistaken. No, there it was again. It came from the west, where the dozen young Federal soldiers were camped. They certainly were practicing early. More shots sounded, seeming to come nearer. Perhaps they were on their way to town. And what would Mrs. Bishop say to this? Edmund's troops had never raised such a commotion, especially at this hour of the morning.

She stepped outside. The sun was just coming up now, in a hot red sky. This was going to be the hottest day in a string of cruel ones, and she sighed a little, thinking of all she must accomplish between the rising of the sun and its setting. Another shot came, nearer this time. Surely those young soldiers were overdoing things.

She could see a figure riding down the deserted street, mounted, bareback, on a mule with a rope halter. As he came, he beat the neck of his mount, first on the right side and then on the left, with the ends of the rope. By now she could see it was a Negro. Involuntarily her mind raced back to Milwaukee and to Mr. Booth, riding to arouse a town.

"Run," the Negro screamed. "Run for your lives—they're here—they done shot poor Brother Snyder—"

He was opposite Fannie now, and she called out to him, "Who—who's here?" But she knew, even before he told her.

"Quantrill," he called back over his shoulder. "They're headed this way. Run—"

Even had she wished to follow his warning, there would have been no time. Scarcely had the messenger passed when a band of horsemen swept down the street.

They were a motley, bearded crew in dirty western shirts and broad hats. But the man at their head—she would have known him for the leader, even had he been hidden within the ranks. He was mounted on a fine sorrel horse and wore a beautifully embroidered hunting shirt. His longhorn moustache failed to disguise the loose, cruel mouth. On his small head, atop its long thin neck, sat a low-crowned black hat decorated with gold tassels. Four pistols showed at his belt. Even as Fannie watched, one of them came out of his belt; there was a puff of white smoke, and suddenly the Negro on the mule swayed a little, caught at the neck of the animal. A half dozen ragged followers fired, too, and the Negro slumped, slid off to the ground and lay there while the frightened mule ran wildly down the street.

Quantrill now turned to his men.

"You have your orders," he said. "Divide into columns of fours. Kill every man and boy you see. What you take is yours. If they give any trouble, burn the house. Forward—"

The troops rode off, the rays of the rising sun glinting on their gun barrels. The hoofs of the horses pounded in the street. Dust rose. The clinking of bit and spur filled the air. The main column swept on, toward town, toward Massachusetts Avenue and the business section. And others fanned out, in the direction of the homes of still sleeping people.

Not all left. Four men remained in front of Fannie's house. "Shoot every man and boy—" Quantrill had said. She felt her knees go to jelly. Arthur, only eleven years old, asleep in the house. Surely they would not—surely no man could be so vile—

"What's the use of wasting time here?" she heard one of the four say. "Lane's house ain't far—let's go after him. He's the one we came for."

"Hell—might as well pick this one up on the way. He's bound to be a damned abolitionist. Town's full of 'em."

"All right—might as well get the one next door, too."

One of them rode toward Fannie now. After a moment, he was joined by his three companions. He was very young—he looked no more than sixteen or seventeen. In his hat he wore a flower, which accentuated his youth.

"Where's your husband?" he asked. The voice, too, was a boy's voice.

"He's not here," she said, wondering that she could speak at all.

"Oh, hell, she's lying. Set the torch to the place. He'll come out fast enough."

"No—" she moved in front of the door as she spoke. It was an instinctive gesture; she was not even aware of having made it. "No —I'm telling you the truth. You may go in and see for yourself. My husband isn't here—my children are asleep inside."

The boy hesitated, apparently willing to take her word for things.

"It's just a trick," a third man spoke up. He was dirty and ragged and common looking. At least the boy seemed to have some good in him. Her hope was to appeal to him.

"Remember," the ragged one said, "we had our orders. Bill ain't going to like it if we fail—"

Arthur, asleep in his bed with a Union flag pinned to his pillow. If they saw him! If it crossed their crazy minds that, in a few years, he would be able to carry a gun . . .

The boy took a step toward the house. At that moment Mrs. Carter came walking across the yard, dressed as carefully as if she were paying a formal call. She went directly to the boy with the flower in his hat.

"Why, good morning, Jesse," she said, her voice cool, yet kind. "How good it is to see you."

The boy looked embarrassed as he removed his hat and bowed.

"Good morning, Miz Carter," he said uneasily.

"How is your mother?" Mrs. Carter went on, calmly as if she walked out every morning to find armed men sitting in front of her house. "Did Frank come with you?"

"Yes, Ma'am—I mean he's in town somewhere."

There was a creaking of leather as men shifted in their saddles. Let us get on with the business at hand, they seemed to urge.

"You must have stopped to see my flowers," Mrs. Carter said wisely. "I remember you people were always great ones to have flowers about the place. Here—let me pick one for you—"

She bent over a patch of marigolds, considered several of them before she finally settled on one which seemed better than the others. This done, she selected another one and then made her dignified way to the boy's side.

"Here—" she said. "Let me give you this for your buttonhole."

The boy took it, embarrassment spreading over his face.

"And this one you can take to Frank," Mrs. Carter said. "Aren't they pretty?"

Helpless to refuse her, he took the second one. Then he seemed to come to himself.

"Yes, Ma'am," he replied. "Yes, Miz Carter, they sure are—too damned pretty to be burned."

He turned, faced his three companions. "I'll shoot the first man who touches this place," he blurted out. "Ride on."

A dead silence fell over the group. Plainly, mutiny was brewing.

"I knew her in Missouri. Besides, we don't touch women," the boy snapped. "*Ride on*—" No boy's voice this, but the voice of a man to be obeyed.

After a moment's hesitation, the horsemen galloped down the street.

Fannie turned weakly to Mrs. Carter. "You saved us," she said, almost in a whisper. "They said they were going to burn the house . . ."

"They spared us," Mrs. Carter said. "But God help the town—"

"Quantrill—" Fannie began. "Those are his men."

"Yes, I know."

"And you knew that boy with him—"

"I lived near his family in Missouri," she said. "They are nice enough people. Jennison came bothering them, and then the Federal troops arrested their mother and sister for sheltering guerrillas. They are hot-blooded folks, the Jameses. I do not wonder that Frank and Jesse have cast their lot with Quantrill."

"I don't see—" Fannie burst out, and paused midway in the sentence, stopped by a terrific sound of gunfire from the direction of Massachusetts Avenue.

"There are many things we cannot understand about this war," Mrs. Carter said. And walked calmly back into her house.

6

Fannie kept the children in and tried to quiet their fears, an undertaking in which she had scant success. Who could hide from them the terror which possessed the town in the hours that followed? Who could pass off as nothing the sound of guns, the agonized screams of the victims, the spurt of flames and smoke rising to the sky? Anyone, even a child, could fill in the facts from his own terrified imaginings.

It was a little after midmorning when the sounds of shooting and yelling stopped. Fannie saw Mrs. Carter coming across the yard, making her way through the flowers, headed in the direction of Massachusetts Avenue, a look of purpose on her face.

Fannie opened the door. When the children acted as if they

meant to follow her, she turned to forbid them with such firmness that they stood back quietly as she went outside.

"Wait a minute, Mrs. Carter," she said. "I'll go with you—there'll be work for me to do, too."

Mrs. Carter considered the matter. Finally she said, "I think it is best that, for the time being, you remain here with the children. I think there will be—well, sights which it is best their young eyes be spared. Already they must be greatly frightened and puzzled."

Children in wartime were spared little, Fannie thought. But while she hesitated, Mrs. Carter continued, "Later on there will be work for us all. Why not wait here until I come back and tell you of conditions in town?"

Fannie could see the wisdom in Mrs. Carter's suggestion. She went back into the house, gave all her strength and purpose into bringing the children back to something like a normal state.

Before long, Mrs. Carter returned. "The men are slipping back from their hiding places now," she said. "Such ones as were fortunate enough to find hiding places. They are taking the dead to the Methodist Church on Vermont Street. There will be work for us there."

"I'll go," Fannie said. She turned to Lillie. "Lillie," she said, "You are a big girl. Do you think you can take care of the children while I go to town to help?"

"Yes, Mama," Lillie said, her eyes enormous in her white face. "You know I can."

Fannie turned to the boys. "Arthur, Pitt," she said, "you are to stay here and do as Lillie says and help her look after Eddie. Under no circumstances are you to come to town, or even leave the house. Do you understand?"

"Yes, Mama—" The promise was given less willingly, but it was sincere.

"I am ready to go now," Fannie told Mrs. Carter. The two women walked off together and as they went, Mrs. Carter filled in the account of the raid, a tale of horror whose reality surpassed anything Fannie's imagination had supplied.

It was a story of pillage and panic, of aimless flights which were seldom successful, of groans of the dying and of the wild terror of the living, pursued and shot down with as little compunction as if they had been wild animals. Street patrols robbed every house systematically. At each gate, two men waited on horses while others dismounted and went, with spurs jingling, up the walk. If a woman opened the door, she was ordered to deliver all money, jewels and watches. If a man, he was shot. The house was then set on fire. If that procedure flushed out a man or a boy, he was shot on the run. Some women struggled with the murderers, others begged and prayed, but, for the most part, few succeeded in having the lives of their sons or husbands spared. Some simply stood, mute and helpless, their children around them, while their loved ones were killed.

Everyone had his own story to add to the general horror. One had seen a Negro man with a baby in his arms running across the street. A bullet found him and he fell forward, the baby still in his arms. A man tripped and pitched forward, down a flight of stairs in a burning house. His wife tried to run to help him up but the raiders held her back, forcing her to watch him burn to death inside the house. One house was set afire seven times, and each time the woman of the house rushed forward to beat out the flames. Finally the looters gave up and rode off, bearing with them some small trinkets which had belonged to her baby, only recently dead.

Quantrill had established himself in the City Hotel during the raid, saying he had once stayed there and liked the place. He ordered a lunch to be brought him, a request which was naturally obeyed. From here he had a good view of the business houses in flames, looted goods scattered under the hitchracks in the streets, smoke pouring out of smashed windows. He could see the offices of three hated newspapers, the *Journal, Tribune* and *Republic,* burst into flames. Doubtless, he also saw young John Speer, Jr., run out the back door of his father's newspaper, the *Tribune,* only to bump into one of the guerrillas. The boy, upon demand, handed over his pocketbook, and the next moment lay writhing in the dust mortally wounded.

By nine o'clock the town had fallen completely into the hands of the guerrillas, all long since thoroughly drunk, for the liquor stores were first to be raided. Quantrill made his way to the street and summoned a few of his henchmen. A short distance away he spotted the livery stable where a few prisoners huddled.

"Select one to drive an ambulance with my wounded men," he ordered. "Shoot the others. Fours right: march."

They rode out of town, whooping wildly, brandishing guns and whiskey bottles as they went, piano covers and damask curtains serving as new saddle blankets. Every rider was followed by a pack horse (stolen from the livery stable) laden with bolts of cloth, shoes, dry goods and loot of all kinds. And in the tail of almost every horse was braided a small Union flag, plundered from poor Menzie Kemp's cherished supply.

Mrs. Carter told the story as they walked along, but even so, Fannie was not prepared for the scene of desolation which spread out on both sides of their path. Already the women and the men who had been spared were beginning the rescue work, while buildings smoked on every side and the wounded and dead lay in the streets where they had fallen.

"We will do what seems to be needed most," Mrs. Carter said simply.

There was no problem of decision here. They helped women find their dead, sometimes with bodies charred almost beyond recognition. They enlisted the aid of five young army recruits, the only survivors of a group of thirty-two who had been sitting waiting to be mustered into service when the carnage broke loose.

"We were unarmed, Ma'am," one of them, a mere boy, explained to Fannie. "When the shooting started we began to run every which way, trying to crawl under sidewalks or into bushes. It wasn't no use—they got most of us. What can I do?" he asked, apparently too dazed to think for himself.

"Help carry the bodies to the Methodist Church on Vermont Street," Mrs. Carter told him. "The benches have been taken up so the place can serve as a morgue. The families will be there to identify them. Mrs. Ross, we had better go to the church, too."

Fannie followed her. The place was already filled with bodies, and more were coming in every moment. Lying among them was little Bobby Martin, still wearing his cut-down Federal uniform. Death had come so suddenly his face still held its look of pride.

For no reason she could fathom, Fannie turned to Mrs. Carter to ask, "And how did Mrs. Bishop come out of it?"

"Fine," Mrs. Carter told her drily. "She wrote 'Southern' in large letters on her front door and escaped harm of any kind."

After the burying was finished (kinfolk carrying off the bodies of their loved ones, the unidentified put to rest in a common grave), the town counted up its losses. More than a hundred and eighty men and boys killed and many wounded. Better than two million dollars in property destroyed. Lane himself, the man Quantrill had avowedly come to get, had escaped, jumping from his window clad only in his nightshirt and taking refuge in a nearby corn field, leaving his wife to face the raiders. When she told them her husband was not at home, they set torch to the house. It burned to the ground, and with it all the fine things Lane had brought home from his Missouri raids.

Fannie, going about the business of helping those who needed her, was conscious of only one clear thought. The Lawrence raid would not escape the attention of the nation. Once more the word "Kansas" would be on every tongue.

VIII

Last Full Measure

1864–1866

THE NEWS of Quantrill's raid on Lawrence hit the front pages of newspapers all over the nation. Never more, cried the eastern ones, must the western border be left so unguarded. Everyone blamed somebody else. Lane raved up and down the border, tearing off his shirt in his frenzy, shouting for volunteers to march over into Missouri for vengeance.

The thing Fannie found best to her liking in the whole horrible business was the fact that General Ewing ordered Edmund to return with his company to Lawrence at once. Fannie, who delayed her return to Topeka, watched the soldiers march back to their old encampment, feeling pretty sure that this time there would be no complaints about getting water from wells, or singing, or anything at all.

The town was broken and frightened; many had left. The ones who stayed were ready to panic at the slightest rumor. Certainly the presence of Edmund and his soldiers would help to give the town some small feeling of security.

"If you had only been allowed to stay here," she told him when he came home, "this never would have happened."

"Yet the raid served one good purpose," he comforted her. "The eyes of the nation are focused on the border once more.

For a while they neglected us, devoting all their time to the conflict in the East. Now we may get some sort of adequate protection."

"Unless Lane takes things into his own hands and marches over into Missouri. Then everyone will be able to say we bring these things on ourselves. Do you suppose he will?"

"No," Edmund said. "General Schofield ordered him to stop his recruiting."

"Lane won't like that," Fannie mused. "General Schofield has just made himself an enemy."

As, indeed, he had. Lane, in disbanding his recruits, told them he was forced to do so because "Skowfield" forbade the vengeance march. Dan Anthony, the fiery young newspaperman from Leavenworth who had approved of John Brown's foray against Harpers Ferry, went beyond Lane's accusation by declaring the Lawrence raid was all General Ewing's fault in the first place.

"I hope they don't force Ewing to do something foolish," Edmund said uneasily. "At the moment, things don't look too good. Lane has gone to Washington to ask for Schofield's removal. Of course he'll try to give Ewing a black mark while he's there. We may be in for reprisals out here, and that won't settle anything."

"President Lincoln won't listen to Lane's demands for vengeance," Fannie declared. Once more she could see that tall, kindly man as he had appeared in Leavenworth.

"Let's hope not," Edmund said. "But the newspapers are making a big issue of Quantrill's raid. They demand to know from the military men why Quantrill got away, clean as a whistle."

"It is something to think about," Fannie agreed.

"And it will give Lane some mighty good ammunition," Edmund reminded her. "People are going to blame Lincoln for leaving the western boundary so poorly guarded. And next year's election year."

According to the accounts in the papers, Lincoln met Lane in the East Room at the White House, gave him a thoughtful and considerate hearing. The President would not approve Lane's request for revenge, but he did tell John Hay that, while radicals like Lane made a lot of trouble, he rather liked them.

"They are utterly lawless," Lincoln said, "and the unhandiest devils in the world to deal with—but after all, their faces are turned Zionward."

Ewing, evidently unable to ignore the general clamor for action, responded with Military Order Number Eleven, decreeing that all people living in Jackson, Cass, and Bates counties, those sections of western Missouri which were said to harbor Quantrill's men, were to vacate their homes within fifteen days and that all crops growing in the fields were to be taken to designated authorities. Any crops left standing in the fields would be burned.

"How awful," Fannie protested upon hearing the conditions. "There's probably not one person in fifty who ever gave Quantrill help, and yet they will all be driven out."

In obedience to Order Number Eleven almost twenty thousand people moved in all directions. They rode bony horses (the good mounts had been stolen by Jennison's Red Legs or commandeered by Union troops), or oxen, mules, donkeys and even milk cows. They traveled in ox carts, rickety wagons and homemade contraptions impossible of description. All conveyances were given to the aged, the ill, the babies. Every able-bodied person more than six years old walked, stumbling along in a state of numbed shock. Behind them were the ashes of their own homes, burned by the soldiers who came to enforce the order; often plundered first by those very soldiers. The refugees scattered with the winds —some a few miles farther into Missouri in an attempt to obtain shelter in abandoned barns, old cabins and shaky dwellings once used for slaves; others finding their way back East; still others, after months of wanderings and enduring privations unspeakable, drifting to Arkansas and Texas. And even as they traveled, death joined every caravan, halting it long enough for burial to be made. Once more, the border was on every tongue.

In the general excitement Quantrill, the cause of it all, slipped over into Indian Territory and prepared to spend the winter far removed from battles of any sort.

In the East, the owners of the house in which Fannie and her children were staying read the accounts of the disturbance and wrote that they were delaying their return. They understood Major Ross was to be quartered in Lawrence once more, and if Mrs. Ross wished to remain in the house, they would be glad to rent it for a year, perhaps longer.

"What do you think we should do?" Edmund asked her as they sat talking together.

Of course, the thing she wanted was to stay in Lawrence. It was all she could do to keep from crying out, "*Of course* we'll stay, close to you." But how would they work it out? There was, as always, the question of money. They owned the house in Topeka. For this house in Lawrence they must pay rent, an added expense which might prove more than they could manage, with Edmund in the army and being paid irregularly. Oh, why must they always shape all their plans around money or, rather, the lack of it?

"Of course," Edmund told her, "there is always the chance fighting will break out again. Prince and Shelby—and Quantrill, if he comes back—will use Order Number Eleven as an excuse for raiding Kansas, if excuse is needed. It stands to reason that, with Grant needing men so desperately in the East, the rebels aren't going to let the fighting stop here. They'll want to divert as many Federal troops as possible."

"And then you'd be off—"

"Yes—"

"In that case, we might as well stay in Topeka." She managed to make her decision without reminding him about money.

"It might be the sensible thing to do. At least, until we have a chance to sell the house there. For do you know what I might do, once the war is over?"

Once the war is over! Her heart echoed the bright prospect his words foreshadowed.

"John Speer said today he would sell me an interest in his paper, if I wanted it when I was mustered out."

Poor John Speer! Well he might feel he could use help, with his two young sons killed in the raid.

"What did you tell him?"

"I said I'd consider the matter."

2

Actually, it was the spring of 1864 before the move to Lawrence was accomplished. Fannie liked the new house on sight. Located in West Lawrence, it was comfortable and roomy, with a fence surrounding it and a wooden sidewalk outside the fence, running the full length of the lot. Fannie settled herself and her family into the house, feeling quite happy.

Evidences of Quantrill's raid were still present everywhere, even though people had started immediately rebuilding the wreckage, both of the town and of their lives. Fannie wished her new house had been closer to Mrs. Carter, but she couldn't have everything she wanted. After all, Edmund could be at home more often now, and that was the most important thing. But in her heart she knew that Edmund would not remain indefinitely in Lawrence.

Grant, concentrating on the relief of Chattanooga, had apparently decided to let the border suffer. And, taking advantage of this decision, Stand Watie, the Indian, had raided southwest Missouri. Lincoln had finally replaced Schofield (and wouldn't Lane rejoice at that, Fannie thought ruefully) by Rosecrans, who had been such a failure in Tennessee. Dapper little Jo Shelby, marching up through Missouri, bragged that he had destroyed a million dollars worth of Federal property, railroads to the amount of eight hundred thousand dollars, and had stolen the Lord only knew how many horses and mules. His proudest boast was that he had diverted ten thousand Feds who might otherwise have reinforced Rosecrans at Chichamauga.

No wonder people found fault with Lincoln and his conduct of the war. There was a demand that the President restore Frémont to command of the Department of the West, if he wanted to be renominated. One group of Republicans even went so far, in a session in late May in Pittsburgh, as to push Frémont for the Presidency.

In June of 1864, Edmund and his company were ordered out of Lawrence to meet the threat southward in Missouri and Arkansas. Amid the rush of preparations for his departure, Fannie would have missed all the stories about the Republican Convention meeting in Baltimore, had not Edmund read the papers and relayed information to her.

"I wish you'd see what Lane has done this time," Edmund exclaimed one day.

"What?" Fannie asked, scarcely looking up from the shirt she was ironing. Nothing that man did would surprise her.

"It looks very much as if he's got Lincoln nominated for a second term," Edmund said. "Listen—"

And while she ironed, he told her about it, reading some, filling in other items for himself. As almost everyone agreed, Lincoln's failure to end the war would prove a handicap to the Republican Party in November. There was a great tide of sentiment to throw him out. Just when it was at its height, down the aisle came Jim Lane, looking very much the polished gentleman (no horsehide vest and tattered hat here, Fannie could wager) and gave a talk which won those rebellious delegates over just as he had used to win rough-and-ready border men to his way of thinking. He didn't talk long, but he spoke well. "If we nominate any other than Abraham Lincoln, we nominate ruin," he told them.

The convention voted to endorse Lincoln and the following day Lane himself made the nomination. Andrew Johnson of Tennessee was nominated for the vice-presidency, a choice which some papers also attributed to Lane.

"But," Fannie asked uncertainly, "isn't Johnson a Democrat?"

"Yes," Edmund said, "but perhaps they think this will be a good move—crossing party lines. Or maybe they've even overlooked the matter of his party allegiance and expect him to think Republican. Anyway, it's not too easy to find candidates on whom to agree in times like this."

"I wonder why Lane would want him?" Fannie mused.

"There's rarely any way of deciding what Lane's true motives are," Edmund said.

But thoughts of Lane did not remain long with Fannie. For that very afternoon Edmund and his company marched away from Lawrence and once more she was left to look after the family.

3

People in Lawrence seemed to know quite well every detail of the fighting. Fannie could not go downtown for a spool of thread or the most necessary items without hearing the talk.

"They say Price is marching up from Arkansas, north toward St. Louis."

Well, at least Edmund was not in St. Louis.

"Jo Shelby's joined him. Between them they've got twelve thousand men, and they've turned west. Heading for Jeff City."

Ah, that was nearer.

"Price brags that he's making Sherman's victories in the Southeast look like nothing at all. He says Lincoln won't dare let Sherman march to the sea, so long as he and Shelby threaten the West."

An old man, who had lived in Leavenworth a long time, looked thoughtful. "Price just don't know Sherman, then," he finally said. "He'll do what he wants."

He fell to reminiscing of the time, long gone, when two young men—Sherman and Ewing—had started a law office in Leavenworth.

A lot had happened since then. And kept on happening.

Westward, toward Lexington, Price and his men marched. Now rumor had it that he was headed for Kansas, and at last Fannie knew that Edmund was with the Federal troops, marching to meet him. There was no weapon left to her save prayer. So close the fighting was, sometimes she fancied she could hear the guns.

"They've taken Lexington—"

People shouted the glad news in Lawrence streets. And then, the next day, "They have been driven from Lexington. Price came, with forces ten to one, and drove them out."

Each day the news was much the same. The Federal forces, and of course, Edmund with them, were retreating westward, giving dearly every inch of ground they surrendered. It was a delaying action. That was the best that anyone could hope for—just to hold off Price's men. Just to slow them up, until help came. But no other word could be given to the thing they were doing except to admit they were retreating.

Fannie was washing the breakfast dishes that October morning when she heard a knock at the door. She said, "Come in," not bothering to take her hands out of the dishwater. It was probably only a neighbor.

The door opened and a young man wearing a Federal uniform walked in.

"Good morning," she said uncertainly.

"Don't you know me, Mrs. Ross?" the young visitor inquired earnestly. "I'm Henry. Henry Lindsey."

"Why, to be sure," she said. "How much you've—" She started to say "grown," but stopped herself in time, thinking this was not quite the right thing to say to a young man in uniform. "It was the uniform," she said. "For a moment it confused me."

"I'm a lieutenant now," he told her proudly.

"That's fine," she said. He must have brought her some word about Edmund, or why else would he come? Why didn't he tell her—quickly—

"Major Ross said for me to come," he said. "He sent some money by me. He didn't have time to write—"

What was money! A thousand times over she would have rather it had been a letter.

"How is he—oh, Henry, how is he?"

"He's fine, Mrs. Ross. And the way he's fought—" The boy

stopped, evidently wanting to review in his own mind the accomplishments of his hero. "All along, he's been the coolest and the bravest. We had to burn a bridge—that was our orders. Shelby's men were right at our heels. We went across it—it looked mighty rickety, but we got over. And then we set it on fire. Piled hay and grass and stuff up on it, and burned it. With the enemy right on us, too!"

He was full of his story. Fannie brought him coffee, made him sit down at the kitchen table and eat homemade bread and jelly while he talked.

"Once we were entirely without ammunition," he went on. "We didn't have a bit—say, Mrs. Ross, you don't know how good this bread tastes after army food—well, anyway, we didn't have one little bit of ammunition. So we just stood our ground and began to cheer. We stayed as long as we dared, covering the retreat of the others, and then, at the last minute we got out ourselves. Oh, I tell you it was wonderful—"

As long as they dared! What if that had been too long? Honestly, sometimes she thought men took these chances just for pure excitement rather than any real need.

"We fought every step of the way," he bragged. "All the way from Lexington, right up to Kansas City. We held the Rebs, and now the reinforcements have arrived, and things are going to be all right. There won't be any invasion of Kansas. Major Ross said to tell you he'd be home when he could. Maybe not for long, but he'd be here—"

"Thank God for that," Fannie said, more to herself than to the boy. The fighting was over, for a while, and Edmund would be home when he could. You lived from moment to moment in wartime; you existed from promise to promise.

"He had two horses shot out from under him at the Battle of the Little Blue and he just grabbed himself a third one, and went right on fighting. And do you know what he said?" Henry paused, giving her time to make a guess.

"I couldn't imagine—"

"He said that if that fool horse, that second one he was

riding, hadn't reared up right when he did, the horse wouldn't have got killed. Yes, Ma'am, that's what Major Ross said." Henry laughed with relish.

Fannie sat down suddenly. She could not remain standing, and think about the alternative, had the horse failed to rear at the moment it did. Yet Henry could relate the incident and laugh about it!

"Well, I thank you for the coffee and stuff, Mrs. Ross. I had better be going. You mustn't worry. Things are going to work out now, and before long the war will be over, and Major Ross will come home."

"Let us hope so, Henry," Fannie told him.

Young Lindsey, of course, didn't really believe the war was going to end right away. He probably would have been a little disappointed had this statement been true. It dragged on. In November, Lincoln was elected for his second term, with Andrew Johnson for vice-president. Lane, so most people said, went in on Lincoln's coattails (he kept reminding the voters that he had been responsible for Lincoln's nomination) and would serve his second term as senator. Samuel Crawford, the officer who had been so impressed with Edmund's fighting at Prairie Grove, was elected governor of Kansas.

In spite of Price's boast, Sherman did march through Georgia, leaving a trail of desolation and destruction behind him until, at last, Savannah surrendered to him.

The war settled down now to a struggle between Lee's and Grant's armies in Virginia. Sterling Price, finally defeated in Missouri, retreated south, joining the Confederate forces in Arkansas. The border war, save for guerrilla sniping, seemed to have ended. Even that had lost its old flavor since Quantrill, so it was said, had ridden east with twenty followers, bent on a great mission. He was going to assassinate Lincoln. (But he was shot like a cornered animal in a barn in West Virginia where he had taken refuge, in May 1865, when the Civil War was over and Lincoln was dead.)

The defeat of Price, besides being a military triumph which saved Kansas from invasion by Confederate troops, had a deeper significance for Fannie. Once more Edmund and his company were stationed in Lawrence, with orders to police the border. They were out of the terrific fighting in which they had taken part during the past months.

Edmund was at home at the time of Lincoln's second inauguration. Fannie thought the whole thing had an undercurrent of sadness. The weather in Washington was cold and forbidding. Johnson, who had been ill for some time with a fever, fortified himself with an unaccustomed glass of brandy and made a great fool of himself, embarrassing everyone, an unfortunate fact that was almost overlooked or forgotten in the impact of Lincoln's address upon his audience.

"—with malice toward none; with charity for all; with firmness in the right as God gives us to see the right—to bind up the nation's wounds—"

According to the papers, people cried, unashamed, at hearing him. Fannie did not wonder. Once more she could see the sad, earnest face, the tall, gaunt figure, on the platform at Leavenworth . . . and, across the years and miles that lay between, she found herself crying, too.

The end came at last, with Lee's surrender to Grant at Appomattox. Fannie, hearing the joyful news, thought first of how Edmund would now be home for good, and then turned to rejoicing of a more general nature. She suspected that a great many wives in the land, both north and south, shared the order in which she rated her own delight.

Then, while the victory celebrations were still in full swing, came the awful news of the President's assassination.

Fannie knew that her own stunned grief and horror were felt by people all over the country. Here was a man whose one thought had been to bring the nation back together without rancor or hatred; to represent only the general good of all the people, not the small, radical group of Northerners who would have vengeance visited on the defeated rebels. Surely the South realized this, too. The things Lincoln had hoped, had planned to do would be threatened now.

How well she remembered her own reaction upon reading the account of his farewell to his friends at Springfield when he left for the inauguration. "He sounds as if he thought he'd never come back," she had said. Now he was returning, in his casket, with Mary Lincoln riding in the funeral train. How must the woman feel, going back to the town where most of their life together had been spent?

Fannie recalled something else. The sad, curiously ugly face at Leavenworth and the sound of the nasal voice saying, "An enthusiast broods over the oppressions of a people until he fancies himself commissioned by heaven to liberate—he ventures into the attempt—"

He had been speaking about John Brown, there in Leavenworth. He had repeated the words at Cooper Union in the speech which was given credit for his nomination. He could not have known then that he was foretelling his own fate. He could not possibly have foreseen that John Wilkes Booth, or one of his kind, would be waiting somewhere around the corner of time, brooding over wrongs he felt he must avenge, any more than he could have realized he was speaking his last farewell to those friends and neighbors in Springfield.

And yet—they said the night before his death he had dreamed it would come to him. Would it be such a strange thing, then, that long ago he would have seen the method of its arrival?

4

The war might be ended in the nation, but out in western Kansas there was no peace. Indian raids were causing as much trouble there as the guerrilla warfare had given the eastern border before and during the war. Cheyenne and Arapaho raced up and down Solomon Valley, killing and wounding settlers and carrying off their stock.

In July, Edmund was especially upset by one of these events.

Sergeant Custard—one of the men in the Eleventh—and twenty-six men were escorting a wagon train to Platte Bridge. The little group was surrounded by fifteen hundred Indians. Custard and his men fought for three hours, and at the end of that time, ran out of ammunition. The Indians bound him and the surviving men to their wagons with telegraph wire and burned them to death.

"Oh, Edmund, they couldn't—" Fannie cried, sickened with horror.

"But they did," he said. "And it's going to happen again. The Indian Bureau is under the Department of the Interior, and they are permitting unscrupulous agents and traders to smuggle supplies and ammunition to those hostile Indians, while all the time another division of the government is trying to stop their raiding. It's the left hand working against the right."

"Why doesn't somebody put a stop to it?" Fannie wondered.

"I'd welcome the chance," he told her grimly. "Wouldn't I just welcome the chance!"

Fannie felt a small chill, somewhere in the region of her heart. Almost he sounded as if he were ready to rush out to western Kansas in order to help subdue the Indians. Not until Edmund was mustered out of the army in September 1865, could Fannie relax.

5

It was a delightful experience, settling down in the house in Lawrence, becoming a family once more.

Edmund looked fondly at Lillie, now past sixteen.

"We have a young lady on our hands," he said. "You must start taking music lessons, daughter. I'll see that you have a piano."

And to the boys, "You are growing fast."

He swung Eddie up to his shoulder, and she laid her cheek against his. "Papa's fine girl," he said.

When the children had gone off on their various activities,

he looked at Fannie keenly.

"You hadn't told me—"

"Told you what?" she asked demurely.

"That you are going to have another baby."

"My goodness," she said, raising her eyebrows, "you surely can't be all that surprised!"

Looking at her obliquely, he smiled. "No," he said softly. "Now that I think of it, I'm really not surprised."

He was silent a moment, and then went on. "I guess that means I certainly *have* to get to work. Five children and a wife to look after."

"Want to trade us off?" she asked impudently.

"You're twinkling again," he told her. "It's been a long time since I've seen that."

"It's been a long time since I felt like it—"

"Luckily, only today I closed the deal with John Speer. We've just about finished making the arrangements to go partners on the *Tribune*, here in Lawrence. With his boys gone—"

Poor Mr. Speer. Two sons killed in Quantrill's raid. Two fine, promising young lads. She could understand how he felt. Of course, there were those who would tell her that the death of one small, frail child was nothing beside Mr. Speer's loss. But when did a mother's heart ever measure love by the size and strength of a child?

The paper was started as Edmund planned. He was proud of it, often taking Arthur and Pitt to the office with him, telling them that they could not learn too early about the newspaper business.

This they enjoyed thoroughly. But, boylike, they were probably more pleased with the drugstore newly opened by young George Leis, who gave them jawbreakers occasionally.

"He's a hero, Mr. Leis is," Pitt reported.

"Because he gives you jawbreakers?" Fannie smiled.

"No—he's been a soldier and he fought against Price and he got a saber that used to belong to Colonel Sumner and he was a surgeon in the army . . ." The list continued. It was a record which Edmund confirmed when he came home.

Edmund found a piano for Lillie, a great dark rosewood grand which easily dominated the living room. She started lessons at once, picking out familiar tunes. Evenings the family often gathered around the piano to sing to her accompaniment.

"You have a gift for music, Lillie," Edmund told her proudly.

"Thank you," Lillie said, pleased as always at any praise from her father.

Everything seemed to be working out well for the Ross family now. The new baby, a boy whom they named Kay, was a joy to the entire family. Fannie was glad this baby was a boy. And that he would have his father with him as he grew up.

With Edmund home, she liked the town even better than she had before. Lawrence was a pretty town, lying in the valley of the Kaw, beneath Mt. Oread. She could look at the river and recall the other bodies of water which she had lived close to without ever a wish to go back.

But in the nation's capital, things were not going well at all. From the depths of her own content, Fannie felt sorry for President Johnson, who had taken over the office after Lincoln's death. Certainly the Radicals were giving the poor man a great lot of trouble because he was trying to carry out Lincoln's policy of leniency and forgiveness toward the conquered South. A bitter battle seemed to be shaping up. For once, Fannie felt proud of Lane and his stand. He had announced to the Senate, "So far as I am concerned, I propose today and hereafter to take my position alongside the President."

And then, close upon the heels of this announcement, he introduced a resolution for the recognition of the new state government of Arkansas.

This the people in Kansas refused to countenance. Memories of Cane Hill and Pea Ridge, those two bloody battlegrounds in the state, were yet fresh in their minds; nor had they forgotten all the men who had been sheltered there, men who had made life so miserable for them—Sterling Price and the Indian, Stand Watie, Jo Shelby and Quantrill. Oh, the list was long. All over Kansas meetings were now held, denouncing Lane's stand. Edmund attended one at Lawrence and himself presented a set of resolutions condemning the senator. Fannie was a little surprised; Edmund was not given to vindictiveness.

"I suspect Lane of not wanting to help the President so much as wanting to cover up his own tracks," Edmund explained.

"Of course," Fannie mused, "I'm inclined to suspect anybody and anything Lane advocates."

"They say a cancelled check has been found proving Lane got twenty thousand dollars in some sort of a crooked deal," Edmund went on. "He's been wanting Johnson to give him a foreign mission, so he can get out before the storm breaks."

"No wonder he's backing the President," Fannie agreed.

"And by the way, Lane's sent word he's coming home this week," Edmund told her. "I suspect he isn't going to find things here much to his liking."

Nor did he. When Lane arrived he found a reception very different from the kind he had been accustomed to in former times. No matter how eloquently he spoke now, all he got was cold, unfriendly stares. Old acquaintances passed him on the street without recognizing him. Political conventions everywhere in Kansas were following Lawrence's lead and denouncing him. It seemed strange that a man so ruthless in pursuing his own ends should have taken public censure as hard as he did. Finally, on a hot July day, Lane walked into a Kansas cornfield, put a pistol to his head, and pulled the trigger.

For eleven days Lane lingered, making that last tenacious fight which he had always put up, whatever the odds. Friend and enemy alike seemed to talk of nothing else during this time, for, whatever you might say about the man, he had never been inconspicuous. Colorful and lusty, evasive and eloquent—his history was interlinked with that of Kansas. He finally died, without having regained consciousness.

Of course, all the time Lane lay on his deathbed, there had

been much discussion of his successor, who would have to be appointed by the governor to fill out his unexpired term.

"Who do you think it will be, Edmund?" Fannie asked.

"There are several men right here in Lawrence who would be good." He named them, men of integrity and ability. "Governor Crawford has asked me to come down and confer with him in the matter. I'm going tomorrow."

The next day, Edmund went to Topeka. Fannie busied herself about the house, but all the time she was wondering which, if any, of Edmund's candidates would be selected. She was proud to think that Edmund would be consulted in a matter as important as this.

It was late when he came home. The children—even Lillie, who thought herself, at sixteen, to be rather too old for early retiring—had gone to bed. Fannie sat with some mending in her hands. She was so intent on her handiword that he had come into the house before she heard him.

Seeing him in the room with her, she looked up quickly. It seemed to her that his face wore a most peculiar expression. Not disappointment, exactly . . . and yet not quite elation.

"Oh, so there you are," she said needlessly. "Well, how did the day go? Did Governor Crawford appoint your candidate?"

"No—"

"Oh, Edmund. He should have listened to you—"

Surely Crawford knew that Edmund was level-headed and honest and, in contrast to many others, not self-seeking. If he said a man was a desirable candidate, it would be foolish of Governor Crawford to ignore that suggestion.

"Who was his choice?" Fannie asked.

That strange look was still on his face.

"A no-account fellow named Edmund G. Ross," he told her, his eyes twinkling.

She was on her feet in an instant. Like a girl she ran to him, throwing her arms around his neck. She kissed him, several times. "Oh, Edmund," she cried. "I am so proud—so very proud."

His arms tightened around her. "You are, are you?" he said, almost in a whisper.

He put his hands on her shoulders, pushed her back from him so that he might look at her better. His eyes, his mouth, his whole face smiled at her.

"Proud of me," he teased her, "or proud of being Mrs. Senator Ross?"

They talked things over, more quietly, now that the first excitement had died down.

"I presented my names," Edmund told her, "and when I had finished, he said that was all very fine, but I was the one he wanted."

"A man of great and good judgment," Fannie pronounced solemnly.

"He said, and these were his very words, 'We need a man with backbone in the Senate. I saw what you did at Prairie Grove, and I want *you* for senator.' When he put it that way, I couldn't refuse."

Strange how things turned out. Edmund was going to be a senator because he had proved himself a brave soldier.

"When do you leave?" she asked.

"Immediately."

Her bright spirits suddenly declined. Another parting; another time of separation.

"Actually, the appointment is for only about six months, until the Kansas Legislature meets in January. They may, or may not, elect me. So, there doesn't seem much point in pulling up the family and moving to Washington."

And, she wanted to add, there wasn't enough money. They had just bought this Lawrence place, and Edmund had only started the newspaper. But all she said was, "Of course not—you go on, and we'll stay here until we see how things are going to work out."

That settled, they turned to another subject.

"Do you remember the Reams—the ones you had for dinner the day we decided to buy the farm?"

Of course she did. How could she forget the little girl with her clever fingers who had shaped the life-like head of Lillie out of a bit of clay?

"To be sure I do," she said.

"I heard today that they're now living in Washington, and run a boardinghouse. And it seems that the girl—the one who liked to model clay—"

"Vinnie," Fannie supplied.

"It seems that Vinnie modeled a bust of Lincoln, before his death, and it's so good they are considering giving her a commission to do a statue of him."

"I'm not a bit surprised," Fannie told him. Nor was she. "Anyway, Governor Crawford suggested that I write and ask them if I might stay in their boardinghouse. Seemed a good idea to me."

"Yes, indeed," Fannie assured him. She liked the thought of Edmund's being among friends in Washington.

"You have your chance now," she said, smiling at him.

"My chance?" he asked uncertainly.

"To put a stop to this Indian situation," she reminded him. "Remember—you said you'd welcome it!"

"Oh, that. Of course I'll do what I can. But I also want to see that we get our railroad. We made the plan in '60, with our Topeka Convention. Now, with the war over, we need to push the plans through."

He and Colonel Holliday had said at the time of the convention that, in order to get the railroads there must be a senator from Kansas who would press the matter upon Congress. Well, they had him now.

"You'll bring us the railroad," she promised. "I can almost hear the engines whistling right down Topeka's Kansas Avenue."

Before he left them, Edmund and Fannie acted as if this was only a temporary thing. Their conversation, carried on in the children's presence, was focused on subjects of common interest and pride. It was a great honor to be a senator and Washington wasn't really so awfully far; the children were big enough to be of help and comfort; wasn't it fine that Lillie was one of the forty students who had presented themselves for admission to the recently opened University of Kansas; Christmas would be here before anyone had time to turn around, and then Papa would be home again.

But when he was gone and night had come, Fannie went to their room and closed the door. No need for pretense now.

Kay slept in the crib which had been used for his brothers and sisters in years gone by. Edmund's old clothes hung forlornly in the wardrobe, as if they, too, felt forsaken.

Edmund had been home not quite a year. And now he had gone again. Three years away, and then home ten months before he was off once more. Fannie told herself she should be proud to have her husband a senator. But a little less honor and a little more of his presence at home would suit her better. She tried to take hope from the thought that he might not be elected by the Legislature for a full term. But Edmund would do a good job, and he would be reappointed.

She might as well get ready to face another period of time when Edmund would be gone more than he was at home. She might as well prepare herself to pick up once more a pattern with which time had already made her familiar.

PART THREE

THE SENATOR FROM KANSAS

IX

Washington

1866–1867

Edmund's first official act as senator had nothing to do with either Indians or railroads, but was something a great deal more to Fannie's liking. He signed a recommendation that Vinnie Ream be given the contract for a statue of Lincoln to be placed in the rotunda of the Capitol.

"It was a joint resolution of the Senate and the House," Edmund wrote Fannie, "signed by President Johnson, members of the Cabinet and members of the Senate and the House, as well as various other prominent people."

Certainly an impressive list of backers, Fannie thought.

"The resolution also provides her with a small studio in the basement of the Capitol, where she may work without interruption." And then he added a note which he knew would give Fannie a sense of pride and satisfaction. "I must tell you that I signed first on the list of Senators."

And who had better right to head the list than Edmund—Edmund, who had known Vinnie Ream longer than had any of those others!

"The Reams send you many good wishes, and urge you to visit them here in Washington. If I am reappointed, you most certainly must plan to do that. You will remember the oldest daughter, Mary. She is married to Perry Fuller and they, too, live here in Washington!"

Then, Edmund plunged immediately into the Indian problem. "The Indian question touches the lives of hundreds of people in western Kansas," he declared in a speech before the Senate. "For years we have urged that the Indian Bureau be taken out of the hands of the Department of the Interior and given to the War Department."

For months Governor Crawford had been appealing vainly to the government at Washington for the protection of settlers in western Kansas. For some reason Fannie could not understand, Pomeroy, the other senator from Kansas, did not back up the request of his governor. If Edmund threw himself now into an all-out attempt to promote the measures Governor Crawford urged, he would probably incur the enmity of the powerful Pomeroy forces, which could easily cost him his election when the Kansas Legislature assembled to vote on the matter in January.

Dear Edmund—he could not settle down to being an inactive member of the Senate and doing only what was expedient. He must have a cause.

"Moreover," he had gone on in his speech, "Colonel Leavenworth ought to be removed—he is unfit for the job as agent for the Comanches and Kiowas. We need to get those trouble-making Indian tribes into reservations outside the state. The army should accept the services of volunteers from western states to put down Indian uprisings. As it is, settlers have to sit still and do nothing to protect themselves while hundreds of people are killed each year and property is destroyed. These sufferers from Indian depredations should be given indemnity."

It was quite a program which he outlined for the Senate. Fannie wouldn't be a bit surprised if the Kansas Legislature decided against him. But the Legislature took no such attitude. Edmund Ross was elected for a four-year term when it met in January, a move opposed by John Speer, who was himself a Pomeroy man. Edmund, at home during a Senate recess, made but one response to the news: "Now perhaps I can get some action in Washington."

"Indian or railroad?" she asked, remembering his earlier enthusiasm.

"Both. But I think the Indian situation should be undertaken first. At least, no one is dying for lack of a railroad."

Edmund went back to Washington. Fannie read with great care all the newspapers she could lay hands upon. Knowledge of the problems he faced brought him closer to her. She smiled wryly to herself upon occasion, thinking that, with the exception of Mrs. Carter, she was probably the best informed woman in Lawrence. Once or twice she thought of calling on the woman who had been of help and strength on the day of Quantrill's raid on Lawrence, but always she restrained herself. All Lawrence held Mrs. Carter in great respect and even a certain awe.

Through Edmund's letters as well as the papers Fannie knew he did not have complete backing on the measures he advocated concerning the Indian situation; however, he was not entirely without success. Congress created a Peace Commission authorized to pacify the Indians by making treaties and furnishing them with more provisions, arms and ammunition.

Edmund did not hesitate to let his opinions of this move be known.

"In this way," he told the Senate, "you may bring about a temporary truce. But it will be only a matter of time before there will be fresh outbursts. People know this—that's why so few settlers are going out to western Kansas. Those who have gone are leaving."

In this prophecy, he was correct. The marauding continued. In an attempt to correct the situation, the Peace Commission finally decided to invite the wild tribes to meet in council at Medicine Lodge in Kansas.

"Governor Crawford and I are to accompany the group," Edmund wrote Fannie. "You must not be concerned—we will be escorted by a strong military guard."

Yet the very nature of the expedition caused concern to the entire nation. It had been formed because matters looked very grave. In Montana the Flatheads and other tribes were stealing stock, plundering settlements, running off with horses, burning crops, threatening to kill or drive away settlers. It was no pleasant little Sunday-school picnic toward which the Peace Commission was headed. Congress knew this. Why else had they detailed a detachment of soldiers to guard the members of the Commission?

Important papers from all over the country were sending their top reporters to cover the story.

The Lawrence papers naturally carried full accounts of the conference. Reading them, Fannie felt almost as if she were at Edmund's side.

The Council was scheduled to last for five days. Among the first tribes to arrive were the Dog Soldiers of the Cheyennes, with their chiefs, White Horse, Little Bear and Gray-Head. Once there, they asked for an interview, saying they were anxious for peace. Then the Penettchetts and Comanches, under Silver Broach, and the Neconees from Texas, three hundred miles away came, led by Chief Horseback. In all, five thousand Indians were on the scene, before the start of the conference.

"All those Indians—" Arthur and Pitt were round-eyed at the thought. "Why didn't Papa take *us*?"

Take them, indeed! Didn't they, or anyone else, see what could come of this meeting? Several thousand Indians, and more coming in every day, with only a small detachment of soldiers to guard the members of the Commission. She remembered poor Sergeant Custard and the men from the Eleventh Kansas, Edmund's old group, bound to their wagons and burned to death by the Indians, and wished again that the government would see fit to put Edmund's own serious evaluation on the situation.

Government authorities, so the papers said, had already issued a week's rations to the Indians present. Then the Cheyennes drifted in, many of them war parties. By this time, ten thousand Indians were on the scene.

The Commission itself, Fannie was relieved to read, traveled with a great deal of circumspection. Certainly they seemed aware of the seriousness of the situation. Scouts rode ahead and rear guards followed, watching warily any place that might offer a possible ambush. When the members of the Commission finally reached their destination, they found twenty thousand Indians waiting for them: Kiowa, Apache, Comanche, Cheyenne, Arapaho.

The Indians presented a truly awesome sight. Wearing the immense warbonnets with lengths of feathers falling to their waists, their faces daubed with war paint, they wheeled about on their horses, also bedecked in the trappings of war, brandishing spears as they rode. The Lawrence *Daily Tribune*, reporting this, took occasion to recall all the dark deeds Indians had perpetrated against the whites. Lillie, reading these accounts, burst into quick tears.

"Oh, Mama—I'm so worried about Papa—"

"There, there," Fannie consoled her. "The soldiers are with him. He's being taken care of. Don't excite the children—"

She wanted nothing more than to indulge in her own fears for his safety, but she must push them aside in order to comfort Lillie. It seemed that she was forever seeing Edmund take great risks and, at the same time, forever prevented from giving way to her fears for him.

The tension mounted. Santanta, that wily and influential Kiowa, spoke at great length to the Commission, his words giving no real promise a peace could be achieved. And then, just when concern was at its peak, a treaty was signed. The St. Louis papers were almost lyrical in their account of this. "The treaty signed at Medicine Lodge, Kansas," they declared, "between the five Plains Indian tribes and the Federal Government, ended a bloody war that has been in progress between the Indians and the white race for three years, one which threatened to go on indefinitely. This treaty has made possible the settlement of all western Kansas, Colorado, Dakota, New Mexico and Arizona."

Edmund, while most certainly relieved, was more practical in his evaluation of the treaty. His account was published in the Lawrence *Journal.*

"It was decided that they, not we, should surrender territory. As a result, we have gained the country between the Arkansas and the Platte Rivers. But we must be alert. The Indians may not keep the treaty. I can only hope that the approaching session of Congress will develop some settled Indian policy."

And to Fannie he wrote that the whole business was a most interesting experience. He met some very fine people. Among them there was a young man, born in Wales, who came out to cover the Conference for the *Missouri Democrat* of St. Louis. He said he had served in both the Confederate and the Union armies during the Civil War, and later reported on naval battles. His name was Henry M. Stanley.

Wasn't that like Edmund—to gloss over the danger and talk only of the interest in the situation?

"And now that I am back in Washington," he went on, "you must come for a visit. I am sending a railroad pass and some money. Take the train at St. Joseph. The Reams are most anxious to have you here, and you may be sure how I feel about it."

2

Fannie looked eagerly out of the window as the train pulled into Washington. Even now, in early February, with the trees and shrubs stripped bare of leaves, she thought that this must be the most beautiful city in the world. The lights of the town were reflected in the Potomac. The dome of the Capitol rose, proud and majestic, into the darkness of the night. Too bad the children couldn't see it.

Lillie had said, when the discussion of the visit to Washington began, "Now, Mama, you must go by yourself and have a good and restful time. I will stay here and look after the others."

"But Lillie—"

"I am eighteen years old, Mama. Surely I can take care of the house and the children while you are away."

"Well—" Fannie hedged. The prospect of a visit with Edmund was delightful. Of course she loved the children, and dearly, too, but it had been such a long time since she and Edmund had really had a chance to be alone. "Kay is rather small," she reminded Lillie.

"He's almost two years old, Mama. And you must not forget that I have helped care for him ever since he was born. Besides, you deserve a vacation. Another time we will all go with you. But now you must have this holiday alone."

"If only Ma were here," Fannie worried, "she could come stay with you."

How many times Fannie had thought that since her mother moved back to Sandusky, so that, as she said, she could "be with the friends I used to know." Fannie felt she knew a deeper reason—when the end came in Sandusky, there would be no question about placing her beside Pa and the two little girls who had died so long ago.

"I really want to do it, Mama," Lillie continued. "It will be good experience for me."

"Oh, yes, it will," Arthur said, with big-brother candor. "And you just might need that experience in looking after a house. With George Leis hanging around the way he is—"

"Oh, Arthur," Lillie protested. But she looked not at all displeased.

In the end, Fannie had agreed. But all during the trip, she had not ceased to feel strange without the children around her. She hoped the feeling would wear off, once Edmund was with her. She hoped, too, that she looked all right; she would not want to embarrass him. Kansas was, after all, a long way from Washington. The latest styles were a little slow in coming West, and when they arrived it was not always easy to follow them with the little bit of money she felt justified in spending. Even with a pass, this trip was costing more than she had anticipated. Her traveling dress had given no real difficulty, since she and Lillie had fashioned it out of an old one Fannie had made long ago. The material was good, and Fannie had always been handy with the needle. And resting inside her carpetbag was a real luxury—a new gray silk dress which the children had insisted upon.

She saw Edmund, even before the train stopped, standing on the platform, looking anxious and eager. She wanted to grab her bag, rush down the aisle and be ready to jump off, into his arms. But she sat still—what an undignified thought for the mother of six—no, five—to have! (Wasn't it strange that always, without thinking, her first count included Flint?) Fannie waited properly enough, and then made her way down the steps of the train. As Edmund saw her and came toward her, his gait was certainly not a slow one. He put his arms around her and kissed her soundly.

"It's good to have you here," he told her. "You look fine."

"I feel fine—"

"And the children?"

"All well—they sent their love—" And then, wistfully, "I wish they could have come."

"Another time—now there was no extra room at the Reams'."

The Ream house, on B Street, was certainly not fashionable. A typical boardinghouse, Fannie thought. But the welcome the Ream family gave her was very warm.

"Oh, do come in, Mrs. Ross," Mrs. Ream urged, drawing Fannie into the living room. A bright fire burned in the grate. Shabby but comfortable furniture was scattered around the room. "We are so glad to see you. It's been such a long time—"

Mrs. Ream looked much the same as she had in Kansas, almost ten years ago, and Mr. Ream, if changed at all, appeared even thinner and frailer. Fannie felt she would have known Vinnie anywhere, for she was much as she had been as a child. Her dark eyes glowed and her hair, long and luxuriant, fell in curls around her face, giving her a childlike appearance. She still had that warmth and charm which had been hers long ago, a vital quality in every gesture she made, every word she said.

"Oh, how do you do, dear Mrs. Ross?" Vinnie said, coming to Fannie to kiss her. "You must be tired from your long trip."

Mrs. Ream was more practical. She sent Vinnie scurrying to the kitchen for "something for Mrs. Ross to eat—she must be starved."

Presently they were all seated around the fireplace, while Fannie ate the good food Vinnie had brought in on a tray and sipped her tea. The fire snapped in the grate; the sound of voices rose and fell. Across the room Edmund smiled at her. Seldom had Fannie felt more relaxed and content.

"How is your little girl, Lillie?" Vinnie asked. "I remember her."

"She's not little now," Fannie said, laughing. "She's eighteen. She remembers you, too, and the little clay model you did of her. Edmund has told me about your statue of Lincoln. I am very proud, but not surprised. Even when you were small, back in Kansas, you showed talent. It was most fortunate that you had the opportunity to study President Lincoln as he was in his last days."

"Indeed it was," Vinnie said. "A number of people are wondering now why he agreed to let me do it. They say it seems so strange that he would allow a young, untrained girl, only recently come from Kansas, to sit in his office and sketch him."

Mrs. Ream beamed lovingly at her daughter and Mr. Ream reached out to pat her hand.

"Senator Trumbull begged the chance for me," Vinnie explained. "Finally President Lincoln agreed that I might come to his study every day for half an hour. I was to make no noise, and under no circumstances was I to bother him. I was so scared—my goodness, I was almost afraid to breathe when I first started."

She laughed like a child.

"I went every day, though, scared or not, and sat in a corner, watching him, as still as I could be. I studied his face, and I made sketches of him. He seemed to have forgotten all about me—I doubt if he knew I was there. That was why I could catch him the way he really was. I'll never forget how sad he looked—as if the weight of the world were on his shoulders."

"And so it was," Edmund told her. "You got him at a time when he could well be sad. Things were going badly for the Union that spring."

"Willie had died, too," Vinnie added. "Once I saw President Lincoln standing at the window, looking out at the spot where Willie used to play. Tears were streaming down his face—it almost broke my heart to watch him."

"I suspect it was your feeling for him that made it possible for you to do so well," Fannie said.

"I did those sketches with my heart as well as my fingers. I was only seventeen, and I was easily moved."

"That was why Congress gave you the contract rather than to one of the well-known sculptors who had also applied," Edmund said. "We wanted the statue of Lincoln to show the same deep feeling."

"Now," Vinnie said, "if only I can give the plaster model that same quality. And if the marble can then be cut as I wish—"

They went on to talk of other things. Edmund was especially pleased to report that Henry M. Stanley, the young reporter who had made such an impression on him at Medicine Lodge was now a foreign correspondent for the New York *Herald*, a direct result of his excellent work in reporting the Peace Commission for the *Missouri Democrat.*

"A bright young man," Edmund said. "He's in Ethiopia now. We're sure to hear more about him."

Presently Mary, the Reams' oldest daughter, and her husband, Perry Fuller, dropped in, and the talk went back to Kansas and how things were there. The Fullers had a house in Washington, and Edmund seemed to be perfectly at home with them.

"Mrs. Ross," Vinnie said, "I'm going to take you to a party day after tomorrow. Mrs. Sprague is having one of her 'At Homes,' and I asked if I might bring you. She said to be sure—she was anxious to meet you."

Fannie looked inquiringly at Edmund.

"By all means go," he told her. "Vinnie's the darling of Washington society now. Since she got the contract to do the statue, people can't seem to invite her to enough affairs."

"Thank you, Vinnie," Fannie said, grateful for the gray dress.

"I sometimes think it will wear her out," Mrs. Ream said. But she was obviously proud at the attention being heaped upon her daughter.

"Just so long as they don't keep me from my work, I don't

mind," Vinnie said. "But they know that once I get into that little studio in the basement of the Capitol, I'm not to be bothered."

"Mrs. Sprague . . ." Edmund mused. "Well, you will be getting into society, Fannie."

It was a statement with which Fannie could agree. Everyone knew about Kate Chase Sprague, wife of the Senator from Rhode Island, daughter of Salmon P. Chase, Chief Justice of the United States. For years she had been trying to ger her father nominated for the Presidency.

"Still running society with one hand and playing politics with the other," Perry Fuller laughed.

"Well," Mary said gently, "she's smart enough and—now that she's married to Sprague—rich enough to do both."

"And don't forget," Mrs. Ream put in, "charming and beautiful enough to make it easy for her to get her way."

"Kate Sprague and her father both are supposed to be solidly back of the President," Mr. Ream said. "They say Kate is one of the few people Mrs. Johnson will receive, and Johnson's two daughters go to the Spragues' often."

The talk continued to flow around Fannie. Parts of it she understood well enough, for even the Lawrence papers had reported these things. There were times, though, when she understood only dimly what was being discussed. She knew, of course, that Johnson was a Southern Democrat, but intensely Union in his sympathies; that he had the same desire Lincoln had possessed —to have the Southern states take their places in the Union with as little delay as possible; that he had been confronted by a bitterly partisan Congress determined not to permit such leniency toward the subdued South. She knew, too, that when Stanton (who was completely familiar with Lincoln's plan since he had himself helped to draw it up) refused to help President Johnson implement the plan for Reconstruction, the President asked him to resign. When he refused, Johnson had suspended him, appointing General Grant as Secretary of War. Grant lasted only until the Senate convened, when the members refused to recognize his right to serve and reinstated Stanton.

"It's Mr. Lincoln's plan," Vinnie said, her voice troubled. "I don't see why it can't go through."

"Johnson doesn't have the force of character Lincoln had," Perry Fuller said. "Nor does he have the following. All along the Radicals have resented Lincoln's idea for Reconstruction. They want the South treated like a conquered province."

"Johnson's a good enough man," Edmund remarked thoughtfully. "He's honest and genial, and he's made a lifelong study of the Constitution. But he's also pugnacious and self-willed and, to a degree, nonprogressive. And now he has Stanton fighting him, and everyone knows he's one of the most powerful men in Washington."

"Yes, Johnson has a formidable crowd lined up against him," Perry Fuller admitted. "Stanton and Stevens, and Ben Wade—by the way, if the President is impeached, Ben Wade as president pro tempore of the Senate would be the one to take his place."

"Oh, they *can't*—" Fannie cried, aghast at the very idea of impeaching a President.

"They certainly could," Mr. Ream said. "There are fifty-four Senators, not including those from Southern states not as yet recognized. The twelve Democrat votes would certainly be cast against impeachment, if for no other reason than to defy the Radicals. But if fewer than six of the forty-two Republicans vote against it, the President can be impeached."

He looked at Edmund speculatively as he spoke.

"The town is full of people who feel sure the necessary two-thirds majority—thirty-six Senators—will vote for impeachment," he went on. "The Willard Hotel is crowded with office-seekers who think they'll get a job if a new President comes into office. Dozens, in fact, for every vacancy. Some of them with good claims, too—former soldiers, who are without work. Times are hard now, and jobs are scarce. They feel they deserve something from the government."

Fannie could understand that. It was a hard thing to come back from the army, after four years of fighting, and find no work or any promise of it. The country owed something to these men who had given much to preserve it.

"They say the top army man of them all has been promised a good rich plum if Wade goes in," Fuller said knowingly. "Grant himself. Oh, there are all sorts of promises, and all sorts of stories, going the rounds. How do you feel in the matter, Edmund?"

The direct question. Edmund hesitated, and Fannie could see that his thoughts went deep. Finally he answered.

"I don't yet know," he said honestly. "After all, I am new to this thing."

3

Fannie, wearing the new gray silk dress, stood with Vinnie at the door of Kate Chase Sprague's imposing residence on E Street. From inside the house she could hear the muted hum of many well-bred voices. A lot of people she had never seen before would be there, most of them famous or well-known. Often, when meeting people, she forgot names or did not catch them in the first place. She hoped Vinnie would allow her to slip off into a quiet corner and watch.

If only Edmund had come, too. Vinnie had urged him to accompany them, saying that other men would be there, some whom it might be advantageous to meet. *Everybody* went to Mrs. Sprague's parties. But he had thanked her kindly and refused, saying he had many letters to write. And Fannie, standing now at the door, was thinking she should have stayed with him.

The butler let them in. Vinnie nodded brightly to him, and he bowed low. She was certainly not a stranger to this house. A memory came unbidden to Fannie—little Vinnie Ream, driving the family cow to Shawnee "because she wanted to." And now, she moved with ease and grace in one of the most fashionable drawing rooms of the nation.

Vinnie led her toward a woman who was obviously the hostess, Kate Chase Sprague. Fannie thought she had never seen a woman so imposingly beautiful. Diamonds flashed from Kate's hands, neck, wrists and hair. No wonder they called her "Proud Kate."

"Ah, Vinnie," she said, extending her hand, "how good to see you. And this must be Mrs. Ross, of whom you told me—"

She smiled, and Fannie felt the full force of her personality. It held little warmth; but, like her diamonds, it glittered for all who saw her. Fannie returned the greeting, thanking her for the invitation, feeling not a little surprised that with all Kate Sprague must have on her mind she would still remember the name of a woman from Kansas whose husband had only recently become a Senator.

Fannie and Vinnie moved away to make room for other guests who seemed also to be well known to the hostess. This ability to remember people must have been something Kate had developed down the years—a quality which could certainly be useful in furthering the ambition people said she had for her father. Fannie wondered how Kate Sprague and Jessie Frémont got along—one wanting the office for her father, the other for her husband. Of the two ambitions, Jessie Frémont's seemed the more commendable, especially since it was said that Kate could scarcely endure her husband, having married him only for his money.

Fannie looked around the impressive room, seeking some quiet corner where she might sit down and watch the show. Presently she spotted a small love seat, partly hidden by tall ferns. A few chairs were drawn up close to it—she would not be stranded and alone if she sat there. Vinnie would feel free to leave her.

"I'm going over there to sit down," she told Vinnie. "You must not feel responsible for me—just go on and have a good time and I'll enjoy watching people."

"I'll go with you."

Together they made their way to the seat Fannie had indicated. Once there, she sat down while Vinnie stood beside her, pointing out people she might enjoy knowing about, waving gaily to many of them as she did so. The short, stocky man fumbling around the punchbowl was General Grant; the pleasant, mannerly woman was Martha Johnson Patterson, the President's daughter and housekeeper. (Poor Mrs. Johnson lay bedridden in the White House and never got out. They did say, however, that Kate went to see her as cozy and easy as neighbors visiting over the back fence.) The extremely tall, imposing man with the huge head and the massive brow, the thick lips and blue-gray eyes was Chief Justice Chase himself. Sprague was nowhere to be seen; Justice Chase was acting as host at his daughter's party.

"Who's that?" Fannie asked, her attention suddenly attacted by a man whose features reminded her of Edmund, except that he was older and looked sick and unhappy.

"Oh," Vinnie said, "that's Mr. Dickens."

"You mean—" Fannie hesitated, "*Charles* Dickens?"

No wonder he looked familiar. She was back in Sandusky, with her mother pointing out the great man to her. How excited she had then been at seeing a real-life author, one who wrote the books the family read aloud evenings after supper.

"The very one," Vinnie assured her. "He's giving a series of readings here at Carroll House, and he doesn't like it a bit. He says the lighting is poor and the ventilation worse and the dogs bark outside the window and people cough and drown out his words. Oh, he has no love for the town or the people in it."

"He didn't like Sandusky, either," Fannie smiled.

"He probably doesn't like it anywhere," Vinnie said. "Oh, look, there's Mrs. Howe—you know, Julia Ward Howe."

She indicated a woman with a wealth of curls falling around her face. The dapper young man talking with her was Phil Sheridan, Vinnie added. The quietly dressed woman standing nearby, looking cultured and kindly, was Mrs. Ben Wade. Who knew what dreams of the white house filled her own mind as she had greeted her hostess?

One by one Vinnie pointed them out—the statesmen, the jurists, the artists, the writers, the bankers, the foreign diplomats and all the other names familiar even in the smallest hamlet of the land, moving about in this setting of flowers and music and impressively dressed women and men.

"Look," Vinnie said, "Mrs. Sprague is greeting the French Ambassador and his wife, and you may be sure she's speaking perfect French to them. No wonder everyone admires her."

She turned to Fannie. "Do you mind?" she asked. "Mrs. Sprague is motioning for me to come to her."

"Now, Vinnie," Fannie said, "I've already told you that you mustn't feel you have to stay here at my side! Go on and have a good time."

The girl moved off and Fannie sat still, listening. She caught names and bits of sentences. Fanny Kemble was giving readings from *Othello*, and Joe Jefferson was delighting everyone with his performance in *Rip Van Winkle*. One woman said the best attraction in town was Ole Bull, the Norwegian violinist. Another declared nothing was so truly amazing as Mrs. Daniels, the spiritualist appearing in Harmonial Hall . . . "Really, it's unbelievable, the things she tells people. She has all sorts of messages for the President, from Lincoln himself . . ."

Someone shushed her quickly. Fannie was sorry; she very much wanted to hear the woman repeating the message with a straight face.

"May I sit next to you?" a voice asked at her elbow.

"Of course." Fannie turned to look at the inquirer. She saw a small, gray-haired woman, attractive and alert. There was something vaguely familiar about her face.

"I'm—" the woman began, and at the same moment there was a stir of excitement in the room. A tall, elegant man was making his way toward Mrs. Sprague, extending a long, delicate, and curiously feminine hand, smiling at her as he came. Either the general confusion drowned out the woman's self-introduction or she was so impressed with the newcomer she forgot to complete her sentence. "It's Edwin Stanton," she said, "the Secretary of War and the most mysterious man in Washington."

"Oh," Fannie said. So that was the man all the trouble was about, the one who could defy a President and emerge unscathed.

"John says there's no telling how it's all going to turn out," Fannie's companion went on. "The town's a powder keg right now. By the way, I don't believe I caught your name—"

"I'm Mrs. Edmund Ross," Fannie told her, wanting to say that she, too, had failed to hear the other woman's name. But before she could do so much as begin, her companion interrupted brightly.

"Your husband is the new senator from Kansas. I've heard my husband speak of him. He thinks Mr. Ross has some very sensible ideas—about the Indian situation, for example. John certainly knows Indians and their ways, and he agrees with your husband."

"I am glad he thinks so," Fannie said. "Edmund also is working hard for railroads in Kansas."

"John has mentioned that, too. He is favorably impressed, since he has long been interested in railroads and their routes. I laughed and told John that no wonder he approved of Mr. Ross—the two of them, actually, are much alike."

The statement made Fannie all the more anxious to know her companion's name, but a natural shyness, plus the fact that she had let the matter go so far as to make her sound foolish if she now inquired, held her back. Besides, there was something about the woman which made it difficult, for all her magnetism of manner, to admit one's shortcoming in her presence.

She was bright and vivacious, but at the same time, her face held a certain hint of sadness, of hopes often deferred. She looked as if she might be no stranger to work, nor even to hardship. She was dressed well and tastefully, although actually without any real pretense to style. But in the way she spoke and gestured there was a certain quality about her which put her above any need for following styles.

"I see Mrs. Howe," the woman said. "I must go speak to her. Will you excuse me? It has been delightful talking with you."

She made her way across the room, nodding and speaking to everyone as she went. Certainly, Fannie thought, I am the only person here who does not know her. Mrs. Howe greeted her warmly, and Fannie, watching, half-expected the older woman to break into the first bars of "Battle Hymn of the Republic." She was smiling at her own fancy when Vinnie came back to her.

"Well," the girl said, "you've been making out fine. I saw you entertaining one of the most popular persons here—"

"Vinnie," Fannie began, both embarrassed and a little unhappy at the admission she must make, "who *was* that woman? If she told me her name, I didn't catch it."

"My gracious, Mrs. Ross—you *are* a little girl from the country if you didn't recognize her—"

"I most certainly didn't," Fannie said, exasperation creeping into her voice, both at herself and at Vinnie. If the woman had been that important, why hadn't Vinnie come over?

"That," Vinnie told her solemnly, "was Mrs. John Frémont—Jessie Benton Frémont."

4

Was she, Fannie Ross wondered as she packed her bag in Edmund's room the last night of her visit, forever to be torn between two loyalties—to her husband, and to her children? She must leave Edmund now and go back to Lawrence. All the time she had been here she had felt, in the back of her mind, concern for the children. Especially for Kay, who was so young to be left without his mother. Of course, Lillie could look after him quite well. But still . . . And Eddie was at an age when she, too, needed her mother.

And now that she was going back to the children, her mind was already turning toward Edmund and the loneliness he would feel when she was gone. She supposed that, under the circumstances, there was no perfect solution to their problem. They must simply do the best they could, and try to forget the deprivations. If only there was enough money to do as so many other senators did—bring their families with them to Washington. She pushed the thought from her, since even to entertain it was being unfair to Edmund. He had not sought this office he held; it had come to him in such a way that he could not refuse.

Through the window she could see the lights of Washington reflected in the Potomac, just as she had seen them on the evening of her arrival. Only it was different then—she was coming to an unknown place with all her visit ahead. Now she was leaving, taking with her some knowledge of the town and the people. When Edmund wrote her about Vinnie and the plaster statue she was working on, Fannie would be able to see the girl in the little basement studio in the Capitol. Kate Chase Sprague would no longer be merely a name in newspapers, nor Edwin Stanton, nor even the President himself, for Edmund had pointed him out one day as Johnson rode away from the White House. And wasn't it strange that she should have met Jessie Frémont without even knowing who she was?

She was folding the gray silk carefully, replacing the tissue paper between the folds, when Edmund walked into the room. One look at his face and she stopped, the gray dress still in her hands.

"Has something happened?" she asked. "The children—"

"No," he said, sitting down on the edge of the bed. "You remember I told you when the President again ordered Stanton's removal last Monday that something would come of it, and fast."

"Yes—" She put the dress into the bag and went to sit beside him. "Everyone said it. Something about the Tenure of Office Act, wasn't it?"

"Yes—well, it's given the House the excuse it needed. Today it has reported to the Senate articles of impeachment against the President, demanding his trial and removal from office."

"Oh, Edmund," she cried.

"The next step is to organize the Senate as a Court under the constitutional provision. That means all ordinary and necessary business of the nation will be neglected. Which will be chaos, in a way."

"Who will preside?"

"Chief Justice Chase, of course. And there'll be lawyers, for and against. At the last, we senators will be called upon to cast our votes. Already the lines are being drawn—one can pretty well tell how the different ones will vote. Before the trial is even started, the thing seems decided."

He laced his fingers together as he spoke, and Fannie thought, as she so often did, how expressive his hands were. She did not need to look at his face to know the depth of his concern; one glance at those restlessly twisting fingers told her all she needed to know.

"If I vote 'not guilty' I can never again hope to be elected to any office, state or national, in Kansas," he went on slowly. "But then, if I think I should vote that way, how can I go against my own convictions in the matter?"

"The Reams are certainly for the President," Fannie said, not knowing why she wanted to plead the man's case. She had seen him only once, and that at a distance. Oh, it wasn't for him at all. It was for the thing he represented—all the dignity and might of the country. All the great men who had come before him—Washington and Adams and Jefferson. Yes, and the tall, gaunt man she herself had heard that long-gone day in Kansas.

"Yes," he said. "And Justice Chase, so they say. And Senators Grimes and Fessenden. I admire those men, and trust them."

Fannie was silent, thinking of the problem Edmund had inherited. Even after death, Jim Lane's shadow came back to haunt them.

"It looks as if everyone but me has pretty well taken a stand in the matter," Edmund went on.

"Edmund," Fannie began timidly, "why should you feel the responsibility so much? After all, yours is just a single vote—no more, no less, than the one any other senator will cast."

"Mine happens to be one of the very few which is still in doubt. For that reason, great pressure will be put upon me by both sides."

"You have not yet decided—" It was a useless question, for had his decision been made, he would not be debating the matter now.

"No, and I shall have to give the situation a great deal of thought before I do. I have a responsibility to my constituents, the people of Kansas whom I represent. However, I feel this matter must be settled, not on party lines or personal prejudice, but on the basis of justice and of what will happen to the nation's laws if a President can be impeached simply because he has offended some of the officers in the government."

He wasn't talking to her, she realized, so much as he was clarifying his own thoughts.

"But on the other hand, I think Crawford appointed me in the first place—and the Legislature later elected me—because of the stand I took in opposing Lane's determination to go along with Johnson. I did that out of distrust of Lane, feeling he supported Johnson merely because he would have a better chance of covering up his own dishonesty by so doing. But still, I must remember that, actually, I came into office on a platform of opposition to Johnson."

Fannie reached out to touch his hand, a gesture of which he did not even seem aware.

"And, since I've been here I've done nothing to indicate I am in favor of Johnson," he went on. "After Stanton's removal, I voted with the majority in adopting a resolution saying the removal was unlawful. If I do not go along with the Radicals, they are going to raise a mighty rumpus."

She was silent, contemplating the gravity of the situation confronting Edmund. If she could remain in Washington during the coming trial, to comfort him and give whatever help lay within her power. But she must go back to Kansas—already her stay here had been longer than she had first anticipated. Or, if only she could think of something cheerful to say now, instead of sitting, silent and helpless, with the clock rapidly ticking away the moments left to them.

"Already I am beginning to have letters from Kansas about the matter," he told her. "One from Dan Anthony came today. Telling me I must vote for impeachment."

"Oh, that man," Fannie cried. "He's such a big, hulking bully! He could break you in his bare hands, and wouldn't mind doing it, if the thought occurred to him. Do be careful, Edmund."

He looked at her, smiling gently. "Since when," he asked, "have I ever run from danger?"

"Never, that I know about," she said, trying vainly to keep her voice light, maybe even to twinkle a little. "But perhaps it's time you started!"

X

The Vote

1868

ON THE wooden sidewalk which ran the full length of the yard Eddie rolled her hoop, her hair flying behind her as she ran. Inside the fence surrounding the yard, Kay followed her, crying with vexation and disappointment at being shut away from the fun. Fannie, paying no attention to Kay's howls, went about her work, her mind torn in a dozen different directions. She supposed she really should go out and suggest that Eddie come in and play with Kay, but that would probably set Eddie off into wails of protest. Surely there must be some way to compromise. But then, when were the Rosses ever the ones for that!

The next few days would be hard on all the children, Fannie realized.

Lawrence, along with the rest of Kansas, seemed united in the belief that President Johnson should be impeached. The storm of hate and prejudice stirred up in Washington was reflected here. Fannie had come back from her visit with Edmund to a town which talked about nothing but the impending trial. People stopped Fannie to discuss the situation in Washington, wanting her firsthand views on the subject. But with all the questions, none concerned Edmund's stand. Apparently everyone felt confident he would vote "Guilty." How could a Republican from Kansas do otherwise?

The trial opened on March 5 in the Senate. Fannie, her perceptions sharpened by her trip to Washington, realized almost at the beginning that here was no court dedicated to justice, but rather a group of radical politicians bent upon deposing an executive because his policies did not agree with theirs. Naturally Chief Justice Chase presided. Fannie, remembering his courteous manners, was pleased, feeling the trial would at least be conducted with decency and consideration. It was a sentiment not shared by the Radicals. Chase was a known friend of the Johnsons—just look at the way his daughter visited with the family. They were entirely happy, however, with the chief prosecutor for the House, General Benjamin Butler (the "Butcher of New Orleans"); nor did they see anything amiss about Ben Wade's participation in the trial even though, as president pro tempore of the Senate, he would automatically become president should Johnson be voted guilty. They did not even criticize Wade and his fellow conspirators for drawing up in advance a list of cabinet officers to be appointed when Wade took office.

Even as Edmund had told her, the lines were pretty well drawn and the votes of the senators already determined. All, that is, except Edmund's. At first the Radicals had not worried about him, their confidence based on his stand against Lane and his earlier vote against Johnson at the time of Stanton's dismissal. Gradually doubts began to arise in their minds, doubts occasioned chiefly by his refusal to commit himself. This hesitancy they attributed to his association with Perry Fuller, the Reams, Tom Ewing, and various other people known to be friends of the President. Even so, they still considered him weak and pliable—if enough pressure were brought to bear on him, he would give in. No real doubt entered their minds until Edmund remarked to Sprague, "Well, Sprague, the thing is here; and so far as I am concerned, though a Republican and opposed to Mr. Johnson and his policy, he shall have as fair a trial as an accused man ever had on this earth."

From that moment on, Edmund had not known a moment's peace. He had been threatened, followed, advised, badgered. Letters and telegrams poured in upon him. Pomeroy kept at him constantly, pointing out the fact that to vote "Not Guilty" was to betray Kansas. All the while the country was busy surmising what sort of man this fellow Ross might be. Would he hold, or would he give way?

Fannie could have told them, had they bothered to ask her. Edmund Ross was a man possessed of that very rare virtue, courage—courage such as few men have. The courage to do the right thing, although the heavens fell. What that would be she did not know. Perhaps, as yet, he did not know himself.

With tomorrow the day set for voting on the Eleventh, and final, Article of Impeachment, Lawrence knew a suspense scarcely less intense than that experienced in Washington itself. Actually, tomorrow's vote would settle the question, for the Eleventh Article was a sort of hodgepodge containing the essence of all the others. If it passed, the President was as good as declared guilty; if it failed, he was, to all intents and purposes, acquitted.

In the mounting tensions brought on by the trial, the people of Lawrence had not hesitated to express their opinions to the Ross family, not even sparing the children. Men, seeing one of them downtown, would take the youngster by the shoulder and say, "Now you write to your Papa and tell him to vote right, you hear me?"

If they had acted with so little restraint when the trial was barely started, how would they behave today, when the verdict was so close at hand? Much as Fannie herself wanted to know how things were going, she would have kept the children home had they not insisted upon going to town, to mingle with the people on the streets, read the bulletins posted outside the newspaper offices, and buy the extras which most certainly would be issued. Finally she gave in to them, and Lillie, Arthur and Pitt left. Before long one of them would surely be coming home to report.

Fannie heard the sound of footsteps running over the board

walk—that would be Pitt. The other two always came more slowly. As the gate opened, Kay's wailing ceased and the sound of Eddie's hoop on the sidewalk stopped, too. She met the three of them—Pitt, Eddie and Kay—at the door, her hands full of cookies.

"Here, Eddie," she said, "you and Kay take these and play under the apple tree."

Eddie ran off, Kay at her heels.

"Mama," Pitt said, getting at once into the heart of the matter. Fannie offered him a cookie and he took it, eating as he talked. "Mama, they say a Senator offered Uncle William twenty thousand dollars if he would tell how Papa was going to vote."

"And what did they say Uncle William told the senator?"

"That he didn't know how Papa would vote."

That was the truth. How could he know?

"And then they said—it's all right to use a bad word if you're telling what someone else said, isn't it, Mama?"

"Yes—I think it is quite all right this time. To me, but to no one else, mind."

"Well, these men who were talking down on the street—I think they knew I was there, Mama, but they went right on—anyway, they said that Butler said if that *damned* scoundrel Ross wanted money, there was a bushel of it."

"Your father wouldn't take money—ever—ever," Fannie cried. "He'll do his duty, or what he believes to be his duty."

"Why of course he will, Mama," Pitt said, looking at her. Fannie was suddenly ashamed of her vehemence. Quiet confidence—that was the cue. She knew Edmund so well, so well—He would never do anything she would need to explain to the children, or condone, or gloss over.

"And a man named D. R. Anthony from Leavenworth sent a telegram to Papa saying that Kansas had heard the evidence and demanded conviction. And he signed it 'D. R. Anthony and a thousand others.' That's a lot of people. Did they all sign their names, do you suppose?"

"No, I'm sure not."

Pitt ran off, calling back over his shoulder, "I left Arthur right in the middle of a bunch of men. I bet he'll have something to tell you—"

"Close the gate after you," Fannie reminded him.

Dear Pitt, Fannie thought, her heart yearning over him as he made his way back toward the hostile town. How like Edmund he was!

Arthur came in a half hour later.

"Would you like some cookies and milk?" Fannie asked him.

"I don't believe I could eat anything, Mama."

His reply did not surprise her. For Pitt, earth had no sorrow —or at least, scarcely any—which food could not heal. But Arthur was beyond that stage, both in age and temperament.

"I was listening to some men, Mama," the boy said, looking old and troubled beyond his years. "They were saying the most awful things about Papa—how his one vote would tell the story, and what sort of a man he was if he didn't vote Guilty. Do I have to tell you what they said, Mama?"

"No," Fannie told him firmly. "You don't even have to remember them yourself. They are not true. Your father is a good and honest man. He will do what he thinks is right. Always that must be your guide, too—what Papa would do, if he were in your place. Then, the right way will come to you."

Arthur straightened his shoulders; his face looked less unhappy. "I heard them talking about Vinnie Ream, too. They said the people against the President were urging her to make Papa vote 'Guilty.' They come to her studio and they go to her home, because Papa's staying there. They say he gets away from the Ream house and hides out in the homes of his friends. They say the men who are against the President are trying to scare poor Miss Vinnie into influencing Papa's vote. Do you suppose she will do it?"

"Your father is not easily influenced," Fannie smiled.

Fannie remembered the little studio in the basement of the Capitol and the statue of Lincoln on which the girl was working with singleness of purpose. What would the great man think of the shady activities going on right under his likeness? And poor little Vinnie—it was too much to ask that she undergo this persecution at a time when she should be allowed to work without interruption.

"And Mama—" the boy's troubled voice went on, "they say Papa will take money, if enough is offered him. That he's probably already taken it."

"Papa will never take money for doing something wrong," Fannie told him sharply.

Of all the charges brought against Edmund, this was the most ridiculous. If only people making such accusations could see the way the Ross family lived—frugally, simply, counting every penny. The way the Rosses lived—that was proof enough of Edmund's honesty.

Arthur turned toward the door. "I guess I'll be going back downtown."

"Why don't you stay here," Fannie suggested. "You could work in the garden. Papa said we must have a good garden to help out with expenses."

"I want to go," he told her steadily. "I want to hear the news as it comes in."

He went off, not forgetting to close the gate behind him, his shoulders set and straight. That was Ross courage for you.

Fannie set about preparations for dinner. Just because she herself could not eat a bite did not mean the children would not be hungry. She believed she'd even bake a cake. She had just started separating the eggs when Lillie came in.

"Oh, so you're home," Fannie said cheerfully, ignoring the girl's tear-stained face.

"Mama," Lillie told her, "I was crying and acting like a big baby, right out on the street." She looked at her mother for the condemnation which she seemed to expect and, failing to see it, went on.

"And then George Leis came out of his store and told me I must not feel bad—that Papa was a good and honest man, and would do what was right. And he said I should come on home. Wasn't that nice of him?"

"Very nice," Fannie agreed, suspecting that, of all the sympathy which might have come to Lillie, this was the most welcome.

The next day Fannie kept Lillie at home. She tried, also, to detain Arthur and Pitt, but they insisted on taking their posts on the street once more, picking up any information available.

Of this there was no lack. It came in by the minute—over telegraph wires, in newspaper bulletins, by word of mouth. Apparently nobody in all of Lawrence could do anything today except discuss the impeachment case. And well they might suspend all their own activities, for the thing which was going on in Washington was without precedent in the nation. Never before had a President of the United States been impeached. Even the people of foreign countries, members of embassies and others either living in Washington or visiting there, could not believe the thing they watched. They might have lopped off a few heads of rulers in their own countries in times past, but this—well, wasn't it carrying democracy a bit too far? And in the general excitement, the city of Washington itself was a madhouse, with anything possible.

"I heard one man say a newspaper reporter had been paid to kidnap Papa and take him off to New York and hold him until the time for voting was past," Lillie reported. Today, with Mr. Leis' kindness in her mind, she could bring herself to discuss some of yesterday's news.

"Oh, he won't do it," Fannie assured her, trying to feel in her heart the confidence she expressed. She remembered the high feeling in Washington when she left. By now, everyone was so inflamed over the issue that rash action could not be completely discounted.

"They said the ones in favor of conviction were hounding Papa day and night—he had no chance to rest and hardly time to eat. They said he was showing the strain, and would probably give in—"

"Lillie," Fannie said firmly, "your father will come through all right. I've known him longer than you have. I've never seen him lose his nerve or his courage. Or compromise on what he believed to be right. He won't now, and you mustn't worry about him. Ah—here's Pitt."

The boy ran, waving a piece of paper in his hand. "There was a telegram posted and I copied it," he cried.

"What is it?" Fannie asked, trying to keep her voice calm.

"It's Papa's answer to D. R. Anthony and all those others." He held the piece of paper, crumpled and dirty, toward his mother.

"You read it to us," Fannie told him. "You deserve to—"

The boy smoothed out the sheet of paper, covered with his own boyish scrawl. "To D. R. Anthony and others," he read proudly.

> I do not recognize your right to demand that I vote either for or against conviction. I have taken an oath to do impartial justice according to the dictates of my judgment and for the highest good of the country.

The boy paused, looked at his mother and sister. "It's signed 'E. G. Ross.' " The pride in his voice showed on his face, even after he stopped speaking.

"Oh, dear, dear Papa," Lillie cried. "If he can be that brave, why should we shed a single tear?"

"Why, indeed!" Fannie said.

The long afternoon dragged by. Fannie did not know how it passed; actually she was not aware that it passed at all. Perhaps, like Joshua of old, the very event itself had bidden the sun to stand still in the heavens. Surely by now—surely the question had been put, to each senator in turn. Edmund, since his name began with R, would be far down on the list.

They were saying in Washington that Edmund was a poor obscure politician, who had sprung up from nowhere to a position where he could cast this deciding vote. How very wrong. Wherever he had gone—Milwaukee, the Lane Trail, Topeka, in the army, Lawrence—he had been a man respected and influential. Oh, he was not a nobody, without balance or judgment or experience. Kansas had become a state under the constitution he had helped to shape. When the Santa Fe Railroad was built —as it would be in time—it would be partly because of Edmund, who had worked so hard for it.

And now when the question was put to him by Chief Justice Chase in his solemn, deep voice, "Mr. Senator Ross, how say you? Is the respondent, Andrew Johnson, President of the United States, guilty or not guilty of a high misdemeanor, as charged in this article?"—when this came, Edmund's answer would settle the question once and for all. And the echoes of it would go beyond Kansas, where she was waiting. It would go out, she felt, to all the world.

Just when she thought she could not stand the suspense another moment—not another fraction of a second—she heard the sound of Pitt's running feet. The boy raced through the gate, leaving it wide open, and came into the house.

"Mama," he cried. "Mama—the President was acquitted. Papa voted 'Not Guilty.' "

It was not easy to explain to Eddie and Kay why they should not play outside, with the weather so nice. Kay was easier to manage because Fannie made him take a nap. She put Arthur and Pitt to weeding the garden, which was back from the street and hidden from the passers-by. There was, really, no way she could protect Lillie; it was foolish even to try. She was nineteen now and must learn to take her hurts. "You could help Eddie sew doll clothes," Fannie suggested. "I am going to do some mending."

"Oh, Mama—" Lillie protested, feeling this was no time for frivolous pursuits like making doll clothes, even for one's little sister.

"Go ahead, Lillie," Fannie told her steadily.

So Lillie hunted up odds and ends of material and set about fashioning a bonnet for Eddie's battered doll.

Lillie was working on the dress, Eddie watching her with adoring eyes, when Fannie became conscious of the sound of footsteps on the wooden sidewalk just outside the fence. Her first thought was that the boys had left their weeding job and were playing there. No—it sounded like a number of people. She dropped her mending and raised her hands quickly to smooth her hair. Perhaps company was coming—it had been some time since she had received any callers. Eddie left her place at Lillie's side and went to the window.

"Mama," she asked curiously, "what are all those people doing out there? They walk by the house, and then they turn around and walk back. And they keep looking—"

Oh, these were not callers. What their business was Fannie did not know.

"And there's one—a man—shaking his fist at the house. He doesn't look like a nice man at all. There, he's done it again and a woman with him is doing just as he does—"

"Come away from the window, dear," Fannie said as steadily as she could. "Don't mind those people—they're just excited about some news from Washington. See—Lillie is going to put bows on the doll's hat."

Lillie lifted stormy eyes to protest she could not sew a stitch—not a single stitch—while those people were out there. Fannie looked at her sternly, nodding her head meaningfully in Eddie's direction. Lillie, after a moment's hesitation, picked up the hat once more, her face white and strained, her hands trembling over their small task. Eddie, apparently satisfied and too interested to think more about the crowds outside, hung over her sister's work. Fannie reached for her mending, her own hands shaking so it was difficult to hold the needle. At that moment Arthur and Pitt slipped in through the back door.

"Those people—" they began breathlessly, only to stop abruptly at the sight of Eddie. The older ones, leagued together with me in order to protect Eddie, Fannie thought. I wish Edmund knew. No—she did not want Edmund to know any of part of what was going on in Lawrence today. His own home town—the one he had guarded during the war, the one whose activities he had recorded in his paper. It was well he was not here to see with his own eyes the behavior of his fellow townsmen.

The boys motioned to her and she followed them. Once they were out of Eddie's hearing, Pitt said, "We heard them talking, Mama. They're planning a mass meeting tonight to talk about Papa. They've got no right—"

"You can't stop them if that is what they mean to do," Fannie said crisply, her own heart aching with the impact of the news.

"Do you want Pitt and me to go tonight and see what happens, Mama?" Arthur asked, looking very white around the mouth.

"Indeed I do not," Fannie told him firmly. "We can't stop them from having their meeting, but we don't have to go ourselves."

Fannie sat in the living room. Someway, she had got through supper, had sent the children, even Lillie, to bed.

"You need the sleep," she said, something in her voice warning them argument was useless.

Across the distance between the Ross house and the mass meeting, sounds carried well enough for her to translate their significance. Angry, excited shouts told her it was a group of no small proportions, so it must include neighbors and people she had once counted friends. More than likely it was swelled by additions from adjoining towns—Dan Anthony would certainly be there from Leavenworth, doing his best to inflame the crowd, already at the point where it was more mob than orderly meeting.

And yet, could she blame them completely? In their minds was still fresh the memory of all the atrocities committed by the proslave groups—the border warfare, with its toll of life and property. Lawrence had suffered especially. Sam Jones and Quantrill, and Atchison—the list was long of those who had tried in one way or another to wreak vengeance on the town. Not seeing the larger issues behind the impeachment trial, most of the people of Lawrence would think that Edmund's vote meant that he condoned those outrages. But Edmund himself had fought the Confederate forces—did no one in Lawrence remember how bravely he had fought? Surely memory was not so short a thing as that!

She did not know how long she had sat there, listening to the noises coming from the mass meeting, when she became aware of another sound. Outside on the sidewalk was a tap-tap-tapping, a sound whose origin Fannie could not place. She made her way to the window. Pushing aside the curtain she saw, there in the dim light, the reason for the noise. A man was walking back and forth in front of the house. He carried a cane; its tapping was the sound she had first heard. He walked the full length of the sidewalk, his footsteps mingling with the tapping cane.

It was the beginning of a pattern of action which was to continue for hours. Back and forth, back and forth. Occasionally there was a pause when the old man would stop to shake his fist at the house.

Finally she made herself go to bed. She lay on her bed and thought—thought—thought. Quantrill's raid. She had feared for Arthur, then, asleep with the little Union flag on his pillow. And now this threat to him and all the family—oh, it would not be over as soon as the raid had been, but it was as hard a thing in its own way. She remembered Mrs. Carter and her quiet courage, and wished for her.

The tapping went on—back and forth, back and forth, as the old man kept his vigil of hate. It must have been long past midnight when she finally dropped off to sleep, too exhausted both physically and emotionally to stay awake longer. The last thing she heard was the tapping.

2

In the week which followed, pieces of the whole picture began to fall into place. Edmund was, in truth, given credit for saving President Johnson. All the Radicals in the north had, as a matter of course, voted "Guilty." Pomeroy, the other Kansas senator, had gone along with them. Even Kate Sprague's husband, the senator from Rhode Island, had joined them. People were saying he relished this way of getting even with his father-in-law, Chief Justice Chase, who had been in sympathy with the President. However, Fesensden and Grimes, although from the north, had refused to line up with the Radicals. It was Edmund's single vote which had swung the balance in favor of the President, and the people who hated Johnson and his policies would never forgive the man who had saved him.

Fannie read every word that was published in the Lawrence papers. She could see, in her mind, the historic room filled with the senators and, in the galleries, the witnesses—beautifully gowned women and men from all walks of life. It had been, according to reports, a spectacle beyond all describing. She could hear, too, the question asked Edmund—"Mr. Senator Ross, how say you—" One account said that Edmund sat tearing scraps of paper as the question was put to others. Well, why not? He often did that when he was thinking. And how he must have thought—oh, what he must have thought—as the names were called down the line. Closer, closer to his own—closer to the point where he must rise and make a stand and, after that, take the consequences. Let him tear paper if he wished. Let him have any help he could fasten upon. They said when he rose to vote the bits of paper fell to the floor. Just as if, Fannie thought, the bits of his life and his family's were falling too.

She could almost hear his voice, that beautiful clear voice of his as he spoke the words. "Not guilty—" Except they said the first time he spoke so low he was not heard and, for a moment, the Radicals rejoiced because they thought he had gone along with them. But then he spoke again, so loud and clear that all the nation might hear.

Of course, there had been a rush of furious comment. Dan Anthony's message went scorching across the wires immediately.

> Kansas repudiates you as she does all perjurers and liars.
> D. R. Anthony and others.

From Topeka another telegram was sent. "Unfortunately the rope with which Judas hanged himself is mislaid, but the pistol with which Jim Lane killed himself is at your service."

All over Kansas, editorials lashed out against Edmund. He had sold himself, they said, betrayed his constituents, stultified his record, lied to his friends, shamefully violated his solemn pledge, signed the death warrant of his country's liberty. He was a Benedict Arnold who loved money better than he did principle, friends, honor, and his country all combined.

In the general outcry, Edmund's statement explaining his vote was almost drowned out.

"I did not vote as I did," he said, "to save President Johnson, but to save the Constitution. Thirty-five senators voted to evict the President and supplant him by a radical politician who would have been as unconformable and as ruthless a dictator as Robespierre."

Fannie read this, finding every word a comfort and a solace. And when Edmund's letter to her finally came, she gathered the children around her so that they might all hear at once.

It was written on a sheet of Senate stationery and was brief, but it was from Edmund, which meant everything.

> Don't be discouraged, dear wife. It's all coming out all right. This storm of passion will soon pass away, and the people, the whole people, will thank and bless me for having saved the country by my single vote from the greatest peril through which it ever passed, though none but God can ever know the struggle it cost me. Millions of men are cursing me today, but they will bless me tomorrow. But few knew the precipice upon which we stood on Saturday morning last.
>
> Your aff. Hus.

"What a wonderful letter," Pitt said when she had finished. "I am very proud of Papa."

"And I am too," Arthur said.

"And I—" Lillie was close to tears, but she wiped them away. "Dear, dear Papa. How cruel people have been to him."

"We'll not think of that," Fannie said. "We'll go about our business. Quietly, mind you. But we will not let ourselves be angry and hurt. If Papa could do his duty and not mind what people say, we can manage to do the same thing."

3

One piece of news gave Fannie a great deal of unhappiness. The Conservative group, Edmund among them, had apparently used Vinnie Ream's studio as a meeting place. This fact, coupled with the opinion held by many that Vinnie had influenced Edmund's vote, so angered the Radicals that they closed her studio. Fannie wondered what the girl would do now. She hoped no harm would come to the statue.

Slowly, gradually, things began to calm down a little. A few letters came to Fannie praising Edmund. One of them she especially liked. It was written hastily, on cheap paper, and the postmark was blurred. But the contents leaped out at her, bright and joyous.

> I thought you would be glad to know what Senator Walker said. It was this: "I'd rather go down into history on the vote cast that day by E. G. Ross than on any other vote ever cast in the United States Senate." I share his views, Dear Mrs. Ross.

She read that to the children, and they cried out their delight.

"I'll bet people are going to praise Papa a lot," Pitt said.

"All along there have been many people who thought your father did right," Fannie told the boy. "We haven't been hearing from them, but nevertheless, they have approved."

She had lost sight of the fact herself in the general clamor against Edmund. More than that—she had not been able to make herself go about her natural round of activities. Even the ordinary errands like shopping, she had delegated to the children, not wanting to meet the people who were saying such cruel things about Edmund and his vote. A real coward, that's what she had been. The sooner she made herself go out and face people, the better off she would be—the better off they all would be. She wasn't at all sure the children would see the reason for what she was about to say, but she knew, and that was sufficient.

"We are going to church tomorrow," she told them. "All of us—"

When morning came, Fannie found she could not so much as lift her head off the pillow. A blinding, staggering headache had struck her. She could not even set her foot on the floor, although she tried.

"Now don't worry, Mama," Arthur said. "We don't have to go—"

"Go on without me," Fannie told them. "You'll be all right. Lillie will be with you."

After they were gone, Fannie dropped off into an uneasy sleep. When she awoke from it she felt a little better. She put a tentative foot on the floor. Her head obligingly stood still. She put the other foot out. Then she stood up, ready to grab for a chair in case she needed it. That was all right, too. She took a step or two. She was weak, but she could walk now. She decided she would feel better if she drank a cup of tea, and so made her wobbly way to the kitchen.

She was almost through with the tea when she heard the children. They opened the front gate and came up the walk slowly, not saying anything, which was unusual. Fannie lifted her head quickly, finding that the sudden motion set it to aching once more. Then the children came in the kitchen.

"Well," she said, "how was church?"

Then she looked at them. Their faces were terrible, stricken, old beyond any telling of time. "Oh, what has happened?" she cried.

"Nothing—" Lillie lied, her mouth set in a straight hard line.

Fannie stood up, holding to the back of her chair. "Tell me everything," she commanded.

The three older ones looked at each other. Lillie still held

Kay's hand and Arthur held Eddie's. The two younger ones looked from brothers to sister, and then back at their mother. They evidently had no clear notion of what was wrong.

"Tell me—" Fannie insisted. The sight of her children's concern had cleared her head, as pain is said to do.

"Oh, Mama," Lillie burst out, "it was the awfullest thing—"

"You mean the people—" Fannie could not bring herself to finish the sentence.

"Well—they were bad, but most of all it was the preacher—I was so embarrassed and humiliated."

And then, bit by bit, by careful questioning and filling in details for herself, Fannie got the story. The children had arrived a little late, to find the only vacant seats were well up front. So they filed in, Lillie placing Kay on one side of her and Eddie on the other, just in case they got restless or misbehaved.

"But they didn't, Mama," Pitt put in earnestly. "They were good—good as anything—"

They managed all right through the song and the reading. But then when the minister started his sermon, the terrible part began.

"He talked about Papa," Arthur said. "He said Papa was a wicked man, a sinful one. He said that Kansas, like Diogenes, needed a lantern to find an honest senator to take Papa's place. He called Papa by name, so nobody would fail to know who he was talking about."

"What did you do?" Fannie asked, keeping her voice level with great effort.

"We just sat there," Lillie said. "I wanted to fall through the floor. I wanted to get up and walk out, but we were so far down front, and there were five of us, and I knew we couldn't leave without making a disturbance. I just sat there, and I nearly died of shame, Mama."

"I wanted to get up and tell him he was a—he wasn't telling the truth," Pitt said. "But I didn't do that, either. I tried to scoot down in my seat, but I felt at least six feet tall."

"And when he was finished," Lillie continued, "we slunk out, before they sang the last song. And nobody—not a single person —smiled at us, or nodded, or spoke. They just stared at us, like they—like they hated us, Mama—"

Her chin quivered and she could not finish.

Oh, no, Fannie thought. People could not act like that in the house of God. People we have known for years. People who had watched these children grow up. They call themselves Christians, and they act like that. She should be telling the children they weren't to mind what these people did; they should not hold in their heart the things the minister had said from the pulpit. She ought to be striving, in her own heart, for forgiveness for feeling as she did.

But no words came to her; no healing forgiveness crept into her own heart. All she could feel was bitterness. At the moment, she doubted that it would ever leave her.

4

Fannie realized, numbly, that the Sunday episode marked a turning point in her life. She kept the ordinary household chores going, and when they were finished, she simply sat in a chair, looking at nothing in particular. Such supplies as were needed the boys brought from town. Not once did she caution them, before sending them on such errands, against talking rudely to people. What did it matter how they acted in this town? People who went to church and professed to be Christians, and then would hurt children as they had hurt hers, were worth neither respect nor courtesy. Let the boys say what they wished, act as they pleased.

No visitors came; even the ones who had, on those first days, walked by to stare at the house had ceased their vigil. Mail still poured in, most of it abusive in nature, although a few complimentary ones arrived, too. She had got to the point where she did not concern herself about opening letters unless they came from Edmund. When Lillie put a small envelope into her mother's hand one day, Fannie pushed it to one side. Just another missive of hate. Judging from the writing, it was from a woman, but women could hold resentment worse than men, and express it in more scathing terms.

"Aren't you going to open your letter, Mama?" Lillie asked timidly.

"You open it," she said. Once she might have wanted to spare Lillie whatever the letter might contain, but there was no way of shutting off the public reaction from her now. It was a thing too apparent, too all-inclusive.

Lillie tore open the envelope, drew out the single sheet, ran down it with her eyes.

"It's from Mrs. Carter, Mama."

"Mrs. Carter—" Fannie snatched the letter from her daughter's hand. The fine, closely written words leaped out at her.

> I want to take this opportunity to tell you I have not forgotten your courage at the time of the Lawrence raid. I have thought of you many times since then, but as you may know, I am out of town a great deal of the time.
> It was signed, "Eloise Carter."

Suddenly Fannie found herself crying. Lillie came to hug her close and the boys stared, chins dropping on chests. Baby Kay ran toward his mother, lifting his wails to the ceiling.

"Mama, Mama, what is wrong!" Eddie shrieked.

"Nothing," she said, wiping her eyes. "Nothing. Not now, there isn't. I've been a weak and foolish woman, but I'm better now."

"Mama's better," Eddie announced to the others.

"Indeed I am better," she said. "And Sunday—we—all of us—are going to church."

Courage at the time of the raid, indeed. She had far greater need for it now. And, just as Mrs. Carter had come forward at that crucial time, so had she done now.

She knows what is going on in this town, Fannie thought. Perhaps she even knows that she, more than anyone else, can help me through this.

Sunday morning she made the children dress in their best, from Lillie on down to baby Kay. She took more pains with her own toilet than she had done at any time since the party she had attended with Vinnie in Washington. Once they were ready, she told each one how nice he looked, watching them brighten before her eyes.

She did not in the least underestimate the difficulties they might encounter. It would, in all probability, be much the same sort of situation from which the children had fled several weeks ago. The difference now was that she would be with them and that she had taken pains to fortify both herself and them against whatever might happen. This she had not told them; it was a fact which was evident and needed no explanation. The Rosses were going to have another try at going to church. They were going with heads high and spines stiff. And, although she hated to let herself think of such a possibility, prepared for a reception less than cordial.

She had timed their arrival with care, and good fortune was with her. They went inside just as the first song was starting. At least that gave the congregation something to do besides stare. She chose a seat not in the front nor yet in the back. Middle ground—that was best for her to take right now. When the minister stood up to read the Scripture, and later, to preach the sermon, she braced herself each time. But nothing disturbing was said. Perhaps he was a little ashamed of himself for his earlier outburst. Goodness knows he should be. Perhaps, which was more likely, he had got his burden of bitterness out of his system and did not need to mention the matter again.

Even so, she found it hard to keep her mind on the sermon, jumping forward to the end of the service and the inevitable difficulties which would accompany their leaving church. When it was over at last, she stood, the children rising with her. Together, they made their way out of the building, into the open air.

She had not known so terrible an experience could greet her here in her own home town. The reception of the news of Edmund's vote had been a different sort of thing, but at least, she could meet that in her own home. But this—this was a public humiliation.

She and the children made their way through lanes of one-time friends, who parted as if they gave a path for despised reptiles, looking above and around and beyond her. No hand was extended in friendship; no voice was raised in recognition. There was only cold and hostile silence and eyes slithering away from meeting hers. She could feel herself going first red, then white. Lillie was ready to cry and even Kay, too young to know the reason back of the hatred but feeling it just as keenly, shrank close to his mother.

Down the line she walked, her children at her side. *If I can only hold to my courage,* she thought, *just until I can get away from here. Not for my sake, but for the children's. God, help me to hold on—*

She did not know a path could be so long; she did not know that seconds could spin themselves into eternities. Just a few steps more—just a few—

And then she heard a voice speaking to her. It seemed to come from far away, and yet it was near. Surely she was not that close to fainting—

"Why, how do you do, Mrs. Ross?"

Fannie turned slightly to meet the cool, detached kindness in the voice and saw Mrs. Carter at her side, a hand extended. As calm as she had been that day the raiders came, and as blandly determined to ignore the real situation.

Fannie put out her own hand, feeling it tremble as she did so. The woman's steady clasp closed over her fingers.

"I have missed you," Mrs. Carter said.

Missed her, indeed! Fannie had lived here four years and, any time Mrs. Carter wished, she might have called. Even so, her words now sounded like the bells of heaven ringing in Fannie's ears. She had regained her composure sufficiently to see heads turning in their direction. She knew, without looking, that faces were beginning to soften. No one in Lawrence would look lightly upon any action of Mrs. Carter's.

"You must come and see my flowers, Mrs. Ross," Eloise Carter went on, speaking clearly and distinctly enough so no one of the waiting group could fail to hear her. "Come and bring the children. Would Thursday be suitable?"

"Thursday would be quite all right," Fannie mumbled. "You are very kind to ask us."

"Not at all. I have been wanting a chance to tell you how much I admire Senator Ross for his courageous stand against prejudice and lawlessness. We have all too few men willing to fight for the highest good of the government, especially when so many hot-heads are demanding less than justice. Well, good day. I shall look forward to seeing you Thursday, at two."

She walked away with great dignity, toward her carriage. It was not until she had driven off that Fannie remembered she had not told her good-by.

Fannie moved toward the sidewalk, finding the whole climate around her had changed. A few people nodded. One woman smiled. Another woman went so far as to say "Good morning," her voice sounding a little defiant as she looked around her, daring anyone to take her to task. Fannie returned her greeting briefly. She could afford to be generous and forgiving. Her heart was light and relieved. It was not until she crossed her own threshold that she knew the reason.

For the first time in days she felt no hate.

XI

"I Will Not Cry for Quarter"

1868–1871

FANNIE DID NOT deceive herself into thinking that everything now would be smooth in the Ross family's relations with the town. She only knew that now she could work things out. Not ideally, of course, but she could face what came day to day. Her one hope was that, when Edmund came home as he would do when Congress adjourned the present session, she would have the situation under control. Not solved—just under control.

When he did return, it was as if a convict, paroled before his time was up, had come back asking for shelter. Nowhere did he find welcome or even understanding. There was nothing but coldness at best, blame and censure at worst. And, hardest of all to bear, the hints, not always veiled, that he had voted as he did for the sake of handsome bribes. Of course he was restless and unhappy under existing circumstances.

"I believe I'll go over to Topeka," he told her one day.

Poor darling—didn't he realize things would be no better there. Almost nowhere in Kansas would he find approval. It was too soon after Johnson's acquittal for him to look for forgiveness; it was too soon after the terrible war which had been fought for reasons underlying the whole trial. But he was restless and if he must have a change, Topeka was as good a place as any to go.

When he came back that evening he looked better than he had at any time since his return to Kansas. Something good had happened to him and her heart rose up joyously.

"I saw Colonel Holliday in the lobby of the Capitol Hotel in Topeka," he told her.

"Oh, that was nice. How's his railroad going?"

My goodness—how long had it been since he and Edmund were working together, trying to bring the railroad through? They had thought and dreamed and hoped railroad. How much had happened since then—how much.

"It goes well. He's just returned from New York where he managed to raise some money. He says they're going to have the first dirt turning day after tomorrow, and he wants me to make a speech."

"Oh, Edmund—" she didn't know whether to laugh or cry. She did both, as a matter of fact, and went over to kiss him, happy as a girl.

He was pleased, too, but he chose to hide his pleasure under brusqueness.

"I told him I had no heart for speeches," he said, "and that people won't listen to me anyway, feeling as they do about the acquittal."

"But you told him you would—"

"Yes. Can you go with me?"

"Yes, indeed," she said. "I want to see this."

They arrived in Topeka shortly before noon. Colonel Holliday and Joe Blunt, who was in charge of construction workers, met them with a livery hack and drove them to a point on Washington Street, between Fourth and Fifth. The day was raw, with a bleak wind blowing, whipping the waters of the Kaw, only a few blocks away, into a muddy gray froth. A few townspeople had gathered around, apparently not much impressed. Reporters from the *Weekly Leader* and the *State Record* were on hand. Did any of these watchers, only mildly curious now, realize the part Edmund had played in bringing newspapers to Topeka, or the railroad venture to its present success? Did they feel, as she did, that here was a moment of history; did they sense, as she did, that this day—October 30, 1868—would be one to remember down the years?

Fannie chose to remain in the hack while the three men alighted, Joe Blunt carrying a new shovel which he now stuck into the earth. The workers stood there watching, leaning on their own shovels.

"All right, Senator," the colonel said.

Edmund cleared his throat, and then began to speak. After three years in the Union Army and two in the Senate at Washington he was glad to be home on this auspicious occasion, he told them. It was a big day—one they'd all been waiting for for ten years. Obstacles were removed—efforts rewarded— But Colonel Holliday was the one to tell them about the big plans ahead.

Colonel Holliday took his turn and, when he had finished, handed the shovel to Edmund.

"Now, Senator—the first shovelful—"

Edmund took the shovel, bore down upon it with one foot, and heaved up a chunk of brown wintery earth. When he had finished, he handed the shovel to Colonel Holliday, who also dug a shovelful.

The people standing around gave a cheer. Above it, Fannie could hear, in her own mind, another sound—the trains of the Atchison, Topeka and Santa Fe, slipping over steel rails, out of Topeka, across the dun and endless prairies to Santa Fe. And then, beyond that, through the purple mountains and across great rivers until they slid at last into the cities on the coast, with the Pacific Ocean washing up against them. Oh, it was a great dream, and Edmund had a part in bringing it to pass. He came to sit beside her now, and she reached out to squeeze his hand.

Dear, dear Edmund. Once more he had done a splendid thing.

"This has been a good day," she told him, as they drove back to Lawrence.

"Yes, I have found it so. For the first time in many months, I have found people approving of what I did."

"My poor darling," she said. "There must be many times when you find yourself quite lonely."

"Quite lonely. But never lonely enough to endorse those measures which I believe to be wrong."

As if she didn't already know that!

"It strikes me that you must often be lonely, too," he continued. "When Congress opens again, you should plan to come to Washington for another visit. It will do you good."

"And be company for you—" she suggested.

"Much company for me—" he assured her, leaning over to kiss her cheek.

2

Fannie went to Washington in April of 1869, leaving the two younger children at home, again, at Lillie's insistence. Things had changed since her visit a little over a year ago. Grant was President now. Edmund was still staying at the Ream house on B Street, but the Reams were not there. Vinnie had at last won over her opponents, had completed the plaster statue of Lincoln, and, accompanied by her mother and father, had gone to Italy to execute its duplication in marble. It seemed strange and a little lonesome without them; Fannie knew Edmund must miss them, as well. It was good that she had come out to be with him, even though she had wondered, when she was back in Kansas, if she ought to leave the family for Lillie to look after.

As soon as she saw Edmund, she knew it was well that she had come. He was deeply concerned about something.

"What's wrong?" she asked.

By way of answer, he handed her a copy of the New York *Herald Tribune*, indicating the portion she was to read. She skimmed down the column swiftly, getting the content of the story. It reported an interview purported to have taken place between Edmund and President Grant in which Edmund asked for special favors for himself. During the interview, abusive language was supposed to have been exchanged between the two men.

The article concluded:

Ross took his departure accordingly in a terrible rage, quitting the White House like one rushing from a plague, and hurried to the Capitol. President Grant threw himself into a chair the moment the door closed and wiped his brow with his pocket handkerchief, evidently very much agitated. Old Zach. Chandler approached and was thus addressed by the President.

"Excuse me for a few minutes, Senator. After that interview I must take a little time to cool off."

"Oh, Edmund," Fannie said, her distress spilling over into her voice, "this isn't true—I know it isn't!"

"Of course it isn't. Well," he smiled at her now, and for that she was grateful. "Well—he may have wiped his brow after I left. But as for that other part—that I asked favors for myself or that either of us so far forgot ourselves as to exchange abusive language—it is not true at all."

"Then why be worried about it?" Fannie said. "This is not the first time a newspaper has misquoted and maligned you."

"That is not what bothers me so much. As a matter of fact, I did go to the President to discuss a matter of appointments, but not for myself. It had become apparent that he was trying to drive out all Kansas officeholders who are my friends. I put the question directly to him."

"What did he say?"

"He said—and I could scarcely believe I heard him aright—that where any man has held office the last year and a half it is presumptive evidence that he is a Johnson man."

"And he considers that sufficient evidence for firing him even though he is doing a good job?" Fannie asked.

"Grant says he does. I tried to point out that, by so doing, he would frequently displace men who had fought courageously for the Union, many of whom were disabled as a result. But he would not listen to me."

"Well, at least you tried," Fannie said.

"And I am continuing to try. Tomorrow I am going to address a joint session and put the matter directly before them."

"Oh, Edmund," she protested, "do you think you must?"

Here he was once more preparing to launch into the middle of a fight, one which he had little or no chance of winning.

"I *know* I must. First of all, I want to deny that story in the newspaper. And then, I will protest this driving out of innocent, capable officeholders in Kansas simply because they happen to be my friends, or have held office for a year and a half. It is unjust, and I cannot stand by and allow it to happen without registering a protest."

"Well—" Fannie began.

"I know what you are going to say," he told her. "That anyone who was given anything by Johnson can now expect to have it taken from him—especially if that person is unfortunate enough to call me his friend. It is not right or fair."

Of course it wasn't. But when in the history of mankind did abstract justice ever prevail?

"At any rate, I would like for you to hear my speech. And on your way over, will you stop and take a look at the picture Mathew Brady did of me? He has been getting up a collection of photographs of members of the Senate."

"I'll come," she said, "and I'll look at the picture."

She stood before the Brady portrait, regarding it carefully. It had caught Edmund not in profile nor yet in a full front view. He was looking off into the distance, as if he were in deep thought, as well he might have been. His hair was long enough so that, at the ends, it showed the slightest tendency to curl and, just at the part—low on the left—it was beginning to recede a little. Just a little. In fact, she had not noticed this until she saw the picture. His sideburns, side whiskers, moustache and chin whiskers were all darkly luxuriant. Edmund was a very handsome man. Perhaps "distinguished" was the better word. His dark suit and vest fitted perfectly. But then, he always looked well in his clothes, even when they had to be, of necessity, of the cheapest cloth and cut. His shirt showed immaculately white and the small black bow tie was neat and exact. It was all so like him. And yet, Fannie felt a sense of disappointment. What was wrong, anyway? It was Edmund, and yet it was not quite Edmund. She stood back to get a better view.

Standing so, she thought she knew what was wrong. In the picture, Edmund looked fat, with even a faint air of complacency about him.

And that was not like Edmund. The relaxed complacent air was not for him. He was a fighter, a nonconformist, a lean, hard man, aloof and alone. Never his the small, safe, uncomplicated ways of lesser men, of ones who must always wait to see which way the army was headed before they decided to fall in step. He would cut his own trails, and move along them. Alone, if necessary, but always moving. Men like Edmund did not grow fat and complacent.

She turned away slowly, and then went over to the Senate chambers to climb the steps to the visitors' gallery. It was not the climb alone which made her breathe quickly as she found a seat from which she could have a good view of the place where Edmund would probably stand to make his speech. She was a little late—she had stayed too long looking at the picture—and the senators and members of the House were already in their places. In fact, the speaker had just rapped for order. There were a few matters of business to be droned over, and then Edmund rose and addressed the chair. He was recognized, and walked to a position out in front, holding a copy of the newspaper story to which he called their attention.

Never had Edmund's voice seemed better to her than it did now as he stood on the floor of the Senate preparing to address his peers. She could look down on him which, especially since he was not a tall man, should have made him look shorter. Strangely enough, it did not; Edmund had never, in fact, seemed anything but tall to her.

"I trust, Mr. President," he said, "that it is not necessary for me to assure the Senate, in which I have had the honor of occupying a seat for now nearly three years, that the statements in this extract are grossly incorrect and slanderous, not only in regard to myself, but also in regard to the distinguished gentleman who is now the Executive of the nation."

Edmund went on to deny the story, saying he did this in justice to the President as well as himself because, "The Chief Magistrate of the nation is here represented as forgetting the dignity of his position and the courtesy which is due a member of the Senate and as having indulged in expressions of passion and resentment unbecoming a gentleman in his capacity."

He was doing this very nicely, Fannie thought. Calmly, and with reason and conviction. She glanced around to see how people were taking his remarks and was pleased to see, or think she saw, that Edmund's words were getting across. However, he almost immediately went on to the other matter, the one about the dismissal of all Johnson appointees in Kansas. Almost at once she could feel the temper of his listeners changing.

Edmund sketched for them much the same picture he had discussed with her—the injustice of throwing out capable men simply because they had held office for a year and a half, or were his friends.

"In fact," he said, "a combination of my colleagues from Kansas has been formed to drive me from political life because I dared defy the dictates of party when I believed that other objects than my country's good were sought. Hence the sweeping and unjust removal of officeholders, chiefly Republicans and old soldiers, merely because they are my old friends."

Again he paused. Then he looked directly toward the ones who, Fannie knew, were most guilty in this respect.

"I neither court nor shun the contest. I have faced many a danger before without loss of nerve or self-respect. I will not cry for quarter or lick the feet of power or abate one jot of heart or hope, however fierce the attacks upon me. I will support the administration just so long as it commands my confidence as representative of the free principles I have sustained from boyhood through evil and through good report."

Whatever his listeners were thinking about his speech, they were listening to it. Fannie could feel the stillness, the attention. Men might not agree with Edmund, but rarely did they refuse to hear him.

"Whether the administration goes right or wrong, I will adhere to the great patriotic Republican party, in station and out of station, so long as it adheres to the life-long championship of freedom and equal justice for all; and I will criticize and oppose all acts of administration or party which I believe to be unjust to my comrades and friends or destructive to the interests of the country to which I owe my first allegiance."

He sat down.

"And to think," Fannie told herself, "I worried because the Brady portrait made my good warrior look complacent!"

She would not have him any different, now, or in the past, or in the future.

"You were good," she told him later.

"You think so?" he said, looking pleased at her words. Almost like the old Edmund. "I'm glad you heard me. I said what was in my mind and heart, and I am always at my best at such times. By the way, how did you like the picture?"

She hesitated a moment.

"You didn't," he accused her.

"I thought it was good," she said, "but you looked a little—well, fat—"

She didn't say the rest of it.

"It was the way the camera caught me," he explained. "Brady's an excellent photographer, but sometimes even he catches a subject with less than a true likeness."

"Oh, yes," she assured him. "I can see now that it was the angle the camera caught you."

And so it was. There was nothing wrong with Edmund's fighting spirit. Nothing at all.

"I miss the Reams," she said.

"And so do I. But I understand that Vinnie is meeting with much praise and acclaim in Europe. There are plans afoot now for a dedication of her Lincoln statue early in 1871. Those in a position to know seem to think that by then the sculpturing will have been finished, and the marble statue shipped back here and put into place."

"I hope all goes well," Fannie said.

"There is no reason why it shouldn't. You must plan to come back for the dedication, once the date is set."

"My goodness, Edmund," she said. "That's almost two years off. A lot can happen between now and then. I can't make plans so far ahead!"

"The years go by before you know it," he told her.

3

Back in Lawrence, Fannie had occasion to remember Edmund's words many times in the months that followed. The days flew by; she seemed scarcely to have started one before she saw its close. And then they had added up to weeks, and in turn, to months. Gradually she began to realize a thing which both frightened and disturbed her—Edmund's absence seemed to be a part of their pattern of life; his presence was the delightful and unexpected pleasure. Always, there was the problem of money. This Fannie handled as best she could, with a skill given by long practice. But she never did learn to accept the loneliness. The most difficult time was late afternoon when the street was full of men coming home for supper, making their way to the light which shone in the window, to children playing in the yard, to neighbors visiting over back fences comparing the size of tomatoes and the number of blooms on the potato vines, and later, to talking things over with their wives after the children were in bed. A light shone in the Ross window, and children played in the yard, but inside the house Fannie would sit with only Lillie to keep her company, once the others had retired.

The summer slipped by, bringing August and its cool evenings. Fannie went rummaging in the trunk for extra covers and brought out the quilt she had finished more than ten years ago. It gave her rather a start to see that some of the blocks were already a little faded. No wonder—the one made from the dress she had worn when Edmund came home was more than twenty years old. But never mind—the material was still good and strong. With gentle fingers she traced the outlines of the block made from Flint's little dress; she touched the one made from the scraps of the bonnet she had worn across the Lane Trail. She sat in front of the trunk for a long time, just thinking, before she got to her feet, holding the quilt in her arms.

What had started as a pretty fancy, she thought, had wound up as a stern necessity. How many times had this quilt protected one or the other of the Rosses from the chill of Kansas winters? It had served its purpose well. Now she was going to make a concession to sentiment. From here on out, the quilt would be used on her own bed. Hers, and Edmund's, when he was home. No matter if time had dealt a little less than gently with it. It was still strong and substantial. Like their marriage. Ma had said it would be a record of her life, and she had been right.

It was on her bed when Edmund came home in early fall of 1869.

"Do you recognize this quilt?" she asked.

Of course he didn't, so she told him, pointing out some of the pieces, reminding him of the occasions they represented.

"A sort of family diary," he said.

Almost Ma's exact words, years ago.

"Well," she said, "at least I can look at it and read much into it."

Although he said nothing, she knew, as always, the attitude of the people in Lawrence hurt him. Hate dies hard, she thought, and even its residue is bitter. And hatred for the South now had to have a new object against which to direct itself; Edmund, casting his vote on the side of sanity, was the logical person on whom to fasten it.

Knowing this, he should have been less outspoken on other issues. For instance, he need not have said that President Grant was a "little man" who might have the strength and wisdom to lead an army in wartime but was utterly incapable of leading his country in time of peace. This remark was widely quoted in Lawrence and just as widely censured. This in spite of the fact that it was an open scandal, the way the President was allowing himself to be manipulated by the big business interests of the country. You'd think the people of Lawrence would see Edmund was right. Perhaps they would, if he didn't keep harping on the subject; maybe they were just as stubborn as he was.

"Couldn't you just—well, keep quiet about these things," Fannie suggested hesitantly. "After all, the people here read the papers and can't help knowing—"

"I can't remain silent while so much of government fraud and double dealing and downright weakness goes on. I do not believe that President Grant is deliberately, or even consciously, dishonest. He has simply let himself be taken in by an unscrupulous bunch of financiers. The facts about Jay Gould and his railroad fraud are common knowledge. It's as I said—Grant is not a big enough man for the Presidency."

"Will he try to run again?" Fannie asked.

"Of course," Edmund told her. "Or, at least, he will be run by big business. I myself do not intend to support him. There is talk about trying to get Horace Greeley nominated instead. I'll support him."

Edmund, with all the prejudice against him—did he feel his support would mean much to any candidate?

"I know what you're thinking," he said. "That I'll be a liability instead of an asset. But here again—I must do what I think right, just as I did when the matter of the voting came up."

"No one can blame you for that," Fannie told him. "There will be some who will admire you for the nerve it will take to stand up against a popular candidate, just as there were some who admired you for the nerve it took to vote as you did."

"I was not aware of any nerve at that time," he told her. "I saw only one right thing to do, and I intended doing it at all hazards. No amount of arguments or threats could shake my resolution at the time nor can any amount of reproach or extremity of poverty ever make me regret."

4

Fannie's seventh child, a girl, was born June 13, 1870. Edmund was as proud of her as if she had been the first.

"I'd like for her to be named for you," he said.

"Won't that make for confusion in the family?" Fannie demurred.

"I have a namesake; so must you. Besides, I cannot think of a better destiny for a little girl than that she bear your name and grow up to be like you."

Fannie smiled. Edmund was always the one to think of a pretty way to phrase a compliment, making it sound all the more meaningful because he spoke from his own convictions. It would seem strange and not altogether right to have a daughter with her name, but if Edmund wanted it—

"We'll spell it with a *y* instead of *ie*," Fannie said. "That way we can at least keep it straight when it's written."

And so the new baby was named Fanny Ross.

The summer seemed to melt away and then, once more, Edmund was back in Washington. Poor little Fanny—like Eddie, her father would be almost a stranger to her. Most of those dear and cherished moments in a baby's life—the first real smile, the dawning recognition of loved ones, all the manifestations of growth and development of personality—would be witnessed by her mother alone.

There was not even the comfort of having Edmund at home for Christmas, for he decided not to come, choosing rather to send money for gifts.

"Besides," he wrote, "Vinnie's statue is going to be dedicated in January. She is most anxious to have you at the ceremonies. I am looking forward to having you, and of course, baby Fanny. I don't want her to forget her father entirely."

5

Fannie went to Washington in January of 1871, taking the baby with her. Edmund was no longer rooming at the Reams'. But when she saw that the Potomac was visible from the window, she still felt at home.

"The landlady will stay with the baby," Edmund told her, "so we can go to the dedication services this evening. Vinnie has sent word that she expects us."

Fannie and Edmund made their way toward the Capitol through the crowds of people standing patiently in the cold January evening. It looked as if half of Washington, with a goodly sprinkling from other places, was standing here now, waiting for the doors to open to the general public so that they could get in to see the unveiling.

"The Rotunda will never hold half of them—" Edmund said. "Excuse me—I am a senator and I have a pass."

The crowd parted good-naturedly enough to let them through.

The several flights of stairs of the western façade of the Capitol were filled with people, with a determined crowd jostling each other for a nearer position to the Rotunda entrance, ready, apparently, for the rush that would come when the doors were opened. She and Edmund made their way to the eastern door, where the senators and their wives were to be admitted at seven o'clock. The steps on this side were also filled, although it was more than half an hour before the public could expect to come in—if there was room.

"It's such an unpleasant evening—I feel sorry for them, standing here," Fannie said.

"But never mind—those who get in will be rewarded," Edmund told her. "I hear it is truly beautiful."

The guard glanced at Edmund's pass and admitted them. They went to the reception hall of the Senate, where they were told to wait. Presently they, with other Senators and wives and guests, and members of the House of Representatives and their wives, who had been waiting in the Hall of Representatives, were moving down the corridor to seats previously assigned them.

Fannie took her place, looking quickly in the direction where the statue stood under its cover of red, white, and blue, a flag, so the papers said, made especially for it by silk weavers of Lyon, France, each one having contributed two sous per individual to pay for it. Everyone agreed this was as much a tribute to Vinnie herself as it was to the martyred President, for she had endeared herself to the people in every country she visited while she was in Europe. The Rotunda itself picked up the colors, with flags and bunting draped over the great doorways or suspended in the hall, while a gas star was placed in such a way as to light up the face of the statue, once it was unveiled.

And, over it all, the shadowy figures of patriots in Brumidi's fresco —statesmen, warriors, and discovers of the past—seemed to belong to the assemblage, taking a part in the honoring of the man so lately added to their ranks. Columbus, de Soto, Penn; the Pilgrim Fathers kneeling on the deck of the Mayflower; Washington, Jefferson, Adams and Franklin—all looking down benignly, as if to welcome a tried and acceptable brother. Above, the vast hall seemed to rise to an almost immeasurable height, the circles of light shading one into the other, giving an impression of infinite vastness. And at the highest point of all, as if in the heavens, the "Father of His Country," seeming to hold out his hand in an attitude of benediction directly over the statue.

And now the platform guests were filing into their places—President Grant, Vice-President Colfax, Judge Davis of the Supreme Court, various senators, and General Sherman. Then little Vinnie Ream and her family.

At half past seven, the doors were opened to the public, that patient waiting crowd through which the more privileged ones had earlier made their way. The clamor of their voices, the sound of their pushing to attain a place in the Rotunda, almost drowned out the music of the Marine Band. As soon as the number that could be accommodated had come in, the doors were closed. The sounds of protest from those left outside echoed through the hall. Fists pounded on doors, and people called loudly for the doors to be reopened so they, too, might crowd in. Fannie looked at those who had gained entrance, those ordinary people whom Lincoln himself had loved. They seemed to come from every class of life, with a great many Negroes in the group.

And then the Marine Band began playing a dirge and silence settled over the crowd.

Senator Morrill spoke; various others also had something to say. Finally, came the part of the program everyone wanted to see—the unveiling.

Judge Davis walked forward, and he too, spoke briefly. At the conclusion of the speech, he reached out to lift the silk flag covering the giant marble statue. Slowly it rose, showing first the base, bearing the simple words "Abraham Lincoln"; then the tall form; and, finally, the face. There was a hush, followed by a tremendous applause. Fannie joined in.

It was as if the living man stood before her, the one she had seen long ago in Leavenworth, before all the trouble set in. Tall and gaunt, without grace; almost slovenly in his dress; with a face sadder than ever worn by any other man, one which must have mirrored all the sadness of the country he was guiding through the storm . . . Oh, everything was there. The nights he must have passed without sleep; the days which were so filled with trouble, both of governmental nature and his own personal grief; the suffering that comes of war, both at home and on the battlefield. His head was bent slightly forward and downward, seeming to look with anxious solicitude on the multitude of newly liberated people to whom he was presenting, with his right hand, the Emancipation Proclamation. A long circular coat covered his right shoulder, falling back to the left, as if he would cover with it all the defenseless ones who had received freedom. Above all there was an air of brooding tenderness and of great dignity. It was difficult to sit looking at the statue and not believe one was in the presence of the living man.

When the applause had died down a little, Senator Carpenter led Vinnie to the front of the platform. No doll-like, dimpled girl —as some reports had made her out to be—stood here, but a Vinnie grown older, with a pale face and earnest eyes and a certain sadness which spoke of the hard work accomplished, the worry and difficulty endured, and the responsibilities far beyond her years. Her hair was still dark and lustrous, her eyes bright, and her face mobile and intelligent. But the years had put their mark on Vinnie Ream; she had not bought her honors easily. That marble statue which now stood in the Rotunda had taken much out of her, both of the flesh and of the spirit.

Vinnie spoke only a few words, and those so low few could hear her. Once the ceremony was over, the crowd pushed around her, pressing so thickly against her it was a wonder she was not crushed.

"I think we'll go home," Edmund said. "We'll never get near her, with all this crowd. They're going to break down the platform if they don't watch out—"

Fannie was disappointed, for she wanted a chance to tell Vinnie how much she liked the statue. But Edmund was right—it would be difficult, if not impossible, for anyone to talk with Vinnie now. At that moment, the girl turned her head. Seeing Fannie across the room, she gestured imperatively to her and then began to push in the direction of the Rosses. Fannie started to make her way to Vinnie, and finally they met.

"Oh, dear, dear Mrs. Ross," Vinnie said, "I am so glad you came. You and Senator Ross. After all, his was the first Senator's name on my recommendation."

"A proud moment," Edmund assured her.

"And you saw one of my first models," Vinnie said, laughing and squeezing Fannie's hand. "Oh, we must have a good visit, now that you are here. I'll want to hear about the children—"

The last was spoken over her shoulder as someone came to take her away. Fannie and Edmund walked back through the crowd, still milling around in the raw January evening.

"Is it worth it?" a man called to them.

"Very much so," Edmund told him. "You must see it for yourself—"

"Mr. Lincoln wouldn't have liked this way of doing it," the man said. "He would have wanted everyone—every man, no matter how poor or underprivileged—to be right in there with the best of them. They've done things all wrong."

"You'll forget about that when you see the statue," Edmund told him.

It was a statement which Fannie could echo in her heart. She felt sure that most people, when their turn came to see it, would feel as she did. Young Vinnie Ream had caught the spirit of Lincoln from the man himself. She had not failed herself or the group who had entrusted her with the commission. Most important of all, she had not failed the martyred President who had allowed her, an unknown girl, to sit and sketch him. Whoever saw the statue was going to feel this deep authenticity; whoever looked would know it had been done with the heart as well as the hands.

She and Edmund talked late after they were back at the boarding place, but not about the statue.

He was pleased that Henry Stanley, the young reporter for whom he had foreseen a bright future when he met him at the Peace Conference at Medicine Lodge, had been given an assignment to go into the jungles of Africa and find Livingstone.

"I've always admired Livingstone because he tried so hard to stop the slave traffic," Edmund said.

"Livingstone hasn't been heard from for a long time," Fannie remarked. "Many people think he's dead. Do you suppose Stanley can find him?"

"He'll do it," Edmund said, "even if everyone else has failed. He's already landed in Zanzibar."

He talked, too, about the fact that his term was almost over.

"I'll be coming home to stay," he told her. "Think what that means!"

Home to stay—as if she hadn't thought a thousand times what that would mean!

"Of course, there would be no chance of re-election, even if I wanted the office."

She let that pass. She was glad, however, that he had realized this himself and would not even enter the contest.

"I'll have a chance to become reacquainted with my family," he said. "It will seem good to be home at last."

"It will be very good," she told him. She hated to ask, but she felt she must know. "Have you—well, any plans?"

"I thought I'd go back to the paper," he said. "After all, I once owned it."

Then, at her silence, he looked at her quickly. "Is there some reason why I shouldn't?"

There was every reason why he should go back to the paper for whose existence he was responsible, even though it was now in other hands. But the Radicals in Kansas did not operate by reason, even as they had not done so anywhere else. She remembered so many things—the people of Lawrence going by, shaking their fists at the house in which the Ross family lived; the minister who preached against Edmund, with his children sitting there helpless while he did so; the mass meeting; the old man walking up and down in front of the house that awful, unforgettable night. . . . Edmund had not shared these things, except in a secondhand way. She had never told him the whole story. She wished she could warn him now; she wished there was some way to prepare him for possible failure in his assumption that he could go back on the paper, once he returned to Lawrence. But, then again, she might be mistaken. Perhaps all would turn out as he had planned.

"You don't think I can go back, do you?" he asked.

"I don't know," she told him frankly.

"I may have to work at the case," he said. "It will be difficult, so far as my own pride is concerned. It will not pay much, so the boys will have to stop school and help out with whatever work we can get. But it will be honest work."

"Oh, of course—" Fannie said. Edmund wanted to be an editor, not a man working in the case. He had gone beyond that. But if that was all he could find, he would do it.

"At all events, it is always best to look on the bright side. We are all young, and we are strong. The world is yet before us. Thank God, we live in a country where there is always work to do."

She looked at her hands, red from the washing and ironing and cooking and dozens of jobs which were necessary each day if she were to keep the family life moving smoothly, and she could agree with him about work always being present.

"And best of all," he went on, "I will be home to stay. Do you realize how long it has been since we have been together, save for little scraps and bits of time?"

Did she realize! What did he think she was made of, anyway? Iron and steel, with a mechanism for a heart!

He went over to the sofa where the baby lay sleeping and touched the small form gently. "My little Fanny," he said, "I hope she'll know me when I come back."

"Oh, she will," Fannie assured him. And so she would—if Fannie had to talk to her all the while she slept, as well as all her waking hours, telling her that her dear Papa was soon coming home. That one thing she could spare him—the knowledge that one of his own children did not remember him because of his absence.

6

That was practically all she could save him from, however. When he finally did come home, after Congress was over in the late summer of '71, it was to find a town not so much hardened in bitterness as set into a pattern of indifference and coolness. The family was socially ostracized. Old friends who once, no matter how busy, had stopped to talk with him now passed him as if he were not there at all. But that was not the hardest thing.

"I'm going down to the *Tribune* today and ask for a job," Edmund told Fannie one morning. He didn't look at her as he spoke; and, seeing him so unsure and hurt, she wished she could call out to him that he must not go at all, even if the children did need new clothes and the food was running low and the house in need of repair. A man shouldn't have to humiliate himself just because his family needed things. But she remained silent because she knew instinctively that protest now would only add to his hurt.

She was not surprised, however, when he came back—oh, it was such a short time before she heard his steps once more on the walk. He could not have had good news, or he would never have been back so soon. When he walked into the house without speaking, she did not need to ask him what his reception had been.

"You knew," he told her quietly. "You tried to warn me, back in Washington."

"I did not know," she said. "I only suspected."

"They would not give me a job on my own paper!"

Yes, that was a hard thing—the worst blow of all. Any other paper but that one.

"They said it was because I did not belong to the printers' union. Of course, that's only an excuse—"

Seldom had she seen him more angry. He got up and paced the floor, his fists clenched. Finally he stopped in front of her and anger went out of him. He took her hand, looked at her tenderly. "This hasn't been easy for you, my girl," he said. "You were in the thick of it, seeing, hearing things I am afraid I did not realize fully until today."

"Oh, I managed," she told him staunchly.

"Sometimes I fear I've thought of you too little," he said gently. "But that is only the way things appear on the surface. I think of you so much—so much. You must know that. Whatever I do, always, is for your sake. Yours, and the children's."

"I never doubt that, Edmund," she assured him.

Silence settled over the room. Outside, in the crispness of a fall night, Fannie could hear footsteps passing along over the board sidewalk. But this was only a passer-by—not like that other awful time. And yet, the hurt they were facing was also an extension of the other episode, stemming from the same roots. Would they never be free of it!

Finally Edmund spoke. "Do you know what I'm going to do?" he asked. And then, without waiting for her answer, he went on. "I'm going to start me another paper. That's what I know how to do, anyway. Start a paper of my own. I've done it in Topeka, and I did it here in Lawrence. I can do it again."

Now it was her turn to ask a question. Where was the money coming from? One didn't start a paper with nothing more than a determination to do so.

"I'll borrow the money," he told her. "I can mortgage this house and get enough money."

Oh, no, not that. The house was the one thing which furnished some sort of security for the children.

"I'll make a paper that will sweep everything before it," he told her. Suddenly he was himself once more—confident, enthusiastic, purposeful. "I even know what my editorial policy will be. It is to expose Pomeroy and his gang of crooks. I can do it, too."

Edmund was off on another cause. Perhaps, of all the ones he had undertaken, this was the most hopeless. Pomeroy was firmly entrenched here in Kansas. There would be no shaking him, with or without the aid of a paper in which to expose him. Had he not voted for impeachment? What if he was in the middle of all sorts of corruption, both state and national?

But of course—Edmund knew all these things better than she did. So, all she asked was, "Where? Here in Lawrence?"

"No," he said with firm decision. "I'm going down to Coffeyville. There's no paper there, and it's always good to start a new paper in a town which has none."

"Coffeyville—" she said faintly. That was miles away, almost at the border of Oklahoma. "Will you take us with you?"

"No, I think not. At least, not until I get things organized. Maybe, though, I'll take Pitt and Arthur with me. I'll teach them to run a newspaper. We'll call it—" He closed his eyes a moment, thinking. And when he opened them again, his face was alight with pleasure.

"We'll call it *Ross's Paper*," he said. "Won't that be fine? *Ross's Paper*, published by Edmund G. Ross and Sons."

PART FOUR

NEW MEXICO

XII

Albuquerque

1884–1885

The wheels of the Cannon Ball Express clicked over shining bands of steel—westward, across Kansas. Outside the window the landscape flashed past, golden and opulent now in mid-July. Wheat was being harvested and fields of corn grew tall and proud. And, intermingled with them, the bright gold of the sunflowers, rank and thick beside the tracks.

Fannie rode with her back toward the engine, Eddie beside her. Fourteen-year-old Fanny and Kay, four years her senior, tremendously excited at this, their first ride in a sleeping car, wanted to have the seat which faced forward, thinking that way they would miss nothing. They acted as if they meant to sit up every mile of the way to Albuquerque, sleeping car notwithstanding. The prospect of a forty-eight-hour train ride held no threat of discomfort for them.

Fannie did not mind riding backward, facing Lawrence, facing Topeka. Memories came to her—slipping out of Put-in Bay as they left Sandusky, knowing she would not return. Sitting in the wagon as they traveled out of Milwaukee over the Janesville Plank Road with the knowledge that the Milwaukee chapter of her life was finished, too. She had looked back both times as she left, remembering. And she looked back now, and Lawrence was with her, even as she knew she would not return there, either.

The years passed before her—those swift years between the Coffeyville debacle and Edmund's going to New Mexico—years that flashed past like the landscape outside the window, melting into each other, blurring a little in their swift passage. The cyclone which dipped down on Coffeyville, destroying Edmund's printing press and leaving him, stunned and bruised but otherwise unharmed. Edmund, coming back to Lawrence without a dollar to his name, and finally getting work as a printer. (A signer of the Constitution of Kansas, a major in the Civil War, a United States Senator who had saved a President from impeachment and a nation from a blot on its record, a man who had helped bring the railroad to his state—a man like that, working at the case!) Edmund, finally managing to buy a paper of his own, the Lawrence *Standard*. Edmund, deciding to run for governor of Kansas on the Democratic ticket because the state needed a two-party system. (And he had come out not too badly either. His old friend and former commander, Colonel Moonlight, made the nominating speech and Edmund's acceptance was greeted with thunderous cheers. When the votes were counted Edmund, while not winning, had polled a third of the votes.) Edmund, serving as an elector-at-large for Tilden and, along with the rest of the nation, being indignant at the farce which defeated him. Edmund, doing well enough so he could afford to buy the Leavenworth *Press* and bring it to Lawrence, where he consolidated it with his own *Standard*. Edmund feeling the patriarch, now that three of the children—Lillie, Arthur and Pitt—were married and had started homes of their own. (Lillie had married George Leis, who had, over the years, endeared himself to the whole family.) Edmund, advocating measures which set conservative people gasping—advising Negroes not to band together distinctly as colored people. ("It fosters a spirit of clannishness," he told them. "You must exercise your own judgment and divide up among all parties, as white men do. If you are to become citizens in the full sense of the term, you must think for yourselves and act for yourselves.") Two other ideas created no less excitement—his recommendation that women be allowed the vote on matters having to do with education and that a woman be appointed as state superintendent of instruction.

"You'll get no end of discussion on *that*," Fannie warned him when he told her about it.

"Women as well as Negroes have a right to representation in the government," he said. "And anyway, who knows better than I do how well women can manage? Sometimes when I think of all the things I have left for you to care for—home, and children and business—I feel that you are far more capable than I am."

"Oh, my goodness, Edmund," she said. "What a way to talk—it's so little I've done. So little, compared to what I want to do."

He came over and took her hand, turned it over and then back again, looking at both the palm and the top. For a moment she felt self-conscious that he should see it the way it was—red from cleaning and cooking and washing; needle-pricked from sewing; knuckles enlarged from much work. The gold band on her finger had grown thinner down the years; it was not exactly the same as it had been when he put it there, almost thirty years ago. But then, neither was she the same.

"A lovely hand still," he told her softly. "It bears honorable scars, which serve to make it more beautiful."

"Oh, you—" she said, laughing a little thickly. But she did not withdraw her hand. At that moment Eddie came in upon them and, with a young girl's characteristic embarrassment at any such behavior on the part of her parents, said, "Excuse me," and turned to go.

"Don't leave," her father said. "I was just trying to tell your mother what a fine woman she is."

"Yes, Papa—" Eddie said. And fled hastily.

Edmund turned to smile mischievously at Fannie. "Now how do you suppose they think they got here?" he mused. "That we picked them out of a Kansas sunflower patch?"

"Perhaps—with a few snatched from a Wisconsin blackberry

row, and one in an Ohio marsh."

They laughed together like children. And wouldn't Eddie have been shocked at that, had she remained!

The years had brought other gains. Papers around the state began to take notice of Edmund, to report favorably on his policies and his activities. And *Scribner's Magazine* wrote to ask him to do an article about the impeachment.

"Oh, I'm so proud," Fannie told him. "People are relenting now. They see you were right."

"Thinking people never questioned it," he told her calmly.

Perhaps the thing which made him happiest was that, at last, he could put on the masthead of his Lawrence paper the thing he had so long wanted.

"E. G. Ross and Sons, editors."

This caption could go on not one, but two papers. The *Evening Standard* "published every afternoon at four o'clock (Sunday excepted) $5.00 a year" and the Lawrence *Standard* "published every Friday, $1.00 per year."

But these things did not come without struggle. It was no wonder that, for the first time in his active life, Edmund's health began to fail. He blamed it on the Kansas winters, but she knew better. No man can stand up for years under a barrage of hate, adverse criticism, privations and worry about money without showing the strain.

It was a great source of satisfaction when his article appeared in *Scribner's* in April 1882. He handed her the magazine wordlessly, but his face showed his pride. She turned the pages until she came to the article, saw "by Edmund G. Ross" under the title, and thought, "This is the story of a life here. What came before was a prelude to his vote; what has come after is a result."

She handed the magazine back to Edmund.

"Read it to me," she said.

"You've read it—and listened to portions of it—until I should think you wouldn't even want to see it."

"Read it to me—" she repeated.

And so, while a Kansas twilight settled around them, he read aloud the story of the trial which, almost fifteen years ago, had shaken a nation and altered his life, as well as the lives of his family.

> At this point the intensity with which the gaze of the audience was fixed upon the figure then on the floor was beyond description. Hope and fear seemed blended in every face . . . not only were the occupants of the gallery bending forward in intense and breathless silence and anxiety to catch the verdict, but the Senators in their seats leaned over their desks, many with hand to ear . . . conscious that I was at that moment the focus of all eyes, and conscious also of the far-reaching effect, especially upon myself . . . it is something morc than a similc to say I was almost literally looking down into my open grave. . . . Friends, position, fortune, everything that makes life desirable to an ambitious man were about to be swept away by the breath of my mouth, perhaps forever . . .
>
> Then the verdict came—"Not Guilty"—in a voice that could not be misunderstood. The die was cast. The historic trial of the age was practically ended. American institutions had successfully endured a strain that would have wrecked any other form of government . . .

When he had finished, he looked up at her.

"Does it read as well as we hoped it would?" he asked.

"Even better," she told him.

As, indeed, it did. Where there might well have been bitterness or even a swaggering defiance, there was only a clear, unprejudiced explanation of what had happened and the reason back of it.

"It is very good," she told him. "I am sure you will receive a great deal of favorable comment on it."

In this prediction she had been right. A great many letters came to Edmund, praising not only his article, but also the stand he had taken at the time of the impeachment trial. Most of them said the writers had always been on Edmund's side. This was all very gratifying, but Fannie wondered why they had waited so long to proclaim themselves. They wrote now, after the years when Edmund had been the target of a flow of hate and abuse such as few men had ever experienced as well as accusations both unfounded and unprincipled and had undergone, for himself and his family, privations it was best not to allow oneself to recall. No wonder his health had failed. It broke her heart to see him so worn and ill.

Actually, the letters seemed to put new spirit in him. He looked better than she had seen him in years. One letter bore a New Mexico postmark. She could see that Edmund was pleased, even before he shared the contents with her.

"They have read my article in *Scribner's*," he told her, "and want me to attend a fair at Albuquerque, with all expenses paid. The purpose of the fair is to promote the development of the region. They'd like me to come out, take a look around, and then do some articles about the country."

Her pleasure was as great as his. "Oh, Edmund," she cried. "How wonderful—"

"I am pleased," he said simply, looking years younger and much stronger as he spoke.

He went to New Mexico. Scarcely had he arrived than he wrote back that he found the place a real land of promise and would like to stay. He could get a job on the Albuquerque *Journal*. His health, he added, already seemed improved, out in this dry sunny climate. He hated the thought of facing another raw Kansas winter.

Fannie sat holding his letter in her hand. I am almost fifty-five years old, she thought, and Edmund is more than a year older. By now we ought to be settling down—two contented, lazy old people, ready to sit by our own fireside while the young people carry on the work of the world. In Lawrence, even as it was in the nation, there had been a definite swing in Edmund's favor; why wasn't he content to stay here?

But when had Edmund ever been content to settle down and let well enough alone?

She answered as he had known she would; as she had answered him down the years when he wanted to move on.

"You must do what you think best, Edmund."

He had stayed, and she had known he would. And Pitt and his

family had joined him.

It was with a real start that Kay's words came through to Fannie now.

"Mama," he asked, "do you suppose Papa will meet us at the train? At three o'clock in the morning—"

"He'll be there," Fannie promised, trying not to sound as excited as she felt. The last time Edmund had met her train was . . . Ah, yes—in Washington. Little Fanny, her namesake, had been in her arms then, and now, at fourteen, the girl thought herself a young lady. Perhaps she was right. When she herself had been that age, she was in Sandusky, just becoming aware of a young lad named Edmund Ross.

Indeed, the years did fly by.

2

Fannie Ross had not realized air could be so light and dry, so clear and bracing, as it was here in Albuquerque. Nor she had known sunshine could be so bright and unfiltered by clouds, nor that at night the stars and moon could look so close you felt you had only to reach up and gather them into a sort of heavenly bouquet. She felt curiously elated, and almost young again, with the delightful undercurrent which is the essence of youth—that each day something good might happen.

Twelve miles to the east of town the Sandia Mountains rose, darkly blue against a bright blue sky and, running through the town itself, the blue thread of the Rio Grande. It was called a river, although there were times when it seemed no more than a mere trickle. Still, Edmund warned her that quick torrential rains would come, sending raging floods down the dry bed. He bemoaned the fact that all that good water must run away in a matter of a few hours from a country which knew a year-round need of it. "We should make some attempt at conservation, at building dams, in order to keep at least a part of it with us," he said each time the rains came. With the first big rain she quite understood what he meant. She watched the water, reaching from bank to bank, rushing down the river bed, urgent and unrestrained, thinking as she did so of the other bodies of water she had lived close to. Each, in its own way, had been flowing away to destinations already determined. In a way this was her life—forever joining the stream of emigrants, drawn to new lands by forces stronger and more compelling than themselves. She and the rivers she had lived by—it was no use to fight their ultimate destiny. Here she was, for reasons strange and complicated, in a new land.

And yet, Albuquerque was not a new town. Some of the long, low, broad adobe buildings which made up Old Town had been built in 1650, when the town was founded. Their flat roofs still held off the sun, drained off the scanty rainfall. And the people who lived in them were, in themselves, alien and strange, but thoroughly delightful to Fannie, the sounds of their liquid voices speaking Spanish a perpetual joy to her. Edmund had already mastered enough of the tongue to communicate with them after a fashion.

For Fanny and Kay, the delights of the town were not made up of the old, quaint characters, interesting as these might be. There was an opera house, open every evening. A roller-skating rink. And, as they said in awe, "Ten thousand people in the town—it's a city, Mama."

The best thing about the whole business was to see how well Edmund looked, and to find him once more filled with enthusiasm. And, of course, that they could be together once more. It was good, too, to see how much Edmund liked the town and the region. It sounded as if, at last, he had found a place where he wanted to spend the rest of his life.

Fannie settled their belongings into the new home. The piano (brought overland by freight, and what a job it had been); the chairs and tables and other furniture which had seen so many moves by now; and, of course, the quilt. She found herself liking the town almost as much as did the others in the family. Old Town, so picturesque and quaint; New Town, growing up around the red railroad station; the jingling, mule-drawn streetcar which connected them. Beyond the town lay the Sandia Mountains, with their blue silvery sides and the Douglas fir, the Colorado blue spruce, the white and yellow pine growing at their base, with some clambering up the sides. And over it all the blue and purple shadows which, for a while at evening, flamed rose and gold only to be displaced a little later by the deep blue shadows once more.

Edmund, while not discounting the charm of the region, was more concerned with practical matters.

"We have the largest city in the territory," he said. "We have buildings which would do credit to St. Louis or Kansas City. We have a trade which is rapidly reaching out into every part of New Mexico and Arizona."

He had found a new cause to advocate.

"There's difficulty, though, about claims," he went on. "An emigrant wishing to make a homestead entry resorts to plats in land offices. By the time he finds land open to entry, and goes to his land, often he'll find it occupied or claimed under Mexican title. Then comes a long contest before land officers can report to Washington—and all that time, the land can't be settled."

Another wrong to right.

"And there's a bunch of crooks—they are called 'The Santa Fe Ring'—down at the Territorial Capitol that have all decent legislation tied up. There's a tooth-and-nail fight between Santa Fe and Albuquerque anyway. It looks as if whatever one proposes, the other tries to block."

He wasn't going to get mixed up in politics again, was he? Surely he had had enough of that.

"And the Indians—they're keeping settlers from coming out here. There's a no-good scalawag named Geronimo who is leading them in all kinds of depredations. The settlers are helpless. Arms are issued to the Indians, but the Territory can't build up a militia. Just the way it was in Kansas."

Oh, exactly as things had been in Kansas. Land difficulties and crooked politicians; towns fighting each other for positions of power; Indians raiding white settlers. He had gone the full circle, back in Kansas, and here he was ready to start all over in this new land.

"We need to become a state," he told her. "Things won't get any better so long as we are a territory, with our affairs administered by men sent out here by the government. Men who, often as not, know nothing at all about our needs."

Yes, it was the same. Almost she might once more be the young matron, Fannie Ross, driving into the little town of Topeka with her three small children playing in the back of the wagon.

When the Democrats, meeting in Chicago in June 1884, nominated Grover Cleveland, Edmund was elated.

"You'll see," he said, "they'll win this time. Cleveland is a good man—honest, fearless, capable. Besides, the Republicans have behind them those years of monopolies and scandals. It's time for a change, and we'll have it."

"The Santa Fe Ring," Edmund went on, "is Republican, too. With the coming of a Democratic administration, they'll be out."

That she could understand. In territories, appointments came out of Washington, and no Democratic president would put back into office Republicans now there, even had they been less corrupt and graft-ridden than the Santa Fe Ring was supposed to be.

"Do you know what I'm a notion to do?" he asked her.

Naturally, she had no idea.

"If Grover Cleveland is elected, and I think he will be, I'm going to ask for the position of Territorial Governor of New Mexico."

"Oh, Edmund—" the words were wrung from her against her will, against her judgment.

"What's the matter?" he asked her quickly. "Don't you want me to have the job?"

"No, no—" she said. "That's not it at all. You know it isn't—"

How to tell him she did not want him facing defeat again? Among all those politicians who would be begging for the job—the Democrats had been out of office for so long, there would be dozens for every available job—among this horde, he would have no chance at all. Besides, territorial governors were usually appointed from among the men close to the new President, men he felt he must reward. Why would Edmund, off here in New Mexico, miles away from the center where such matters were decided, think he had a chance? His years in Washington, his experience with appointments in Kansas should have taught him that. Now just when they were settled in Albuquerque, with things going smoothly, why did he even want to think of risking this new-found peace and security? Well, perhaps the thing would be solved by Cleveland's defeat. She need not rush to meet trouble. Besides, no Democratic President had occupied the White House since Buchanan. The party was probably dead, and would never come back.

She couldn't have been more mistaken. In November, Cleveland was swept into office. Edmund at once began making his plans.

"As soon as the inauguration is over, I'll go out and press my claims," he told her. "I know enough to realize the man on the scene has more chance. And by the way—that's my best argument for appointment—the man on the scene knows best what the Territory should have in the way of government."

"I suspect that's right," Fannie agreed. But what a situation he would be facing if he did get the appointment! Crooked politicians in the government, Indian troubles, land scandals, graft. Why did he want the place? Why didn't she rise up and say, "Edmund—get this foolish idea out of your head. Live your last days in peace and comfort. You are almost fifty-nine years old. You are entitled to take things easy."

And, even as the question came to her, so did the answer.

Years ago when she had seen the Brady portrait of him she was concerned because it made him look less than the good fighter he had always been. She remembered her relief at hearing his speech on the Senate floor. Across the years, his words came back to her. "I have faced many a danger before without loss of nerve or self-respect. . . ."

She was proud then, and she was proud now. That was why she made no protest.

3

The inauguration over, Edmund went to Washington. He wrote back that President Cleveland had received him very kindly. Of course, the Albuquerque papers snatched at every bit of news, rumor, or fact which they could settle upon. The *Evening Democrat* reported, and with good reason, that until a governor was appointed, all politicians would be in a state of suspense. They further stated that the contest clearly lay between Judge Trimble and E. G. Ross, with Ross' chances being greater. The paper went on to say that New Mexico wanted and needed a man from the Territory rather than an outsider. It also said (and Fannie read the lines several times) "Ross is a good man. He knows the Territory and will represent it well. We want no outsider in the Governor's chair. Ross will represent all."

She was not really surprised when she had his letter from Washington. "Dear Wife," he wrote, "I have had a great victory. Only eight days after my arrival I was confirmed, and that almost without opposition."

She did what any other woman would have done at the news which told her that her husband had won a thing he very much wanted. She had a good cry.

When the news was announced officially, the *Democrat* broke into headlines, giant in size and lyric in quality.

GOVERNOR ROSS—THE MAN WANTED BY THE WHOLE TERRITORY

NO MORE LAND STEALS, NO MORE RINGS

A PURE AND HONEST ADMINISTRATION—FIRST IN THE TERRITORY FOR MANY YEARS

HONESTY IN POLICY: HONESTY IN EVERYTHING

Fannie read the article which followed. Kay and young Fanny read and reread it.

"Oh, Mama," Fanny said in awed wonder. "You will be the wife of the Governor of New Mexico Territory. Aren't you proud?"

"I'm proud and pleased because your father wanted it," she said. "But then," she added honestly, "I've always been proud of him."

"Does that mean we'll be moving to Santa Fe?"

"I imagine so—"

"To the Governor's Palace—Oh, Mama, it is all so wonderful—"

"Yes," her mother agreed. "Yes, it is, my dear."

And so it was, but not for the reason the young girl had in mind. Not because now they would be the wife and children of a governor, living in that lovely and historic Old Palace in Santa Fe; nor yet because they would be people of consequence in the Territory, if not in the nation. Rather, to her, it was because she felt that, at long last, Edmund was on his way to being justified in the step he had taken at the time of the impeachment, the step which had cost him so much trouble in the years since. The appointment would bear the stamp of a public vindication, almost a public apology for the treatment Edmund had received for performing an act which he believed not only to be his duty, but one which would save the honor of the nation.

It was too much, of course, to expect that the papers of Santa Fe would share the delight of those in Albuquerque. To begin with, there was a running feud between the two towns and little of good could be found by either with anything the other did. This disapproval was extended to the residents of the towns. And then, naturally, the Santa Fe Ring would certainly not be pleased at the prospect of being unseated. The Santa Fe *New Mexican Review* referred to Edmund as "Albuquerque's Patron Saint." But it also said, "Even those who most roundly abused Ross for his vote at the time of impeachment have found time to repent in the sixteen years that have elapsed since then and have joined in popular request that he be appointed."

Perhaps, Fannie thought, they are trying to smooth over their guilty consciences at the way they acted. All over the country, the papers took up the cry of approval. The New York *Times*, remembering the impeachment trial, labeled Edmund's vote as "one of the bravest ever cast." The Leavenworth *Evening Standard* had kind and glowing words to say. Approval poured in from every side. Letters from people they had known in former days came now to Albuquerque. Perhaps of all of them, Fannie cherished most the one from Colonel Holliday.

My very dear old Friend,

The most sincere note of congratulations I have ever penned, I pen today in offering you my earnest, cordial, hearty and enthusiastic congratulations upon your being appointed Governor of the Territory of New Mexico. . . . This is not clap-trap; I mean all I say and a thousand times more.

I should perhaps add, what you already know . . . that your appointment meets the approval of everybody in Kansas. Your political (for you have no *personal*) foes join me in congratulations. The "Old Timers" are simply jubilant.

Your Sincere Friend,
C. K. Holliday

Fannie wondered if the good colonel realized while he was writing that, in order to arrive in Santa Fe from the east, Edmund would come swinging across the plains of Kansas, into the bright clear atmosphere of New Mexico, over the rails of the road that he and Colonel Holliday, in the years gone by, had helped to establish. Could either of them have foreseen then the destiny which would be served in its making, he would have thought it too strange a thing to believe.

There were some who believed that Edmund should be inaugurated in Santa Fe at daybreak, following the tradition of the coming of Montezuma at sunrise. He was to be a Democratic Montezuma, arriving at sunrise, in all the glory of a new day to lead his Democratic warriors to victory and additional triumphs in the great Territory of New Mexico. The whole idea sounded a bit fanciful and high-flown to Fannie, but evidently either Edmund agreed or decided it could do no harm, for he went along with it. His train was scheduled to arrive at 1:00 A.M., and according to the plans, as soon as he was there, he and his party would take their places in the Old Palace, where he would be sworn in. When this was accomplished, he would come on to Albuquerque where his family awaited him. Because of the early hour, as well as the fact that the plans had been made hurriedly, the family did not plan to attend the inauguration. Pitt, however, announced his intention of going.

"You know there'll be all sorts of business for him to attend to," Pitt pointed out. "Papa certainly won't be here before evening, and maybe not even until the next day. You'll want to know how it went, anyway."

With that she could heartily agree.

She had not realized how anxious she was to hear about it all until Pitt stood before her giving the accounts.

"It was tremendously impressive, Mama. It took place in the Old Palace, as had been planned. Even as early as that, the Plaza was busy and excited—"

He sketched in the details, knowing she would want to hear every single bit he had to say. The sun was just coming up from behind the snow-covered mountains, the pinkness spreading over the laurel and spruce as well as the town itself. Cannons boomed and fifty American flags whipped out in the fresh morning air. The Thirteenth United States Infantry Band played martial music, and half a hundred young men, both Democrats and Republicans, were on hand to congratulate the new governor.

"When the time came for the ceremony," Pitt went on, "the Honorable Henry Vincent said, 'Governor, the hour has arrived.' Papa stepped into the center of the room. The Honorable Chief Justice Vincent took his place slightly in advance of Judge Waldo. Everyone became very quiet and then the chief justice administered the oath to Papa. When it was finished, Papa was Governor of New Mexico Territory. It was all dignified and impressive. I was proud of Papa."

"Of course," Fannie said. Why shouldn't he be!

"Anyway, it's just as I said. He won't be here until tomorrow. He'll come by train. I think half the town is planning to meet him. And there'll be a reception following. It's a great time, Mama."

A great time, indeed! How great, neither Pitt nor any of the children could know except in part. Only she and Edmund could look back over the long years from Sandusky to Santa Fe, and know all that lay back of the moment when Edmund Gibson Ross, the new Governor of New Mexico Territory, stepped off the train at Albuquerque, to be greeted by family and friends and the enthusiastic citizens of the town.

4

Fannie, from her place on the platform at the station, decided that Pitt had been right when he said half the town would be down to meet Edmund. There was a banner at least nine feet long proclaiming in great red letters, "Welcome, Governor Ross." There were scores of young girls, their hands full of summer flowers with which to pelt the governor, once he got off the train. The band was standing ready to start playing, the moment the train came into sight. And, at the Hotel Felipe, the preparations for the reception were in full blast.

The children stood around her, all dressed in their best, scarcely able to control their excitement. Pitt and Arthur and their wives; Eddie and Kay and Fanny. Only Lillie was not there. Lillie, and Flint—

"There she comes—" someone cried.

Sure enough, the train was a speck in the distance. It came nearer, a plume of smoke curving backward over its length. The band struck up, after a few false notes, for even its members shared the excitement. The girls raised the flowers in their hands, just so they would not be caught unready. Horns began to blow.

The train drew to a triumphant stop, the engineer leaning out of his cab, conscious of his part in the drama, a wide smile on his face. The conductor opened the door and came down the steps. Then, there was Edmund, looking dignified and happy. A great cheer arose from the welcoming crowd. The banner of welcome was raised high. The band played loudly.

Edmund did not seem to be aware of any of these things. His eyes swept the platform, restless, searching, and then, across the crowd, Fannie and Edmund exchanged glances.

Without a word to any of those others waiting to do him honor, Edmund made his way across the platform, pushing aside those who would detain him—not rudely, but with purpose. Then he came to her and without a word took her in his arms. There were tears in his eyes, although how she knew this she could not say, for her own were filled with tears. The others might be cheering their heads off, but neither she nor Edmund said a word.

Why should they? This thing went beyond the need of speech.

XIII

The Governor's Lady

1885–1889

THE OLD PALACE in Santa Fe, flat-roofed, gray, made of adobe bricks, stretched out a good four hundred feet along the north side of the Plaza. Built in a hollow rectangle, it had a grassy plot in the center. The recent renovations undertaken by Territorial Governor Lew Wallace (who wrote his famous novel *Ben Hur* while in residence at the Palace) had done little to change the essential character of the building. He had added white pillars and scrollwork corbels and, along the entire front, a low white balustrade of wooden pegs surmounted by white wooden urns in line with each pillar below. These innovations seemed to fit into the ancient structure and, rather than changing it, were absorbed by it so that the whole impression was one of ancient dignity, Spanish in flavor.

Fannie Ross, moving into the quarters provided for the Governor and his family, had a sense of belonging. The rooms with their beamed ceilings and corner fireplaces enchanted her. Three bedrooms and a sitting room formed one unit which opened into a hall. To the right of this hall were the dining room, two kitchens (each with its own pantry), the parlor and, opening off it, Edmund's office. She needed only to open the connecting door in order to be in the room with him. Of course, she would never do this without good reason, but it was a comfort to know he was as close as that.

Eddie was acting as his secretary, a position which kept her occupied and gave Edmund a source of much-needed help. Kay divided his time between Santa Fe and Albuquerque. It was young Fanny who found time to explore the place, finding it full of excitement and wonder.

"Mama," she asked in awe, "did you know this Palace is two hundred and seventy-five years old!"

"Yes," Fannie told her. "That's what they tell me."

"And the flags of four countries—Spain, Mexico, the Con federacy, and the United States—have flown over it."

"Yes—" Fannie said. "It's not only old; it's historic."

"It's the oldest capitol now within the boundaries of the United States."

"I hadn't thought about that," Fannie told her.

"Well, it's true," the girl said, quite pleased that she could pass some information new to her mother.

Indeed, Fannie thought, there was a sense of history in all Santa Fe, so far as that went, for here was blended, more so than in any other part of the nation, the diverse strains of three different cultures—Indian, Spanish, and American. From the time when Don Pedro de Peralta, third governor of the "Kingdom and Province of New Mexico," founded it at a spot known to the Pueblo Indians as Kuapoga, "the place of the shell beads near the water," the town had been important to the various countries who held it. Peralta had built the Old Palace as a fort, laid out the Plaza, and planned a walled city. Young Fanny said, "And do you know, Mama, that even now people occasionally find sections of the old wall? They say this used to be the site of a Tano Indian village. Since then it's never ceased to be the seat of a government."

"Yes, I know—" Fannie said. Sixty Spanish governors had lived here for a period of two hundred and twelve years, ruling a vast territory, maintaining the Spanish against invasion from the north. This occupation was interrupted for a twelve-year period when the Pueblo Indians revolted, drove the Spaniards out and themselves occupied the Palace. In 1821, when Mexico gained its independence from Spain, the flag of the new republic waved over the Palace; in August 1846, General Kearny marched his United States troops into the town, raising his flag over the Palace and making the territory, in a bloodless revolution, a province of the United States. In February 1862, Confederate forces under General Sibley took the town and, for two weeks, the Stars and Bars proclaimed the Palace southern property, only to be superseded by the Union Flag when the United States troops, stationed at Fort Union, chased the Confederates out of Santa Fe. Yes, Fanny was right when she said she could feel history as she walked the streets of the town.

"And Mama," Fanny went on, "I am simply fascinated with La Fonda!"

"And well you might be," her mother agreed.

It stood on the southeast corner of the Plaza, a one-story building built around a central patio with large corral and stables to the south. The Americans had used the place for an inn since the beginning of their occupation in 1846. Here the Santa Fe Trail ended; here Kit Carson stayed; here Spanish grandees, trappers, freighters, traders, merchants, soldiers—all the various kinds of men (and women) who made their way to Santa Fe—had found lodging.

"I just get shivery with excitement, looking at the place, remembering all those people who have stayed there. And there are lots of interesting people coming in all the time, right now. I stand on the corner of the park, and watch—"

The Plaza itself was of intense interest to all the Ross family. Fannie in her sitting room and Edmund in his office could look out on it. The park in the center had been surrounded by a white wooden picket fence. On the Palace side was a hexagonal bandstand with a pointed roof topped by a carved urn. The edges of the hexagon were finished with wooden lace. The Plaza seemed to be the center of the city's public entertainment. In the daytime people sat resting in the shade of the giant cottonwoods; in the evening they went walking there, seeing what there was to see. On the streets surrounding it the Indians, wearing their native costumes, displayed their wares.

On Tuesday, Thursday, and Sunday evenings, from six to seven, the regimental band of the United States garrison gave concerts. Red, white, and blue bunting fluttered from the lacy points of the hexagonal stand while the musicians (Negro soldiers in uniform) and their German conductor went through a program made up of martial airs, overtures, waltzes, and selections from grand opera as well as light opera.

"Mama, look," Fanny said, the first time the family strolled over to listen to the music. "Look—all the musicians except the drummer are wearing white gloves!"

And indeed they were.

"How well they play," Edmund remarked. "Fannie, we must start the family singing together once more. What a good thing you brought the piano—"

It is all good, Fannie thought—the town itself, nestled in the little valley of the Rio de Santa Fe, where it emerged from the foothills of the Sangre de Cristo Mountains on the east; to the south, the Sandia Mountains, and to the West, the Jemenez Range. Lying inside these snow-covered peaks was a land of vast distances and the deep colors of the mesas, standing up like medieval cathedrals out of the red sand around them. And at their base, the wild verbena covering the hills with a blue and rose and purple mist.

Fannie never tired of watching the mountains, which seemed to change color constantly as shadows passed over them or the sun lighted them up, shifting as the waters of the sea would shift. She was glad, also, for the little stream running through the town. Again, she was living close to water. She was enchanted with the ancient, narrow streets of the town itself, the brown adobe houses; patios with hollyhocks and towering cottonwoods and fruit trees; crumbling gateways or ancient walls where adobe bricks showed through broken earthen plaster. In the evening, the fragrance of the piñon fires filled the air. Each room in the Palace had its own corner fireplace where the sweet-swelling piñon logs were burned.

Edmund was delighted with the town.

"I am going to do myself the honor of calling on Archbishop Lamy," he told Fannie.

Almost from the first, New Mexico had been a missionary area, its history linked with that of the Roman Catholic Church and Mexico. Priests had gone to this region, working with the Indians, sometimes converting them, sometimes being martyred by them. It was Bishop Lamy who had made truly great strides since his appointment in 1850. He had done much good, and was revered and loved by all. Largely through his efforts, the Cathedral of St. Francis was built.

Edmund came home from his official call as Governor to say, "That's a fine man. He received me most kindly. I have a great deal of respect for him, and hope we shall see more of each other."

2

In the fall young Fanny was enrolled at the Loretta Academy.

"I've never been so happy in all my life, Mama," she said. "When I listen to those bells in the Cathedral ring out—did you know they are supposed to have been made from silver captured from the Moors?—well, when I hear them they seem to tell me I ought to be thankful for being here. And, truly, I am."

For Edmund, the days had a more sober note. Geronimo, the wily Apache, at the head of his murderous band, had returned from Old Mexico and was making his way into New Mexico Territory. The residents of Santa Fe shivered at the sound of the name; how must the settlers perched on the very edge of civilization feel at hearing the news?

Repeatedly the tales came in, of atrocities against women and children; of burning of crops and homes; of destruction of property; of stealing of horses and cattle—almost it might have been western Kansas twenty-odd years ago, so much alike the stories were. Then it had been Fall Leaf and others; now it was Geronimo. No Peace Commission now, as then; just Edmund Ross, the Governor of the Territory of New Mexico, to decide how the threat must best be met.

"Can't you call on the United States Army forces to help out?" Fannie suggested. "They're close enough."

"Close, yes. But who are their scouts? Apaches, and the settlers have no faith in that breed. And with good reason. There is need for a Territorial Militia as well. The Indians need to know that the settlers will be able to protect themselves, that acts of murder and pillage will be punished, and swiftly. There are too many people in the region now for us to abandon the country. Nor can we allow it to become worthless because new settlers will hear of the raids and be discouraged about settling here."

She was relieved—but not at all surprised—that Edmund should take quick and decisive action.

"I have published orders to the Militia commanders in the Territory to have authority to put scouting parties in the field," he told Fannie. "Especially at the water holes. We are going to show the Indian we mean business."

He fired off letters by the score—to the army commanders in the region, to Secretary of War Endicott in Washington. To the latter, Edmund pointed out that the Militia members needed decent weapons. The ones they had were of inferior quality while the Indians themselves had the best of army rifles, furnished them either openly or by stealth.

"That's the big trouble," he told Fannie. "Renegade whites. They slip the Indians rifles and whiskey. Sometimes they even take part in the depredations against their own kind. It's no new problem—every state in the Union, since Plymouth, has had to meet it."

"How can white men betray their own kind!" Fannie protested.

"No need to act as if we thought the white race had a monopoly on all the virtues," Edmund pointed out. "If I had my way, there'd be a law punishing white men who went on reservations without authority just as there is, supposedly, one to punish Indians who leave without permission. That's a two-way street, as I see it."

"When you consider everything," Fannie mused, "it's amazing that the priests have accomplished as much as they have down the years. With whites, as well as Indians."

"It is indeed," Edmund told her. "And by the way, I heard today that Archbishop Lamy has announced his retirement."

"But who will take his place?" Fannie asked.

"Archbishop Salpointe," Edmund told her.

3

From the first moments when the twenty-seventh legislative assembly convened in December, it was evident that the members meant to give the new Governor a hard time. The assembly, overwhelmingly Republican, ignored whatever policies Edmund favored; it was only with the greatest of difficulty that he was able to put through any measure which would be to his party's credit.

At every turn, the members set up frustrating and humiliating restrictions on Edmund—unseating enough Democrats so that the Republicans could at all times command a two-thirds majority and thus be able to override the Governor's veto. But this did not prevent Edmund from exercising his right—he vetoed laws whenever he felt them unwise and unjust. Fannie thought he might as well have saved himself the effort it took to do it.

"Couldn't you go along with them—" she suggested, and then, seeing the black look on his face, went on hastily, "Oh, I mean, just a little—enough to—well—" She could not finish. She knew what she was suggesting was compromise, and with that Edmund never had any patience.

"Listen, Fannie," he told her, "the affairs of the Territory are a disgrace. You know yourself the scandals which have come out of speculation in territorial warrants. It's pretty generally known that a few men in Santa Fe have grown rich by taking advantage of time payments on these debts. I won't compromise there; I'm going to see that the finances of the Territory are put on a cash basis."

There was the drought, which came soon after he went into office.

Fannie, looking across the sun-scorched plains around Santa Fe, could almost believe herself to be once more in Kansas, with the dry cracks opening in the earth and all living vegetation seared and brown. The blazing wind, sapping the life out of humans as well as crops, could have been a Kansas wind, and the deep despair was an old one, known long ago to the young Rosses in another land, another time. Now, as then, Edmund did not lose courage. He talked of conservation and building up better herds. "A rancher with a few head of good cattle is better off than he would be with a thousand poor ones. And the sorry cattle eat as much, or more, than the good ones."

In the midst of the Kansas drought he had talked railroads, now it was better cattle he urged. Always the forward look, forever the hope that refused to falter. And, when the rains did come to New Mexico Territory, even as they had done in Kansas, Edmund was the first to begin talking of water conservation.

"Floods do a great deal of damage, washing out crops and even railroads," he said. "There should be storage basins at the heads of various rivers, especially the Rio Grande. Canyons could well serve as places for storage, and later the water could be used for irrigation."

Would he never get over planning big things for the land where he lived!

"By the way," he said, "do you know what Archbishop Lamy is doing?"

"Taking a good rest, I trust," Fannie said.

"He's in Old Mexico begging contributions for the Cathedral here," Edmund told her. "He's riding horseback and muleback and they say by the time he's finished he will have ridden better than ten thousand miles."

"Some men don't know the meaning of the word 'rest,' " Fannie said, smiling slightly.

"It pleases me a great deal to be able to send in a good report to the Secretary of the Interior," Edmund went on, quite missing her point, as she had known he would. "I can tell him that since last April, since General Miles assumed command of the Militia Department, not a single instance of depredation by hostile Indians has taken place against the lives and properties of settlers."

"That's a great thing you have done, insisting on a well-armed militia," Fannie said warmly.

"We have only to contrast it with last year," he said, "when not less than one hundred people were killed and many thousands of dollars of property were lost. Business was stagnant and settlers were afraid to come in."

Certainly things were better now. At long last Geronimo had been captured and sent to Fort Sill, in Oklahoma, for the rest of his life. No more would his fearful shadow spread over the homes of innocent settlers. Also, the finances of the Territory were finally in a more favorable state. People were at least beginning to think of conserving water and planting alfalfa; of smaller herds of good stock feeding on better grass.

Perhaps there were some men who were not supposed to know what the word "rest" meant.

She was reminded of this thought again when Archbishop Lamy came back from his travels in Old Mexico to report the success of his mission.

Indeed, there were some men who should not take their rest, so long as there was work for them to do.

4

"Mama," Fanny said, "there's going to be some sort of celebration tonight. I heard about it at school today. We must watch out for it."

Santa Fe was a town of celebrations, of feasts, and of processions, swaying slowly along, carrying their sodality banners, their candles, their statues. Invariably the clergy, richly dressed, brought up the rear. December was the time of celebrating the feast of the Virgin of Guadalupe, but it was October now, with the golden aspens splashed across every canyon, showing all the brighter against the evergreens of the mountains with their snow-covered peaks.

"This is the Feast of St. Francis," the girl explained. "They say he's Santa Fe's patron saint. Did you know Santa Fe is really named 'The Royal City of the Holy Faith of St. Francis of Assisi'?"

"Somewhere I'd heard it. Of course we'll watch for the procession this evening."

The celebration started at dusk. Young boys with torches of burning pine lighted bonfires of short sticks of piñon wood laid in hollow squares. Firelight sprang up in front of shops and houses looking up toward the cathedral at the head of San Francisco Street, crowded with people in spite of the sharp evening air.

"Look—it's started," Fanny said as she stood with her mother and Edmund in the park.

The procession came slowly forward from the cathedral doors, the marchers carrying candles, singing plaintive Spanish hymns as they came.

"The Sisters say it won't be just their own people in the procession, but other townspeople, as well," Fanny explained.

Of course not. For several hundred years the good Brothers of St. Francis had labored here among the people, at first suffering great danger and disappointments in their work. No one in the entire Territory could fail to recognize the contributions of these men.

Certainly as a Democratic appointee Edmund could not expect to be popular with the Republicans. But one would think that, when he advocated worthwhile measures, he might have had some support. Rarely was this the case. Sometimes she thought Edmund was also to blame for the stormy times that went on within the Legislature. He was not the most tactful of men; he would not budge an inch from the thing he thought should be done. But, even so, there were some gains. She went over them in her mind, feeling courage and pride as she did so.

Edmund, addressing the New Mexico Education Association, telling the members that "ignorance is slavery; intelligent education is freedom. No community can long preserve its freedom that fails to provide for the education of its youth." Edmund, advocating woman suffrage in school affairs on equal terms with men. (And what a furor that had raised—a condition which disturbed him not at all. "I have only to remember how you handled the home and the family while I was gone," he told her, "to provide my answer. To what better hands can we entrust the education of the young than to their mothers?") Edmund, signing a decree "Establishing within the Territory of New Mexico an institution of learning to be known as the University of New Mexico" (how proud he had been, more than twenty years ago, when Lillie enrolled in the newly opened University of Kansas); Edmund, journeying down to Albuquerque, where the new University would be located, in order to give the formal address when Whittin Hall was opened. Edmund, writing a recommendation suggesting that the Old Palace be "preserved as a museum, public library and archaeological curiosity, since it is looked upon by every native New Mexican with respect and veneration." Edmund, pushing hard for statehood, disappointed when the Congress refused, the House voting for, the Senate against; Edmund, writing his protest to Congress, "New Mexico was settled years before Jamestown, New Amsterdam, or Plymouth. For over forty years it has been electing its own legislature." Edmund, pointing out that New Mexico's mixed population—Indians, Spanish, Mexicans and restless, enterprising Americans—was a good and stable mixture to add to the nation.

These were the accomplishments on which she should concentrate, rather than on the frustrations and difficulties which he had to undergo.

5

Just before eight o'clock on the morning of February 13, 1888, all the church bells of Santa Fe began to toll. No need to ask the reason. For some days now Archbishop Lamy had been gravely ill; the bells could signal but one thing, his death. Santa Fe immediately went into a state of mourning.

For three days he lay in state on a high catafalque in the Chapel of Our Lady of Light at the Loretta Convent which he had dedicated only eight weeks previously. Edmund was in Washington at the time, looking after certain matters of business touching on the welfare of the Territory, but Fannie and young Fanny filed past the bier.

On the morning of February 16, all the city turned out to mourn their old and good friend as he was borne by six priests in a solemn processional, led by Archbishop Salpointe, to the Cathedral. From Loretta Academy to Cathedral Place they went, bearing their solemn burden, over to Palace Avenue around the Plaza and up San Francisco Avenue, through the main doors to the spot which was to be his tomb.

It seemed to Fannie that all who watched, or all who took part, must feel as she did—that an era had come to an end.

She said as much to Edmund when he came home from Washington.

"A good man," Edmund said. "I shall miss him."

"How were things in Washington?" she asked.

"I think people are almost beginning to forgive me a little," he said, smiling wryly.

Almost, but not quite. The old hurt still lingered; the old barbs were still being cast. In all honesty she must admit that Edmund himself was not without blame for the things which had come to him and to his family. He had never been a tactful man; he had always resented restraint. And even in the honors he had experienced—and there had been many of these—there was forever an undertone of failure, of work unfinished, and, worst of all, of goals misunderstood. Sometimes she wondered if he might not accomplish more if he would be less outspoken, would agree to compromise here and there.

But that was not Edmund's way, and perhaps it was just as well. Somewhere she had read that when an army crossed a bridge the marchers are ordered to break step lest the combined rhythm of their marching break the bridge. Perhaps this was true in other circumstances—a few men needed to be out of step with the multitude if the structure of society was to be preserved. This might well be Edmund's role in life—breaking the exact conformation of other, more circumspect individuals. And if he listened to a different drum as he marched, who was there to say he was wrong? Different, perhaps, but not necessarily wrong.

"Somebody did call me 'the moral grandeur of the Fortieth Congress,'" Edmund broke in on her thoughts. And, at her look of delight, "Oh, I've long since learned not to pay overmuch attention to words, either good or bad. Now if the President would just back that idea up with action and reappoint me governor of the Territory."

"Of course he will," Fannie said. "If he did once, he will again."

"And so Cleveland would—if he is re-elected. But already it looks as if the Republicans will nominate Harrison and win."

"And he'll appoint a Republican?"

"I'm afraid so. And just when I had so many plans for the Territory."

"In that case, what will you do?"

She hoped he'd say he would take a good rest, and perhaps write some of the articles he had been asked to do.

"Oh—I'll find something. Work on a newspaper once more. Maybe even start one of my own. There's no paper at Deming—I might go there. I could ask for a job as Secretary of Immigration in New Mexico. And I've always wanted to study law and be admitted to the bar."

A good rest, indeed! Here were plans enough to keep a young man busy for a lifetime, and Edmund was past sixty.

"Then, there is always my writing. *Forum* asked me to do an article on the impeachment. I've had several other suggestions about writing pamphlets and articles."

The *Forum*. That had a good and substantial sound.

"Oh, Edmund," she said, making no effort to conceal her pleasure in the recognition given him. "It's just as I've always said. People are sure to recognize what you've done for them. In Kansas, in Washington, and in New Mexico."

She had felt as she watched the solemn procession bearing Archbishop Lamy to his tomb that the people would forever after remember the good man and follow the paths he set for them. Now she was equally as sure that in after years they would remember Edmund, too. Certainly he had not accomplished the legislation he had hoped for, but he had set many to thinking. Afterward, when the measures he had advocated came up for reconsideration —tax reforms and soil conservation and irrigation and woman suffrage—they would remember Edmund. Every settler living without fear in his lonely home would bless him. Students crowding into the great university which was certain to grow up in Albuquerque would have cause to thank him. And when the Old Palace was turned into a museum for the preservation of New Mexico's proud and fascinating history—that, too, would be a thing in which Edmund had played a part.

"People are recognizing you for what you are," she told him. "A great man."

"Oh, I wouldn't say that," he told her, but this time his smile was warm. "Because I've been asked to write a history of the impeachment doesn't necessarily mean I've been forgiven. Just that some people want to hear my side of the story. I do believe, however, that in time I will be vindicated. Yes—in time, the whole people will vindicate me."

"Of course," she said. "And soon. When your article is published—"

"No—" he interrupted her gently. "No, not then. Later on perhaps, but not as soon as that. Probably not in my time. You'll see, Fannie," he told her, "you'll see—I'll be a greater man dead than I am living."

Edmund, talking about dying, assuming she would be here after he was gone! What a way to talk. She would hear none of it. "Don't talk like that," she said sharply.

He looked at her, smiling quizzically. "My, my," he said. "What big talk from such a little woman."

He walked over to her side and put an arm around her. With his forefinger he touched her nose, her hair, the corners of her eyes.

"Same perky little nose, same brown hair, same black eyes," he said. He gave her a gentle squeeze. "Same spunky little girl I married. Now tell me—why shouldn't I say what is true?"

"Because," she began and then hesitated. How was she to explain that she wanted no more talk about his going away and leaving her, now or ever? Already there had been too many partings in their lives; too many times when she must stay at home and wave good-by.

"Because," she explained, "there's no sense in your saying you won't be great until after—after you are gone. You're a great man now."

"Now—?" he raised his eyebrows.

"A very great man," she assured him. "Now, and always."

Even then she had known she would go first. That was quite as she would have it. He had books to read and articles to write, and his complete justification yet to come. There was work for him to do. But without him, she had nothing.

He was thinking it strange for her to leave now when always she had been the one to stay at home, waiting for his return. He was most certainly worried; she could sense it. She must find some way to explain to him that she was not as homebound as he might think. She had never failed to follow him, either in the flesh or in the spirit, and so had taken many a splendid voyage, tremendous in scope and promise. True, she had not gone willingly at times, for she was small and weak and sometimes frightened. But never frightened enough to turn back, or to urge him to do so.

She must tell him this. Strange, though, how difficult it was to say these things. Perhaps it was because she knew it was not really herself—Fannie Lathrop Ross—who lay under this faded quilt. The shell, the semblance was there; the real person was quite another woman. She was the sum of all that had happened to her down the years. She was the children and their children, busy and active, carrying on their own lives. She was Edmund and the life they had led together.

Many there were who would say it hadn't been a very good marriage. Just a long series of poverty and separation and humiliation and bereavement. But, oh, they did not know. They could not see how these very things, in themselves and of themselves, brought about a depth and richness; they could not know that the sum of a marriage was greater and better than any of its individual components.

She would like to tell Edmund that, just as she would like to say to him that this voyage on which she was going now must be undertaken by herself. In a way, however, he would be leading her still, for he had taught her the greatest lesson any human can give another—to stand alone. He must not think, either, that because she was going he must hurry to join her, leaving any necessary work unfinished.

It was vitally important that she make him realize this. With considerably more effort than she felt like expending at the moment, she raised herself on one elbow. "Don't hurry—" she shaped the words carefully.

Still she was not completely satisfied. There was more that she needed to say. It had something to do with going away and coming back—strange she should fumble with the thought, for that had been the pattern of their lives. This, however, was different; it involved some old obligation, some long unfulfilled promise. Something to do with welcoming—

Suddenly it was clear. Clear as could be, for she was in Sandusky and Edmund was disappointed. She knew exactly what to say.

"I'll be waiting at the gate," she told him.

She lay back on the pillow. She could rest now.

Author's Note

THIS IS frankly a novel. It is, however, a novel based on facts which I have verified by careful and exhaustive research. I began the book through no wish of my own. In the spring of 1954 Mr. Raymond Bond, president of Dodd, Mead, brought to my attention a book printed some fourteen years earlier in which Edmund G. Ross was mentioned. It was to my great discredit that I had never heard of the man before. Said Mr. Bond, "There's a book for you."

I read the material, found it extremely interesting and dramatic, and agreed that Edmund Ross' story did, indeed, hold the germ of a book. But not for me. Even so, I could not dismiss the idea and from time to time did further reading on the subject. Then in 1956 Senator John Kennedy's book, *Profiles in Courage*, was published. It devoted one chapter to Ross and his historic vote at the time of the impeachment trial of Andrew Johnson. I felt this had covered the situation, making unnecessary any book of mine on the subject.

"On the contrary," Mr. Bond said, "the field has just been prepared for you. Go ahead."

So, ahead I went, choosing, however, to see the story from the point of view of Fannie Lathrop Ross, his wife, rather than that of Ross himself. It was an undertaking in which I could never have succeeded without the aid of the following people:

The staff at the Kansas State Historical Museum at Topeka, Kansas, who not only gave me access to the vast resources of their organization, including the Ross letters and papers and much other source material, but also answered my questions, often the naïve mirror of my own ignorance; the staff at the Public Library of Milwaukee, Wisconsin, who made it possible for me to have a look at rare manuscripts, books, maps, and newspaper collections; various members of the staff of the Public Library at Amarillo, Texas, who opened for me the fascinating world of interlibrary loan and who became so interested in my project that they sometimes ran ahead of me in research; Nell Snead of the Kansas City *Star* who suggested that I check the Public Library in Kansas City, where I found a copy of an interview with Lillie Ross Leis in which she gave the poignant details of the day the news of her father's vote came back to Lawrence, Kansas, where the family lived; Lucile Hutson of Sandusky, Ohio, who discovered several obscure but interesting items, including an account of a high school program in which Edmund Ross took part; the staff of the New Mexico Historical Museum in Santa Fe, who helped me uncover vast richness of material; members of the staffs of several libraries in New York, where I read newspapers of the period; several librarians in the Library of Congress who could answer, with ease and dispatch, the most unbelievable questions; the Chambers of Commerce of all the towns from which I needed background material; former Senator Henry Ashurst of Washington, D.C., who, as a young newspaper reporter, once interviewed Edmund Ross; the staff at the Albuquerque *Journal;* the members of my creative writing class at West Texas State College who, with youthful candor, pointed out my errors in such portions as I read to them; my family, who had to put up with me while I wrote the book. The list, long as it is, is only a partial one.

Especially am I indebted to Barbara Kamb of Dodd, Mead whose patient, careful and devoted editing of the manuscript has been of immeasurable help; and to my agent, Maurice Crain, himself a knowledgeable and astute student of history, whose wise guidance has saved me from many an error in fact and spirit.

Mr. Edmund G. Ross of Albuquerque, grandson of the original Fanny and Edmund, contributed invaluable information. At the time of Fannie's death he was about ten years old. He remembers her well. According to him, she was a small woman, "perhaps five feet two inches tall, with brown hair which grayed little and remained abundant and lovely until her death." She was "a spunky little thing, and, even at the last, had a twinkle about her." She had the "only truly black eyes" he has ever seen. She was an expert seamstress and pieced quilts; she played the piano and had a lovely singing voice. Once she hid an escaped slave, a feat made especially difficult when one of the children almost betrayed his presence. Her husband adored her. She died in her son Pitt's house where all the children came to be with her in those last days. Evenings they gathered around the piano and sang. (The piano, brought across the plains in a freighter wagon is now at the University at Albuquerque.) Patiently, carefully, I dug up the facts, weighing one against the other where there was conflict, choosing those which seemed to come from the most dependable sources (a decision often aided by my friend in the Kansas Historical Museum), until I felt I knew how the story had happened. In only a few instances have I taken liberty with facts as written. I do not know for sure that Fannie was in Lawrence during Quantrill's raid since, from the best records obtainable, the family lived in Topeka at that time. Edmund and his troops were stationed in Lawrence the spring of 1863, and from there he wrote Fannie urging her to bring the family to Lawrence and spend some time with him. I do not believe she would have ignored the plea. He had marched away from Lawrence the day before the raid, but I choose to believe that she was still there. The details of the raid itself I have checked from many sources until I feel they are entirely accurate.

Nor do I know for sure that Fannie was in Washington at the time Vinnie Ream's statue of Lincoln was dedicated. But Edmund, who had remained in Washington during Christmas of 1870, wrote early in January of 1871 that he was sending money and a railroad pass and urging Fannie to join him in Washington.

If she did as he asked, she would most certainly have gone to the dedication, for the friendship between the Rosses and Vinnie Ream lasted all their lives.

For the most part, I have told things the way they happened, insofar as I have been able to reconstruct the course of events from reading the vast amount of source material at my disposal.

Primarily, however, I am indebted to that amazing man, Edmund G. Ross himself, whose letters and writings I have studied with great care. It is in these, I believe, that he shows his true self, a man different in many ways from the one historians and politicians have pictured him to be. They portray him as a man who rose out of obscurity to cast his vote, and, this done, sank back into obscurity once more. Actually, during all his long and eventful life—he lived to be eighty—he was about as obscure as the steam calliope in a circus parade. He played a prominent part in shaping the destinies of every region in which he lived. Nor is his grave forgotten and neglected; it is carefully tended by proud and devoted descendants. Well they may feel pride, for he was a devoted, even ardent husband; a loving, wise father; a courageous, dedicated politician; a clear-thinking writer and student of current affairs; a wise and thoughtful leader; a brave and fearless soldier; a gifted, even dedicated, editor; a selfless, stubborn patriot.

A man of great vision and foresight he was, yet alas, never to reap financial benefit from his own ideas, some of which realized fortunes for other men associated with him. He had great personal dignity and integrity, but was not given to tact or compromise. And, unfortunately for him, although he always chose the side which he believed to be right, he was rarely on the popular one.

In spite of all the research I did, I was able to find only three recorded facts about Fannie Lathrop Ross, my heroine. These were the date of her birth, the date of her marriage, and the date of her death. I found only one good likeness of her—a picture taken with her husband when she was in her sixties. Somewhere there may be other pictures of her, or even letters she wrote but if such exist, I was unable to find them. Even the spelling of her name is not always the same, being at times "Fanny" and at others

"Fannie." Her monument in the cemetery at Albuquerque, where she lies buried by her husband's side, uses the former. But the record of her marriage certificate in Sandusky, Ohio, uses the latter, as does Edmund Ross in writing his own account (in longhand) of his life. So, I decided to use the latter spelling as well.

There is no doubt in my mind, however, that she must have been an extraordinary woman. She would have needed to be to have lived with that remarkable man, Edmund Gibson Ross, past their golden wedding anniversary. Through him, in one way or another, her life was touched by almost every great national event during those tumultuous years, 1848–1889, the time span covered by this book. In it I have tried to reconstruct Fannie Ross as I myself believe her to have been.

Perhaps there are readers who would like to explore further the fascinating era covered in this novel. Here is a partial list of the references I consulted in writing *Many a Voyage:*

George B. Anderson, *History of New Mexico: Its Resources and People,* 1907; Edward Bumgardner, *The Life of Edmund G. Ross,* 1949; Claude G. Bowers, *The Tragic Era,* 1929; Richard S. Brownlee, *Gray Ghosts of the Confederacy,* 1958; Thomas Graham Belden and Marve Robins, *So Fell the Angels,* 1956; F. W. Giles, *Thirty Years of Topeka,* 1886; Paul Horgan, *The Centuries of Santa Fe,* 1956; R. L. Hoxie, *Vinnie Ream,* 1908; George W. James, *New Mexico: Land of the Delight Makers,* 1920; William A. Keleher, *The Fabulous Frontier,* 1945; John F. Kennedy, *Profiles in Courage,* 1956; Lew Larkin, *Bingham: Fighting Artist,* 1954; Meridel Le Suerur, *North Star Country,* 1945; James Marshall, *Santa Fe: The Road That Built an Empire,* 1945; Jay Monaghan, *Civil War on the Western Border,* 1955; George Fort Milton, *The Age of Hate,* 1930; Allan Nevins, *Ordeal of the Union,* 1947; Alice Nichols, *Bleeding Kansas,* 1954; Miguel Antonio Otero, *My Life on the Frontier,* 1935; Sara T. D. Robinson, *Kansas: Its Exterior and Interior,* 1857; Hannah Anderson Ropes, *Six Months in Kansas: By a Lady,* 1856; Edmund G. Ross, *The Impeachment of Andrew Johnson,* 1896; Ishbel Ross, *Proud Kate,* 1953; Carl Sandburg, *Abraham Lincoln: The War Years,* 1939; Leverette Spring, *Kansas: The Prelude to the War for the Union,* 1885; Federal Writers' Projects—*Iowa: A Guide to the Hawkeye State,* 1938; *Kansas: A Guide to the Sunflower State,* 1939; *New Mexico: A Guide to the Colorful State,* 1940; *The Ohio Guide,* 1940; *Wisconsin: A Guide to the Badger State.*